I0601717

For Melissa

Mary & I: The Real Story of Miss Mary Mack: The first Witch, is a work of fiction. Names, characters, places, and incidents are the product of the author's imagination or are used fictitiously. Any resemblance to actual events, locales, or persons, living or dead is entirely coincidental.

2025 Rabbooks Publishing First Edition

Copyright © 2025 Alexander G. James

All rights reserved. Published in the United States by Rabbooks, a division of Rabbit Studios Graphics. No part of this book may be reproduced in any form or by any electronic or mechanical means, including information storage and retrieval systems, without permission in writing from the publisher, except for a reviewer who may quote brief passages in a review.

ISBN-13: 978-0998247465

Illustrations by Alex James

marymackandi.blogspot.com

MARY & I

The First Witch

The Real Story of
Miss Mary Mack

MACKNOWLEDGMENTS

Special thanks to all the people who helped in one way or another, either by inspiration or perspiration, to place this book in your hands.

A special thanks to Melissa Ehman, Luke Neher, Azusa James, Mikaela James, and Elijah Hernandez for their support.

Contents

Photo taken in 1915 of Mary Elizabeth of the House of White

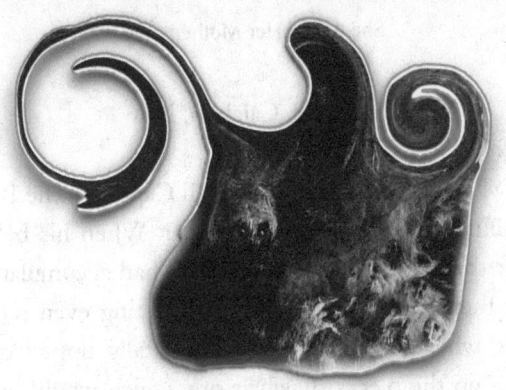

PART ONE

SHE ASKED HER MOTHER

February 13, 1898

The gondolier handed young Leopold Bianca some bread. Leo was more mentally upset than physically hungry. Within minutes, his Aunt Gwenhwyvar had sent him from the isle of Great Britain to the canals of Venice simply by throwing him into a well. He didn't know about the forge called 'Vorago' she used to transport him; there were many forges he never learned about and never will, banished from the White household; an orphan again.

Leo looked up at the face of the kind-hearted gondolier. To this man, he appeared to be just a child drowning in the canal at night. This Dayfide has probably never heard of Forgers or Smithing. Giving Leo food or shelter was all this man could offer; there was no way he could help him return to England in a minute or help Leo take revenge and rescue Mary.

"Sei un orfano?" The man asked."

"What?"

"Er-ah—orphan. You orphan?"

"Yes."

"I take you to my brother, they have lots of kids like you, take you in, okay?"

Leo nodded in agreement. He knew he didn't have a choice.

July 14, 1898, Calabria, Italy

The man who forced Leo to call him Il Capo or 'The Boss' was the furthest thing from a respectable leader. When his belt struck Leo's back for the third time, the sweat Leo had accumulated from working near the forge caused the blow to sting even more. Leo picked up the wheelbarrow he had accidentally tipped over and started picking up the pieces of silver ore, which would be melted down and turned into the coins they made. He had no idea where the rocks with silver in them came from. Now and then they would melt jewelry and eating utensils down to make the same coins. When he read the necklace inscribed with the words: 'For my love, never forget I will always be yours' he was hit again for pausing his work.

Now and then, the man with the monocle and bushy sideburns would appear to inspect the foundry. Il Capo was afraid of this man, but Leo never understood why. The man and I'll Capo were around the same build. The man with the monocle and sideburns never yelled or seemed unpleasant until he asked Il Capo in his French accent what had happened to 100 coins not included with the last order.

"I-I-don't know!" Il Capo scrambled around in a panic, looking for something nonexistent. He called all of the boys over. The workers stopped what they were doing and lined up in a row. One by one, he patted them down and came up empty. When he got to Leo, he rummaged through his pockets and placed a handful of coins in them. "I knew it! It's this boy! He's been stealing all along!" He reached into Leo's pocket and pulled out the coins. The man with the monocle walked over to see the discovery. Il Capo opened his hands, revealing a handful of useless rocks. "What? No, wait! He stole the coins! I saw him!" Leo walked over to Il Capo, reached into the man's coat pocket, and presented the coins. "Wait–what? How did you do that–"

"It appears Monsieur you are the thief," the man with the monocle said.

"I didn't—" Although they were standing far from the furnace, Il Capo appeared to break out in a sweat, unrelated to the heat. "... What did you do?—This boy, he steal them, not me!... I" He grabbed Leo around the neck and started choking him. In a panic, Leo punched and kicked at him. He landed a blow between the legs. The man let go of him and backhanded Leo, sending him onto the ground. Il Capo looked around and picked up a large brick. He walked over to Leo. "I smash you skull!"

Leo pointed at the man, grabbed his crucifix necklace with his other hand, and said: "Roydldldll!" Il Capo looked confused, trying to figure out what Leo had just said. He got closer and closer and prepared to bring the rock down. *"Roy dldl"* Leo repeated.

The man stopped approaching. He was confused again, but something was different. He threw the brick onto the ground and searched around his body. The open furnace had transferred flames onto his body. Whenever he patted out a flame, another one ignited. He thrashed around in a panic and screamed in agony, before collapsing onto the ground and convulsing until his burning mound of flesh yielded to its fateful demise.

The man with the monocle took a cigar out of his pocket, clipped the end of it with a cutter, and handed it to Leo. "Garçon, if you don't mind?"

Leo looked at the cigar for a moment and then grabbed it. He walked over to the burning heap of his proprietor and used the flame to light the cigar. He returned to the man and handed it to him. The man looked very pleased with what Leo had done. "You know how to forge?"

Leo nodded and looked back at the flame. Other boys had surrounded the pyre, but no one attempted to put it out.

"Did you use forging? To transfer the coins back into his pockets?"

Leo shook his head. "No, just reverse pickpocketing."

The man chuckled. "What is your name, garçon?"

"Leopold Wh...Leopold Bianca."

"My name is Maximillian Blanc. Come, you will work for me now." Maximillian turned around and started leaving. Leo followed closely without looking back.

April 1, 1915, London, England

Leo knew they were getting close to The White family building. Their auto was much faster than the numerous horse and buggies or the double-decker motor buses crowding the streets of Westminster, but this still put their arrival time within 15 minutes. Leo nervously tapped his foot. Maximilian took note of this.

"Leo, is something wrong?"

"Ah, uh, just feeling a little anxious."

"No need to worry. Our mark is a very powerful Forger. But even he will not be able to defeat all of us, especially her." Leo looked backwards at the black-clad pale woman with white hair and gauze wrapped around her eyes. Leo could sense the power emanating from her. He put her at least a level 9.

"How did you find this place?"

"No need to worry about that, my friend. The important thing is we found him."

"Are you sure this is the right place?"

"Why do you ask?"

"Uh, I don't know. I don't like the thought of raiding the wrong house."

"Well, there is a rumor about a place somewhere in Wales, but we weren't able to pin its location as we were this one."

"But what if...?"

"If we find anyone here, we will kill them and torture the rest until they give us what we want."

Leo's thoughts were of Mary. He clenched his sweaty fist.

Their taxi parked in front of a gated house. Leo knew Maximilian was staring at him.

"Allons-y (let's go)", Maximilian said. They disembarked the car. Another taxi, a luxury Model T, and a truck pulled up behind them.

Four men emerged from the truck, two holding rifles. A chauffeur opened the door of the luxury auto and helped a young blonde woman in a frilly white dress out.

"Who is that?" Leo asked.

"Shirley Blanc—or now Blanche. She is the new leader of the Golds…and our boss."

"They picked her instead of you?"

Never before had Leo ever seen the leader of the Golds. He put herself and his ages around the same. 'How could someone her age be bossing us around?' he wondered. 'That's gotta eat Max alive. She must be a powerful Forger to get in that position.' "But—"

"What is done is done…" Maximillian said. "She is la patronne (the boss) now—for now…" Maximillian said.

Shirley walked up to the gate. She lifted a pair of opera glasses to her eyes. "To think they had a place so close to the royal palace, right under our noses," she said. After scanning the building, she put her glasses away, turned around, and gestured to Maximillian. "Ouvre la porte, s'il te plait. (Open the gate, please)."

Maximilian unsheathed a sword from his cane. With one swipe sliced it between the gate lock.

"That was forged…" Leo said, "How did you…"

Maximum opened the doors and was about to enter the courtyard; Leo stopped him.

"Don't!"

Max and Shirley looked surprised at him.

"What is it, Leo?" Max asked.

"I…it…it may be a trap."

"A trap?"

"No, it's nothing…" Leo realized he had said too much.

6

Shirley walked over and stood next to Maximilian. "Maximilian, qu'est-ce qu'on attend? (What are we waiting for?)"

"Leo a dit quelque chose à propos d'un piège (Leo said something about a trap)" Maximilian answered.

"And how would you know anything about a trap?" She asked Leo.

"Er–ah…It's nothing, I'm just being precautious," Leo answered.

"Are you afraid?" Shirley asked, raising an eyebrow.

"No of course not."

"Then please proceed to the front door." Shirley turned to Maximilian. "Max, give poor…Comment s'appelle-t-il? (What is his name?)"

"Leopold."

"Give poor Leopold a few babysitters so that he will feel safe. Maybe one can hold his hand or get him a bonbon." Everyone but Leo chuckled.

"You two…" Maximilian waved a couple of henchmen over to join Leo.

Leo recognized them as part of the group they had busted out of jail five years ago. They moved forwards past a fountain embellished with a 10-foot-tall statue of Theseus holding the severed head of Medusa in the air. Water dripped from the neck of the gorgon, like clear blood, into the pool below.

The men bravely strutted, holding a rifle and a bat. Leo timidly bought up the rear, constantly looking around for the expected and ignoring their conversation about all the loot they wanted to pillage out of the swanky mansion. One hoped there would be a female he could assault. Imagining the man capturing Mary, Leo resisted the urge to kill him right then and there. Leo looked back. Behind the gate, Shirley lowered her eyes and smiled slightly.—A scream interrupted his speculations. When he turned his attention back to the front, he saw one of the men wrapped in thick roots, instantly growing out of the ground, covering him. The other man rushed to help him. He hit the roots with the baseball bat over and over. The bat bounced off. He picked up a dropped rifle and shot at the vines; it did insignificant damage. By the time he had cocked the gun for another shot, the roots had wrapped around him too. Leo stood still, knowing this was the right decision to make. If he backed away, he could escape completely unharmed. Looking back, he saw the confused look on Max's face. Shirley was smiling coldly.

"Aren't you going to help them?" Shirley yelled.

Leo did a short back and forth and then reached out and tried to pull the vines off the men. Leo knew this was a mistake. The vines turned their attention to him and lunged towards his legs. He leaped up onto the shoulders of the statue of Theseus. The vines reached for him. He held his crucifix. *"Qwithie gwint!"* A gust of wind blasted out of his hands and briefly repelled the vines. The plants relentlessly edged towards his neck. Leo looked over at Shirley, Maximilian, and the White Haired woman. Neither one of them made any movements to aid him. When his attention turned back to the vines, it was too late to notice how they had wound themselves around his legs and were twisting towards his chest. Leo leaped over it. The vines lunged at him and grabbed on. He was yanked back and pinned against the statue. Water from Medusa's neck dripped onto his head as the vines tightened around his chest and neck, making it impossible to breathe. Leo gasped for air and avoided taking in water. His thoughts were of his death and how he was in a similar situation at the White Manor in Wales when he tried to rescue Mary. The protective vines would have killed him if he had not said one sentence. It was a gamble that he was still considered a member of the White household. After his attempted attack on Gwenhwyvar, they would have changed the conditions of the forge to keep him away from anything remotely connected to them; surely no part of them still considered him family; would they forgive him? The vines were too powerful for him to handle. In a few moments, he wouldn't be able to talk. With his last breath, he said: "It's ...me...Leo..."

The vines retracted from his neck and then the rest of his body. Leo fell limp into the fountain and breathed in heavily. He rubbed his neck and chest. The vines retreated into the ground, dropping the dead bodies of Leo's unfortunate escorts. Leo climbed out of the fountain, looked back at the bodies, and then at the faces of Maximilian and Shirley. She still had a slight smile. Maximillian expression was the same he had seen on Professor White's face more than once: a look of concern and disappointment. He looked at the bodies of the two men again, wondering if that was upsetting them. When he started walking towards the others, Max grabbed his cane as though he was going to use it and Shirley stepped back and let the White Haired Woman move forwards and stand next to Maximilian.

"What is it?" Leo asked.

"Did you see that, Max?" Shirley asked.

"I did." He gave Leo a stern look.

Shirley started walking forward. Once she entered the gated area, the vines reappeared from the ground and reached up to capture her. The White Haired woman said: *"Heahweed!"* and slammed her cane down. In an instant, all of the vines and some of the surrounding cobblestones froze in a layer of ice. The crystallized vines formed a frozen tunnel, stretching from Shirley to where Leo stood. Shirley gracefully walked towards him without slipping on the frozen ground.

"They didn't attack you," she said to Leo.

He felt more unnerved. "What?"

"The vines…they retreated from you. Why?"

"I…I don't know. Maybe I taste bad."

Shirley chuckled and looked back. "Did you hear that, Max? He tastes bad."

Some men behind him laughed, Maximilian never cracked a smile. Shirley turned her attention back to Leo. "No, I'm sure you're quite a delicious morsel. But the plants didn't attack you."

More plants tried to curve up and lunged towards Shirley, but the White Haired woman froze the vines and created another arch of frozen stalagmites.

"I don't know why," Leo said.

Shirley moved closer and examined his face. "Well, I do." Leo resisted the urge to push her away from him. "It's obvious. These plants were created to defend this estate from intruders like us. Us... but not you."

"Are you saying I live here? That's ridic—"

"No, but the people that lived here wanted to be sure you will always be welcomed, like a friend...or family member n' est pas?"

"I've never had anything to do with the White household—"

Shirley turned to Maximilian. "Max, did you ever tell Leo here which house we were going to raid?"

Max sadly shook his head. Shirley looked at Leo with a slight smile. Leo didn't know what to do. He wasn't sure what kind of forging powers Shirley had, but he was sure Maximilian and the White Haired woman could kill him if he attacked. He said: *"Qwithie gwint!"* causing an immense gust of wind to blast the area and propel him upwards 10 feet into the air. Leo landed on the shoulder of the Thesis. With one more leap, he could make it over the fence and be out of the distance of a lightning attack. Just as his feet left the statue, ice anchored him to it. The ice on his legs spread to his shoulders and bound his arms to his sides. He thought he could shake it off, but it was no ordinary ice; it was as hard as stone and colder than anything he'd ever felt. He felt a flash of numbness. The ice petrified his muscles and rendered him immobile; all fight left his imprisoned body.

Everyone gathered around Leo in a circle.

"Shall ah shatter him?" the White Haired woman asked with a Scottish accent.

"Not yet," Shirley answered. "I'm sure he has lots of information about the Whites then we could have found out otherwise...Isn't that right, Leo?"

Leo tried to do a fire forge; it was hard to concentrate with his fingers feeling so numb.

"I doubt he's going to talk, he's very resilient," Maximillian said.

"We'll see…"Shirley gestured to his head. Without hesitation, The White Haired Woman said: *"Heahweed Kamai!"* A set of ice stairs reached up to Leo. Maximillian walked to the top and put his hand on Leo's head.

"No!" Leo yelled.

"You lied to me, Leo!"

"I…I didn't!"

"All this time you knew we were looking for Professor White. If I'd known you were related to him, I would have tortured you sooner,"

"I'm not related to him! I've never seen him before in my life!"

"If you're going to lie, do it in a way that I can't tell!"

"But I'm not—"

Shirley snapped her finger. Maximilian said: *"Oo-aid vell ur woove ur aid dwaid!"*

"No!" Leo yelled. His body slumped down in compliance and his eyes turned red.

"What should I do with him?" Maximillian asked.

"Ask him about everything he knows about Professor White."

"Leo, are you related to Professor White?"

"Yes," he answered.

"He's your father?"

"He adopted me."

"Passionnant (fascinating)," Shirley beamed. "Are there any other kids?"

"Was it just you?" Maximillian asked.

"No,"

"Who were the others?" Leo was silent. "Leo?" There was still no answer. "He's not responding."

"Incroyable (incredible), Shirley said. Even forging can't reveal that part of his memory. He must care quite deeply for the others," "Now, ask him where Professor White is."

"Is Professor White here?"

"No...he's in America."

"He answered that rather fast," Maximilian said.

"Not as much loyalty and love for his adopted father. Ask him where."

"Where in America?"

"He likes to spend April in New York City."

"Where in New York?"

"Hotels"

"What does he do in New York?"

He works out of an office in the Flat Iron building."

"Well, there is our next destination," Shirley said... We're running out of time. Ask him about the book."

"Does he have the Siv Myrddin?"

"I don't know."

"We have no more use for him." Shirley walked around the scene and headed to the house. "Blank his memory of anything he has seen today, and then throw him into the Thames."

"Why blank his memory of today?" Maximilian asked.

"Because, when you kill him, he will have no idea why someone —I assume he considered a...father figure—will be killing him. He will die confused, and what he feels is a meaningless death of betrayal, the worst kind of death." Shirley continued on her way towards the house. More vines tried to attack her, but the White-haired woman froze them into a spiky arch. Maximilian put his hand on Leo's head and commanded him to forget everything that had happened that day. When Leo came to, he was more confused by Maximilian's sad eyes than waking up encased in a block of ice. "Max? What is this? What's going on?"

Six men broke the base of Leo's ice sculpture with bats and axes, gently lifted it, and started carrying it to the truck. "Max!

What is this? Max, why are you doing this to me? What did I do? Max? MAX! NO! MAX!"

Photo of Maximillian of the House of Blanche(Blanc).
Taken in 1898

PART TWO
FOR FIVE CENTS MORE

June 7th, 1915

A German soldier disguised as an American dock worker handed Captain Walther Schwieger a spyglass. The Captain focused it on the large, black helium balloon with a single figure in its gondola floating far in the distance over the New York skyline. Schwieger tucked the spyglass back together. "Hold your fire, it's her!" he commanded. Some men lowered rifles. The balloon descended to the dock, rapidly deflated, turned silver, and shrank until it became the size of a golf ball. Mausi the Coppersmith tucked it into the pocket of her black dress. She clumsily climbed out of the gondola holding a globe-sized sphere and walked down the gangplank to join Schwieger and his crowd of German workers.

"Very daring floating around in that thing while the sun is still up," Schwieger complained.

"Balloons aren't that uncommon."

"How did it go?"

"We leveled the White mansion and found a safe, but the only thing inside was Shirley Blanche. Maximillian was there as well, sporting a new arm."

14

"So, no book?"

"Looks like."

"Is that the end of it? With the death of that Mary frau, we wasted all of this time!"

"Maybe. But just to make sure she's dead, I'm going to test this out." She set the sphere on a crate.

"What do you have there, Mausi?"

"Something which will make our lives a lot easier, this is what we took from the Federal Reserve."

"Is that one of the crystal balls?"

"Yes. The Eye of Graeae. With this, we can locate the owner of the Siv Myrddin. In an instant."

"Sehr gut!" Let us do that. Then we can get out of this God-cursed country!"

"Patience! Unfortunately, it can't tell us where it is because that thing has so many bloody protections on it—can't even be photographed..."

"Then this is useless!"

"Calm yuh self! Since we know who owns the Siv Myrddin, all we have to do is find out where they are. Assuming they survived."

Schwieger sighed. "Yeh really are homesick, aren't yuh?"

"My country is at war! I'm supposed to be out there sinking ships! Not looking for magical books and constantly being attacked by hexen!"

Mausi put her hands on the sphere and concentrated: "Dùbailte, saothair dhùbailte agus trioblaid; losgadh teine agus builgean coire...Mary Elizabeth White of the House of White." The sphere glowed at first and then showed a visual image of Mary on the bridge of the Virginia, talking to Thomas and Abel. "Well, I'll be! She survived!"

"We are lucky. Now, where is she?"

"There's a view of water outside a porthole window. On a boat? Could be around here, hopefully not in the middle of the ocean."

In the gold-trimmed, red velvet, and mahogany-lined salon of the Virginia, Mary, Thomas, and Abel hashed out a plan while watching Flapper, the Japanese magpie, hopping on and off his perch inside a cage.

"How is that bird going to help us?" Thomas asked.

"It follows Leo everywhere," Mary answered. "It's like it always knows where to find him."

"Then we should use him for the location forge," Thomas suggested.

"It has to be a personal, non-living object," Mary informed.

"Can you talk to this bird?" Thomas asked Mary.

"Converse with him?"

"Yes."

"Maybe, but I don't think I'd learn anything but bird knowledge."

"Then how can he tell us where Leo is?"

"We let him go."

"What?"

"Let him go. I noticed that everywhere Leo went, this bird was sure to go. It's like they have a forged connection. Flapper will instantly try to find him the second we let him go. Then, all we have to do is follow him to wherever Leo is."

"Hard to do if he flies over trees or water."

"Wouldn't matter with the Silver Ghost," Abel informed.

"Really? Even over water?"

"That car can go almost anywhere."

"Okay then," Mary said, "it's settled. Abel, can you summon the Silver Ghost?"

"The second I start to mention it, it sets off to find me; it's funny in that way."

"Good. Let's reload and go save Min," Thomas said.

16

They began to go downstairs. Abel stopped. "Oh, what about the book?"

"Pardon?" Mary asked.

"If we leave the book here unguarded, the ship may get attacked."

"Does it really matter?" Thomas asked. "No one will ever be able to get into that safe without a key which may not exist."

"But it still won't stop them from trying, even if they have to destroy all of New York," Mary said, thinking about something Gwenhwyvar told her.

"True. Are you suggesting one of us should stay behind?" Abel asked.

"Hmm, which one?" Thomas said.

"I know all of the secrets of the Silver Ghost. Perhaps one of you should stay here." Abel suggested.

"No, Mary said. You're also more familiar with the ship—assuming Father taught you how to operate it."

"He did."

"Then, take the ship somewhere safe. We'll rendezvous back here within four hours."

"Are you sure?" Abel asked

"What do you mean?"Mary asked.

"Leaving me with the Siv Myrddin?"

"Why wouldn't we?"

"Because of…what the Belgian and Shirley did to my mind… What if there's another hypnotic suggestion in my head, ready to do harm?"

Mary thought for a moment. She put her hand on his forehead and closed her eyes. "Hmm, I don't sense the presence of any more welding, bending, or hypnosis in your mind. You're fine."

"Oh…" Abel said, a little happy. "Alright. If you run into trouble with the Silver Ghost, press the exclamation mark on the wheel and say: "Dianc!" It'll take over and choose the best course of action."

"Sounds simple enough, let's depart before Leo gets too far." Mary hugged Abel. "Be safe!"

"You as well," he answered.

Mary and Thomas walked outside. Behind them, the CSS Virginia raised its gangplank and disembarked from the shore of Battery Park.

Off in the distance, a silver 1907 Rolls Royce raced down the street and headed towards them.

"Your powers seem to be expanding by the minute," Thomas said. "I didn't know you could read minds, too."

"I can't," Mary confessed.

"What?" Thomas looked shocked. "Then what was all of that hocus-pocus you just told Abel?"

"I told him that to encourage him."

"Encourage?"

"Quite. He's been through a lot. He's probably feeling a little vulnerable right now. I'm sure Shirley got into his head because the Belgian had already weakened his mind. I felt he needed something to boost his courage, to make him stronger. There are two different types of people in the world: Those who want to know and those who want to believe." As long as he believes I helped him, he will be better.

"Oh…Well done."

"Thank you."

The Silver Ghost parked itself next to the curb. Thomas opened the front passenger door for Mary, walked around, and climbed into the driver's side. He examined all the buttons on the steering wheel: one had an elephant head on it, another, three spirals converging into one, a two-headed snake, and another had the button Abel had explained with an exclamation mark on it. "Hope I don't blow the horn and accidentally turn someone into a frog," Thomas complained.

"Don't be silly. The frog button is on my side." Mary countered.

Thomas looked over before realizing she was joking.

"Ready?" he asked.

Mary paused in deep thought.

"Mary, what's wrong?"

"What am I going to do?"

"What are you going to do with what?"

"Leo. What am I going to do with him once I catch him? Am I going to kill him? If you arrest him, he'll just escape from jail—he's right, you can't keep someone in jail if they know how to forge. So that leaves only one option. For him to stop bedeviling us for the rest of our lives, we have to kill him. I don't know if I'm up to that. It's one thing to kill a man turned into a monster, but it's another to kill a man acting like one, especially a man you've grown up with who you've considered a brother." Mary sighed.

Thomas reached over and clasped her hand. "Sometimes you have to do things you're not proud of. Because if you didn't, something far worse would happen. For now, all we have to do is find those kids—that's all—one thing at a time. If or when we reach a point where we have to take his life, we'll deal with that when it presents itself. For now, let's go find Min and the boy— concentrate on that."

She nodded to him and opened Flapper's cage. The bird cawed, hopped onto the steering wheel, cawed again, and flew up and forwards towards some buildings. Thomas put the car in gear, and they hurried after the bird.

In the area where White Manor used to be, the late afternoon sun cast a yellow hue on a black crater caused by Mausi's barrels of TNT. At the very bottom was a mound of dirt and soot. The mound shifted around and exposed a soil-covered giant sword. The sword moved, and underneath it, two dusty figures, buried deep down in the center of the pit, awakened. Elzbieta was lying on top of Helga. Helga helped push her off of herself. Elzbieta wiggled around and removed the blackened dirt from her body. Helga lifted and spat out a handful of dust. "Blimey! Me ears are still ringing, 'ow about you?" Helga asked.

"I fine; want to kill Boom-Boom lady."

"Me too, luv, me too." They both struggled to stand up and leaned on each other for support. "Looks like I owe yuh one, Luv. That sword is quite versatile: weapon, broom, and shield."

"I love my Cali."

"How'd yuh get it?"

"I found it in a lake."

"Of course...appropriate."

They climbed out of the pit and saw the large crater, which used to be White Manor.

"Bloody hell!" Helga jogged over to the pit and looked over the edge; she saw the exposed Clo Keffin vault. "Mary!...Min!... Abel...Thomas!...Leo!" She yelled. "Oh what happened here?" Helga nervously wrung her hands.

"Fritzy!...FRIT-ZY!" Elzbieta called.

Helga ran down the debris-laden crater to look for clues of the earlier events. She frantically tossed large pieces of house debris into the air in case anyone was trapped underneath. "Mary!... Min!...Abel...Thomas!" She yelled louder than before. After a long pause, she took a deep breath to calm her nerves. Looks like a hell of a röw 'appened 'ere after we wuz taken out...." She stumbled over something. She kicked some dirt off it and discovered a buried metal wheel."

"What's that?"

"That's Mary's old wheelchair—Coor, wherever she is, I 'ope she doesn't need it." She noticed the open vault. "...Oh no! They got the Siv Myrddin!"

"The Siv Myrddin's here?"

"Guess yeh really did just want the boy." Helga saw the body of Maximillian nearby. "Who's he?" They walked over to examine him. "Hmm...don't recognize him."

"That is Piggy Man. He stabbed me with cane. Lucky I don't get to him first. I was going to make him eat his own eyes so he can watch blade go through stomach."

Helga made a scrawled face. " 'old on a tick…" That white suit …That's part of 'ow Thomas described—this is the Belgian!"

"What is Belgian?"

"This bloke! He's missing facial hair and a fancy cane, but looking at that arm made out of solid ahrion—only a rich Forger could replace an arm like that. 'e's been giving us a heap'a trouble. Guess they won that part of the battle, and if the safe is open, perhaps they took it with 'em."

"So Fritzy alive?"

"Hopefully. Plus, I gave Thomas a forged coin, and since it 'asn't come to me for help, he must be okay.

"I trust Fritzy. I'm sure he alive as well."

"Who is Fritzy to you?"

"Fritzy is my boy."

"The dog boy is yuh son?"

"No, Fritzy is…Fritzy. So, since they okay, we can fight now to find out who strongest?" Elzbieta lifted her sword.

Helga lifted her hands. "Give it a rest, Deary! I 'ave to find me friends first! Don't yuh want to make sure yuh boy is okay?"

Elzbieta bought the sword down fast and hard, jabbing Maximilian's heart. "Okay: First I find Fritzy, then I kill Dee-tech-tive Vanderbilt, then I kill blonde, Black blood, then kill other Black blood, kill Boom-Boom lady, then Helga of Pendle."

"Don't yeh like anything else besides killing?"

Elzbieta thought for a moment. "I like pie."

"Looney as a…Tell yuh wot, if yeh can hold off on yuh killing the red 'eaded Black Blood and Thomas—I'm rather indifferent to the blonde one, then I'll fight yeh before yeh can bump them off, s'all right?"

"Doesn't matter what order."

"Good, then off we go then."

"Wait." Elzbieta walked over to the corpse of Maximilian. She kicked his body until it was face down and then used her sword like a shovel to cover him in a pile of dirt.

"A proper burial? That's nice of you."

"No..." Elzbieta said. She changed her sword back into a parasol. " I bury him face down. That way, he go to hell faster."

"Oh... s'all right." Helga looked around for any witness to their meeting. Despite having a hole in it caused by Mausi, the wall of cars Elzbieta had made to keep most of today's activities from the site, was still blocking their view of Central Park. A few interested people were walking down the street and looking at the car wall, but no one investigated. "I wonder why the police or fire department never showed any interest in an army of anghenfels, a flying elephant, and huge explosions on Fifth Avenue?"

"New Yorkers no care. Dayfides are easily distracted."

"Perhaps." They walked out of the yard, through the gap, and arrived on the sidewalk. "It's not dark enough to fly without spooking the Dayfides. We had better walk."

Helga turned her teclyn into a walking stick and headed towards Fifth Avenue. Elzbieta followed closely behind with her parasol.

For most of the journey, Flapper was cooperative enough to fly straight over main roads and turn down different avenues with enough time for them to change directions and continue following. Mary's task was to keep her eyes on the bird while Thomas prevented the car from rear-ending other autos, horses, or trollies that inevitably blocked their path. The plan mostly worked until they slowed down to prevent themselves from colliding with a wall of women Suffragettes.

Over 30 women, some from Mary's voting rights group, held torches while staging an impromptu protest on Fifth Avenue near the Flatiron building. The few police officers not assigned to guarding the Federal Reserve were not too happy to be in charge of corralling protesters. There was much yelling between the groups, causing it to become the nucleus of the calamity, spreading out to multiple cars involved in a traffic jam, spilling outwards to at least two blocks.

Thomas looked at the steering wheel and wished he knew which button was the horn.

"Oh no! We're going to lose him!" Mary yelled, watching Flapper flying onwards. Eventually, the bird made a right, and they lost track of him. "We have to hurry before he makes it too far!"

"What can I do?" Thomas gestured to the crowd of women blocking the street.

"Just blow your horn!" Mary reached over and pressed the exclamation point button. *"Dianc!"*

"Mary! Not here—"

The auto misbehaved as if it were being possessed by spirits. It backed up, went around another car, and headed towards the sidewalk. Once it reached the curb, it tilted up on its two right wheels. It hurriedly drove around the traffic and crowds in the street, down the sidewalk, scaring pedestrians out of the way and causing the few police officers to yell, blow their whistles, or briefly give chase on foot.

Mary was caught off guard. She had expected something like a loud car honk or an alternative road to being chosen. Thomas tried to remain calm. He tightly gripped the wheel with one hand and held Mary's arm with his other. Everyone viewing the stunt backed away and stood in stunned silence. Among the many protesters, Juliet and Sarah dropped their picket signs and watched their friend's car travel along the sidewalk on two wheels.

"Hello Juliet, hello Sarah!" Mary chimed. Juliet and Sarah hesitantly waved their hands at her. "VOTING RIGHTS FOR WOMEN! VOTING RIGHTS FOR WOMEN!" Mary yelled.

The crowd burst into cheers and waved. When the car reached the end of the traffic obstruction, it fell back down onto four wheels and steered back towards the street. Behind them, they could still hear cheers and police whistles.

"That was the cat's pajamas!" Mary yelled.

On the spiky top of the 60-story Woolworth's building, Helga and Elzbieta searched the city below for signs of anything unusual. Helga came close to noticing the car chase Mary, Thomas, and Leo were engaged in but got distracted by the sounds of screams from below. Elzbieta was more concerned with dropping coins onto people's heads and laughing as they screamed in pain than being of any help.

"Can yuh please stop that!" Helga said. "Do yeh want to find our friends or not?"

"Last time Fritz sent me cockroach made out of coin. I sure he do it again."

"Unless you don't have the coin on yeh—like the ones yuh been dropping on the Dayfides!" Elzbieta had a look of shocked realization.

Helga shook her head and used forging and her fingers to form two loops to create a telescope. She looked all around the East River. Something that looked like the Virginia was in New York Harbor, " 'old on a minute, is that...?" She was distracted by Elzbieta's loud fart. Helga lost her concentration, sighed, and looked down. "I can't work like this." She wondered how she could lose Elzbieta. "Now then...Yeh want to kill Mary and Shirley because they are from the Black family. What does that have to do whiff yuh?"

"Black Blood descendants of Maria."

"Who's Maria?"

"Maria, my siostra—sister. She was on the make with my husband, Samual Black, and they drown me as witch."

"So, it's revenge—wait, descendants? When was this?"

"1692."

"1692! Then...Yeh said they killed yeh. Yuh really are a reincarnate?"

"I suppose."

Helga looked at her. "Blimey, a cursed reincarnate! No wonder yuh a looney! Having to start over, again and again!" Helga spotted something dramatic off in the distance. "Hold on a tick..." Elzbieta walked over and tried to see what Helga had sighted. "Is that...the Federal Reserve?"

"Looks like building on fire."

"It does. We should get a better look. It's dark enough to fly there."

"Why? We not fire—men!"

"No, but that's also where me friends and Boom Boom lady works."

"Oh! Let's see her! I want to make her sad." They jumped off the roof, straddled their teclyns, and flew towards the smoking building.

"There it is!" Mary pointed at a gas-lit Flapper, flying a block away, just over the trolly wires. Her eyes scanned from the bird to the street. "...And there's Leo! On his motorcycle! He has something in his sidecar in a large sack—it must be the kids!"

Thomas sped up and passed a couple of horses and buggies.

Flapper cawed, getting Leo's attention. He looked up and then back at Mary and Thomas, closing the distance between them.

"Damn bird!" He yelled. He revved the throttle and sped away from them.

Thomas accelerated the Silver Ghost and tried to keep up. Although they could match Leo's speed, the agility of his motorcycle through the traffic increased the possibility of him escaping.

Mary remembered when they were being chased by henchmen, how they had evaded them. "Be careful, he's probably going to turn into a narrow alley! Or someplace we can't follow!" She yelled.

"Got it!" Thomas acknowledged.

As Mary had predicted, Leo turned the cycle into a narrow alleyway.

"There he goes!" Thomas complained. He slammed on the brakes and watched Leo disappear down the alley. "We should drive around."

"No, by the time we make it over there, he'll be long gone!" she reached over and pressed the exclamation button again. *"Dianc!"*

"Mary!" Thomas complained. The car backed up and then hurried towards the narrow alley. Thomas and Mary braced for a collision. She and Thomas were drifting apart from each other. She looked down and saw the car was stretching. "What's going on?" Thomas asked.

"This isn't going to work." Mary panicked. The car widened, and then, like elastic metal reaching a breaking point, it snapped along a seam and became two halves. They briefly reached out their hands to each other but missed connecting when Mary's half moved ahead. "Thomas!" She yelled. Her part of the Silver Ghost changed and transformed until it became a two-wheeled motorized vehicle. The tires narrowed, and a bike steering mechanism stretched out of the glove compartment area. Mary grabbed onto it to keep herself from falling off the new vehicle. It completed changing and became an advanced 1917 model of a four-cylinder Henderson motorcycle—the fastest bike on the road. Mary looked back at Thomas, sitting on a similar model.

"I don't know how to ride a motorcycle!" He complained.

Mary's bike lurched forwards by itself and sped between the buildings. "I think it's driving itself!" She yelled. Thomas followed close behind her.

A couple of people scurried out of their way when they burst from the alley and skidded onto the avenue in front of traffic. The cars honked and slammed on their brakes. Without wasting a second, Mary and Thomas accelerated in the direction she hoped Leo had gone.

Around the Federal Reserve building, despite being equipped with water wagons, a group of firemen seemed disinterested in putting out fires. Wooden crates of gold and silver were being loaded onto dozens of trucks, while hundreds of police officers stood guard over the operation.

Tibuta stood guard in front of the burning structure that used to be the vault. The large-framed Black woman put her hands on her hips and surveyed the scene. She sensed something coming, turned around, and looked into the sky. Helga and Elzbieta flew towards her. With two shakes of Tibuta's arms, two large, spike-covered iron balls on chains dropped out of her sleeves and thumped onto the ground, cracking the sidewalk.

Inga walked over, stood next to Tibuta, and patted her shoulder. "It's all right, it's me friend, Helga."

Tibuta shook her arms, and the balls on chains retracted into her sleeves.

Helga and Elzbieta landed and dismounted their teclyns. "Who is that?" Inga pointed to Elzbieta.

"She's an Ironsmith," Helga answered. "She wants to kill me— it's a long story—what in Goddess' name 'appened 'ere? It's like yeh 'ave every copper and Coppersmith In town, 'ere; no wonder no one showed up at the manor."

"It was Mausi—she betrayed us."

27

"I'll say, she threw a barrel uh gunpowder at me and destroyed White Manor, she might 'ave even taken the Siv Myrddin…" Inga sadly looked down. "What is it, Inga?"

"Heide, Christina, and Betty…They're all gone."

"Gone?"

"Mausi and some Dayfides, armed with ahrion bullets; probably the Followers…" Inga started to cry.

"No…Betty too?" Inga nodded. Helga walked over and put her arms around her.

Inga recomposed herself. "They didn't even take any metals!"

"No metals, then what was this about?"

"The Eye of Graeae."

"They took the Eye?"

"Yes. I guess we were so busy protecting the gold and silver that we forgot about the most valuable item."

"It's not yuh fault, Sweetie. Mausi betrayed us. We'll get the Eye back. And then black the eyes of the Followers!"

"I wish we could."

"What do you mean, wish? Let's go! Now!"

"We can't. We're under orders from the government to serve as security while they move the metals to a new location."

"Babysitting?"

"Pardon?"

"The government is going to let the Followers of Myrddin get away with this?"

"The Followers are working with the Germans! If we aren't careful, attacking them could drag the United States into a war!"

"THERE'S ALREADY A BLOODY WAR! Those bloody Dayfides in Washington are okay whiff our friends getting killed as long as the lovely metals are intact! Whiff the Eye of Graeae, they'll be able to watch us! And if they don't 'ave the book, they'll be able to find the owner! And then what? Sod all this! I know exactly where they're located! If you 'ave any Coppersmith 'onor in yeh, yuh follow me and go put some boots into arses!" Inga looked down. Helga was sad. She marched over to Tibuta. "You! Whiff yuh 'elp, it could be over in seconds! We can bring the Eye back! And punish the ones that did this!" Tibuta looked Helga in the eyes. Her face showed no emotion. Helga shook her head. "Bloody government quiffs yeh are, the whole lot of yuh!" She started walking away, stopped, and turned around. "Betty, Inga! Betty! She was yuh sister!" Inga turned her head and tried not to tear up. Helga turned back around and mounted her teclyn. "I understand if yeh gave yuh word to protect the Dayfide treasures, but a friend reminded me. Sometimes, you have to do the right things. Not because of honor, but because it's the right thing to do!" Helga lifted and flew away. Elzbieta turned around, stepped on her sword, and flew after Helga.

Tibuta stared intensively at the women. When they were out of sight, she paused in thought, smirked, and then turned around to continue guarding.

Mary searched the ground for Leo and the air for Flapper. She saw the bird about a block away, flying over some trolly lines. "There!" she yelled and pointed. The self-driving motorcycles weaved between cars at tremendous speed.

Leo heard the two machines approaching, looked back, and grimaced. On the sidewalk was a paperboy selling the latest edition of the New York Times. Leo held his ahrion-coated crucifix necklace, pointed at the boy, and said: *"Dol bwide!"* The newspapers flew out of the child's hands, into the air. The sheets of paper folded and twisted themselves, forming origami cranes the size of seagulls. The paper gulls began a series of distracting dive bombs on Mary and Thomas. They slowed down. Thomas came close to having a head-on collision with a truck, avoided when his motorcycle took control.

Mary swatted and hit a paper crane. It flew out of striking distance and dived down with two others. She spread out her fingers. *"Roy dldl"*. Within a second, the cranes burst into flames, rose, and quickly dissipated into black ash. She did the same on the other cranes and incinerated them from Thomas' path. He pulled his motorcycle beside hers. "You can set things on fire?" he yelled.

"Not until a moment ago," she responded.

"Good job!"

"Thank you...where did he go?" Leo was no longer in front of them. They looked all around. Mary was worried they had lost him.

"There!" Thomas yelled. He pointed to a parallel street to their left, one block over. Leo was going in the opposite direction.

Ignoring the screams and whistles of a traffic officer in the middle of the street, Mary and Thomas made sharp turns leading to car honking, screeching, and more whistle-blowing. Mary's bike rotated clockwise, and Thomas swerved counterclockwise. Their back tires met in the middle of the street and almost touched. Before the officer could run over to them and speak, they were already gone and had maneuvered to the same street as Leo, who had gotten further away.

"Can you throw a fireball at him or something?" Thomas yelled.

"I don't want to hurt the kids!"

Leo looked back at them angrily, spread his fingers, and said: *"Ne Weloeed!"* Grey smoke began to billow from his palm. The smoke flowed into Thomas and Mary's faces and blinded them. The pair moved their bikes to separate lanes, which gave them a break from the smoke. It increased its volume and coated them once more. Mary coughed and tried not to tear up too much. She wanted to turn around but knew catching up to Leo again would be too hard. She spread her fingers and said: *"Qwithie gwint!"* Suddenly, a gust of wind burst from her fingers and swept the smoke away from her face. The massive amount of smoke ahead had become so thick it was turning into a fog bank. The best Mary's Wind Forge could do was create a clear 10-foot path in front of her.

Thomas moved his motorcycle behind hers to slipstream her clear visibility. All around them, the fog was causing calamity: Cars swerved out of the way—one hit a telephone pole, pedestrians ran across the street right in front of them, and panicked, horse-drawn carts cut across their path.

Mary was losing patience with Leo. If he didn't have the kids, she imagined all kinds of forges she could do to cause him bodily harm.

The wall of fog curved to the left. Within a second, she and Thomas had passed through the fog bank and reached a clear area. Leo had made a sharp left turn in front of a wall of the women suffragette protesters they had interacted with earlier. Mary and Thomas skidded their tires and stopped 5 feet away from Juliet and Sarah. Thomas quickly turned his bike and continued chasing after Leo. Mary's bike was unresponsive. She began to hit it and yelled: "Go! Vamoose! Skiddo!"

Like trying to play catch up, the cycle's front tire lifted into a wheelie and roared away after Leo and Thomas. Mary held on for dear life but had enough dexterity to raise a fist in the air and yell: "VOTING RIGHTS FOR WOMEN!" The crowd burst into cheers again and waved.

Juliet and Sarah watched her disappear down the street.

"Never a dull moment with her," Sarah commented.

"Indeed." Juliet agreed.

Abel steered the Virginia around the base of the Statue of Liberty. He looked up at the copper-colored, majestic monument designed by Bartholdi and Eiffel. Something heavy came down onto the front of the ship; he could feel the back lift briefly and then come down again. Elzbieta stood on the bow with her back to him.

'She's returned!' He took out his magnifying glass. *"Eh-ha- gu avuh!"* The magnifying glass turned into a cannon gun. He held it tightly and tried to be as quiet as possible. He cautiously walked out of the bridge to the outside deck. She remained on the bow, looking around and enjoying the view. Abel snuck over to the exit and hunched out of her sight. With one step, he would be exposing his presence. He inhaled deeply and prepared to rush on her, imagining what his attack moves would be. After a final breath, he stepped outside. She was no longer in sight. He looked back and then to the water. He knew this left one more option. He quickly jumped forwards and avoided the sword coming down on him as she attacked from above. Her sword embedded itself In the ship's deck. He fired the cannon gun at her. She quickly removed the sword from the deck and blocked the golf ball-sized bullet. She brought the sword down on him. He dodged. She continually swung in all directions. Each time, Abel avoided the hits, damaging parts of the ship around him. He needed to close the gap between them and remove the chance of the sword chopping him in half. She swiped downwards. He rushed forwards and aimed the gun so that the bullet would strike her in the face. Elzbieta moved her head slightly, just enough so that the gun ended up on her shoulder. She grabbed the barrel and his hand and lifted with such force Abel rose with it over her shoulder in a suplex, causing him to land on his back. Her heel kicked down on his chest like a 240-pound weight. Abel grimaced and tried to bear the pain. Elzbieta spun the sword around and pointed it at his chest. 'This is it!' he thought, closing his eyes. Nothing happened. When he cautiously opened his eyes, he saw her holding her sword at his chest. He waited for something to happen. "Huh?" he said. She didn't respond. "What are you waiting for?"

"Do you want to die?" she asked.

"Pardon?"

"You're fighting like a man who wants to die, and the weak don't get to choose how they die!"

"I'm…I'm confused."

"If you want to die, kill yourself! Don't use me to kill you."

"Wha—what are you talking about? I'm not trying to kill myself! You're the one trying to kill me!"

"You attack first, I'm defending."

"You attacked my car and our house, and now you're landing on my ship! Of course, I'm going to attack you!"

"I only want to kill Black bloods and get Fritzy. Helga say Fritzy may be on funny black ship. I find funny black ship, and you attack; not say: welcome aboard, matey."

"I'm not going to—wait—Helga? Helga's alive?" he yelled. He looked away, smiled, and appeared to want to cry.

"Helga fine. We work together to find friends. I kill her later."

"You? You're working together?"

"For now."

"But, Why? Didn't you attack her too?"

"Helga spy on me when I find ship of blessed metals—ship is mine!"

Abel looked at the tip of the sword. "If you're not going to kill me, can I get up now?"

"You can. But you try to kill yourself again. I let you."

"Why do you keep saying that? I'm not trying to kill myself!"

"You are. Your moves are dangerous for a Stryker."

"What are you talking about?"

Elzbieta lifted her sword upwards. "Why you try so hard to be what you not?"

"I d—" Abel was interrupted by a propellor sound from the sky followed by another thump on the ship. "Helga!" He yelled, getting up. She unmounted her teclyn. He ran over and they tightly embraced. "Are you all right? Look out! She wants to kill you!" He pointed to Elzbieta.

Helga almost laughed. "It's all right, Luv. Where are the rest?"

Photo taken in 1913 of Abeo (Abel) of the House of White

"Great Scott!" Thomas yelled when Mary passed him, doing a wheelie.

She closed the gap between herself and Leo to make it within shouting distance and brought the vehicle back down to two wheels.

"LEO, PULL OVER!" She yelled.

Leo took an apple from his pocket and lifted it over his head.

Mary knew what he was about to do. He threw the apple into the middle of the street, and she shielded her eyes before it exploded in a blinding light in all directions, causing her motorcycle to wobble from the shock wave.

She regained control of the bike and was about to accelerate to be near him.

A truck driver on her left had succumbed to the effects of the light flash and struggled to maintain control of his vehicle. He veered the truck towards Mary, potentially sandwiching her into a trolly on her right.

She looked around for an escape; behind her, an auto whose driver was also steering blind cut off her escape route. "Is this Leo's intention? 'Did he mistakenly put my life in danger?'

A gust of wind caused her bike to float upwards. When the truck and trolly came close to sandwiching her, she lifted over the vehicles before they made contact.

The truck driver righted his vehicle and quickly sent it rebounding to the left.

Mary looked down and saw Leo pointing his hand back at her. 'At least he doesn't want me dead.' He periodically looked back and forth between her and the road as her bike floated higher and higher over the traffic, looking around to see where his forge had sent her. 'He doesn't have any control.' She remembered the time he made her float in her wheelchair. 'He still doesn't know how to master that forge. I'm going to keep floating until I'm 100 kilometers up.' Like the other forges, the correct words came into her mind to stop herself from ascending. *"Duhc welleg deef thi hav!"* The bike started to go downwards towards a pair of subway tracks on top of an iron trestle.

She turned the handlebar back and forth, again and again, but her trajectory remained the same. 'I've got to get off of this thing!' The parallel tracks had approaching trains; she had to think quickly; she was almost on a collision level with one of them.

With one smooth motion, she stood up on her motorcycle seat and launched herself up into the air.

The train collided with her Silver Ghost motorcycle and tumbled it away, producing sparks and the sounds of squealing train breaks. Mary noticed her speed of descent was fast yet still controlled and almost graceful. She could maneuver a little with her arms out. "Can I fly without a teclyn?"

Leo didn't expect to see Mary land between his motorcycle and its sidecar. She steadied herself to keep from falling backward and raised her sword over her head.

He raised his arm to block her. She brought the blade down between the cycle and the sidecar and severed the vehicle in two, then jumped onto the sidecar as it wheeled off to the right. She grabbed the back of the sidecar and held on to prevent it from hitting a lamp post. Her shoes skidded on the concrete and brought the car down to walking speed. It hit the post with a light tap.

Mary shook the burlap sack. "Min? Little Dog Boy? Are you all right?" Muffled sounds were coming from inside the bag. "Are you bound and gagged?" The muffled sounds had a tone of agreement in them. "Right, stay still, I'm going to cut you out!" Mary lifted her sword and prepared to slash the bag open. A massive spray of water hit her in the face and pushed her into the wall of a nearby bookshop. She thrashed around and tried to release herself from the stream caused by Leo forging the escaping water of a nearby uncapped fire plug. It didn't matter where she moved, the water moved in that direction and kept her pinned against the wall. "LEO…" she struggled to say, "…S-s-stop this!" Leo ignored her and kept up the assault. He was concentrating so much on Mary, that he was unaware of Thomas. Before Leo could act, Thomas punched him in the face, sending him off his bike and onto his back. The spray of water released Mary. She gasped and shook the water from her hair.

Leo crawled away from Thomas, who was marching in anger towards him. "You cur!" Thomas yelled, walking over the top of a manhole cover.

Leo said: *"Urf ur caa fael"* and pointed at the metal disk. It shot up into the air, and Thomas somersaulted backward off of it and landed on his back. The disk spun high into the air, then flew downwards towards his head. It made it within five feet until it was split in two by an upswing from his sword. The halves crashed to the side of him in metallic thuds.

"Good Show!" Mary yelled. She busied herself with releasing the kidnapped children in the bag; it was very difficult to open. "This bag has been forged!" she said. "It's as tough as iron!"

She lifted her sword and prepared to slice the bag open; a gust of wind prevented her from doing so.

Leo pointed at her and used hurricane-strength winds, concentrated at her height to push her away from the kids. He walked over to the sack and kept his eye on Thomas, getting up to stop him.

Leo rubbed his cheek where Thomas had punched him. "I owe you one, chief," He stopped his wind forge on Mary and pointed towards the bookstore. *"Papier-heholee!"*

Mary recomposed herself, pointed at Leo, and yelled: *"Bêl tân!"* A fireball came out of her hand and traveled towards him.

Something jumped in the way and took the impact; a humanoid figure made entirely from books. It burst into flames and thrashed

37

around, then lunged towards Thomas and came dangerously close to grabbing onto him.

Thomas slashed away at the flaming bookman, cutting it into large pieces.

Leo used the distraction to walk over to the sidecar and started pushing it towards his motorcycle.

"Don't forget about me!" Mary yelled, feeling insulted. She pointed her hand at him and was about to launch another fireball.

Something grabbed Her wrist and yanked it upwards; her fireball shot towards the sky and eventually dissipated; another man made out of books had snuck up from behind her.

She grabbed the creature's right hand, trying to strangle her around the neck, flipped her sword back in her right hand, and impaled it into the bookman's side. The creature released her neck, and she swiped fast, severing its head.

She read the cover that used to be his head: Metamorphosis by Franz Kafka. "Oh, I read that!"

While Mary was struggling with her assailant, Thomas cut his into enough pieces so that it stopped advancing.

Leo was having difficulty reconnecting the two halves of his motorcycle. "I wish I knew more forging!" He pointed towards the entrance of the bookstore. "Papier-heholee!"

Thomas and Mary ran towards him.

Four more book people lunged out of the shop at them. Thomas flipped one over his shoulder and immobilized it with a stab to the chest. "These creatures—I thought paper dolls couldn't hurt you!"

"These are books!" Mary yelled while cutting one of her attackers in half. "But if you make it human, it's going to die like a human!"

Leo settled with hoisting the large sack over his shoulder. He started his motorcycle, revved the engine with his other arm, and tried to speed away but only made it three feet. Mary's sword was thrown at his back tire and wedged in the spokes.

Her book creature backhanded her, and she fell. It grabbed her around the neck and started choking her. She remembered her combat lesson from Min and Thomas. 'Spread my fingers, put them under his wrist, and lift!' As she was lifting the creature's arm, it used its other one to punch her in the jaw. Her anger concentrated into a powerful kick to the thing's chest, sending it flying across the street into a lamppost. It didn't get a moment to rest as she had already set it on fire. The rising flames licked the side of a building.

Leo struggled with removing the sword from his tire. Thomas, brought his sword back to kill him. Leo used the escaping water from the hydrant to spray sideways and knock him away. He noticed Mary was getting dangerously close to him.

"Give it up, Leo!" she yelled. "You know you can't do more than one forge at a time!" Mary pointed at her sword. *"Oomestin raff!"* Her sword melted and reshaped into a silver rope, wrapped tightly around the cycle's tire and seat.

"I guess you figured that one out," Leo said. "I didn't stick around White Manor long enough to master that," he tried to pull the metal rope off his bike. "Guess I've got a lot to…learn!" He took out an apple and was about to throw it onto the ground to create a blinding flash.

Mary yelled: *"Crafanyo dül lo!"* and pointed at her sword. It elongated into four skinny metallic arms and snaked itself around Leo's body, binding his arms to his sides and causing him to drop the apple before he could cast a forge.

The water spray holding Thomas at bay returned to an upward direction, freeing him and doused the pole Mary had set on fire earlier.

"Where in the world does he keep all of those damned apples?" Thomas asked.

"Magic," Leo answered sarcastically.

"Well, it's going to take a lot of magic to get you out of jail for attempted murder and kidnapping."

"Ha!" Leo scoffed. "Didn't I tell you? The hoosegow can't hold me?"

Mary went back to trying to open the sack. "He's right, if he goes to prison, he'll just use forging to escape."

"I guess we'll just have to kill him." Thomas reared his sword back.

"Thomas, no!" Mary yelled.

"Ahh, you do care." Leo cooed.

"No, I need the sword to cut the kids out of this sack, mine is busy binding you." Leo looked disappointed. Thomas handed her his sword. "Well, the third time's the charm; my word, every time I try to do this, I get interrupted!"

"Then I suggest you hurry," Thomas said.

She lifted his sword. There was a metallic plop sound near them. They looked towards the street and saw a softball-sized black metal ball.

"What is that?" Mary asked"

"A cannonball?" Thomas answered.

The ball started to wiggle around a bit and then sprouted eight skinny metallic legs from its sides.

"A spider? How did Leo do that?" Thomas readied himself for an attack.

"Don't look at me," Leo said. "Insects aren't really my thing."

Mary looked around. "He's right, with his arms like that, he can't reach his anvil."

"Anvil?" Thomas asked.

"...His magic wand? Leo uses his necklace to forge!"

The metallic spider remained still.

"Where did it come from?" Mary asked.

"More importantly, why is it here?"

A tiny white rope sprouted from the top of the spider. Mary, Thomas, and Leo stared at the thing in fear and fascination. The little rope on its head sparked and started fizzling. The spider started rapidly crawling towards them.

"It's a bomb!" Leo yelled.

"Leo, if this is another one of your tricks—"

"It's not me, it's a bomb! Let me out of this!" He tried to squirm out of his restraints.

"I for one, don't believe you!" Thomas said.

"I agree…" Mary said. She walked over to the spider. "Enough of your Tom foolery! Just come along quietly!"

She kicked the spider across the street into the open manhole. The spider fell in, and a second later, there was the sound of a small explosion. A plume of smoke came out of the hole. They all flinched. "Bloody hell!" Mary yelled.

"A dangerous attempt to escape," Thomas said.

"It wasn't me!" Leo complained.

"Who else would have done that?" Mary asked.

"Her!" Leo answered, nodding his head up towards the sky."

They saw Mausi riding in a canopy, suspended underneath a large black balloon.

"She was the one who killed Helga!" Mary yelled. Mausi waved her hand over the basket and seemed to be guiding something. "What on earth is she doing?"

Thomas looked around. "The children!" Behind them, the sack with Min and Fritz floated towards Mausi's gesturing hand.

"She's taking the children!" Mary yelled.

Thomas ran over and tried to jump up to grab the sack but it was too high.

"Let me try!" Mary yelled. She hunched down and braced herself. With a huge leap, she sent herself skywards towards the floating sack. She came within three feet of the children. Mausi said: *"Qwithu ar wahân!"* and threw a little black ball in between Mary and the sack. The explosion sent her flying backward into the window of an office above the bookstore.

"Mary!" Thomas yelled. He ran into the building and looked for the stairs.

"I'm okay!" he heard her yell. "Save the children first!"

"Right, of course!" When he ran back outside, he felt something sharp go into his back near his left shoulder blade. It took a few seconds before the excruciating pain of being stabbed registered with him. It brought him down on one knee. He looked to the right and saw Leo holding Mary's sword. "You dis... honorable..." Leo let go of the blade, and Thomas fell forwards onto his hands.

Leo got down and whispered in Thomas' ear. "The only person I care about is Mary! The rest of you are in my way!" He stood up and pulled the sword out. *"Dückweh luhg!"* The sword turned back into a pen. "I remember this pen, it belonged to Professor White." He tucked it into Thomas' shirt pocket. "You can have it back, I want nothing to do with him."

"They seemed to be after you and this sack!" Mausi shouted down to Leo. "Who are you?"

"Leo Bianca." He shouted back. "I used to work for Maximillian Blanc."

"Maximillian? Ronin Goldsmith?"

"Ronin? Yeah, I guess. How did you know what was going on"

"Let's just say we have eyes everywhere."

"Are you working for the Follow—"

"Is the Siv Myrddin in this sack?" She held up.

"No, but it's valuable enough to Mary White that she'll trade what's in it for it."

"O'right...that's good to know...We'll keep in touch, Leo Bianca." She lifted her hand underneath the opening of the balloon.

Flames billowed out of her hand, sending the balloon craft high up into the sky.

Model T police cars pulled up with their sirens blaring and surrounded Leo and Thomas.

"Get your hands up!" An officer yelled, pointing a gun at them.

"Officers, arrest tha—at man!" Thomas struggled to say. He felt a stream of blood trickling down his arm.

"You too! Get your hands up!" He pointed his gun at Thomas.

"Sorry…rather difficult right now."

Two more officers got out of police cars, weapons drawn.

"I…I'm Detective Vanderbilt of the NYPD…formally." Thomas tried to take out his copper badge.

A shot ricocheted on the sidewalk. "I said don't move!" The lead officer yelled.

"Officer, I'm telling you the truth."

"Alls I know is: there was a crazy car chase involving motorcycles and reports of massive property damage—including a wrecked subway train! Looking at that fire hydrant, that balloon, and those wrecked trucks behind us tell me you two are involved In this, somehow!"

"I saw the whole thing, officer. It was him!" Leo pointed at Thomas.

"What? You—he just stabbed me!"

"With what?" Leo asked.

"A sword!"

"What sword? Do you mean that ink pen in your pocket? See! Officers! He's either five sheets to the wind or off his rocker."

"Leo, I swear, I'm going to…" there was a familiar hissing sound near them. Thomas looked down the street in the direction Mausi had traveled in. Hundreds of heavy little black balls rolled towards them and transformed into a swarm of spider bombs. The ones closest to them automatically ignited their fuses. Thomas counted at least three, about to explode. "Look out!"

"What is that?" The officer asked.

"They're bombs!"

Leo pointed his hand at the ignited bombs. *"Qwithie gwint!"* A concentrated wind blew the bombs off to the side, underneath two of the police cars, and they exploded within seconds, sending the cars flipping into the air. Leo ran over, mounted his motorcycle, and took off, down the street.

Thomas struggled to get up and took out his pen. *"Dückweh luhg!"* The pen turned back into a sword just in time for him to swat a spider bomb that had come dangerously close. He screamed from the pain of having to move so fast. All around him, officers were either injured, firing guns at the bombs, or lying down dead near burning cars. Over 50 spider bombs ran into the building Mary had crashed into. "Oh, no!" Mary! He lumbered towards the building, but it was too late. A series of explosions came from upstairs, sending debris and smoke at him. When he went outside, there was another explosion. Mary crashed out a window, barely ahead of a fireball, and came down fast. On the last three meters, a ring of air blew under her feet, spread outwards, and her body slowed almost to a stop and then floated to the ground. She brushed herself off and noticed her shoulder was on fire. Looking annoyed, she patted it out.

"Are you…okay?" Thomas asked.

"I am. I was injured. I was about to take some ahrion, but my body healed itself! On its own!" She kicked a spider across the street and it exploded on the sidewalk.

"On your own? How—never mind, we have to get out of here, that woman went…that way!" Thomas tried to gesture down the street with his left arm, but it was too painful.

"Thomas, you're injured! Take this, and drink it!" She handed him the ahrion.

He bit the cork top off and drank it. His face winced in distress. "My God! That's horrible, I feel worse!" He grimaced. "It's burning…"

"Sorry! Hold on." Mary put her hand on his shoulder: "Gwessla orga-na." Nothing improved. She said it again and again. Each time he felt worse and worse. 20 spider bombs crawled towards them.

"I don't…want to rush you…but pain is …making me faint…" Thomas passed out.

"No-no-no-no-no!" Mary yelled. She bent down and put her hand on his head. "No! Why is it so hard to master healing? Thomas, don't pass out! We have to save the kids!" She closed her eyes and concentrated. Thomas' eyes shot open, and he gasped as though he had been holding his breath. "Mary, spider!" he yelled. One of the bombs crawled onto Mary's back. She tightly hugged Thomas, shut her eyes, and prepared for an end. They heard an explosion behind her.

"Mary.........Mary......MARY!" Thomas yelled.

Mary opened her eyes and released Thomas; he was in shock. "Thomas, what is..." She looked back to see what he was staring at and saw a large pair of silver mechanical angel wings. Moving her shoulder a little, she discovered the wings were attached to her back. "Thomas?" Within an instant, the wings shrank, folded, absorbed into her back, and disappeared. She felt her shoulder blades; there was no evidence of angel wings ever appearing except two small slits in the back of her blouse. "Thomas? What was that all about?"

"You had wings—they pushed the bomb off of you!"

"I...No time to lose, more coming!" She pulled him up and pointed at the spiders.

The surviving police officers fired their guns at the bombs, exploding them prematurely and causing various street damage.

Thomas looked around. "We need to catch up to them! What happened to my motorcycle?"

"It probably went to join with its other half and turn back into a car. Look!" Mary pointed to the Silver Ghost weaving between the wreckage behind them. It pulled up and opened its doors.

"I really do love this car!" They got in, Mary took the driver's seat.

"Mary, I..."

"What, you're injured! Do you have a problem with a woman driving?"

"No, of course not, I have more of a problem with you driving!"

"Thomas, I'll have you know, I'm a perfectly safe—"

"Hey, where do ya think yuh going?" One of the policemen yelled"

"Away from the chaos!" Mary yelled. "And if you want to live, I'd suggest you jump onto the runner." The officer hesitated for a second and then gestured to the other policeman. "Let's go, Sullivan!" They hurried over and jumped onto the car's runner, and kept firing at any spiders."

A spider bomb hopped onto the hood and lit its fuse. Mary slammed her foot on the gas, and the car skidded into reverse.

The bomb rolled off and exploded a second later.

Hordes of spider bombs filled the street and skittered after them. Mary zigzagged the car around the truck wreckage, and they continued to reverse down the street. The policemen jerked, swayed, and held on for dear life, too busy holding on to fire at the bombs. Thomas used his derringer to shoot three spiders when they crawled too close. "This gun is inefficient! I need something better!" he complained.

"Thomas! Remember! You have a teclyn!"

"It's a sword."

"It becomes a sword by default! It can be whatever weapon you want, you're a Stryker!"

"Okay then, what are the words for making a gun?"

"Eh-ha-who gwen—My word, how do I know that?"

He took out his pen and looked at the hundreds of bombs running after them. "Eh-ha-who gwen!" The pen turned into a Lewis light machine gun, used by the army to mow down countless soldiers in the war. "Oh! that's much better!"

"What are you people?" a policeman yelled.

Thomas started a barrage with his machine gun; moving it from side to side, aiming at the bombs. Some of the closest ones exploded, and the others burst into black sparkling powder. All of the spiders had been eliminated, by the time they had traveled three blocks.

The path was now clear. Mary stepped on the brakes, forcing Thomas back into his seat and causing the officers to fall onto the street. She floored the gas again and they sped forwards in the opposite direction, leaving the officers and their pleas to stop.

"We've lost her!" Mary complained.

"Doesn't matter, from the direction the balloon is headed, I know exactly where it's going!"

"Where?"

"The docks, to the RMS Olympic. That's where Helga was attacked!"

"Sounds like a good place to start!" Mary looked over at Thomas. She was never gladder he was with her. "Thomas?"

"Yes?"

"Thank you!"

"For what?"

"Everything!"

They sped down the street towards the docks.

On a nearby building, dressed in a long black dress and a long red scarf, the White Haired Woman, with her face completely covered in gauze, watched the Silver Ghost speed away from the destruction.

After the car was out of sight, she leaped off the building onto the roof of another and ran in their direction at an incredible speed.

So which direction did Mary and Thomas go?" Helga asked Abel.

"I'm not sure. I was pulling the ship away at the time," Abel answered.

"Well, ne'er mind all that, I can track Mary using a personal item on this ship. Unfortunately, Leo escaped. I'd sure like to rip off 'is bollocks for what 'e did to you. And taking the kids to boot."

"Is Leo man who throw apple at my head?" Elzbieta asked.

"One and the same."

"Ohhh. I save him for last! See how long he survive without skin!" Helga and Abel grimaced.

"Anyway..." Helga continued. "...Why didn't you go whiff them?"

"Well..." Abel looked over at Elzbieta; preoccupied with tasting a metal mapping compass. He lowered his voice. "Tell me, do you have the key to the..." He lowered his voice even more. "...clo kefin for this ship?"

"Clo kefin? I honestly didn't know this ship 'ad one. Why, wots in it?" Helga whispered.

Abel whispered as quietly as he could: "The Siv Myrddin."

"The SIV MYRDDIN is on this ship?" Elzbieta yelled.

"Crikey! Ears like a bloody dog—that one!" Helga complained.

"No, I read lips." Elzbieta corrected.

"Cor blimey! Now she's going to be after it, too!"

"No, I already tell you. I no care about gulpi (stupid) book, kochaine (darling), I just want to kill Apple Man, Boom Boom Lady, and Black Bloods and get Fritz back!"

"Forger's honor?" Helga asked her.

"Forger's honor—wasting time with talk-talk, we should be hunting!"

"She's right," Abel agreed. "I'm going to hide the ship somewhere while you two fly on to join Thomas and Mary... provided she doesn't try to kill Mary?"

"I told yuh, we 'ave a truce," Helga assured. "But, hide all yeh want luv. The ones that blew up White Manor had the Eye of Graeae in their office."

"Wait...is that the thing that can see into the past?"

"No, this one was a huge crystal ball..." she gestured with her hands to indicate a globe, "...about this size that can spy on anyone in the present. If they 'ave that, they'll find you, no matter where you 'ide this ship—could be watching us, right now."

"But you can't: record the Siv Myrddin, copy it, film it, or transport it. There's no way they'll know it's on this ship."

"Unless Leo tells them who's guarding it." Abel had a look of panic on his face. "If we don't find Leo before he contacts the Followers—doesn't matter where yeh hide this ship, if yuh on it, they'll be able to find the book by looking for where yuh are."

"Besides, you no protect book." Elzbieta added. "You bezsilny."

"Bezsilny?" Helga asked.

"Weak."

"I'm not WEAK! Abel yelled."

"You fine for protection from Dayfides and anghenfēls. But if Followers send someone level 10, and you here by yourself..." Elzbieta stamped her foot down. "...they smash you like bug!".

"He's not weak!" Helga defended. "Abel is a good fighter!"

"He can fight, very well—most opponents would be red mist by now. But, Strykers can't beat Forgers alone, it's the way it is. You try to beat us alone, we'll kill you! Do you not know what Stryker for?" Elzbieta asked Abel.

"Yes. We're like Forgers, without the casting powers."

She began to laugh hysterically. "Silly Stryker, no one tell you? Did you no tell him?" she asked Helga. Helga looked down, embarrassed. "You are servants! You support the Forgers! Stryker help the Smiths! Silversmiths use the word Stryker, Coppersmiths call you familiars, and Goldsmiths call you minions or slaves! But you no act like support. You try to act like equal who thinks he's Forger! This why I beat you easy!"

"Elzbieta! That's enough!" Helga yelled.

"She's right," Abel said. "I couldn't defeat her when she boarded the ship."

Helga sighed. "That's not a fair test, Luv. She's a level seven berserker!"

"And who are they going to send to get the book? A level one? Shirley—a Normalu, was able to use me! And the Belgian easily got the drop on me or—"

Helga put her hand on his shoulder. "Let's shove off then. The sooner you can 'ide this ship before they track yuh, the better. Then, when the coast is clear, we can all rendezvous."

"And how am I supposed to get back to shore? Row?"

"Just draw a bath in the tub, Dearie. We can Vorago to you and out when the coast is clear."

"A bath? The ocean is full of water you can use."

"The ocean is too turbulent, Luv. Unless you're a high-level, fast-moving water is too unstable for the rest of us. Yeh can end up 1000 kilometers off course."

"That's why I row boat across ocean," Elzbieta added. "But where you hide ship?" she asked Helga.

"Don't know. We can sink and raise it if we 'ave to, right?"

"I supposed," Abel answered.

"Then we'll do that. If we can get it to the middle of the ocean, we'll sink it. Even if they can see you it'll be harder to locate you without seeing any landmarks."

Mary and Thomas hurried along the street. When they reached the shoreline, Mary drove carefully past busy dockworkers, recent travelers, and fishmongers. "Didn't Helga say there was a boat full of Germans making ahrion bullets around here?" she asked Thomas.

"She did. She got into a fight with the Ironsmith around here; said the Germans also had an anti-aircraft cannon, a foundry, and men unloading crates of precious metals onto trucks."

"Not much of that going on around here, now. Everyone here seems unaware of anything out of the ordinary."

"I think she said the ship was the Olympic—said it looked like the Titanic."

"Titanic? I don't look forward to seeing that again."

"Your family does seem cursed with naval mishaps."

"All caused by those seeking that book."

"Do you think the Followers sank the Titanic?"

"Perhaps not the Followers. I don't think they had much power until the war started. I believe the Gold Forgers probably did that."

"I'm rather confused. With the exception of that short woman who killed Helga, the other Coppersmith working in the bank seemed pretty chummy with Helga. And yet, they said that they were working with the Goldsmiths. Doesn't that mean the Goldsmiths aren't evil?"

"The Coppersmiths have always been a rather neutral group, and the Goldsmiths, minus the greed, can sometimes be no more evil than the other foundries. All histories are stained." Mary spotted something in the air. The gondola underneath Mausi's black balloon flying four miles away. "Look, about 6 kilometers!"

"I see her!" Thomas pointed to an area populated with warehouses. "Looks like she's headed to the pier further down that way!" Mary drove the car while looking up at the basket. All around them, entire missing sections of the dock showed signs of massive damage; evidence of the fierce battle between Helga and Elzbieta. The balloon descended out of sight. Mary craned her neck around to see if she could see where it had landed. A cloth-covered cannon was being lifted off a truck, blocking her view. Thomas drew her attention to the security guard she was about to run over. She slammed on the brakes before the bumper hit his knees.

The armed guard stood in front of a barricade made of steel drums, tires, and wooden crates, preventing anyone from advancing. Behind the barricade stood another man, smoking a cigarette, and holding a machine gun.

"What's all this then?" Mary asked.

"Roads closed, lady!" the man said coarsely with a German accent.

"Why?"

"Because I said so, now scram ya floozie!"

Mary looked over at Thomas. "Er-ah, Mary, why don't we turn around? We'll go another way."

"What? She asked angrily."

"It's fine, let's go." He pleaded with her, using a widened eye expression to implore her to let it go. Mary looked at him for a second and then at the guard. Her face showed obvious frustration. She put the car in reverse and backed it away from the area until they were out of listening distance of the guards. "Why didn't we just ram through them? I'm sure they can't offer any resistance remotely close to our abilities."

"True, But if we go crashing through there, we don't know what kind of trouble we could run into. Sometimes, the subtle approach is the best."

"Hmm. Perhaps you're right.

"Maybe you can turn us invisible, and we'll sneak in."

"I can try. Do you still have that coin Helga gave you?"

"Of course. I'll always carry it. It saved my life; as did she."

Mary held out her hand. Thomas put the coin in it. "Now then: *'Dooes loose la god.'* She handed the coin back to him. "Once you repeat those words, the forge will activate, and you will turn invisible."

"Remarkable. That must be how those goons were turned invisible when we were attacked on the beach."

"Quite. But, remember: slow, gentle movements; no dramatic gestures, or it'll break the forge. This is why it's hard to attack while invisible—also, no speaking, that will definitely break it."

"The large amount of knowledge coming out of you lately is astounding. Is this all from what you learned as a child?"

"Some of it, But most of it is coming from the vision memories I was having—it's like someone else's knowledge is also flowing into me."

"The memories of a skilled Forger."

"Most likely our of yet seen level 11—anyway, let us park the car somewhere and sneak in."

Leo pushed his motorcycle into an alleyway next to some garbage cans and covered it with an old discarded blanket. With extreme caution, he looked around before proceeding into his apartment building. Once inside, he shut the door and breathed a sigh of relief. He walked over to a small table to pour himself a stiff drink. There was someone else in the room watching him. He grabbed his crucifix and pointed at the figure, trying to imagine the most painful way to harm them. He was surprised; Shirley Blanche was not on his list of possible attackers.

She sat in his only good chair, sipping alcohol out of a metal tea cup.

"What are you doing here!" Leo yelled.

"I've come to see you, Mr. Bianca."

"Why? I'm sure you figured out that book wasn't in the safe—you should be hunting it down."

"How did you survive the explosions?"

"Mary's father had a canal in the basement. We sailed out just in time."

"Does she still have the book?"

"Yes…" Leo looked pale.

"What's the matter, Mr. Bianca?"

"It's in another clo kefin, with a different key."

"Then we just need to get her to—"

"How did you find me? I thought my apartment would be too obvious of a hiding place."

Shirley smiled. "I have many resources."

"You mugs have been trailing me the whole time, haven't you? Why are you here?"

"You shot Abel White."

"Yeah, so what! He survived and ratted me out!"

"He grew up with you and Mary, right?"

"Yeah, so."

"Yet, you did it so easily, just to make sure I got into the safe to get the book."

"What's your point?"

"I need a new minion, I think it should be you."

"Really? Sure Maximillian won't like that idea."

"Oh, I killed him."

"WHAT?"

"It's true."

"You? You killed a Forger?"

"Yes."

"How?"

"I gradually poisoned him with ahrion mixed with arsenic, and then I stabbed him."

"In the heart?"

"No."

"Did you cut his head off or nail the corpse's mouth shut?"

"No, he was a Forger, not a vampire—I have his sword cane back at my hotel room if you require proof."

Leo chuckled. "You know less about us than you think."

"The Forger library was at my orphanage. I've studied you, people, for years. I know all of your weaknesses."

"Oh really, and what's mine?"

"I told you, amour."

"And I told you, I'm not doing it for love!"

"Really? Tell me, if there was a way to make Mary fall in love with you—forever, would you use it?"

"If...if you're talking about a mind bend, that can't happen, they already bent Mary's mind. Once someone's mind is bent they can't be hypnotized again."

"Incorrect."

"What are you talking about, you crazy Dayfide? It's one of the first lessons they teach you at the foundry."

"Mary's mind was welded just like mine. Professor White used a forge called Calculus Remotio to suppress, not bend our memories. Otherwise, neither of us could walk around for all those years with glowing red eyes. He changed our memories, but he never forced us to do anything. Do you understand? She's still vulnerable." Leo looked shocked and settled into silence. "I can see by your reaction that you never considered this."

"I guess...I...I didn't. So that's why Helga was able to question you."

"Pardon?"

"Never mind, they found out nothing about you. But even so, You can't have someone walking around with the red-eye thing. Who would want someone like that?"

"True, But when it comes to mind-bending, there is more than one way to do it. When they restored my memories, the Goldsmiths didn't have that book; how do you think they opened an unbreakable vessel holding my memories without a forge?"

"I don't know. Someone must have known what to say?"

"No, they used a Chamfer."

"A Spell Breaker? Those are real?"

"Quite real."

"The Golds have a Spell Breaker?"

"We had three. We lost one to the Germans when they invaded. I assume that means the Followers of Myrddin have it now."

"What does a Spell Breaker have to do with mind bends?"

"One of the forges In that book is not a mind bend or weld but is called prolongation and can only be used with those special weapons. It's the same forge used by Tristan and Isolde—a love forge which will bind someone's heart to yours until the day they die—a lifetime of love…from your heart's desire, with no red eyes."

"Why are you telling me all this?"

Shirley stood up and walked over to Leo. "That book has that forge, that Ironsmith has Calibur—a Chamfer. Help me get them. Then we'd both get what we want!"

"Even if I wanted to—assuming we can get that sword without being chopped in half, I'm already planning to make a deal with a bomb-throwing witch in a balloon, hoping Mary makes a deal with her for the book—actually, if you ask me, I'd rather work with her. 'cause she looked a lot more powerful than you and your dead assistant.'"

Shirley laughed.

"What's so funny?"

"That must have been Mausi from the Followers of Myrddin. They want to give the book to the Kaiser in Germany. Can you imagine the damage he could cause with that kind of power: armies of Forgers and soldiers with ahrion bullets and weapons?"

"No better than you Golds."

"We want wealth. We have no interest in taking over countries and having to govern, we'd rather pay others to do that job. The Followers want to bring back the over-romanticized reign of Pendragon: An insecure, incestuous hypocrite who destroyed his kingdom over an affair —ignoring the advice of the man who wrote the book we're all fighting over. I on the other hand, just want to end this terrible ordeal for my cousin; for you both." She put her hands on his shoulder. "Don't you want to be with her? Never worrying about Forgers and that cursed book? Don't you want her to love you and only you…and not Detective Vanderbilt?"

Leo removed her hand. "She doesn't love him!"

"Of course she—"

"You let yourself in, you can let yourself out the window!"

Shirley sighed, walked over to the table, and finished her drink. She went to the front door, opened it, and turned around. "I have a plan to get close to Mary again."

"You are nuts. Abel knows you hypnotized him! He'll kill you on site!"

"Let me worry about that. Just go. Do your little business with the Followers. And when they fail—and believe me, they will, you come to see me, and we'll do it my way. I'll be at the Waldorf"

Shirley departed without closing the door behind her. Leo watched her walk down the hallway

The Virginia cut through the Atlantic Ocean, heading east at twice the speed of any sea-faring craft available in 1915. Turbulent splashes under its iron belly created a trail of mist and waves in its wake. On the stern, Elzbieta stood with her arms spread out, letting the wind rush over her.

Helga and Abel were on the bridge watching the act. "Saw a boy do that when we were on the Titanic..." Helga said. "...'e died."

"Hopefully the Virginia will fare better than the Titanic," Abel said.

"Hope is good," Helga, picked up a little girl's dress, held it to her chest, and closed her eyes.

"That's the personal item you're using to track Mary?"

"Yes. Professor White gave this to her on her 8th birthday...It was the last time all of us were together, with Leo, and the last time she was Mary Black. I assume it means something to her since she 'adn't donated it."

"Probably an accurate assumption. Where is it telling you to go?"

"The last reading has somewhere near the docks. Maybe Leo is going to give the kids to the Germans. They are rumored to be working with the Followers."

"Leo has no alliance, does he?"

"Only to himself."

"Ohh!" Elzbieta yelled.

"What's she going on about?" Helga walked outside onto the deck to investigate.

"Big metal fishy, big metal fishy!" Elzbieta yelled.

"Metal what?"

"Metal fishy, under the water! Same one that throw bomb at Elzbieta when I try to kill Elyan White on ship!" She pointed to the water.

"A metal—you mean a submarine?"

"Same one that blow up Elzbieta and Elyan White!"

"The Lusitania? A German submarine? Why is there a German submarine off our coast? And how do you know it's the same one?"

"Ironsmith can feel machines; machines have spirits; that how I find you. In water is same one that blow me up—now I get revenge!" Elzbieta grabbed her parasol, walked to the stern, and jumped overboard.

"What In Goddess's name!? Where are you going? Yuh looney?"

"Fishing!" Elzbieta answered before disappearing behind the waves.

"She's not very dependable, is she?" Abel yelled from the bridge.

Mary avoided coming into contact with one of the German dock workers. With controlled, slow movements, she turned her body just enough for the man to walk to her left. She knew with one nudge, he would cause her to turn visible again. She wasn't sure if Thomas was with her. She hoped his goal and trajectory matched her own. If he was near her, he could also cause her to turn visible if he ran into her. Talking would also break the forge, so communicating with him was impossible. She wished she could ask him if he had also seen the foundry outside on the dock, with a smith pouring molten silver into bullet molds. Or the crate-loads of what she assumed were precious metals to be shipped back to Germany.

Her goal was to board the ship and look around for the kids. She made it to the gangplank. Its narrow width lent itself to perfect timing and fear. If she were in the middle of it going up, and someone was coming down, there was no way they would pause in their stride. After watching two men carry a large wooden box up and a man holding a rifle coming down, she felt enough time had passed for her to feel safe. She walked up onto the plank and cautiously ascended. Out of nowhere, another man with a gun appeared at the top of the plank, preparing to come down. Mary looked back and considered retreat. 'But, what if Thomas is walking behind me? If I bump into him, we will both be exposed!' She looked at the man who had started downwards. 'If he runs into me, I'll have to deal with him! But what do I do? If I toss him over the side or jump, that will cause enough ruckus to render my plan awash in chaos!' The man got closer. 'Okay, prepare for trouble…' Another man appeared at the top of the plank. '…make it double.' The second man called out to the first man in German. Mary didn't catch what he said. For whatever reason, the first man reversed course and walked to the top to join the second one. As fast as she could go, Mary treaded lightly behind the first guy as if she would explode if jostled the wrong way. She took the first opportunity she could at the top of the plank to slip around the two guys and continued.

On the bridge, Mausi and Schwieger gazed at the crystal ball stolen from the Federal Reserve. The projection in the ball was black with intermittent wisps of grey smoke.

They had looks of disappointment and worry on their faces.

"I don't get it!" Mausi's said, "I said all the right words, and it still won't work."

"Does it have sound?" Schwieger asked.

"You mean like a talkie? If you want to hear, yuh have to do scrying using a crow or raven."

"Then this thing is useless! Without it telling you where she is or what she is saying—this plan is a waste of time and money: making all of those silver bullets, having to deal with that crazy sword lady; that's it, let's pack everything up and set sail!"

"Not until we find that book!"

"We never should have trusted this job to hexen. We should contact the Kaiser!"

"We can handle this—and don't call me a witch, German slag! We can track the book down!" Mausi slapped the side of the inanimate object. "Come on! Bloody rubbish yuh are!"

"Why isn't it showing where she is anymore?"

"She must be invisible or something."

"Then she could be anywhere, including on this ship! What was her last position?"

"Last I saw of 'er was downtown. When I got back 'ere this is all I've seen."

"We need to assume she's coming here to get that sack!"

"Wonder whot's in here?"

"Now is a good time to find out."

Mausi walked over to the sack and picked it up with one hand. "Should we just drop it over the side?"

"Why would you do that?"

"Make sure it's not a curse or something."

"That doesn't make any sense. Just put it in the cargo hold, place lots of guards around it, and open it."

"Alrighty, then." Mausi dropped the sack hard onto the ground and dragged it out of the room.

Mary had no idea where she was going. The Olympic's layout was similar to the Titanic's, but she had gotten lost on that ship numerous times. 'Now, where would they take the kids?' She wondered. 'Min and...Fritzy; think that's what the Ironsmith called him, would be too strong to lock in a cabin room, they'll put them someplace with reinforced walls...someplace like a brig. Does this ship have a brig? I wish I had one of Min's items. It would be easier to find her.'

An announcement came from Schwieger over the boatswain's pipe:

"Achtung! Ich brauche fünf Elite-Wachen, um mich im Laderaum zu melden. Wiederholen, ich brauche jetzt fünf Elite-Wachen, um mich im Laderaum zu melden (Attention! I need five elite guards to report to the hold. Repeat, I need five elite guards now to report to the hold)."

'That sounded important. I have a vague idea of what he said—I should have learned more German. Something about going in the hold.'

A couple of men in the hallway stopped what they were doing and walked back towards Mary. She slid out of their way and watched them interact with a third man at the end of the hall. The third man handed two of them handguns. All three proceeded together down a stairwell.

'That was very suspicious. I don't know where they are going, but it looked important enough to carry guns. All of that could be related to the kids.' Mary moved as fast as she could and gave chase.

Thomas looked inside the bridge. Two Germans, their backs to him, tended to some machinery near the wheel. Off to the side, he saw the globe-sized sphere, still displaying a cloudy grey surface. There was something familiar about the object. 'Wait, isn't that the crystal ball from Stones office?' As he had learned to do, with slow and controlled movements, he made his way over to the crystal ball. It showed the same dark, smoky view Mausi and Schwieger had experienced. 'What should I do?' I wonder if there is a way I can get this out of here?' If what Helga said is correct, having this here will definitely give them an advantage. I'm sure they've been spying on us the whole time, predicting our every move. That would explain why that balloon lady showed up and started throwing bombs at us.' He reached down to gauge how much effort it would take to lift a glass sphere the size of a globe. He grabbed the sides and lifted. The object was remarkably light. 'I did not expect this. Either this thing doesn't weigh that much, or I've recently become a lot stronger.' He moved the object away from its housing and walked gently towards the door, hoping the seaman would not turn around and notice the floating sphere traveling towards the exit. His heart beat faster, and he started to panic the closer he got to the outside. 'Calm down, Thomas. If I panic, I could become visible!' He took a few deep breaths. It seemed to do the trick, and he quieted down. Just as one of the seamen turned around, he left the bridge and carried the sphere out of site.

He checked left and right on the deck; A crewman was looking over the rail and pulling something up. As fast as Thomas could travel, he tiptoed with the sphere towards a set of stairs. Right when he was about to descend the stairwell, two armed men made their way upwards. At the moment, they were too busy in their conversation to notice the floating ball. It was only a matter of time before they did. Next to the stairs was a bunch of rope and spherical-shaped buoys. Thomas lowered the sphere onto the pile. The men reached the top of the stairs and regarded the objects as any other equipment on the deck. Checking to make sure no one else would get in his way, Thomas picked up the sphere. Moving as quickly as he could, he carried it down to the next deck. 'What exactly am I going to do with this thing? There's no way I'll make it to the car without being spotted. But I'll have to try to get as close as I can; they can't have access to this!'

Down below, Mary followed the armed men. They reached an open cargo hold full of large wooden crates. The men descended some stairs to the bottom and joined other armed men. Mary remained on the top railing. Mausi entered from the other side of the room, carrying the huge sack. '

'It's them!' Mary thought. She considered rushing and grabbing the bag. 'I have to time this perfectly. If I act now, I'll lose the element of surprise!'

The men looked up at Mausi and seemed clueless as to why they were there.

"Do any of you speak English?" Mausi yelled down. The men looked at each other in confusion. "Eng-lish?" Mausi frustratingly repeated, leading to the same response. Mausi rolled her eyes, then lifted the bag. "Do you see this?" She pointed to the bag. The men looked at each other, then back at her, and nodded. "O—pen? Do you understand open?" There was only one head nod of comprehension. "Oh, for Christ's sake!" Mausi threw the sack over the side.

Mary started to jump for it, but it was too late. The sack hit the ground with a heavy thud. 'Oh god, no! They might be hurt—but they are tougher than that, right? I can't reveal myself just yet, for their sake!' It took all of her strength to stop and calm herself down. She moved to a stairwell and crept downwards.

"Open it!" Mausi commanded. The men were confused again. Mausi pantomimed untying. One of the men understood her and explained it to the others in German. They nodded comprehension and started working on the rope, holding the bag closed. After a long moment of them trying to open it, Mausi lost patience with them. "What's taking so bloody long!" she yelled at them. One of them explained in German how difficult it was to open it. Mausi cursed under her breath and jumped over the side of the railing, landing a few feet from the activity. "What a bunch of milquetoast Dayfides!" She pushed one of the men and sent him to the ground off to the side. "Out of my way!" She went to work on the rope and arrived at the same snag as they had. "Bloody thing! Must be forged!" She looked around and then walked over to a nearby wall adorned with a bucket and ax used in case of a fire. She grabbed the ax off the wall, took it to the men, and gave it to the tallest one. "Here! The rope may be forged, but the bag could be normal!" He stood still for a second. She did a chopping motion. He quickly nodded and lifted the ax. "Wait a minute!" She jumped and returned to the high railing. "…No need for me to die too if it's 'as a curse on it." She gestured for the man to start chopping away.

Thomas had made it to the deck for the gangplank. Thanks to sheer luck, he wasn't caught. A quick look around let him know he had a window of time that would allow him a fast walk. When he was sure the timing would also allow him a speedy descent down the plank, he hurried as fast as he could to the exit. When he was within five feet of it, he heard a gun cock its trigger. Its muzzle touched him on the side, and he reappeared instantly.

Down below, the tall German man lifted the ax in the air and swung it down in the middle of the sack. Mary didn't care which child was about to be cleaved in half. With a sudden injection of adrenaline, she immediately materialized, sprang into action, and extended her sword, blocking the ax mid-swing. Lately, she had gained quite a bit of strength. Even if he kept swinging the ax down, she could have stopped him from going further. The man stumbled away from her and almost fell to the ground. He yelled something in German; Mary recognized it as a vulgar curse word. She took a defensive position and looked up to see if Mausi was descending to attack.

Mausi held her ground and looked pleased. "I knew it!" she yelled. "I knew that was how you disappeared off the Eye!"

"What are you going on about?" Mary yelled.

"Never mind all that—get her!" The Germans all looked up at Mausi. She looked confused about why they hadn't moved. Mausi figured something out and rolled her eyes. "For Pete's sake...how do you say: 'get her!' in German?" She looked at Mary.

"I know the answer, but don't expect me to help you."

Mausi rolled her eyes again and then started making grasping gestures at Mary.

"Uhhh, greif sie (grab her)?" One of the Germans said.

"Yes, greif sie!" Mausi agreed.

One of the men tried to grab Mary's shoulder. Without thinking, she swiped the arm away with the flat part of her sword and followed it up with a kick to the man's chest. He flew back into a metal pole, bounced off, and landed on his face.

"Oh my," Mary said. "Did you see that? Sorry, that was a little impulsive," she said.

The other Germans didn't seem too pleased at having their friend fly across the room. Another one rushed at her and tried to grab her around the neck. Mary turned her body sideways and pushed him in the chest, shoving him away. Someone grabbed her from behind. She instinctively whipped the flat part of her sword over her shoulder onto his head. He staggered backward with a stinging red mark on his forehead. The last three men, being as impatient as the first two and lacking a solution in how to deal with Mary, chose murder as an option. Before Mausi could finish saying: "No! Don't shoot her! We need her alive!" The men had already pointed their pistols at her and fired.

Mary felt time slow down around her. Sounds became muffled, and things moved at 1/8th their normal speed. Everything was in sharp focus: the room, the men, their guns, and the bullets slowly moving towards her, cutting the jelled air. She remembered when Fang had thrown a knife at her and how she deflected it back at him with incredible speed. Under a different situation, she would have been so fascinated by this scenario she would have watched as the bullets came close enough to hit her. Mary positioned the sword to deflect the first bullet. Although she was moving faster than anything in the room, her movements felt slow and sluggish, like trying to swat something while underwater. When the sword hit the bullet, it ricocheted off the blade and sent it backward. She did the same to the others, sending them to the attackers. Satisfied she was no longer in danger, her mind suddenly switched back to the speed of the real world. She witnessed the three men recoil from getting shot in non-vital parts and hit the ground in pain.

"Core, blimey!" Mausi yelled. "Nobody can do that! Unless…"

Mary looked up at her and almost smiled but remembered what she was there for. She reached down to open the bag. There wasn't enough time to loosen the rope because a small round black bomb with a lit fuse landed near her. She grabbed the bag and leaped into the air. The bomb exploded to the size of her and the sack. Mary landed on top of one of the crates and set the bag down. 'It's remarkably light. These kids should weigh at least 90 kilograms.'

Mausi threw another bomb. Mary used her sword to knock it away, and it exploded against the wall.

"Home run!" Mausi yelled.

"You should be more careful! If you blow a hole in the wall, you can sink this ship!" Mary yelled.

Mausi panicked and looked at the wall. There was no leaking. Mary used the distraction to close the distance between them and was about to do a cross-slash to separate Mausi's head from her body.

Mausi yelled: *"Troiy les murgur!"* causing herself to turn to smoke, and Mary's blade passed through her. Mausi reappeared behind Mary and jabbed her fist into her back. Mary slammed into the wall.

Mausi looked at Mary and was about to produce another bomb, but something felt wrong. She reached up and felt her neck; there was blood. It wasn't a serious injury, but it was still painful. "What the? 'ow you manage to hit me? When I was turned into smoke?"

Mary refused to answer, as even she had no idea how she had done it. She righted herself and turned around. "You're the one that killed Helga!"

"Yea, that's right. Either 'er or me!"

"You ambushed her! Helga would never do something so dishonorable!"

"Honor? Helga?" Mausi scoffed. "Me and Helga go way back, Luv, I've seen her do some pretty dishonorable things."

"You were friends? That makes your attack even more treacherous!" Mary lifted her sword. "Perhaps it's time someone showed you the proper way to duel!"

"This isn't a duel, Luv—this is a murder!"

Mary looked down and noticed the small bomb Mausi had rolled at her.

With extreme caution, Thomas turned around to see who was poking him with a gun nozzle.

Schwieger stood impassively in front of him. "So that is why the Eye couldn't see you. The power of you people never ceases to amaze me, " he quipped.

Thomas was almost at a loss for words. "Who are you?"

"I do believe I am the one who asks the questions, mein freund. You are, after all, the one sneaking aboard my ship."

"This is not your ship! This belongs to the British! I'm quite sure they wouldn't permit you to use it!"

"On the contrary, all those hexen have to do is touch someone's head, and the next thing you know—ker-poof! They're swimming back to submarines and signing over boats!"

"I thought so! There's no other way the richest families in New York would ever do business with riffraff like you!"

"Not all were forced. They know which direction the wind is blowing."

"What? Who? What family would dare sign on to Germany's madness?"

"Enough talk. Please drop the sphere before I have to shoot you."

Thomas looked at the sphere, Schwieger, and then back at the sphere. He deliberately moved it sideways until it was over the railing. "You mean…this thing?"

Schwieger had a look of panic. "What are you doing? Stop!"

"Be quite a setback if I were to drop this over the side."

"Swing that back over!"

"Pretty sure even your balloon friend would have a hard time retrieving this from the bottom of the river!"

"Bring that back, or I'll shoot!"

"Or what? This?" Thomas let the sphere go. Schwieger watched it fall into the darkness, followed by a splashing sound. He turned to look at Thomas. By this time, Thomas' fist was already en route to Schwieger's jaw. The fist made contact, and Schwieger reeled back onto the ground. He fired his gun into the air and then fell into unconsciousness.

Thomas confiscated the gun. It wasn't long before he had to use it. A crewman leaned over the side and pointed a rifle at him.

Thomas fired a shot into the man's shoulder, and he fell back out of sight. Another man peered over the top railing and also fired. Thomas moved out of the way just in time; the bullet missed him by an inch. He returned the volley, and the man ducked down. Thomas hurried away as the sound of running boots approached him from all directions.

In the cargo hold, Mary hopped from crate to crate. Like a bird jumping from perch to perch. Behind her, explosions caused by Mausi throwing small round bombs at her. With each blast, pieces of silver and sometimes gold would burst out of the crates and spray onto the floor in a metallic scatter. 'She doesn't seem concerned about blowing a hole in the ship!' One after another, Mausi continued to throw the bombs at Mary, sometimes ahead of Mary's trajectory, but she still dodged the explosions. 'She never tires of throwing those bombs at me, yet she hasn't used any other type of forging. Is she saving that for when I tire of dodging the bombs? Or are her powers limited to explosions? I didn't see that balloon outside; This means it's her only way to fly. When she killed Helga, she dropped one of the bombs on her. Meaning she can levitate heavy objects. The only way she could have caught them off guard was—by making the bomb—invisible!' Mary looked up just in time to see the large crate full of precious metals reappear. The object fell hard onto her back, mid-jump. She came crashing down, as did the massive box on her back. After the loud sounds of wood and metal pieces had subsided, Mary lay immobile under a ton of rubble. She was in pain. 'Are my legs broken, or have I missed the opportunity to wind the rivets on my back?' She wiggled one of her toes.

Mausi's sinister grin foretold of whatever misfortune was to follow. She leisurely walked over to Mary, who was struggling to release herself from the weight, crushing her legs.

"Rather brave of yuh two, coming 'ere all by yuhself.' Mausi stated.

"Calling a party of two, 'all by yourself,' is as grammatically flawed as your morals are virtuous."

"Well, excuse me, muh lady. I was never privy to a high education as yuh fancy upbringing."

Mary struggled to pull herself out. "Education and morals…are not an inseparable pair.…I'm sure Helga had a similar upbringing…And she was the most upstanding person I knew!" She winced in pain and had to relinquish escaping.

"So what! She's dead, it'n't? And whot? Yuh think yuh gonna come in here and kill me? With yuh fancy jumping and level four antics? I'm a level seven yuh silly tart!" Mausi held out her hand, in her palm, a black bomb inflated to the size of a bowling ball. "Now then, are Yeh gonna tell me where the Siv Myrddin is, or am I gonna have tuh blow pieces of yuh off, one at a time, starting whiff yuh legs?"

"I don't know what you're talking about."

"Don't play daft, dearie. We know all about yeh.…'cept yeh being a Forger. Now, whot's it gonna be? Yer legs or the book?" The fuse lit on the bomb. Mausi held it up in the air.

The sounds of shooting above deck and explosions below deck roused the curiosity of the German crew. Dozens of men scoured the ship, looking for the source. Thomas knew Mary was the cause of the second disturbance. A large group headed for the stairs to rendezvous with her. He distracted them by firing at a lifesaver on the wall; this succeeded and drew their attention to him. They pointed their guns in his direction, and he took cover behind a tubular-shaped ventilator just in time to avoid several bullets ricocheting two inches near his face. He fired a few times, ran out of bullets, and switched to his sword pen. 'Let's see, how did I do that machine gun?....' "Eh-ha-who Gwen!" Once again, the pen turned into a Lewis light machine gun. Thomas took cover behind a lifeboat and fired the gun. It hit a man in the legs, causing him to collapse. A moment later, it stopped firing. "What in God's name?" He tried to fire again but it just made clicking sounds. "What's going on? Is it out of bullets? Is that even possible?" He hit the side of the gun, but it produced no desirable effects. "I thought these weapons were magical!"

Sensing the lull in the fighting, the Germans unleashed a barrage of gunfire at him. Bullets came closer and closer to hitting him, chipping wooden pieces of his shield away. While he focused on his gun, a few feet away, a crewman snuck into his blind spot and was about to fire. Thomas turned the machine gun around and used the butt to hit the man in his head, sending him reeling back into a wall. Thomas did a leg sweep, and the man fell to the ground. He followed up with a knockout punch to the jaw. Before another crewman got too close, Thomas stole the rifle from the unconscious man. He fired a shot into the other crewman's hand causing him to drop his weapon and take cover. Fearing Thomas' rifle skills, two others withdrew to the other side of the ship.

'They're probably going to find a way to circle back and trap me in a pincer move.' Thomas looked around for a place to escape and avoid a trap. There was a clear path to a door leading inside of the ship. The second he left his protected area to make a run for it, a barrage of gunfire showered upon him. He returned to his starting place and realized there were more hidden adversaries.

He knew he was surrounded, out of bullets and out of options. The nook was now occupied by two men firing handguns at him, and other men were taking chances and dashing to areas close to him. He looked at the machine gun. He said: *"Eh-ha- gu avuh!"*, and the machine gun turned into a sword. 'This won't do too well against guns, but at least it requires no bullets.' A bullet ricocheted three inches near his face. 'I guess this is it. Perhaps I can get one of them before I go. I do hope Mary is having better luck than I am.'

"I would rather die than let the likes of you take possession of that book!" Mary yelled.

"Legs it is!" Mausi threw her arm down towards Mary to blow off her legs. To Mausi's surprise, the bomb never left her hand. Mausi looked at it and then tried again; the bomb remained connected to her. "Whot did yeh…?" Upon closer examination, Mausi looked at her hand and realized the bomb was now attached to it by a silver rope. The rope extended downwards and across the room and ended at the hilt of Mary's sword. "What?" Mausi tried to remove the rope, but it was impossible as it had been for Leo to remove it from his motorcycle. Mausi looked at the lit bomb in her hand and then back at Mary. "Think I'm gonna blow me 'and off?" She leaned over and blew on the bomb fuse, immediately snuffing it out. She smiled at Mary. "You lose, level four!"

"Not yet!" While Mausi was distracted by the bomb in her hand, with the words *"Kwifflo em lime"*, Mary forged a large crate of silver bars on a tall stack behind Mausi to teeter forwards. Mausi never had enough time to turn around to register what was happening. Tons of weight landed on her head and back. Crate after crate followed and reinforced the impact on her spine.

Armed only with his sword, Thomas counted to three and jumped from his hiding place.

A lightning bolt ignited a box of ammunition near one of the groups of crewmen, and it exploded. They flew through the air and out of sight. A second later, a lifeboat fell from the sky and landed on top of three others. There was the sound of a whirling propellor chopping the air up above. Thomas looked up and saw Helga steering her teclyn overhead.

"Helga! You're alive! How?"

"Save the hugs for later Detective! Where's Miss White?" Helga asked. She gave air cover by throwing fireballs, causing several screaming men to scurry around wrapped in flames.

Thomas continued his advancement. He punched a man in the jaw when he tried to fire at Helga, another received a kick to his chest. " We have to get to Mary; she's down below!"

In the cargo hold, neither woman moved; they were in similar positions underneath their piles of treasured weights. Mary felt a sudden change in her condition; she was able to move one of her legs and then the other. After a few moments, she could pull herself from underneath the rubble, and eventually, after a while, she stood up and straightened out her posture. 'It's the same thing as when I was thrown into the building. I can self-heal! And with a shorter recovery time than other Forgers! What did you do to me back then, Father?' She limped over to Mausi to make sure she was incapacitated. Mausi stirred and moaned and offered no resistance. "It's not all about how powerful your enemy is, it's all about the ability to be incapable of taking one's enemies, one's accidents, even one's misdeeds seriously for very long."

"Oh really…" Mausi groaned. "Then perhaps you'll take this more seriously…" Mausi shakily stretch out her hand, Mary readied herself for whatever attack was about to come her way. Something materialized behind Mary—a small wooden barrel with a lit fuse hovered over the sack which contained the two kids. Realizing they were now in danger, Mary started to sprint towards them. The barrel dropped onto the bag. Mary tried to think of a forge that could prevent it from exploding—anything, including something which would sacrifice her very life. The bomb exploded. The blast sent her against the far wall with lots of debris. As quickly as she could move, she picked herself up and staggered over to the explosion site. The scene she beheld was heart rending and unbelievable. Pieces of the sack surrounded two charred figures, holding each other for support. Mary's legs became weak, and she dropped to her knees. She felt like crying, the feelings of dread were very heavy. 'I can…can I…is it too—Butterfly?' Her thoughts were a jumbled mass of possible solutions to make this all go away; a way to fix this horrible situation; nothing would work.

"Yuh see," Mausi said. "Yeh don't know what you're going against! Level four!" She tried to laugh but ended up coughing a little.

Mary glared back at her. The bomb was still attached to her hand by the sword rope. Mary pointed at it. *'Roy are don!'* With a sparkling flair-up, the bomb reignited. Before Mausi could blow it out again, it exploded and she shrieked.

After the smoke had cleared, Mary saw the damage Mausi had sustained: one side of her face burned, and a missing right hand. Mausi screamed in agony. Mary ignored her cursing and complaints and walked over to the charred remains of Min and Fritz to mourn the loss of the two children. The tears were about to appear again, but she held them in. 'I will not cry until all truths and adversaries on this ship have been dealt with!' She knelt and examined the charred remains of the bodies. She touched her shaking fingers to the part that used to be Min's head. It disintegrated into black flakes and lifted into the air.

"Hold on a second..." She rubbed some flakes between her fingers. "This is not burnt flesh...this is...this is paper—why would it be paper?... Leo!

Leo dragged a large sack into his apartment and lifted it onto his bed. He pointed at it and said: *"Dadfino!"* The sack unraveled and separated into a clump of threads. On top of the web mass, Min and Fritz were gagged with handkerchiefs and bound by two thick silver chains. The children began to writhe around as much as they could. When he removed their gags, they began to yell at him. Min cursed in rapid-fire Mandarin, and Fritz stuck to threats related to what he was going to do to Leo.

"I know, I know, calm down! Shush!" Leo pleaded. He put the gags back on their mouths. "Sorry, I had to dump you in that alley, but your friends were closing in on me, and I had to give 'em the slip. You ragamuffins hungry?"

He unwrapped their handkerchiefs. Min immediately spat at him. He quickly moved his head to the left. The spit hit an oval mirror on the wall, causing it to fall to the ground and break.

"Whoa! That's some powerful loogie ya got there, Chinese Kid. Wait until you taste it first." Both children tried to wiggle out of the chains. "Don't bother trying to squirm your way outta those chains, they're ahrion."

"What are you gonna do with us?" Fritz asked.

"Don't worry Dog-Boy. I'm not gonna harm ya. All I want is for Mary to fork that book over to me—or somebody, and then you two are free to go."

"Once I'm free, I'm going to bite your head off!" Fritz said.

"And I'm going to decorate the end of my spear with it," Min added.

"Such violent ankle-biters. Whatever happened to stickball or playing with dolls? Growing up with Forgers really frazzles your upbringing."

"You are a dishonorable traitor!" Min said.

"That's war for you. Sometimes, you do what you have to, to get what you want. You'll learn that soon enough."

"I would never betray my friends!"

"You say that now, but I bet if you had the opportunity to get everything you wanted, you'd turn on everybody in that house for it."

"Never!"

"Elzbieta is going to have fun slugging you!" Fritz threatened.

"That crazy dame? Where did you two come from, anyway? Why is she so hell-bent on killing Mary?... And you, what are you? You're not a Forger or a Stryker. Yet anghenfèls can't be healed with ahrion." Fritz was quiet. "No answer, eh, keep the enemy in the dark? Well, tell you what. You think about your answer. I, on the other hand, have some business to do. I gotta trade you to the highest bidder. Pretty sure by now that balloon dame has figured out that sack was a ruse."

Leo looked at something crawling out of the space between Fritz's neck and the chains; a silver and gold cricket nudged its way out and crawled onto the bed. It worked its way to the floor and started skittering to the door. When it reached the middle of the room Leo's foot came down. He smashed it flat. When he removed his foot, the cricket had transformed into a coin.

"Calling for help, eh! Nobody's coming to rescue you!" he said with a bit of anger. "There's nothing you can do!"

Fritz and Min looked at each other and then started yelling: "Help! Kidnapper! Masher! Pervert! Fire! Call the polic—" Leo quickly put the gags back in their mouths. "Couple of weisenheimers, eh?" He grabbed his motorcycle goggles and left the apartment.

Thomas appeared at the top railing of the cargo hold. "Mary!" he called out. She didn't respond. He ran down the stairs and navigated over rubble until he reached her location. "Mary, are you all right?"

She realized he was there and broke out of her shock. "Thomas?"

"Yes, how are you? Did you find the kids?"

"No, Leo gave us the slip. The bag was a decoy; he used Paper Doll on us."

"What? He's definitely a cunning rat." Thomas walked over to Mausi and examined her body.

"Is she alive?" Mary asked.

"Barely. Who is she?"

"She's the one that killed Helga."

Thomas grinned and tittered.

"What? Is something amusing?"

"Oh, am I dead?" A voice called out. "Funny that, I don't feel dead,"

Mary looked up and saw Helga looking down from the top railing. She wondered if this was a mind trick perpetuated by Mausi. She glanced at Mausi, lying unconscious under the rubble, and then up at Helga on the railings. Helga held her Teclyn overhead and used its propeller blade to float herself to the ground. Mary stood up and cautiously walked over to her. "I'd thought...I...I thought I'd lost you," Mary said.

"fraid not, luv. I hazard a guess you'll have to deal with me a wee bit longer." Helga smiled.

Mary wiped away a tear and quickly walked over to hug her. She stopped herself.

"Eh?" Helga asked. There was a pinging sound. "Oh, do you need to tighten yuh buttons?"

Mary tearfully nodded yes.

"For heaven's sake! Turn around."

Mary took off her necklace, handed the key to Helga, and turned around.

"What are these rips in the back of yuh dress?" Helga asked.

"Oh, that. Apparently I have wings."

"Huh…Always something new, eh?" Helga lifted the bottom of Mary's blouse, and tightened each rivet using gentle, motherly movements. Mary has always felt pleasure whenever her buttons were tightened, but the added joy of finding Helga alive pushed her into bliss. When Helga finished, Mary turned around and was about to hug her but stopped herself.

"Eh?" Helga asked.

"The last time I tried to hug you…you wouldn't let me; I wanted to be respectful."

Helga frowned. "I think under these circumstances, it might be o'right." Mary advanced a little more but she stopped again. "Huh? I said it's okay, Luv." Helga held out her hands.

"No, it's—I can't move," Mary complained.

"Is it yuh back, luv? Do we need me to wind yer buttons? Again?"

"No, I— "

" 'old on a tick," Helga said, wiggling her shoulders. "I can't move either!"

Thomas also tried to move but couldn't. "What is this? Is this a trap of some sort?"

They heard the plucking sounds of multiple metallic violin strings. A webwork of silvery threads became more and more visible as the plucking continued. It wrapped around their arms and legs and attached to the walls and floor like spider webbing.

"What is this; did Mausi do this?" Mary yelled.

"No, this is beyond 'er level," Helga answered. She tried to reach for her teclyn; something pulled it out of her hand and encased it in a cocoon of string. "Bloody hell! Fine then!: *Mell—*"

"I wouldn't do that if I were you!" yelled a voice from the top railing.

They all drew their attention to a woman in a long black dress. On her blouse was a copper badge engraved with three spirals converging into one.

Thomas recognized her. "You! You worked the ticker tape machine in Benjamin Strong's office!" He said.

"I see," Helga said. "Mausi wasn't the only traitor that robbed the Federal Reserve!"

"I'm not with her," the woman said. "I'm Patience Muffet, an undercover government law enforcer, here to apprehend her." She spread out her arms. In her hands, she held two knitting needles. Stings spun out from the needles, attached themselves to the walls, and lifted her over the railing. She used the strings to levitate to the ground level.

"If you're here to apprehend her, you should let us go!" Thomas said. "We came here to stop her and rescue two kidnapped children!"

Miss Muffet landed on the ground in front of Mary. "I'm afraid not. You three are also under arrest!"

"What?" Mary yelled. "For stopping criminals from murder, kidnapping, and from the look of all of these containers of silver —robbery?"

"Unless you are deputized members of the law, none of you are authorized for the numerous assaults, murders, destruction of public property—including a New York subway, a bookstore, and now a ship belonging to the British." Patience waved her hands, and the strings on the walls detached and started wrapping around the three captives like a spider cocoon."

"Balderdash!" Mary yelled. "Detective Vanderbilt here is an officer of the law!"

"Not since days ago."

"What are you talking about? Thomas, tell her—" Mary looked over at Thomas, his head was low. "Thomas?"

"I'm sorry, Mary…I forgot to tell you. I got fired after the Ironsmith wrecked the police station and my apartment looking for me; Police Chief O'Riley blamed me."

"But that's not your fault! I should have a word with him!"

"It's okay, I'm doing something more important now." He smiled at her.

"Thomas—"

"Mary, it's fine."

"Bollocks to this!" Helga tried to expand her arm and break the strings. She gave up after an exhausting exhale.

"There's no use in struggling; you can't break my yarn," Patience said.

"Don't need to break it…" Helga said: *Troiy les murgur!*" Her body started to turn into smoke."

"My yarn will cut through the other two like butter if you resist anymore!" Muffet yelled.

The webs around Thomas and Mary tightened significantly; they screamed in pain. Helga returned to her solid form.

Miss Muffet raised her arms. *"Urf ur caa fael!"* All three captives rose into the air. As she walked away, they floated behind, like a trio of bizarre helium balloons.

Outside, a dozen Model Ts and numerous Paddy wagons were parked on the docks, and black-dressed military soldiers armed with bayoneted rifles, hand grenades, and in some cases swords, searched the ship and dock. Helga noticed something about the bayonets and swords. "Mary, can yeh sense the same thing I can about them blades they're carrying?"

Mary studied them and then understood what Helga meant. "Are those…ahrion?"

"Quite. And I'd bet yuh a pound, their bullets are also ahrion."

On their way down the gangplank, Thomas saw Schwieger talking to a tall, curly-haired man in a suit who seemed to be in charge.

Schwieger pointed at them. "There he is!" he said.

"What? What is this all about? Who are you?" Mary complained.

"I'm the captain of this ship!" Schwieger said.

"The last I checked, this was a British vessel! And not one being used for smuggling and kidnapping!"

The man in the suit walked up to their group. He showed no reaction to their floating. On his lapel was a copper badge engraved with a two-headed snake. "I'm Stanley Finch, Chief of the Bureau of Investigation for the Justice Department. You four are under arrest!"

"We know! Apparently for doing the right thing!" Mary said, rolling her eyes.

"You call coming onto this ship and killing dozens of his crewmen the right thing?"

"That man has tons of weapons with ahrion bullets!" Helga yelled.

"And he's working with someone that has tried multiple times to kill us—" Mary said. "Can you let us down, please? Rather disorienting trying to talk in the air like this!" Finch gestured, and Patience lowered them to the ground. "Thank you. I'm Mary Elizabeth White of the House of White—"

"We know who you are, Miss White." Finch interrupted.

"If you know so much about me, then you should already know that man, my cousin Shirley, and the Belgian have turned my life into utter pandemonium!"

"Who's the Belgian?" Finch asked.

"You might call him The Ronin," Helga answered.

"Oh right, Maximilian. Miss White, if you were having trouble with him, you should have come to the police early on instead of trying to solve it on your own."

"I tried to!" Thomas said, but my chief dismissed it all as poppycock!"

"So instead, you run around like a group of vigilante cowboys with no regard for the law, destroying New York, hurting innocent civilians, and attacking foreigners?"

"THAT German and the Belgian were gathering stolen silver from New York's wealthiest families and turning it into weapons!" Thomas said. "Most likely to use against us!"

Schwieger pointed at the boat in anger. "That silver was withdrawn, legally—"

"They probably used a mind weld to force the wealthy to sign over that silver as well as this ship!" Thomas interrupted.

Schwieger pointed at Helga. "That hexen attacked my ship earlier, and now she has come back with her friends!"

"Yeh dodgy prat!" Helga yelled. "Let me loose so I can turn 'im into a frog!"

"You see Officer? I am the victim here of these violent thugs!" Helga tried to lunge at him, but the webbing restrained her movement.

Mausi was carried off the ship on a stretcher, heavily bandaged and wrapped in silver chains.

"Mausi!" Helga yelled. "Yeh, bloody traitorous slag! How could yeh kill our mates like that?" Mausi closed her eyes and turned her head away.

"What did you do with the Eye?" Finch asked Mausi. She didn't answer.

'Should I say anything?' Thomas wondered. 'If I don't, the Germans and the Followers will retrieve it. If I do, these G-men will use it to keep spying on us. "I guess I have no choice—," he said. Before he could speak, he was interrupted by Mausi.

"I don't know that German man…" Mausi said, "I was working with Miss White and her acquaintances to steal the Eye, and then we were going to steal this ship to use as a getaway."

"You lying slag! I owe you! Thrice!" Helga yelled and struggled.

"Mr. Finch, you have to believe us! We came here to find two kidnapped children!" Thomas pleaded.

"Did you or did you not come onboard this ship and kill dozens of his crewmen and go on a rampage through the streets of New York?"

"We did, but it…"

"Then those are crimes, and you are all under arrest!"

Everyone started arguing. Finch gestured for all of them to be thrown in a paddy wagon.

A strange rumbling noise drew everyone's attention. A pier next to the Olympic began to shake as waves broke on its sides. An explosion erupted from beneath the pier, unzipping the wooden planks along the center. As the planks splintered apart, wooden boards, crates, and cars were sent flying sideways. A long black shape wedged itself towards the crowd at great speed. Soldiers and dock workers scrambled to escape its path, with some even leaping into the harbor to avoid the oncoming danger. A gigantic black object lurched onto the top of the dock like a seal beaching itself on the shore and came to a slow rest with a screeching whine and a grinding halt. Sparks of blue electricity lit briefly around, small rapidly spinning propellers on its bottom gradually twirled to a quiet stop.

Everyone paused.

"Is that…?" Mary asked.

"It is," Helga answered.

Elzbieta walked along the top, stopped, and stabbed the object with her sword. "I find Big Fish!" she said proudly.

"I hazard a guess she found her submarine," Helga said.

"Muffet!" Finch gestured to the web woman and then at Elzbieta. She sent out a string of yarn that attached to Elzbieta's leg. Elzbieta looked down and formed her face into a scrawl. "What's this, Spider magic? I hate spiders!" She pulled her sword out of the hull of the submarine. With one swipe, she cut the strings away.

"She cut forged webs!" Mary said.

"Chamfer!" Finch warned.

Patience tried again and spun out more webs. They got within a foot of Elzbieta but were cut away from her. With a look of frustration, Patience turned to Finch for guidance.

"Tibuta, if you'd please," he said.

Tibuta stepped from the back of the crowd.

When Elzbieta saw her, she smiled with joy. "Ooh! It's Silny Dziewczyna! (Strong Girl!)" She assumed a fighting stance.

"Elzbieta! Watch yourself!" Helga yelled.

Tibuta walked heavily away from the others and stood, looking up at Elzbieta.

"Always wanted to fight a level ten!" Elzbieta gleamed. "Okay, Big Dziewczyna, let me see what you can d—"

A bowling ball-sized black sphere covered in spikes burst through the top of the submarine between Elzbieta's legs, hit her in the chin, and sent her flying high into the air. Trailing under the sphere was an ever-extending amount of black chain. Tibuta stood still and had one arm down with the endless chain feeding from her sleeve, flowing down under the dock. Her other arm was up in the air, also feeding an endless chain. On the other end of that chain, another iron sphere came down on Elzbieta's head and sent her crashing onto the top of the submarine, imploding its top.

"Is she...all right?" Mary asked.

Elzbieta lay motionless in a dented outline of her body on the top of the submarine. Her arm ungracefully stretched outward. Her fingers uncurled and released her sword. It slid over the side and hit the ground with a metallic resonance. The sword returned to its parasol form.

"Grab her and wrap her in chains," Finch commanded.

A group of soldiers ran over and started climbing up the sides of the submarine to reach Elzbieta. One of them reached down to pick up her parasol. When he grabbed the handle, he screamed in pain, purple smoke emitted from his hand, and he hunched over and vomited.

"Nobody touches that teclyn!" Finch ordered.

"I knew it had a curse on it," Helga muttered.

Sitting on a nearby dock piling, Flapper the magpie cawed and flew off into the sky.

Tibuta of the House of Salem worked for the Bureau of Investigation for the Justice Department's Forger Division

PART THREE
TO SEE THE ELEPHANTS

June 8th, 1915

Victoria Vanderbilt heard the voice again. The first time, the words were indecipherable from the screaming of her baby brother in the next room, but the second time she heard it, the person could have been in the bathroom with her. She looked around the room. The only other person in there was one of her younger twin sisters. The child continued to sloppily brush her teeth with toothpaste, unaware her older sister was panicked from hearing voices in her head. 'Perhaps it is a prank.' Victoria thought, 'Or it could also be the downstairs neighbors.' It was common for their voices to occasionally seep through the wooden floors, especially when they were arguing. She settled on that explanation, finished her bath, and dried herself off.

There was little time between her leaving the bath and the next child entering to take her place. There were five of them and their mother. She hadn't seen her father in weeks; often, he would disappear for long periods. For now, she refused to panic unless the brutish men showed up again looking for him. Mother never told her anything about Father's business or how he sometimes contributed financially. But Victoria knew a lot more about the family secrets than they thought: She knew her mother was now working two jobs because she refused to accept any more money from her uncle or their rich cousins, and her baby brother cried more than most because he had the colic, her uncle had been fired from his job because a crazy ex-girlfriend made a scene at the police station, and Victoria knew most of all, she wasn't an average teenage girl.

She passed the little ones' room and saw her mother sprinkling her baby brother's bottom with talcum powder. She must have stopped and stared too long because her mother asked her if anything was wrong.

"Pardon?" Victoria asked.

"You look like you've seen a spook?" Her mother repeated.

Victoria didn't realize her face conveyed that message. Her inability to hide the evidence of hearing a voice say: 'Help me.' in her ear would cause anyone to stand and stare into emptiness. "No, I'm...I'm fine, just tired."

"Ok then, off to bed. Don't stay up too late reading."

"But, I like reading."

"I bet you do. The library's gonna run out of books if you keep taking them all."

Victoria retired to her bedroom. It wasn't a proper bedroom but the laundry room. She accepted its small size and occasional interruptions by her mother coming in and out on Mondays, the official wash day, to use the metal wash tub, hang clothes on the line outside the window, or make laundry soap out of lye, which took months to do. Today, she had her privacy, and it was just a bedroom.

She lay down in a bed made for toddlers. As she has gotten taller and older, she has learned how to sleep in a fetal position and read with her knees upright. She started to read the Bible. Her mother insisted a chapter before bed gave you better dreams.

When Saul saw the army of the Philistines, he was afraid, and his heart trembled greatly. And when Saul inquired of the LORD, the LORD did not answer him, either by dreams, or by Urim, or by prophets. Then Saul said to his servants: "Seek out for me a woman who is a Medium..."

"Medium? What's a Medium? Do they mean a witch?" The phone rang, startling her. No one called after the sun went down unless it was bad news. She heard her mother's footsteps in the hallway. 'Who would be calling?' She knew her mother would hide the information from her and the children. To protect them, she figured. Even her older brother, Otto, was kept in the dark about their parents' troubles. But when she recently turned 13 years old, Victoria had developed a way to eavesdrop. When her neighbors argued about something, followed by the sounds of breaking dishes and wrestling, if she put her fingers in her ears to pretend they didn't exist, it made the sounds worse. She was able to hear the husband yelling and the wife begging not to be hit again. Over time, she had learned to fine-tune this ability and follow any conversation from as far away as half a city block.

The caller was Roselyn, one of her mother's friends, or, as she called her, 'The Notorious Gossip'. She was very excited to be reporting the news about someone Victoria was also interested in: Mary White. Apparently, after a gang fight and gas explosion, the land where the lighthouse on Fifth Avenue once stood had collapsed. There was also an enormous wall of wrecked cars in front of it.

"Maybe there's some kind of construction thing going on there?" Her mother reasoned.

"But, didn't that Mary White woman live in that lighthouse?"

"Roselyn, don't be ridiculous, that's just a rumor. No one can live in a lighthouse. Even lighthouse keepers live in a little house off to the side—there's no room! Surely. It was placed there as some kind of monument. She probably lived in the house next door."

"That's the Astors'! I'm telling you, Thelma, there were all these police cars and things heading in that direction, and no one starts a construction project at night!"

"I swear! The stories I've heard about her would make her a crackpot!"

"The rich don't go insane. They go to sanitariums or talk to those head-doctors like that doctor in Germany, Dr. Freud."

"Whatever the reason, my brother says she's as normal as you or me, just a little eccentric."

"How is your brother? By the way?"

"He's fine, why do you ask?"

"I heard he got fired from the precinct."

"What? Where did you hear that?"

"Oh, I have my sources."

Victoria was worried: 'Could I have been the one to mention Uncle Thomas had been fired after I listened to his conversation the last time he had visited? But there would never be a situation I would talk to Roslyn or any of my mom's friends.'

"Don't be absurd!" Thelma said. "If that happened, I'd be the first to know!"

"Are you sure, Thelma? I heard he's spending too much time with Mary White after her father died."

"If you're done, Roselyn. It's getting late, and I have to give the baby its bath."

"Okay, Thelma, I'll let you go. If you find out more about Mary White from your brother, you let me know."

"Will do. In my overflowing amounts of spare time. Goodbye." Her mother hung up the phone. As Victoria removed her fingers from her ears, she heard her mother say: "Why is New York so obsessed with that woman?"

When the sun rose over the apartment building across the street, its beams awakened Min. She looked at Fritz' face sleeping next to her. She had seen him many times, but this was her first time studying his features. His expression was soft while he slept. She continued staring until the beams traveled across his face and awakened him. He opened his eyes, he and Min looked at each other. After a while, she quickly averted her gaze away from his and looked around the room. Leo was not in the apartment. Min took this as a good opportunity for escape. She tried again to wiggle out of the silver chains. They hurt after being wrapped around her for so long. Fritz did his best to get out of the chains as well. He stopped when he saw a strange expression on Min's face, unsure if it was a look of anger or shock.

"Mmm?" Fritz asked through his gagged mouth.

"Mm-ah-en!" Min answered.

"Mmm?"

"Mm-ah-en!" She repeated.

Fritz's expression of confusion caused Min to roll her eyes and turn her head away from his. She wildly began to shake her head around. Fritz stared in confusion until he realized she was talking about her hairpin.

"Ah-en?" he asked.

"Yuh!"

He moved his head closer to hers and looked at the pin. He could smell the ahrion in it. "A tuc-Lin?" He asked, referring to a teclyn.

"Yuh! Itz muh Kang, elp muh gib et!"

Fritz wiggled over to her and stretched his forehead as far as he could until it touched her hair. She moved her head back to give him better access. Moving his head around for a long while, he was able to loosen the hairpin out of her ponytail. Min was wondering what was taking too long. She spun her head around to look at him. When she did this as he was moving forward, they shared an accidental indirect kiss through the gags. Both of their eyes widened. Her face turned a bright red, which transferred into anger. Without a second thought, she head-butted Fritz and knocked him unconscious.

"Ritz?...Ritz?" She asked, trying to awaken him; it didn't work. She tried to loosen the pin on her own, and after more head wiggling, she caused it to fall onto the bed in the space between them. Min took a deep breath and rotated her body so her bound hands could reach the pin. She grabbed it, but it slipped out of her fingers. Another try caused it to stick in her palm. She winced in pain and used her fingers to pull it out. She took another deep breath. *"Eh-ha- gu avuh!"* The pin turned into her large spear and wedged between her and the unconscious Fritz. Her eyes widened with excitement and fear when the blade appeared right next to her head. With more wiggling, she repositioned the chain wrapped around her shoulder against the spear blade. She moved around to create a sawing motion. She was able to cut halfway through one of the links.

Leo entered the room carrying a sack of potatoes. "What the hell?" He ran over and yanked the quiang away from Min. "Where did this come from? You're sneaky! ain't ya kid?" Min scowled in disappointment. "Got any other tricks up your sleeve? I'll just put this one over here." He leaned the spear against the wall. "It doesn't matter. You can't cut forged chains." Min raised an eyebrow. "You hungry? Gotta go to the bathroom?" He looked at the bed. "...whoops! Guess it's too late for that. Sorry kid, I'll get you gussied up before I trade you for the book." Min glared at him. "Guess you wanna clobber me, eh?" She nodded. "I can't blame ya, I wanna clobber myself sometimes. But once that book is away from Mary, you guys can have a nice boring life without people trying to bump you off every second."

Leo sat in a chair and poured himself a glass of water from a metal, pitcher. "Thirsty?" Min ignored him and looked at Fritz. "You know, I didn't want to kidnap you two…it's just…sometimes you have to do whatever you have to do to survive; it is what it is." Min rolled her eyes at him. "Yeah, I know, crocodile tears, right? But don't you wish you could go back to your old life? Like, I'm sure you had a rough life back in China, but I'm sure there were some good parts before you got mixed up in all this. I miss those days. We had six years before she got turned into Mary White. Even though Professor White and Gwenhwyvar spent more time punishing me than talking to me, we used to play, travel to exotic places, experiment with forges, and have fun—did Mary tell you about the time in Persia she rode a flying carpet?" Leo chuckled. "Never understood why Professor White took us to all those weird places…That was…that was the last time I had fun…Leo shook his head as though he had been asleep. "Look at me, talking like a grouser; those days are gone, for me at least. But you guys still have a chance." Leo sighed. "Just wish Max was still around…he was always much better at this type of stuff than me.

There was a tapping outside on the window. Leo walked over and opened it. Flapper flew inside the apartment, circled the ceiling, and finally came down and settled onto a chair.

"There you are, you double-crossing bird! What do you have to say for yourself?" Leo leaned down to the bird. *"Alad droth!"*

Flapper immediately started repeating the events at the docks, doing an impersonation of all of the voices. When he got to the part where Helga said: 'Mary, can yeh sense the same thing I can about them blades they're carrying?' Min's eyes widened with excitement and joy. She looked at Fritz, who had awakened. He nodded to acknowledge her happiness.

"Looks like Helga's alive," Leo said. "That is one tough broad."

Flapper continued to speak. When he said: 'I'm Stanley Finch, Chief of the Bureau of Investigation for the Justice Department, and you four are under arrest!' Leo cursed and stood up. "They all got arrested? Why didn't they just fly away or do a Vorago in the river? I can't make a deal for the book if the mark is in jail and can't deliver!" He groaned and put his head in his hands. "This was all for nothing! You two are useless, I might as well get rid of you—"

Leo's entire window exploded. Debris flew over Min and Fritz and sprayed Leo with a painful glass shower. He hit the floor and did his best to shield himself from further assault. After all of the scraps had settled, Leo started to stand up. He was hit in the side of the head by something. He attempted to stand up again, and was hit on the other side of the head. He grabbed his crucifix to try a defense forge. A sharp object wedged itself between his neck and his necklace. He looked down and saw a hooked red blade of a spear. With one swift pull, the hook yanked his necklace away. It flew across the room and landed on the floor, next to the White Haired woman.

Leo stood up. "Who…Don't I know you?"

She turned her back to him, and with one arm bent down, picked Min up, and hoisted her over their shoulder.

"What do you think you're doing?" Leo yelled. He started to rush towards her. Something hit his jaw, and sent him flying into a wall. He shook off the blow just in time to receive another to the other side of his head, and then another, and another. After what felt like the fiftieth blow, he fell to his knees. Right before he lost consciousness, he saw, through his squinting inflamed eye, that the woman had used a red sledgehammer-like weapon with a large decorated ball on the end. It turned soft, draped down like cloth, and took the form of a long red scarf. The woman looked down at Fritz, paused, and jumped through the hole where the window used to be.

Fritz regarded Leo, lying unconscious on the floor. He could hear Leo's heartbeat; he was alive. Fritz didn't know what Leo would do once he woke up but knew it would hamper his escape plan. With such a large public disturbance, It was only a matter of time before the police arrived. Fritz couldn't be bothered being delayed by Dayfides. Across the room, he could see Min's quiang spear leaning against the wall. It was impossible to cut ahrion chains even with forged weapons, and yet when Min started sawing away at them, it seemed to leave a gash. Whatever the reason, he knew using it would be the best means of escape. With as much effort as he could muster, Fritz moved his body back and forth until he rocked on the bed. With one big shoulder thrust, he rolled off the edge of the bed and landed on the floor with a rattling thump. He was amazed and frustrated by how much noise had come from the apartment without anyone investigating. Perhaps this is the reason why Leo had chosen to live in this particular apartment. Rocking back and forth, created enough momentum to roll himself across the floor. When he reached the spear, he looked at Leo to ensure he remained incapacitated. Fritz bumped the bottom of the staff. It toppled and embedded itself into the floor, narrowly missing Leo's leg. After a few more rolls, Fritz arrived next to the blade. After rubbing his chains against the blade, he cut through one of the links, wiggled out of the chains, and stood up. He grabbed the shaft of the spear. With a little tug, he removed the blade from the floor and started to head out but paused and looked down at the unconscious Leo. "If I leave you alive, you'll keep causing us trouble." He lifted the spear and prepared to kill Leo. The spear shimmered, shrunk, and returned to its hidden form as a hairpin. Fritz held the pin up and looked at it. 'If I plunged it right into his eye, I may still be able to kill him.' He considered this gruesome option but felt the spear was sparing Leo's life.

There was a noise from the outside. Fritz put the pin in his pocket and ran to the hole in the wall. In the streets below, three black-suited men wearing top hats exited an EMF model 30 touring car. The men rushed into the building. Fritz could smell the blessed metals with them. It wasn't pure ahrion but a mix of tin and steel. He could also smell the gunpowder from their pistols. Whatever business they had with Leo would probably contradict his plan to escape. Fritz stepped back, took a running start, jumped out of the window, and grabbed onto a nearby light pole. He slid down to the ground and, without wasting a second, ran down the street away from the potential drama. Several blocks away, he stopped and smelled the air. He picked up Min's trail as well as the abductor heading in the direction of Central Park. If he transformed into a giant dog, he could probably catch up to them, barring the civil unrest he would cause. A bigger priority took the place of rescuing Min. Fritz turned and ran in a different direction. East, where he had picked up the faint scent of Elzbieta

June 9th, 1915

"Victoria!"

Now Victoria was being awakened by the voice; it knew her name. She was more than scared—she was terrified.

She got out of bed and got dressed for school. Today would be the last day before she would get two weeks off for summer vacation. This break was something Victoria looked forwards to. But there would be no vacation. She would have to go with her mother to the garment factory. Even if she were lucky enough to be in the 6% that graduated high school, what was the point? If she was going to end up working in the factory when she finished school? How would she ever be a female detective for the New York police department, like her hero, Emma Goodwin, if she ended up as a textile worker?

After washing her face, she sat down for a breakfast of cold porridge made with rice, water and brown sugar. After breakfast, Miss Flo arrived. She was a middle-aged Black woman who watched the three youngest children while Victoria and Otto went to school and her mother went to work. Victoria has heard that some parents merely gave their kids alcohol to put them to sleep while they went to work at the factories; she was glad the youngsters had the luxury of the nanny.

Thelma, Otto, and Victoria walked to the trolly stop to see Thelma off. She was the only one to ride to her destination. Otto and Victoria walked two miles to their Catholic school.

Usually, she and Otto never spoke, but today he was rather chatty. "You were screaming in your sleep last night," He said.

"What?"

"I could hear you. All the way from my room."

"I don't remember that. What did I say?"

"I don't know…something like free me!"

"Free me?"

"Or maybe feed me—I wasn't sure."

"Maybe I was hungry."

Otto snorted. "Yeah, that was probably it. Mom knows you've been sneaking pieces of her pie at night."

Across the street, Victoria saw what looked like a member of the Tonawanga tribe standing on a street corner, pointing towards a building. She looked at the building; there wasn't anything particularly interesting about the tobacco shop. She assumed he was some type of advertisement. After all, she has read stories of Indians smoking peace pipes with cowboys in the West. Otto ignored the man as though he didn't exist. 'How could he ignore something like that?' She wondered.

At their one-mile mark, they saw a man trying to pull a horse off of the ground so that it may continue pulling a cart. No matter how hard the man pulled the horse, it remained on the street.

"I wonder if they're going to have to shoot it?" Otto asked.

"Golly, I hope not."

A policeman joined the coachman and they began to talk. The policeman took out his gun. Victoria knew what was coming next. She closed her eyes, grabbed her brother's suit jacket sleeve, and tried to walk faster. When they were half a block away, they heard a gunshot. Victoria looked back, out of morbid curiosity. To her surprise, the horse was now standing and looking in her direction. "Thank goodness, he's all right." She sighed with relief.

Otto looked back. "What are you talking about? He's not all right!"

Victoria looked at her brother and then back at the horse. Now it was lying in the street, dead.

Further down the street, she spotted another figure pointing west. A woman was wearing a bloodstained 1600s colonial dress. "Golly!" Victoria yelled.

"What?" Otto asked.

"That woman, it looks like she's hurt!"

"What woman?"

"That one on the street corner!"

"Where?"

"Right there!" Victoria pointed at the woman who gazed into her eyes.

"Where?"

They walked away from her. "Right there! Don't you see her?"

"No."

"What? She's right behind me! Are you blind?"

"Applesauce! I think you're the one that's blind! There's no one there."

"Stop being a dingbat! Don't you see her?"

"All I see is a lamp post and a goof of a sister."

Victoria looked back at the woman in the bloody dress. She peered at Victoria but was still pointing in the same direction. "Otto?"

"What? Keep walking, or we'll be late for school!"

'Am I a dumb Dora, or is he playing a prank on me? But that woman looks like she needs h—' When she looked behind her, the woman was no longer there. 'Am I seeing things, too?'

Gertrude Helfta was shorter than Victoria, with a pudgy doll-like face and a pair of gold wire-framed glasses. In class, despite Victoria's trust in her best friend, she kept her morning hallucinations to herself. Gertrude related the information about the big explosion on Mary White's property and some new information that there was also a police shootout at the docks. She had a desire to be a lady journalist one day and combined with Victoria's desire to be a detective, the two had chronicled every odd event since 1912; the year the Titanic sank and the arrival of Mary Elizabeth White to New York City.

When Gertrude relayed the story about a gigantic dog terrorizing people, Victoria found this story far too fantastical.

"Where in the world did you hear this story?" Victoria asked her.

"My uncle lives in an apartment on Sixth Avenue."

"Is he the one that claimed to see a giant bat flying after a witch?"

"That was my aunt. No, he claims he saw a giant dog running down the street and he said there was someone on its back."

"Gertrude, that sounds like a man riding a horse."

Gertrude thought about it for a minute. "Well, just in case, I did a drawing for our book." She took a sheet of paper out of her book bag and showed it to Victoria. Victoria noticed Gertrude had a huge purple bruise on her arm. Victoria inquired about it.

"It's nothing," Gertrude said.

"Did you fall again?"

"I said it's nothing!" Gertrude angrily repeated.

She showed Victoria her sketch. The crude drawing was of a demonic-looking dog monster with sharp fangs and claws, blood dripping from its mouth. On its back was a black-clad figure resembling a vampire. Victoria studied the drawing and wondered if such a creature could exist. She reached into her bag and pulled out a large book, its cover decorated with illustrations of witches, spirits, and the words: "The Mysterious Book of Mysteries by Victoria Vanderbilt and Gertrude Helfta." Some pages contained samples of leaves, feathers, or any object which offered evidence of the validity of the occult. Victoria slipped Gertrude's drawing into the book and was just about to close it and put it away; their teacher, Sister Consulata, grabbed it.

"What is this?" She yelled.

"It's...uh," Gertrude said.

"Is this school related?"

"Er...no," Victoria answered.

"Then it doesn't need to be in this class!"

"But, it's lunchtime."

"If it's not related to school and learning, then it shouldn't be in this class!" The nun took the book and started to leave.

"NO!" Victoria yelled."

"I beg your pardon?" the nun yelled and menacingly turned around.

"It's ours...we spent a lot of time on that," Gertrude said.

"Young lady, don't you take that tone of voice with me! You two are always causing trouble—questioning the word of God in Bible studies, talking back to your elders, singing inappropriate songs!"

Victoria stood up. Her height put her two inches over the nun. "Sister, my mother listens to Irvin Berlin, and I don't question—"

"See! There you go again, talking out of turn! Tell you what, stick out your hands!"

Victoria uneasily stuck her hands out. Within a second, a 12-inch wooden ruler rapped her knuckles three times. It hurt and Victoria felt tears well behind her eyes. She refused to cry; 'Not here and not in front of Sister Consulata!' Three more hits struck her hands. The nun looked at Victoria as though her entire goal was to get her to cry, but Victoria's face remained stern and defiant. This made the nun angrier.

"You will stay after school and write 1000 times: I will not question the word of God, over and over!" The nun returned to the front of the class, taking their book with her. Of the entire experience, this hurt Victoria the most.

Victoria calculated she had written: 'I will not question the word of God.' 378 times before Sister Consulata got bored of watching her and left the room with a stern warning she would return. When she was sure she was alone, Victoria opened the nun's desk, took out her book, and carried it over to the window. She opened the window and tossed the book outside. She walked over to the blackboard and erased the last five sentences of her written punishments. For an hour, Victoria waited around for the nun to return. When she heard Sister Consulata coming down the hall, Victoria started rewriting the last five sentences of her punishment. When she entered the room, Consulata witnessed Victoria writing what she assumed was the last of the 1000 sentences.

"Now go home and pray for forgiveness!"

"Sister, can I have my book back?"

"Of course not." She walked over to the desk and opened it. "You will never see…" The nun looked puzzled.

"Sister?"

"What did you do with the book?" she yelled.

"I don't have it."

"Of course you do!" The nun walked over and frisked her. Aggravated, she went through Victoria's book bag and also found nothing.

"Sister, did you lose my book?"

"Of course not! I swear, I put it on my desk!" She frantically searched every drawer of the desk. "What did you do with it?"

"You took it from me Sister, remember? Did you lose it?"

"No—get out of my sight, insolent child!"

"Sister?"

"I said get out!"

With the sound of the nun searching around the room, Victoria took her leave, walked outside, and found her book under the window. She put it in her book bag and left the school grounds.

Her brother Otto was waiting outside the gate. "It's about time!" he complained.

"Sorry, I got into trouble."

"Again? You really are a rabble-rouser."

On the walk home, Victoria noticed another woman on the street corner, dressed in pioneer garb and pointing towards the West. Victoria's curiosity finally got the best of her. She approached the woman and asked her what she was pointing at. The woman stared at Victoria while pointing. Victoria repeated the question. The woman remained silent and pointed.

"Victoria?" Otto asked.

"What is it?"

"Who are you talking to?"

"What?"

"Who are you talking to?"

"This lady." Victoria gestured to the woman.

"What woman?"

"Otto, are you blind?"

"Are you nuts?"

"Excuse me…"Victoria turned her attention to the woman. Can you tell my brother…" She reached out to touch the woman's forearm. The second she did, the woman's arm dissipated into ashes, followed shortly by the rest of her body.

Victoria screamed, backed away, and tripped. She fell on her bottom and shook in fear. Something touched her shoulder; she scream again.

It was Otto. He had a concerned look on his face. "What's wrong with you?" he asked. A couple of pedestrians glared at him as though he had harmed her. "It's okay…" he implored them. "she's my sister—get up, you're embarrassing me!"

Victoria pointed and continued to panic. Otto forcibly picked her up and dragged her away from the scene. When she looked back, there was no evidence of the event.

Back home, she went straight to the bathroom and shut the door. She was terrified the woman would follow her home. She thought about the other pointing people. 'Were they also spooks like that woman? And the horse! Was that a spirit too?' She paced around the small room and burst into tears, thinking about the woman's face coming apart.

"Victoria?" her mother asked behind the door.

She wiped away the tears and tried to compose herself. "Ye—yes?"

"Otto said you were kept after school and ran into trouble on the way home."

"It's okay …I was talking in class…there was no trouble on the way home."

She could feel her mother's presence behind the door. She lingered for a long moment and then her footsteps on the squeaky wood floor announced her departure.. When Victoria was sure her mother was gone, she looked in the mirror at her red and swollen face. She filled the sink full of water and splashed her eyes. She looked up again, she could see her reflection; something felt off, as though someone was standing behind her. She turned around quickly. There was a man dressed in colonial clothing standing behind her, pointing. She screamed and tried to push him away. The instant she touched him, he crumbled into nothingness.

A second later her mom knocked on the door. "Victoria! What's wrong? Are you all right?" she yelled.

"I'm fine…I saw something…a rat. I saw a rat?" She crouched down and cried as quietly as she could.

Early in the evening, again, Victoria was visited by an apparition; this time, standing next to her little bed was an old gentleman dressed in Edwardian clothing. He pointed as the others had done. "Victoria!"

"Who are you?!" she yelled.

"Victoria" It repeated.

"Go away!"

"Victoria!" She grabbed her pillow and threw it at him. When it hit him he disintegrated as the others had.

Victoria was about to exhale in relief until she noticed a woman, sitting next to her, her face close to hers. "Victoria—"

The woman never finished her sentence because Victoria screamed and pushed her away into dust.

Her mother turned the key on the electric light and hurried into the room. "Victoria?! What is it? Is it the rat?" she yelled.

Victoria searched her imagination for an answer, anything other than the word spirit or haunting. Her emotions overcame her thoughts and she burst into tears. Her mother quickly crouched down and embraced her. "There, there." she soothed. "It is only a rat, one of God's creatures, for better or worse." Victoria shook her head no. "Not a rat? Not a prowler is it? 'cause I left my poker in the living room." Again, Victoria indicated no. "Then what is it darling?" She pulled away from Victoria. "What is it? You can tell me." Victoria almost spoke but wept some more. Her mother shushed her until she had calmed down. "Is it...you know... lady's issues?" Victoria indicated no. " Then what is it? You seem to be out of sorts lately. What could be bothering you? It's okay, you can tell me."

"Y-you won't believe me."

"Take my word for it Victoria, I've seen some things." Now tell me what is it."

Victoria wiped her tears on her nightgown and paused. "I've been seeing some things too."

"What kind of things?"

"Awful, terrible things."

"I'm sorry darling, like what?" Victoria didn't answer. "Victoria?"

"You won't believe me."

"Did someone hurt you?"

"No...not really."

"You can tell me, dear. I'll get your uncle to run 'em in."

"No, I don't think he could."

"Why is that?"

"Because...because they're dead."

Thelma was silent for a long moment. "You're seeing spirits?" Victoria nodded. "Where?"

"In the streets...in the bathroom..." She started to choke up. "...in my bedroom."

Thelma hugged her and let her cry for a moment. "What did they look like?"

"Like...like people...grey, pale people from a long time ago; pilgrims, cowboys, and Indians."

"Do they say anything or do anything?"

"They point and one said Victoria." Thelma looked very worried. "You don't believe me."

"Don't worry dear, I believe you...at least I believe what you saw was as real as anything else."

"You think I'm off my rocker."

"I don't know, Victoria. I don't understand things like this. I mean: one part of me has to believe in spirits because they're even mentioned in the Bible, but another part of me knows that sometimes the mind plays tricks on you, like those people who saw all of the crazy things recently: giant flying bat, giant dog."

"It's not like that! It really happened!"

"I know. But this all makes me think about my lost aunt."

"Who?"

"Aunt Helen. When she was young, your grandmother used to have a sister named Helen."

"Used to, did she die?"

"No...actually, I don't know."

"What happened to her?"

"My mother—your grandma told me one day Helen claimed that she could float one inch off the ground but only when she's alone."

"Float, as in fly?"

"I'm not sure but it was hard to prove because she claimed she could only do it when no one else was around."

"How old was she?"

"Right around your age, actually. So, it's not like she was a small child making up a story."

"You have to believe me, Mother, I've seen them—they're real!" Before Victoria could get upset again, Thelma comforted her. "I know, I know. Like I said, I believe whatever you've seen is real, but sometimes the mind plays tricks on you."

"I'm not mad!"

"If you're my daughter, we're all a little mad."

Another long moment of silence was interrupted by Victoria's question. "Why did you say: 'lost aunt'?" Thelma thought for a second, deciding if she should share more information. "Mother?"

"Aunt Helen kept telling people about what she could do, and eventually, the local priest heard about it. They said she was possessed by the Devil, and only they could cure her."

"Did they?"

"They came, and they took her away."

"Away, to where?"

"I don't know, but my mother told me she never saw her again."

Victoria fearfully looked at her mother. "I…I don't want them to take me away!"

She held Victoria tighter. "Don't you worry darling, ain't nobody going to land a hand on you, we'll figure out what to do. If we can't call a priest, we'll find one of those special brain doctors like that man in Germany Roselyn talked about, Dr. Freud."

"Won't a doctor that far be expensive?"

"I don't care how much it cost! I'll work overtime at the factory, I'll borrow money from my rich cousins—I'll do whatever I have to, to get your brain fixed. They tried the church, we'll try a doctor. There's no way anybody is going to take you away like they did my aunt!" Thelma put her hands on the sides of Victoria's face. "You're my daughter, and I'll be damned if I'd let that happen!"

"Mother, language!" Victoria and her mother laughed a little and then embraced.

June 10th, 1915

In the morning, as soon as her eyes opened, Victoria saw another apparition. This time it was a girl her age dressed in rags. For a while, she watched the pointing little girl. Unlike the others, Victoria wasn't afraid of her; she felt calmer, less terrified. She wasn't sure why she felt this way despite finding a deceased stranger in her bedroom. As smoothly and quickly as she could, Victoria put on her clothes and crept outside before the others in the house woke. Another one of the dead pointed towards the east. She traveled in that direction and eventually came to another figure and then another a block later. After many blocks, it became apparent the spirits were taking her on a journey too far to walk. Lacking funds, she realized she couldn't afford to take a trolly. On several occasions, she had seen Otto and his friends get around a lack of funds by jumping onto the back of the trolly and ducking down so the Brakeman wouldn't see them. When the train passed by her, she took a running start and hopped onto it, held on for dear life, and ducked down. Block after block, the trolly passed by the pointing figures in various period outfits, sexes, races, and ages. This continued until Centre Street, bounded by White, Elm, and Leonard Streets.

She jumped off the back of the trolly and ran out of the street before another trolly coming in the opposite direction could run over her. She looked at the latest round of spirits. Five souls were looking at a building off to the side. They ignored Victoria and were more interested in the structure.

The building had a chartreuse facade with conical towers, like a castle, and was connected to another building by a walkway. When she got close to the spirit, almost in a choral way, all of them said:

"Help me, Victoria!" This time, on their own, they disappeared into dust.

"W-Wait!" she yelled, realizing how odd it was she wanted them to stay. She walked closer and closer to the building.

One apparition remained, a younger boy staring at the building. Curious as to why he hadn't disappeared, Victoria walked over to him. She almost tapped him on the shoulder to get his attention but remembered what happens to the dead when she does that. "What am I doing here?" she asked him. The boy didn't respond so she said it louder. "Excuse me, why did you bring me here?" A confused Fritz turned around. Victoria noticed his skin was far from pale, letting her discern he was probably alive. She felt a wave of embarrassment run up her spine.

"What?" he asked.

"Er—ah, nothing, sorry!" She turned around and started to walk away. She hoped to get back home before everyone noticed her missing. Looking around, she realized where she was. It was the location of Tombs prison.

June 11th, 1915

Fritz spent the night on the street, squatting on the sidewalk and staring at the building. Inside, hundreds of men and women made hundreds of sounds and produced hundreds of smells. His ears occasionally heard misery—torture? he wondered. Among the Dayfides, the smells inside had the distinct aroma of Forgers and Strykers. Besides Elzbieta, he picked up the Black Blood, the Peppermint man, the Old Woman that smelled like licorice, and later in the day, the man that smelled like pepper, who had held him captive. Some in the building had a scent of delve like the Dayfides with the top hats. Far below the building, there was also the scent of death, an absence of smell, only distinctive to his nose—the largest he had ever not smelled, like a black hole of the living. Its existence made him shiver.

He needed to maintain his strength. He would not be able to rescue Elzbieta if he was weak. He needed to be strong enough to get her out of this building. He might be able to pick up smells and sounds from the inside, but lots of concrete and iron hindered this, and one area was devoid of life, the same type he had picked up in the room with the large door in the Black Blood house where Quing Min had showed him her dance. He took a whiff to see if she was still alive. Within a few minutes, he picked up her scent. She was with the blonde Black Blood and the blindfolded woman who smelled like ginger and ginseng. He was glad Min was alive. He wasn't sure why this made him happy. The only person he had ever been concerned with was Elzbieta.

Two policemen approached him.

"What are you waiting here for lad?" One asked.

"Probably for his pa to be released," the other officer answered for him.

"Go on, scram ya ragamuffin!" The other one shooed him away with his baton.

Fritz used this break in his time to go to the shopping area and beg for food. He waited outside a deli, held out his hand, and put on his saddest face. If he could avoid the police or the Truant Officer, he would usually be able to gather enough handouts or food to last another day. Today, someone gave him half of a ham sandwich which made him grateful; sometimes, the Dayfides could be generous. After he ate the ham, he relieved himself on a fireplug, returned to his spot, and continued to wait for Elzbieta.

The strange Dayfide girl had returned. He observed her as she paced around the building. She seemed to be confused. Fritz stopped in his tracks when he realized something. He thought he was mistaken when she confronted him yesterday but was now sure he had been right about her. Without her noticing, he crept up behind her and sniffed around. His analysis was almost terrifying; she had no smell.

He usually ignored the dead; they were just areas of nothingness, surrounded by the onslaught of the living and inanimate, filling in the gaps. But he noticed the girl because when she moved, she created a void in the other scents, like an eraser moving around on a page covered in graphite. It didn't take long for the girl to realize he was walking around her and smelling.

"What are you doing?" she asked as he continued to circle and sniff. Finding this annoying, she pushed him away from her. "Stop that! What are you doing?"

Fritz stepped back, "You have no smell."

"What?"

"You have no smell."

"I should hope not, I took a bath last night."

No, I can smell the Ivory soap you used on your skin. I can smell the Lux soap on your clothes, but the rest of you have no smell. It's like there's a shell of soap covering nothing."

"Oh! Dry up! You're a crackpot, go away!"

Fritz started to walk away but stopped. He had to find out what she was. In his long life, he had never run into this situation. A spot of quiet in all of the noises in the world. "Are you dead?" he asked.

"No," she said, annoyed. "Are you?"

"No. Are you a spirit, a ghost, or an awakened?"

She seemed startled by this question. "No, are you?"

Fritz shook his head.

"Why would you think I was dead?"

"Because you have no smell."

"What? Can you smell dead people?"

"I can't because they smell like you."

"Who are you?"

"Who are you?"

"I asked you first."

She looked annoyed again. "I'm Victoria Alexandria Vanderbilt. Who are you?"

"Fritz."

"Fritz, what?"

"Just Fritz."

"Are you an orphan or something?"

"I have Elzbieta."

"What's an Elzbieta?"

"She takes care of me, and I take care of her."

"Is she your mother?"

"No."

"Does she know you're out here sniffing girls?"

"No, she's in there." He pointed to the building.

"In prison? Your mom is in there?"

"She's not my mom."

Victoria thought for a second. "Can she talk to spirits or is she friends with them?" Fritz shook his head. Then who's asking for help? It's not him. Am I really just crazy?

"What are you?" Fritz asked.

"What?"

"You don't smell like a Dayfide, a Forger, a Stryker, or anghenfēl."

"I have no idea what any of those things are. What do they smell like?"

"You don't know what you are? Maybe you're like me."

"Unless dead people are talking to you, I doubt it."

Fritz realized something. "You smell like that thing."

"What thing?"

"I don't know what it is. It's far below this building and has no smell."

"It's like me?"

"Yes, but 1000 times bigger."

June 12th, 1915

"Victoria, you've hardly touched your chicken pudding," her mother said.

Victoria was too deep in thought to be thinking about chicken in creamy batter. Yesterday, the strange boy with one name told her she had no smell, but he wasn't talking about a normal smell. She didn't understand what he meant exactly, but he could tell she was different. 'What are Dayfides, Forgers, Strykers, and anghenfêls?'

After dinner, she asked to borrow the family dictionary. She looked up all of the words, but the only one in the book was Forger:

For"ger (?), n.[Cf. F. forgeur metal worker, L. fabricator artificer. See Forge, n. & v. t., and cf. Fabricator.] One who forges, makes, of forms; a fabricator; a falsifier.

2. Especially: One guilty of forgery; one who makes or issues a counterfeit document.

'Falsifier? Was he calling me a liar? I'm obviously not a metal worker.'

Victoria helped do the laundry by turning a large crank on a wringer washing machine to squeeze the clothes through two rollers, transferring them to a waiting metal pale. Her mother looked at her with a concerned expression. "Victoria, any more airings of...you know?"

"I...no...it's fine."

Her mother stopped scrubbing a shirt on a washboard and walked over to her. "Victoria, I told you, you can tell me anything, I won't punish you."

"I know...it's just..."

Her mother hugged her. "Go on...you can tell me."

"They...they lead me to the prison."

"The prison?"

"The one near White and Elm Street."

"Tombs?"

"I reckon."

"They told you to go into a prison?"

"No just the outside of the building, and then they disappeared."

Her mother thought for a second. "Are they asking you to do something bad?"

"No, it's always…it's always …pointing…and sometimes they call my name." Her mother let go of Victoria and sat down in a chair. She looked worried. "You're giving me a look like you don't believe me."

"No, it's not that. I believe you are seeing what you are seeing. But you also have to con…"

The twins came into the room, chasing one other.

"You two stop playing in here. If you spill the wash pail, I'll skin you alive!" The kids exited faster than they came in. "You have to consider how the brain plays tricks on you."

"I have. But there's also a boy."

Her mother stood up. "A boy! What boy?"

"Down by the prison, hanging out, he told me he can see…or smell the same things I can."

Her mother rolled her eyes. "Well, there you go; this is all about a boy and your feelings getting all mixed up."

"It's not like that! I don't know him, especially in that way!"

"But the fact that this is happening, and now there's a boy involved. This could all be because you're going through… womanly things."

"Mother! I've only just turned 13!"

"My point exactly. Your body is all scrambled right now. It happens—it happened to me. I spent hours crying one minute and happy the next."

"This has nothing to do with that!"

"Of course it does. The timing is impeccable."

Victoria fumed. She wanted to tell her mother she could also eavesdrop on conversations if she put her fingers in her ears but withheld. 'The lord only knows how she'll feel about that information.'

For the rest of the evening, they did the laundry in silence.

Before she turned in, Victoria started writing down everything that had happened recently in her Book of Mysteries.

While she slept, although her mother tried to come in quietly, Victoria could hear her enter the room. She tiptoed over to Victoria and lightly placed her hand on her head. she paused at the entrance and sighed before leaving,.

'I'm putting her under a lot of worry. I can't make her worry. I should be helping her, not scaring her. I'm going to have to solve this mystery myself.'

She lit a lantern, opened the Book of Mysteries, and continued writing.

June 13th, 1915

Gertrude was not as graceful as Victoria when it came to hitching rides on the back of the trolly car. In the few trips Victoria had taken, she had become quite adept at hopping on and off the under-ride guard with ease. When the train came to a stop, Victoria jumped off, and Gertrude fell and rolled onto the ground. Victoria quickly picked up her friend before she could sustain any serious injuries and led her across the street to Tombs prison. On the walk, Victoria noticed another new bruise on Gertrude's wrist, "Did that just happen?"

"It must have. Now, please! Drop it!" Gertrude said.

Victoria saw Fritz sitting in his same spot, looking at the building while eating another free ham sandwich.

"Is that the boy?" Gertrude asked.

"Yes, sitting in that same spot every time I come here."

Taking the lead, Gertrude walked over to have a better look at Fritz and stopped outside of listening distance. She opened their book and started to sketch a picture of Fritz. "You said he's waiting on his ma?"

"I'm not sure. Maybe a sister. Someone named Elzbieta."

Gertrude wrote the word 'Elzbieta?' over the portrait of Fritz. She looked at the prison. He's gonna be waiting a long time. Nobody goes to prison unless it's for a very long time."

"I know."

"Let's get a better look at the prison. Maybe there's a clue about why spirits are calling you here."

They walked under the walkway that crossed four stories above Franklin Street, connecting the prison to the Manhattan Criminal Courts building. They glanced up. Victoria felt a cold breeze on top of her head. She looked at Gertrude. "Did you feel that?"

"Feel what?"

"That cold breeze coming from the walkway up there."

"I can't feel anything."

A car came close to hitting them and blew its horn. The girls scrambled out of the street and ran to the prison entrance.

One of the guards blocked their path. "Hey! You dumb Doras! Don't go galavanting around in the streets!" he yelled.

"We're sorry. We were just looking at that thing!" Gertrude pointed to the walkway.

"The Bridge of Sighs?" he asked.

"The what?"

"Bridge of Sighs. That used to be where prisoners walked across to get to the gallows. Before that, they would hang people from it."

Both girls turned and looked at the walkway again. Victoria studied it intensely.

"What is it? Do you see something?" Gertrude asked.

"No...I...No, it's okay."

Victoria turned around and looked at Fritz. He was still in his spot, eating his meal for the day.

When Victoria looked up at the bridge, she saw three bodies hanging by their necks, suspended underneath. She almost let out a scream but covered her mouth.

"What is it? What's wrong?" Gertrude asked, squinting to see what Victoria was looking at.

"Bodies! Three of them—hanging by their necks!"

"You can see them now?"

"Yes!"

As much as she strained her eyes, Gertrude couldn't see anything. Victoria looked at her. "You do believe me, right?" Gertrude's skeptical look gave her thoughts away. "I'm telling the truth! There are three hanging bodies under the bridge!"

"What do they look like?"

"Their skin is gray like the others…they're all pointing"

"Where?"

Victoria looked down. "Towards the ground." The bodies were speaking. She couldn't hear what their decaying mouths were saying from so far away, but she knew what it was. 'Help me Victoria.'

As fast as she could without appearing to run away, Victoria grabbed Gertrude's arm and walked across the street to where Fritz was sitting.

"Where are we going?"

"I had to get away from there, I can only take so much!" Gertrude walked over to Fritz. He ignored her.

"You! Victoria told me your name is Fritz!" He didn't respond until he had finished his meal. He looked up at Gertrude. "She said you could tell what soap she used!" He looked away from her. "Well, I don't believe a word! Not like there are many choices of soaps out there! What's your game?" No response. She looked at Victoria. "You see! He's a fraud! Unless he's a dog, there's no way he can smell things like that!"

"He said there's a giant version of me underneath this building. All the spirits I've seen, seem to be calling for help and pointing towards it. He knows a lot about what's going on."

Gertrude was distracted. "Take a gander at that car!" She pointed.

A luxury auto pulled up next to the prison entrance. Three men with top hats got out of the car. Fritz stood up and looked like he wanted to run.

"What is it?" Victoria asked.

They continued to watch the prison entrance. A few minutes later, the three men came outside, pushing a woman in a wheelchair to the car. She stopped briefly and looked across the street at them. Fritz started to walk forward. The woman seemed to shake her head no, and he stopped advancing. She transferred herself into the car. One of the three escorts witnessed their interaction, looked at Fritz, and began to walk over to them.

"Who's that?" Gertrude asked.

"I don't like the way he looks!" Victoria said. She turned around and was about to tell Gertrude that they should leave. She almost ran into the chest of one of the men. She staggered back in fear and surprise. She was less confused how he had made it across the street so fast than what his intentions were. The man looked at her briefly and then walked around her to where Fritz was standing; he was gone. Gertrude, who had also been distracted by the presence of the top hat man, didn't see Fritz leave and looked around perplexed. Another top-hat man joined the other. They did a quick gaze around the area.

"Where did he go?" the first man asked.

"Probably ran off. Was that Cŵn Annwn?"

"Most likely. Always the faithful dog."

The two men walked back to the luxury auto. When the car traveled past them, the girls could finally see the face of the woman as she craned her head to look at their faces.

"Where did that boy go…and so fast?" Gertrude asked.

Victoria was too enthralled to answer. "That was her!"

"Who?"

"That woman! That was Mary White!"

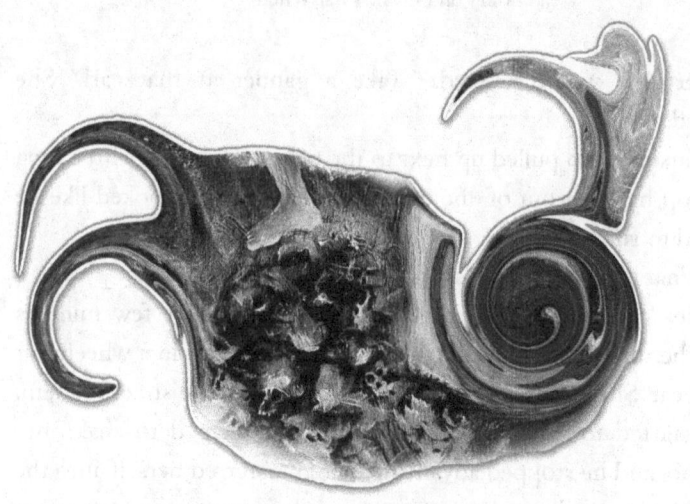

PART FOUR

JUMP OVER THE DOOR

June 14th, 1915, 11:02 AM

Mary was alone in a jail, surrounded by empty cells. If she ignored the stone walls and steel doors, it didn't feel or look like a jail cell. After she was arrested a while ago for protesting for women's right to vote and put in a dirty, crowded cell with potentially dangerous women, compared to that, this was pleasant.

This enclosure was clean, furnished with a comfortable twin bed, a desk, a vase and flowers, and a bookshelf stocked with five novels she wanted to read. She sat at the table in a wheelchair, drinking her cup of tea. It wasn't the best cup of tea, but as horrible as it was, she was sure the other inmates would literally kill for it.

A guard approached her cage. She didn't remember requesting anything. He unlocked her cell and opened the door.

"Miss White…" he said, gesturing to the exit.

"Pardon?"

The guard walked over to push her chair for her.

"It's perfectly all right. I got it, thank you," Mary said.

"This way, please," he repeated, gesturing down the corridor.

Mary felt there were only two reasons someone would want you to leave your cell in prison: exoneration or execution. If it were execution, all of the niceties up to this point would make sense as a drawn-out last-meal scenario. She finished her tea, imagining it to be her last, and rolled her chair out of the room. The man didn't explain where he was leading her, and she had no interest in asking.

She prepared herself for death. On multiple occasions, she had felt her life was ending. But this felt different. This event had only one ending unless she made a bold move like escaping. When they entered another hallway, she noticed something about this area that made her more nervous; she could tell the bars of the cells were hi-yaguh; forged iron. "We're going out a different way than I came in," she said.

"Sorry, other elevator's out of order—this way," the guard said, trying to hurry her through the hall. They went inside a caged elevator. The car lowered to the bottom floor. Mary noticed that the ground level of this particular elevator was not the last stop. This elevator had buttons for sub-levels, reaching all the way down to negative 13.

Upon exiting the car, on the ground level, she saw a large man with a bushy mustache, wearing a tan suit come out of a small room furnished with a bed in its corner. Mary wondered if he occasionally slept in there. "Miss White," the mustached man said. He gestured to a door.

"Are you the warden?" Mary asked.

"That I am," he answered.

"What is the meaning of this, is there an electric chair behind that door?"

The Warden chuckled. "Not yet." He opened the door to the atrium and reception area. They escorted her from the lobby to the outside. A luxury auto awaited her.

She turned around. "You're letting me go?"

"Not quite," the Warden said. "If you can, please slide into the car, or do you need help?"

Mary refused their help. After a little bit of struggling, she transferred herself from her chair into the car. Before they closed the door, Mary looked at the Warden. "In the future, I assume I have your permission to come back inside and visit?"

The Warden looked confused. "If you want, of course."

While she waited for them to put her wheelchair in the back of the car, something caught her eye. Fritz was across the street with two other children. He was about to make a move towards her. She didn't know what Fritz was about to do, but this was neither the time nor the place to do it. She shook her head no and hoped he got the message. He stopped his advance; she breathed a sigh of relief and sat back in her seat. The car pulled away and passed by the youngsters. Mary recognized Thomas' niece Victoria, but not the other girl. 'Why is she with Fritz, hanging around a prison?' And where is Min? If Fritz managed to escape, maybe Min didn't make it! Dear lord, I hope she's all right!'

In the roundabout driveway near other fancy cars, the luxury auto parked in front of Vanderbilt Manor. A top-hatted man tried to help Mary out, but she refused and got out of the car and into her wheelchair by herself. Police officers and a couple of top-hatted men armed with swords and rifles peppered around the area. "Is all this security to protect me? Or to protect someone else from me?" Her escort ignored her question, pushed her to the front stoop, guided her into the parlor room, closed the door, and left her alone. "Curiouser and curiouser."

While waiting for whomever was about to make an appearance, Mary rolled around and examined the various porcelain figurines and vases decorating the room. There was a photo of Alfred Vanderbilt, flanked by several men on the fireplace mantle. She stretched, grabbed the picture, and noticed her father was in the photo, standing in the background.

The parlor door opened. Mary nervously put the photograph on a side table next to a candlestick.

Shirley entered the room, and they studied each other for a moment. Without showing emotion, Mary took the heavy candlestick off the side table, held it like a club, and prepared to hurl it at Shirley's head. Shirley's calmness took Mary off guard but didn't stop her murderous plan. Alva Vanderbilt Belmont entered the room and instantly halted her assault.

"Mary?" Alva asked, looking at the candlestick.

"I—I was just admiring it—late 1700s, am I correct?" She pretended to study the bottom before putting it back on the table.

"Y-yes...Oh, dear Mary!" Alva walked over, leaned down, and they tightly hugged. "I was so worried about you after hearing about your house having a gas explosion, and then you got arrested again for protesting and hurting yourself—"

"Protesting?"

"Yes. Sarah and Juliet said you and Thomas were drawing attention to the plights of women by roaring through town on a motorcycle; I assume that is how you injured yourself, then you were put into jail again."

"I wouldn't say that it—"

"That is correct!" Shirley interrupted. "That is what everyone is saying, and I believe the best explanation for your incarceration, n'est pas?"

Mary narrowed her eyes at Shirley and turned her attention back to Alva. "So, do I have you to thank for my comforts and my prison abatement?"

"Oh my, no. You have a much bigger benefactor, he'll be here momentarily. Poor Mary. Such a tumultuous year this has been for you."

"Alas, the year is only half over," Shirley said.

"Well, let us hope the rest of 1915 will not be as dramatic. Here, Madam Blanche, have a seat." Alva gestured to rococo chairs arranged in a circle. On the table between them, a tea service had been set. "Mary, you won't believe who is here to see you!"

"Without information, my guesses are quite limited."

"It's—perhaps I should just show him in." Alva stood up, opened the door, and gestured for someone to come in. Two of the security men entered the room and stood in the corner. An older gentleman followed; it took Mary only a few seconds to recognize who he was.

"President Wilson?"

"Hello, Miss White," he said, smiling.

Mary smiled for a second but reined in her enthusiasm. He reached out his hand; Mary reluctantly shook it as fast, and as uncongenial as she could. "Charmed" was the best greeting she could muster.

President Wilson seemed surprised by her attitude. He sat next to Alva. "I've heard a lot about you, Miss White."

"And I've certainly heard a lot about you."

Alva looked confused by Mary's tone.

The President cleared his throat. "Sorry to hear about the passing of your father. I heard he was a real humdinger."

"Yes, quite the humdinger, thank you." Mary sipped some tea. It was so much better than the stuff in prison. She refused to allow pleasure to change her mood. "So, what brings you here, Mr. President?"

"I have business to attend to, Miss White, some of which involves you."

"Oh, are you finally going to give women the right to vote, allow Asian women into the country, or perhaps civil rights for colored people?" His face soured and then turned into a smile. "I'm afraid not. That's a heap of legislation that I'm sure will take quite some time."

"Time flies apace. We would fain believe that everything else flies forward with it."

"Pardon?"

"Nietzsche. You're the man in charge. You have the time and resources to make good things happen; you just choose not to."

"Mary!" Alva said.

"I'm sorry, that was slightly impertinent. Please, tell me, what business could you have with me?"

"It's about your father and pertains to...secretive information..." The President gestured to Shirley and Alva. "...If you ladies don't mind, I'd like to speak to Miss White alone."

"Well, of course," Alva said.

She and Shirley left the room.

President Wilson stared at Mary for an uncomfortably long time. "Miss White, let me get straight to the point. We want the book."

"Silly me. I thought you wanted to discuss a fundraiser for your reelection."

"I'm afraid not. You don't sound much like a supporter."

Mary narrowed her eyes. "What on Earth gave you that idea?"

"Your father was also not my biggest fan, but—"

"President Wilson, just because you're a staunch defender of segregation, refuse to grant women the right to vote, had the five Chinese survivors of the Titanic expelled from the country as soon as they arrived thanks to your Exclusion Act, are a huge fan of the ideology of the confederacy and the K.K.K., called slavery a 'gentle patrician affair' and praised that celluloid feculence: Birth of a Nation—what's there not to like about you?"

The President's face had turned red. "Okay, that's your opinion. Getting back to the book—"

"What book?"

"Listen..." The President calmed himself and lowered his voice. " Your father brought the Siv Myrddin to New York in 1912. Apparently, it was in a safe in your underground manor. We didn't

122

know until a ronin goldsmith named Maximilian destroyed your house with a gang of anghenfêls. We searched the wreckage, and all we found was an empty safe. Meaning when you escaped, you took it with you. Am I missing anything?" Mary didn't answer. "Good. Now, as your president, I am ordering you to tell us where the book is. When you do, you can go home—or to wherever, and this will all be over."

Mary took a sip of tea and put it down daintily. "What...book?"

President Wilson clenched his fists onto his knees and then relaxed his hands. He took a deep breath. "I see you like to play games. Here's a little game for you and your gang!"

"Gang?"

"Yes, your gang is responsible for multiple deaths and multiple property damage."

"We were chasing after someone who kidnapped two children!"

"One of them is an illegal China-man! Add that to your charges, I don't know who you think you are, or why everyone seems so enamored by you, but to me, you and your gang don't have the authority of the police department!"

"And yet someone like you is in control of an army."

He took another deep breath. "A real wise apple, aren't ya, woman? Listen to me! You have 24 hours to tell us where that book is! If you do not, we will execute Thomas Vanderbilt by gas chamber, Helga of Pendle will be burned at the stake, Abel White will be sent to a Southern prison plantation in Mississippi, where he'll be worked to death, and 'Men King' will be sent straight back to China where the royal family will most likely execute her! Now, you still don't know what book I'm talking about?"

Her lips quivered. She came very close to confessing; in reality, she had no idea where the book was, as Abel was at an undisclosed location. But she knew the President wouldn't believe anything she told him unless it was attached to exact coordinates. "What... book?" With the look in his eyes, Mary would not have been surprised if the President of the United States hit her.

He composed himself and stood. "Miss White...Mary, from what we can tell, your father was going to hand that book over to England to help them against the Germans. But he was tragically struck down on the Lusitania. Even though I'm trying my damnedest to avoid it, in less than a year, the United States, your adopted country, may get dragged into that war. In that book, there could be some forges that can quickly end that war and save millions of lives. Your father's last action was trying to stop a war. I think it'll be prudent for his daughter to respect his wishes and continue where he left off. Tell us where the book is...please... please."

"Carrot, then stick."

"Pardon?"

"Carrot, then stick."

"I'm sorry, I don't understand."

"When you want to persuade somebody, you offer them a pleasurable outcome, and if they don't comply, you use the threat —the stick." You threatened the lives of my friends, and now you are appealing to my dutifulness? It now makes sense why you admire the K.K.K. They're bad at positive motivation as well.

"24 HOURS!" The President stomped out of the room, followed by the security men. They slammed the door behind them. Mary rolled her chair over to the window and drew open the curtain. She saw at least 12 armed men scattered around the grounds. "Another prison." She saw the President and Alva walking outside. Alva seemed to be apologizing, most likely for Mary's attitude. She was sure he shared no part of their conversation.

Shirley entered the room, closed the door behind her, locked it, and sat at a coffee table adorned with glasses and a bottle of sherry. She smiled. Mary rolled over to the coffee table. She looked at one of the glasses and then glared at Shirley. Mary filled a glass with sherry, downed it in one shot, and smashed it against the table's edge. She pointed the glass shard at Shirley's throat. Shirley remained still. Mary thrust the jagged glass edge towards Shirley's jugular but stopped one centimeter away from touching her skin. Without flinching or changing her smile, Shirley looked Mary in the eyes. The look of such confidence and defiance puzzled Mary on many levels.

"Why are you smiling?" Mary yelled. "How can you be so calm when I am about to end your life for what you have done!"

"And what did I do?"

Mary put the glass against Shirley's neck. "You and Leo were working together! All that time you were scheming and playing on our sympathies! Because of you, Abel was almost killed—"

"Almost? So Leo didn't kill him? That's a relief."

"Yes, he's still alive! Who are you really? Are you the Belgian? Are you one of the Followers?"

"I'm your cousin Shirley."

"Very soon you're going to be my headless cousin Shirley!"

"Then, by all means, do so if it will make you feel better."

It took every bit of self-control Mary had to pull the glass away from Shirley's neck. "Argh! You know I won't!"

"Actually, I wasn't sure. But I hoped."

"Hope is for the innocent and fools…" Mary rolled around to the other side of the coffee table "…the worst of all evils. I'd rather see you rotting in prison!" She replaced her broken glass and poured herself more sherry..

Shirley rubbed her neck and checked for damage. She served herself some spirits.

"Don't get too comfortable…" Mary said, "…just because I didn't kill you now, only means I haven't killed you yet."

Shirley took a sip of sherry. "Oh. I am quite sure in the future, you will thrust your sword into my heart. But…"

"But?"

"But you and I both know if you kill me, you will be missing out on a plethora of information."

Mary silently agreed and calmed her nerves by drinking the liquid. "Who are you, really?"

" I really am your cousin Shirley."

"I assumed that was true by your disreputable character."

Shirley giggled. " I suppose I deserve that. But the only thing I did was hypnotize Abel to let me into the safe, and that was it."

"That was it? You lied to me!"

"About what?"

"About everything! Being attacked by the Gold Leader, who I assume is you! About my father taking you away to an orphanage!"

"Ah bon, that part was all true."

"My father would never have done th—."

"He did it because I stabbed him."

"You...you did what?"

"I know. It was a deplorable thing to do. I had been raised by Robespierre up to that point. They were brothers and bitter rivals at the same time that Elyan was raising you. Your father invaded our foundry and killed all of my friends and the first man I'd ever loved."

"You were kidnapped! Robespierre killed my parents!"

"I know. He was a monster. But in our time together, I developed real feelings for him."

"Be that as it may, it's not normal! You were a child! He abused you more than my father ever could—and you tried to paint my father as the monster—to play on my sympathies, and all that time, you were taking advantage of us!"

Shirley stood up, walked over to the mantle, and retrieved a match. She placed a dried leaf on a silver platter and set it on fire. The leaf went out and smoldered.

Mary recognized the smell. "Are you—" She was quieted by Shirley's raised finger.

Shirley fanned the smoke of the leaf around the room before speaking. "It's sage."

"Why are you burning sage?"

"Do not concern yourself with it."

"Curious and curiouser."

"I was quite surprised the President's threats had failed. I thought you would have considered a trade to save your friends. Definitely, something I would expect from you."

"They're not dead yet."

Shirley smiled. "You have a plan." Mary didn't answer. Shirley took a sip. "I wish to give three reasons as to why you should surrender the book to me instead of President Wilson."

"I see. The fix is in. The double cross has finally made its appearance. Well, at least you're consistent."

"I am not deceiving him, as I have never made any kind of contract with that boorish man. He assumes just because I am a guest in this country, alliances are all to his whims. We may or may not have the same goal of stopping the war in Europe, but I'll have to agree with something someone said to me: arming American Forgers with the book would bring about peace as much as arming German Forgers. Peace is nothing more than enough destruction on the other side for them to surrender."

"I would never expect you to be concerned with the innocent Normalu."

"I'm not. I'm merely playing on your sympathies to such matters."

Mary rolled her eyes, "Your brutal honesty is both unnerving and refreshing." Shirley smiled. "Alright then, give me reason number one."

"Of course. Number one: They don't know about you."

"About what?"

The Americans have no idea you're a Forger. And I haven't told them. Did you notice? The heavy security is more for protecting the President than to keep you from escaping? The fact that you're out of jail means they don't think you'll just fly away or turn invisible." Apparently, that part of you was concealed."

"By whom?"

Schwinger rubbed his cheek where Thomas had hit him. It angered him to be hit by an American. He hated them and their country. His deepest desire was to complete his mission and depart this country. So many obstacles prevented this. The hexen, or witches as they say in English, ruined everything. On the deck of the Olympic, he watched as a replacement 37mm QF1 pounder pom-pom cannon was lowered onto the deck by ropes and a crane to replace the one destroyed by Elzbieta on the first attack. He sighed and turned his attention to a wide net cast in the waters off the port side. There was a little good news. After searching the ship, the Americans didn't find their crystal ball. He didn't know why the one who had punched him didn't tell them where it was, but he was glad. He would be going to Germany without the book. But he had tons of silver and gold, some turned into ahrion bullets, and he would have the crystal ball, which would allow the Kaiser to observe the actions of their enemies—a partial victory for Deutschland.

"Aufzug! Aufzug!(Lift! Lift!)" He commanded a couple of Germans. The words made his jaw hurt. He held his cheek and gestured with his hands instead. When they lifted the net, dripping with water and mud, there was nothing of value in it, only a metal garbage can and an old tire. A moment later, a man in a diving bell underwater suit, connected to a long oxygen hose, was lifted by ropes from the river. When the diver saw Schwinger, he gave him a thumbs-down sign.

"I don't understand?" Schwinger yelled at his crewman. "We've looked everywhere…for days! I saw him drop it over the side right HERE! Where could it be? I can't go back without something!" Schwinger hit the handrail. "Keep looking!"

1,357 miles out to sea, the CSS Virginia bobbed up and down on the waves. Abel rotated the knob of the claw-footed tub and turned off the water. The tub was half full. He knew he only needed less than an inch of water for Helga to do a Vorago forge, but every day he had added just a little more water; better to be safe than sorry. "They should have been here a week ago," he said to himself. 'Either they were captured or killed. At times like this, I wish I could do forging and then travel through this thing directly to them.'

He stood up and walked out of the bathroom. If he were a Forger, he imagined he could also rescue them. Or, at the least, avenge their deaths. As a Stryker, his only plan of action was to wait. He walked through the bridge and glared at the painting that covered the safe holding the Siv Myrddin, one of the reasons he had been waiting for someone to show up. "If I go anywhere with this ship that gives the slightest clue about my whereabouts, the enemy could use the Eye of Graeae to pinpoint my location." He would continue to wait, but for how long? The ship had enough provisions to last three months at least, and he could always fish for food. 'How long? A year—forever—until death. I could always sink the ship and go down with it. Is the book that important? Professor White seemed to think so.'

Abel went out onto the front deck and grabbed a fishing rod. He wound the reel and pulled in his latest catch; it was a jellyfish. He groaned in disappointment. 'Another one? This is all that I seem to catch out here! That's going to make fishing for decent food tough.' Undeterred, he baited his hook and cast out his line again. He sighed and tried his best to relax. 'I have to have faith in the others; they're strong. I will wait for however long it takes!'

After a while of casting and reeling in his line, there was a large tug; the catch was heavy. He pulled harder and brought it closer and closer to the starboard side of the ship. 'This is a big one! Perhaps I underestimated the middle of the Atlantic.' With one more heave, he should see the face of his prey. The action did not yield the result he had expected. He was unsure if it was human, but the shape was human-like; a mound of seaweed and mud draped the figure entirely, dripping green water and slime onto the deck as the creature crawled onto the side.

Abel looked for a weapon; he found a boat hook. He picked it up and readied himself. Two more creatures joined the first, and they crawled onto the deck like inhuman crabs. "Stay back!" Abel yelled. More joined them, and they lurched towards him in a mass of dark green seaweed. As a warning, Abel jabbed at one of their shoulders. The sharp edge of the hook pierced the muck and kept going into nothingness. The creatures were all sea debris, covering an invisible human form. The word 'spirits' came to his mind as well as 'demons'. He had never seen any, and even in his world of forging and defying science, he was always skeptical of this part of the occult. He swiped at the head, sending slime over the edge when he made contact. The remaining material on the monsters let him know all he had done was remove their covering, but they were unharmed and still advancing. 'They can touch me, but I can't touch them.' was the reality.

He pushed his way through the weakest point in their growing army and rushed inside the bridge. Slamming the door saved him from whatever plan they had for him. More and more of them gathered onto the deck. They put green hand prints onto the windows and roamed the deck, looking for a way to get inside. Abel considered his options: 'They can't pass through walls, which is reassuring! Or perhaps they can't pass through the walls of this particular ship! Do I have anything to fight spirits? Are they here for the book? Can they get into the safe?' Abel never wished more that he was a Forger or someone with powers to set attackers on fire or hurl them away with the wind. 'But would that even work on those that can touch you and you can't touch them?'

There was multiple thumping on the metal door as the things tried to get in. Abel looked through the port hole and saw more and more of them climb onto the deck, increasing the banging on the door. He grabbed his revolver teclyn and prepared himself, in case they broke down the door. He knew the bullets would be useless, but the gun steadied his nerves a little.

For almost a minute more, the thumping continued and then abruptly stopped.

Abel waited and then peered outside. One after another, he saw the brown and green beings retreating into the ocean, producing the same splash a human body would. He held steady just a while longer and then cautiously opened the door. An anticipated ambush was not to be. He was about to look around the deck, but something was blocking his path. He jumped back and fixed his gaze on the object sitting on a mound of seaweed and mud. Like a pearl surrounded by darkness. "What is that? Did they give me a gift?" He bent down to poke it, making sure it was not an illusion or trap. Feeling confident, he reached down and picked it up. "Wait…Helga said…is this…Is this the Eye of Graeae?"

"…I have my suspicions about what the Americans have been using to gather information, but I'm not going to disclose it," Shirley said.

"And why not?" Mary asked. "You told me you want me to trust you."

"That doesn't mean I'm going to reveal all of my cards to you," Shirley smirked.

"Then, can you reveal anything else?"

"Number two: I can help you to escape."

"What?"

"You can Vorago out of here, use the tub in my room; you can do that, right?"

"Yes, but if I did without the use of my legs for swimming to the surface, I might drown if I end up in deep water."

"Ah, yes…How did that happen? Was that from fighting with Mausi?"

"…Yes…Yes, it was. She dropped a box on me."

"Ah, I can still help you run away…or roll and never be seen again."

"We both know I'm not going to abandon my friends."

"Then find a way to rescue them."

"If I rescue my friends, we'll all be refugees, constantly running away from those wanting the book for the rest of our lives. It would never end."

"I don't envy you. No matter what you do, you're going to lose."

"So far, the reasons you have given me to trust you have been unworthy of consideration."

"Then perhaps this one will whet your appetite. Number three: The President was bluffing when he said: 'Min would be deported, back to China.'"

"He didn't seem like someone overladen with threats"

"The reason I know is because I have Min."

"What? Now I know you are lying. Leo has Min and Fritz; or at least Min—How would you have Min?"

"I had her rescued from his apartment before the government men got there. Who is Fritz?"

"The giant dog."

"He must have escaped before they rescued Min. There was no one else there when they apprehended Leo."

"That explains…Where's Leo?"

"In the same prison with Thomas, Helga, and the Iron Smith—Abel is not in that prison; that was a bluff as well."

"What proof do I have that she is in your custody?"

"Trust me. She's in a safe and secure location. No matter what happens, I won't turn her over to the President."

"And I'm supposed to believe you? I can't trust anyone else to have the book, especially you!"

"Then I think I have the perfect solution."

"And that is?"

"Destroy the book."

"I've already thought of that; it's impossible—and why on Earth would the leader of the—what are you exactly? Are you a Minion?"

"No, I'm the leader of the Western European Golds."

"Why would someone in your position want to destroy the book? With it, your foundry would be the most powerful force in the world! I would believe you more if your solution was for me to throw it into the Hudson River!"

"It wasn't until Maximilian betrayed me, that I realized even if I got the book, I would have spent half of my life searching for it and the second half defending it. Not just from the other foundries but those in my own ranks, thirsting for power. I would never get to enjoy the benefits. I have no interest in watching my back for the rest of my life."

"Then you should just walk away from this whole situation! You're like a child that doesn't like ice cream, so they want to take it away from all the other children in the world instead of just leaving the parlor!"

"Yes, we are the same. I don't feel comfortable with anyone else having the book; it really is the Sword of Damocles."

"Be that as it may, it cannot be destroyed." Mary sighed.

"I beg to differ. You forget that at one point that book was split in half. Something was able to do that. Perhaps your father wanted to finish the job."

"Preposterous! He was going to give it to England for the war."

"Then why did he leave the book back in the States when he traveled abroad?"

Mary was silent.

"Exactly!"

"In his letters to Asquith, he mentioned a weapon to end the war. That could only be the book!"

"That he left behind? He was not delivering a weapon. He was most likely going to procure one."

"But he said it was for the war!"

"Unless the war is not the one with the Germans. At that time, the United States was and is still not involved. Wouldn't it make more sense for England to hold on to a special weapon? Perhaps the weapon is something that can completely destroy the book and end the war between Forgers?"

Mary paused in thought for a moment. "I have no interest in giving anything to England or the United States."

"Then the best solution is to give it to me. I'll find a way to destroy it and end it all."

Mary chuckled. "My faith in you forces me into atheism."

Shirley's eyelids lowered. "Then your only path shall be: they will kill you, Helga dies, Thomas dies when they find him; Abel dies, and as for Min, killing one with her talents would be a waste. I will get a Forger to perform Calculus Remotio on her. Perhaps I'll raise her as my daughter, a perfect killing ma—"

Mary reached across the table and slapped her. Shirley unfazed, turned her head back towards Mary. There was a speck of blood on her bottom lip. She touched it with her white-gloved hand and looked at it.

"How—how—dare—you think of putting her through the same thing we went through!" Mary fumed.

Shirley took a handkerchief and wiped the blood from her lip. She stood, walked to the entrance, and stopped. "If all choices are bad, everything is equal, then there are no bad choices. N'est pas? You and I both know you'll have to choose one. At least with mine, Min gets to live, oblivious but content." She started to leave but stopped. "By the way…" she lifted her fisted hand and opened it. A necklace unraveled, dangling three keys. "These were confiscated from you when you entered the prison. I made sure to procure them before they figured out their importance. The real reason you can't walk is because your buttons have to be tightened every six hours, by these keys. It has nothing to do with Mausi dropping a box on you." Mary's heart beat faster. "I haven't told anyone, not even my foundry. So you see, you don't have to lie. You can trust me. Take my deal, and I'll let you literally walk out of here." She replaced the necklace in her closed fist and left the room. After the door was closed, Mary looked down and felt a wave of panic and pessimism.

March 14, 1910

St. Petersburg, Russia

Leo had come to see Maximilian as a father figure, a weird feeling because his father had abandoned his mother long before he could ever form a relationship with him. Thanks to Elyan White adopting him, Leo received an exuberant upbringing. He provided Leo with opulent homes, delectable meals, and forging courses to further his education.

If Leo had stuck around the White household, he was sure he would have grown into a proper gentleman and would have continued to have the best things life could offer. But there was always something missing; he felt unrest. Elyan White rarely smiled at him as he did for the girl in the wheelchair and the African boy. The others never questioned Elyan and Gwenhwyvar, but what is the purpose of accepting things at face value? Why should they constantly put their lives in danger over a book? Why have so much power if you don't use it to cure all of the sicknesses in the world, make it rain in the desert, or end wars with a deadly strike at the people causing it? They raised him to believe Silver Forgers were good and the Golds bad. But Maximilian was the most truthful person he'd ever met. What he said, he meant. And what he did was done without guilt or a second thought.

Together, they had stolen, killed, and caused mayhem on many occasions. In the many countries they had traveled to, there was never a plan for what they'd do if caught.

Leo needed to ask him: Why were they in jail? Why did they even allow the weakling Dayfide police to lay their hands on them and shove them into a cell with a group of weakling Dayfide convicts? Maximillian was taking the situation in stride. He was more concerned with finding a cigar than spending the rest of his days in jail for murdering the two men back at the bar. Leo noticed most of the other men in the cell had their gazes set on Maximillian. No one in the cell dressed as well as he. He was still clean, even after violently killing someone.

"Max…why are we here?" Leo finally asked.

Maximillian regarded him with a slight smile. "We are here because I murdered two men who were annoying me."

"I know that, but why did you let them capture you? You could have done plenty of things to avoid being here."

"And you as well, oui?"

"Yes…I was just following your lead."

"You're a good soldier, Leo."

Maximillian observed the other prisoners. "Take a good look around, Leo. What do you see?"

Leo did as he said. "A bunch of depraved roustabouts?"

"Mostly. Mixed in with the occasional drunk or downtrodden tramps."

"And us."

"And us. You are probably thinking, like gods among the sheep."

"I am."

"But among these men, there is a chance for one of them to be something better. Something stronger, more dangerous, more powerful. All we have to do is introduce a little bit of silver."

"Ahrion?"

"Yes. Now, they are no longer just useless parasites on the back of society. Now, they have the potential! Not only to cause mayhem but to change history! If you put them in the right place at the right time!"

"I don't understand."

"Armies, Leo. One dangerous man with a weapon is a nuisance, four is a gang, 100 is a force, but 1000 anghenfēls is an army! Capable of taking over a city."

"You want to turn these men into anghenfēls."

"Not all of them. They must be men you can trust. Otherwise, they'll betray you, and you know what I say about trust?"

"Never trust anyone, not even yourself."

"Correct. So we must pick and choose our loyal soldiers, and there's no better soldier than one given his freedom."

"Why would you purposely turn men into an anghenfēl? Anghenfēls are always accidents or curses— mistakes of God. The Gold foundry won't like you causing chaos."

"Exactly the reason I'm going to do it. For thousands of years, the Golds and Silvers have been playing a game of friendly chess with the other foundries and their Dayfide pawns. Taking turns ruling the world, and now fighting over that cursed book. I'm going to end this game once and for all. I will unite all foundries under one flag—mine."

"You'll need more than 1000 anghenfēls and a lot of ahrion to do that."

"In a few years, the European Golds will have an election to choose a new leader. The only candidates are me, a teenage girl, and Augusta. Now, who do you think will win? Me, a little American brat, or that German cow? Once I become the leader of the Golds, expect to see thousands of anghenfēls bringing order to the world under my flag!"

"But, anghenfēls are unpredictable! I saw what happens when you turn elephants into them! How do you know which one of them will follow your orders?"

"Simple. Watch…" Maximillian stood up and walked to the middle of the room; all eyes were on him. "Gentlemen, I have a proposition for you. I am looking for ten men to help me with an assortment of projects, not limited to robbing, murdering, and terrorizing. Who's with me?" No one said a word; a couple of men snickered. An awkward pause was interrupted by one of the men telling him to sit down. Maximilian spread out his arms "No one? What if I told you whoever says yes will be freed immediately from this jail?'"

"Oh yeah, how?" asked a large man with an eye patch.

Maximilian pointed at the man. "Him! that's one," he told Leo. "As soon as he asked me 'how', he has just opened negotiations meaning he is interested. He desires the illusion of freedom. Those that play into the illusion are always the easiest to control."

"No one controlling me!" the man yelled.

"No, of course not, my good fellow. But you are interested in joining me if I can get you out of here, no?"

"You're nuts!" The man sat down on the bench.

"You see, that's a yes."

"He said he didn't believe you," Leo corrected.

"Yes, but we both know…" Maximillian walked over to the bars. His body became smoke, and he wafted through the bars to the hallway. Serenaded by screams and sounds of disbelief, he reconfigured into his regular form. "…getting out of here is as easy as that." Maximillian ignored the men as they pressed themselves against the bars, reached out, and begged him to let them out.

"How did you do that? They took all of our rings and coins away?" Leo asked.

"It's my Unus."

"Your what?"

"Unus—your natural ability you can do without the blessed metal? Didn't your foundry tell you about that? When you were trained?"

"No."

"Tsk-tsk-tsk, they really didn't trust you. Anyway, now everyone wants to join me. But you see, unlike that first man, they don't believe in freedom. They just want to get out—like rats! They are living in the moment, with no imagination for dreams! They are not worthy of being warriors—the worst kind of soldiers; brainless Dayfides!" Maximilian gestured for Leo to approach the bars. "If everyone in this cell kills at least two people, I will set you free!" They all looked around at each other.

"Wait, what about me?" Leo yelled.

"If you want to be free, you'd better start killing too."

"What? Max! Wha—" Someone grabbed Leo's shoulder. The man took a fist in the face and then a punch in the throat. With a quick twist, Leo broke the man's neck, and he fell dead. The cell was quiet for a second; the prisoners turned their attention to each other. A second later, they began to fight violently.

Maximilian walked away. "I'm going to get the key and our items, I'll be back."

The convicts continued to punch and grapple with each other. Anyone who came close to Leo to fight for their freedom didn't stay on their feet for too long. Maximilian had taught him well. With a combination of boxing and wrestling moves, he severely injured two men and ended the life of another.

Maximilian returned, wiping blood off his hands. He looked neither shocked nor surprised to find Leo and the man he said desired freedom were the last ones standing. He calmly unlocked the cage and allowed Leo and the man to exit.

"I can't believe you left me in there!" Leo yelled.

"I wanted to make sure my training wasn't a waste of time; apparently, you exceeded my expectations."

A loud bell started ringing, and a handful of guards entered with guns and clubs. "Now, to test my theory!" Max grabbed the back of the convict's head and emptied a vile of liquid ahrion into his mouth.

"Don't move!" one of the guards yelled, and he pointed a rifle at them.

The convict gagged, coughed, and fell to the ground on his hands and knees. After more coughing, he collapsed onto his face.

"Oh well...there are some that just die if they drink ahrion." Maximilian quipped. "I'll have to recruit twice as many to compensate for that."

"Reach for the sky!" The guard yelled. He was joined by two others pointing guns and rifles.

"I guess it's time to leave." Maximillian gave Leo his crucifix necklace and gestured to go forward. "After you."

They walked towards the guards. The guards opened fire. Maximillian spun his cane like a propeller and deflected any bullets that came close to hitting them. Leo reached out his arms and said: *"Dat glo-wey!"* Every door that Leo touched opened and released the prisoners, who immediately rushed out towards the guards in a suicidal attempt at freedom. Some of the convicts were shot and killed, but the rest reached the guards, creating a chaotic scuffle. Leo continued to open cages, and the influx of convicts got the upper hand. Leo and Maximilian easily made it outside and leisurely strolled down the sidewalk away from the building. Scores of hooting freed men poured out of the prison and followed them while others scattered away like bugs.

"I don't think you should use convicts as henchmen," Leo said.

"You might be right. But it's all about the quality."

A couple of blocks later, Maximilian broke out of contemplation. "You know, in America, in the city of New York, they say there is a prison especially built for Forgers."

"Really? How can they do that?"

"I'm not sure. Perhaps all of the bars are forged. But if that's true, imagine what would happen if we could free the most dangerous Forgers in the world? Getting them to swear on their honor to follow me! Now, that would be an army!"

June 14th, 1915, 2:11 PM

Leo was whistling inside the prison Maximillian had always dreamed of, one made especially for Forgers. Only one prisoner was allowed in each cell, probably to keep them from doing a congregation forge, as some Coppersmiths could, even without metals. There were no windows, to keep Forgers from turning into smoke and slipping outside. The bars on the exit were all forged metal, and judging by their teclyn rods, some guards appeared to be either Forgers or Strykers.

The cell next to him had been empty for a week. A guard escorted Thomas down the hallway and locked him inside it. Thomas realized who was sharing his cell block and sighed.

"Hello, Detective. Fancy seeing you here," Leo quipped.

Thomas ignored him and sat on the hard mattress.

Leo walked up to the bars. "Why'd they put us next to each other? So we'd kill each other?"

"No. If they wanted a gladiator scenario, an arena would be a more fitting setting," Thomas said.

"You're overthinking it, hawkshaw. Sure you don't want to take a swing at me?"

"As pleasurable as that would be, it's impossible from this distance. They obviously put us together so that we'll squeal."

"About what?"

"What do you think, idiot? Everything. We used to do this at the precinct, usually with someone else in the same cell, to gather information."

"I don't see a stool pigeon in this block. Actually, you're the first person I've seen in days."

Thomas ignored him and looked around. "This cell is different than the one I was in."

"That's 'cause this area is for Forgers. Bars are hi-yaguh."

"Hiya?"

"Forged iron. No sign of other metals; even the furniture has wooden nails."

Thomas picked up the small safety razor sitting on the sink. "What about the blade in this razor?"

"It's ceramic, not deave."

"Deave?"

"Steel—didn't they teach you any of the names of Blessed metals?"

Thomas noticed the razor's white blades. "But steel is an alloy."

"What?"

"It's not pure..." Leo looked confused. Thomas sighed. "Steel is a mix of iron and something else...you can't use it for your forging if it's not pure metal, right?"

"Not good for forging, but good enough to move stuff around."

"I guess. But, if you can use anything to forge, you can use the toilet as a Vorago. That seems appropriate for you."

Leo chuckled. "It won't work. And neither will the sink or showers."

"And why not?"

"Because if that were possible, they wouldn't let us take a shower or use the toilets, right?"

"That's strangely logical, coming from you."

"Thanks, Chief."

Thomas felt the bars. "If these bars are hiya—iron—whatever, which is an element and not an alloy, can't an Ironsmith just forge using them?"

Leo scoffed. "You really are wet behind the ears. Once a forge has been cast on something, like the bars or our Vorago-proof toilets, only the original Forger can remove it, unless they're dead or you use a Chamfer,......hmm."

"A what? What's a Chamfer?"

"Nothing...I...did—so, that Ironsmith is locked up in here too, right?"

"Probably, we were all arrested together. Why?"

"Nothing…just good to know."

Thomas took off his shirt.

"What in the world are you doing? Are you ossified?" Leo asked.

Thomas held his shirt by one sleeve and swung it around like a propeller while walking around the room. After circumnavigating the entire cell, he stopped and put his shirt back on.

"Do you wanna tell me what you were doing?"

"Checking for invisible persons in my cell."

"Not bad, Flatfoot." Leo went to the far end of his cell and sat on the floor. Thomas started to examine the cell walls. "What are you doing now?"

"Seeing if the walls are heeyeeguh also."

Leo laughed. "Hi-yaguh. You're gonna do a jailbreak? You? I never imagined a copper would not only be locked up in Sing Sing but would also try to escape!"

"I will gladly serve out my time and accept my fate if found guilty after my trial."

"Ha! Do you think there's gonna be a trial? Have news for you, Flatfoot, you notice in this wing how there's no other Forgers? Why do you think that is?"

"This is not a normal part of the prison."

"You can say that again."

"I'd prefer if you said nothing at all."

Leo scoffed. When Thomas finished examining his cell, he sat down on his cot. "Given up escaping?" Leo asked. Thomas ignored his question. "That's okay. I have a feeling that not one Forger or Stryker has ever escaped. Notice how few guards there are? That's how confident they are." Thomas closed his eyes. "Even if you were to get out of here, then what? Do you and Mary go riding off into the sunset like a motion picture show? Settle down? Have some rug rats? Live happily ever after?"

"Please be quiet!" Thomas complained.

There was a few minutes of silence. "You have no idea what you're dealing with," Leo said.

Thomas sighed. "Risking aggravation, I'm going to ask you to elaborate."

"You've known Mary what, three years?" Thomas didn't answer. "The one you knew was always the fake one, the jolly optimist! I can see how you'd fall in love with her. But now she's quick-tempered, dark! Probably sad. All the things you've never experienced. How's that make you feel? Are you still in love with her?"

"How I feel about her is none of your business."

"You're right, it's not. But, how would you feel if I told you you're responsible for all of this!"

"What the devil are you talking about?"

"You're the reason Mary got involved in this in the first place."

"Horse feathers! I'm pretty sure it started with your appearance in New York!"

"Sorry to be a wet blanket, Chief, but Maximillian would never have found Mary if it wasn't for you."

May 29, 1915

Leo knew Maximillian wasn't leaving the Astor's party through the front door. After Detective Douglas' failed murder attempt on Mary during the piano recital, she and Thomas were waiting outside for an appearance by any nefarious characters. Leo watched from his perch on one of the gables as a little Chinese girl ran to Mary and Thomas, to talk to them. A moment later, the three departed with the rest of the guests. "I guess they couldn't find him." Leo walked along the roof until he found a spot over a balcony, and jumped down. As luck or a curse would have it, in the room, Maximillian, Fang, and Knuckles were in the office. Leo wondered if this were the same room he had seen Madam Blanche enter earlier in the evening but immediately put the idea out of his head. After all, she had just saved Mary from the people in this room. Without any clandestineness, Leo opened the double French doors and presented himself. The Henchmen jumped into a defensive position. Leo noticed Fang's monstrous appearance. "An anghenfēl? Is he part of the army you're building, Max?"

"Who the hell is this palooka?" Knuckles complained, walking over to confront Leo.

"Think you're going to need more than three goons if you're going to take over the world," Leo said.

"Goon? Who are yuh calling a goon you—"

"Excuse me," Leo interrupted Knuckles, "I'm here to talk to Max, not some low-life heel."

"Knuckles swung at Leo's head while yelling: "Heel?" With ease, Leo blocked the punch and redirected Knuckle's arm until it was behind his back, then grabbed him by the back of his neck and slammed his head onto the desk, instantly rendering him unconscious. His body slid off of the desk and flopped onto the floor.

Fang made a move towards Leo until Maximilian held up his hand.

"But boss, look at what he did to Knuckles!" Fang complained.

"I am aware," Maximillian said. "And he will do the same to you."

"Not me." Fang said, exposing his teeth."

"Better listen to him," Leo added. "I'm in a bit of a bad mood."

"How did you survive?" Maximillian asked.

"They threw me into the Thames. I guess nobody told those simps that ice floats. I just floated along until it melted."

"Hmm, a stupid oversight. But this must be very important for you to expose yourself."

"Very."

"Is this about that woman?"

Leo nodded. "How did you know?"

"Because of all the information we tried to gather, not only was it difficult to find the home address of Professor White, but in the city records there are no records of him living with anyone else. I assume he is responsible for that...or was it you?"

"I won't take all of the credit."

"We didn't know about the girl until the policeman downstairs tried to arrest me out on the street; the strange thing is, I sent him to his death in front of a street car. I guess he is more resilient than I thought."

"What do you mean you found out from him?"

"He is friends with that woman and has an ahrion weapon he used on Fang. We put two and two together and figured out she lived in a lighthouse on Fifth Avenue." Maximillian lit up a cigar and exhaled smoke in Leo's direction. "That policeman who got shot downstairs has something in common with you."

"And what's that?"

"You both tried to hide the existence of that woman." Leo looked off to the side. "Who is she, and why is she so important? She is quite lovely, but I'm sure it goes far beyond that. Is she your lover?"

"It's not important. I just came to cut a deal."

Maximillian chuckled. " A deal, you say? You betrayed my trust in you! You never told me you knew Professor White!

"And you tried to have me killed!"

"Touché, so I guess we are all even, no?"

"No, but I think we can set aside our differences and find a way for both of us to win."

"Go on! I am waiting with anticipation for what you could propose that will keep me from jumping over this desk and slashing your throat!"

"I'm not going to apologize. I told you, I'm here to cut a deal."

"Fine, then. Tell me, what do you want?"

"I can get the book for you if you let the woman live."

"And how would you accomplish that?"

"I can get her to trust me—I can find out where the book is—steal it and hand it over to you."

"And if you fail?"

"I won't! If I do, I'm sure you'll kill us both."

"True. But why would you do this? Is she that important to you? Do you love her?"

"Do we have a deal or not? Because if not, it's going to be a lot harder for you to get that book! Take my word for it, I guarantee, they got it locked up tight!"

Maximillian sat back in his chair for a moment and thought. "How do I know you won't just take the book and the girl and disappear?"

"I won't do that, Forger's honor."

Maximilian stood fast. He and Leo regarded each other with stern expressions.

"What's Forger's honor?" Fang asked.

"It means if Mr. Leo breaks his word, he will die instantly," Maximillian answered.

"What, with just those words?" Knuckles asked.

"With just those words," Maximilian said. He held out his hand. "If you can get the book, I will see that the girl survives."

"Forger's honor?" Leo asked.

"No." Maximillian withdrew his hand.

"What? Then why should I make a deal with you?"

"Because you haven't been killed, and will leave this meeting alive. I will give you six days. At that point, I may take matters into my own hands."

"I need more than six days! I'm not exactly on good terms with her right now!"

"Then I suggest you get on good terms with her. After six days, I can't guarantee her safety."

"I'll get the book. Just keep your little army at bay until then."

"I'll do what I can…or want, whichever comes first."

Leo started to turn around. He backed out of the room instead, onto the balcony.

"It was nice seeing you again, Leo," Maximilian said.

"And I hope I never see you again." He jumped out of sight, off the balcony.

June 14th, 1915, 3:10 PM

It was useless for them to lodge Mary in the lavish suite with a canopied bed, tonight, she will not be sleeping. She put her hands over her face to keep from screaming in frustration. 'No, I must remain calm and control my emotions. What can I do? Shirley is right; there are no good choices! She metaphorically and literally has all the keys—except one. Let me think about all of my options. I guess I should choose the one that causes the least suffering: One: give it to the President, everyone gets saved, America saves England and France—and most likely, the uncouth President takes over the world and brings back slavery! Two: Run. Constantly being hunted. Three: Give it to Shirley. She takes over the world, but Min gets saved—all outcomes are terrible!'

A knock came to the door. "Come in."

Alva entered. "Hello, Mary."

"Alva, I'm glad it's you. If it were the President or Shirley, they probably would not leave the room unscathed."

"Oh my! You seem like you've been having a difficult time lately."

"You have no idea."

"I'm completely in the dark about everything from Cousin Thomas' inquiries about possible foul play to a report of explosions and gang activity on your property. Would you mind telling me more?"

"I...I can't."

Alva put her hand on top of Mary's. "You know you can always confide in me. What's bothering you, Dear?"

"Alva...there's so much—I can't tell you because then you would be involved."

"What exactly did the President say to you?"

"I can't discuss it."

"It must have been quite uproarious to have him leave so abruptly and in such a tizzy."

"Believe me, even without the other stuff, I still would have given him an earful!"

Alva chuckled. "I'm sure you would have. Is it something illegal?"

"Not on my side. Just trust me. If I tell you everything, your life would literally be in danger."

"So many things have happened to you this summer, I feel I've been neglectful of you in your time of need; I've been a terrible friend."

"Alva Vanderbilt Belmont! I will not have you spouting such nonsense! You have been exceedingly gracious since I arrived here three years ago!"

"I remember it well. When I was driving past your front lawn, I saw you were doing cartwheels, and when I asked what you were doing, you said: 'I'm trying to find the best place to put our lighthouse so that it looks good at all angles, even upside down.'" Alva laughed. "You've always been a nonconformist; you remind me of my younger self."

"You?"

"Yes, of course. I wasn't always so fortunate, you know. I grew up in the South and married into the Vanderbilts. But, despite all of our wealth, we were considered nouveau riche, and the Astors refused to acknowledge us as one of the 400. We had quite a passive-aggressive relationship with them. So, I decided to get back at them by throwing the most extravagant party New York had ever seen. Everyone RSVPed, but I mistakenly forgot to send an invitation to the Astors." Alva winked. "Lo and behold, they finally contacted me and asked what happened to their invitation, and I said I thought it would have been rude for someone of my standing to introduce myself first to someone higher up. So the next thing you know, a member of the Astor household comes over to introduce themselves to me."

"Alva Belmont! That's not passive at all!"

Alva laughed. "It's true, but compared to you, belonging to high society was never a priority for you. Yet, with your charm and, shall I say, your fervor, you prevailed. You reminded me to be more of my old self. Even though I've been told I can be quite the harridan sometimes.

"Oh, bushwa! Of all of the neighbors, only you have acknowledged my suffering. And for that, I thank you. The fact that you're still talking to me after so much hullabaloo is a testament to our friendship."

"I'm glad to hear that. Is there anything I can do to help?"

Mary thought for a second. "Let me see something—excuse me." Mary put her hand on Alva's forehead. *"Oo-aid vell ur woove ur aid dwaid!"*

"Mary? What are you doing? What language was that? Mr. Bianca tried to do that to me at the Astor's party."

"Oh? Is that so? It's—just—just a parlor game."

"Oh, how do you play?"

"I'll explain later…when I explain everything else. Perhaps one day over tea. But I do suggest you take a look at your financial records; to make sure there are no anomalies."

"Peculiar. That's what Cousin Thomas said."

Mary sighed. "Poor Thomas, I haven't seen him in a week! I feel terrible dragging him into my troubles!"

"I'm sure he feels it's worth it."

"My aunt told me it's okay to depend on him and my friends, even if it takes them into danger."

"That should include me, right?" Mary agreed with silence. "Where is your aunt Gwenhwyvar these days?"

Mary looked nervous. "She's still in—Eng—Europe!"

"That's good. Which part?"

"Tuscany—Alva, I'm feeling rather wearied. Do you mind, I'd like to retire."

"Of course…I'll see you for breakfast." Alva left the room.

Mary sighed. 'I'm sorry, Alva, I know you mean well, but I can't trust you right now.'

The temperature in the large Palm dining room in the Waldorf Hotel was warm and stuffy. The three-story high ceiling was decorated in the Renaissance style and gave the impression of being spacious and lavish, with a big chandelier and tinted glass domes. Balconies at the various floor levels overlooked everything. Off to the sides of the room, large potted palm trees seemed more appropriate for the temperature. The unpleasantness did not prevent Shirley from wearing her usual lacy white dress, as she sat at the long table with men in suits. The only other female was the White Haired woman. Through her gauze-covered eyes, she looked just as uncomfortable as Shirley. Adding to their discomfort, one of the most powerful men in North America, President Wilson, sat at the end, flanked on his left by the leader of the New York political organization, Tammany Hall, Charles Francis Murphy, also known as Boss Murphy. On the President's right, Stanley Finch from the Bureau of Investigation for the Justice Department.

Although it was a dinner embellished with dishes such as Lamb pot pie, boiled capon, boar's head, succotash, potted shrimps, and rolled ox tongue, nobody was eating. President Wilson used his fork more as a tool to accentuate whatever talking points he had.

"I want that book and the Eye of Graeae back before I leave," Wilson demanded. "This little cat and mouse game with the White family has gone on far too long—no idea why Taft put up with them. If we had that book, there's no way the Kaiser would have sunk the Lusitania and tried to steal the other eyes. I want to make sure he keeps his little war in Europe. With that book, we could get the witches to burn his little country back into the Stone Age!"

The White Haired woman cleared her throat.

"Got a problem?"

"The word: 'witch,'" Shirley interrupted.

The President glared at Shirley and then looked at the White Haired woman as though he wasn't expecting them to speak. "Why do you people have a problem with that word, Miss Wayward? You especially should be out there finding out what happened to the Eye. It used to belong to you and your sisters." Wilson turned his attention to Shirley. "Miss Blanche, what are the chances of Mary White handing over the book?"

"She's very stubborn, but she has many emotional weaknesses. I'm sure she's not going to let her friends die. She'd kill herself before letting that happen."

"Torture?" Wilson asked.

"Maybe as a last resort."

"What about the Oriental, the Dog, and that negro Stryker?" "Have we found them?"

"Not yet, sir," Finch answered. "We thought we had spotted Cŵn Annwn outside the prison, but he got away, we're setting a trap for him right now. As for the rest, without the Eye of Graeae, it's difficult." He sighed.

"How's that possible?" Wilson asked. "She said the Germans had it on the Olympic?"

"We didn't find it anywhere on the docks or the ship. We even searched the water around it, and found nothing."

"Did she lie to us? A thousand years old and can't locate one crystal ball? If the Kaiser has the Eye of the past and we have nothing, that may give him a huge advantage!"

"We know Mr. President, we're still searching."

"If you can't find the Eye of the Present, focus on the Eye of the Future!"

"Gwenhwyvar is nowhere to be found."

The President slammed a fist onto the table. "She is only one Silversmith! Go, talk to the old witch! Tell her to find Gwenhwyvar or the Eye! Or I'll have her burned at the stake—over and over!" Wilson threw his napkin down and stood up. He noticed Shirley smirking. "What is it now, Mrs Blanche?"

"Oh, I find it interesting that those burned at the stake are considered villains, but ne'er the ones setting women on fire."

"Don't be a wise-apple, woman, or you'll join them," He left the room in a huff, followed by Finch and Strong.

Before speaking, Shirley, Boss Murphy, and Miss Wayward waited until they were sure the President was gone. As Shirley had done before her conversation with Mary, she lit some sage and set it smoldering on her plate.

"Sage? Do you still not trust her?" Miss Wayward asked Shirley.

"I have no idea where her loyalties lie, but we can't assume she is on our side, even though she does seem to be hindering the President."

"I seriously doubt she'll assist the Americans. She didn't tell them that the Federal Reserve was going to be attacked, and she hasn't told them where the Oriental girl and the Colored man are."

"But the president can make her wish come true with one swing of that sword," Boss Murphy said.

"As long as that sword has that curse on it, there will be no relief for her—no one can touch it but Elzbieta," Shirley said.

"They can just kill Elzbieta."

"For some reason, she told them not to," Miss Wayward said.

"Must have a plan. But, without death, the President has nothing to offer her," Shirley said.

"The useless Dayfides never have anything to offer us—no offense," Miss Wayward said.

"None taken. I understand how much it infuriates you Forgers to take orders from the powerless. Throughout history, the Normalu leaders gave you just enough reward to quench rebellion...one Forger at a time, until you were trained, like dogs."

"Is that what you're doing?" Miss Wayward asked.

"None of the sort. As one controlled most of her life, I'd never wish that on anybody." Shirley turned her attention to Boss Murphy. "Monsieur, If you'd be so kind as to talk to her on your own and let us know if we can still trust her." He nodded. "Mademoiselle Wayland, would you mind camping out at the prison? Focus on capturing Cŵn Annwn before the government men do."

"But why? I had the chance to capture him earlier. If I had known—"

"He wasn't useful at that time. But he's a bargaining chip with Elzbieta. If we can't touch her sword, maybe we can use the sword through her." Shirley rose. "As for myself, I'm going to continue to work on Mary White's bargaining chip."

Murphy and Miss Wayward watched Shirley exit the room.

"That woman acts like we work for her. Can we trust her?" He asked.

"I trust everything she does. But nothing she says."

Boss Murphy took a puff on his cigar and looked at her face. "How can you see through that blindfold?"

"In a world of forging you're asking me to explain something?"

"Oh, right. It's your thing."

"Miss Wayward nodded."

"I thought you would sound much older and wrinkled. I mean, you've been around for 400 years."

Miss Wayward stood up and headed out the door. "Again, you're questioning. Now, if you'd excuse me, I have to go kidnap another child."

Victoria sat in her bath with one of her little twin sisters, thinking about her recent weeks: Learning about her ability to see the gray people, the boy who seemed to know about her, and seeing Mary White released from prison. She scrubbed the child's hair with LifeBoy soap until the child complained about the stinging in her eyes. Victoria apologized and did her best to wash out the chemicals. The child eventually calmed down, and Victoria focused on scrubbing herself. She looked at the child, playing with a soap bubble, and wondered if she had any abilities—did this thing run in the family? What about her Mother and Uncle Thomas? She remembered walking in on Helga doing a magic trick with light. "That was not a trick," she said.

"What?" the child asked.

"Nothing, just talking to myself."

Her mother bought the baby into the room; it was time for his bath. Victoria and her sister exited the room, and Victoria helped the child dry herself off. She regarded Victoria's face with sincere happiness and wonder.

"What is it?" Victoria asked.

The child didn't answer but instead moved in and hugged her; this caught Victoria off guard. She didn't realize how much stress had been building up inside. She hugged the child tightly and let out a few tears. The child was released, turned around, and ran into their room to play with their brother. Victoria remained crouched on the ground, thinking about what to do.

As everyone was turning in, on her way to brush her teeth, Victoria passed by her mother, reading a book in their room. Victoria paused at the doorway for too long.

"Yes, darling?" Her mother asked.

"Nothing...." she turned and was about to leave.

"Victoria?" She returned to the doorway. Her mother held out her arm. She walked over, crawled into bed, and cuddled into her mother's embrace. She almost cried again but held it in. Despite trying to hide her misery, her mother made a shushing sound, the same she used when rocking the baby. "It's okay," she said. "We'll get through this."

"But what is this?"

"That's what I'm going to find out." Thelma showed Victoria her book: The Interpretation of Dreams by Sigmund Freud.

"Does that tell you what's wrong with me?"

"No, I was hoping if I read some books by smart people about our brains, perhaps some of it would rub off on me."

"But you're already smart."

Thelma kissed Victoria on the head. "Thank you, dear, but I think I need help with this. I don't know anything about brains except how to cook them."

Victoria laughed.

Shirley exited the elevator of the Waldorf Hotel and ignored the maid giving her a slight bow. After a quick look around, Shirley unlocked the door of one of the rooms and entered. "Ah, I see you are still here," she announced.

Min sat with her arms crossed on a large canopied bed, wearing a white dress, which could almost be a child's version of the one Shirley was wearing. She ignored Shirley's statement and continued to sulk on the bed

"You haven't tried to escape."

"Because you haven't told me about my mother."

"So you believed me when I told you she's alive?"

"Fang said the same thing, but he's a liar, and so are you…" Min unfolded her arms. She had something red in her hand. "But you had this."

"Yes. I was wondering why that's so important to you."

Min held up the red folded fan. "It's a symbol of the Hongdeng Zhao." She unfolded it. On it were paintings of clouds and Chinese characters. With a quick flick of her wrist, the fan sent a blast of air towards the window. The curtains gustily rose and gently settled back down. "This one belongs to my mother. We use it when we are separated, and need to let others know we are alive and will find each other one day to reclaim it."

Shirley took it and examined it. "Charming. Finding her was actually easy. I just got a Forger to do a tracking forge on this fan."

"Who would dare give you her fan?"

"Your aunt. She was quite eager to hand it over when we offered her enough gold."

Remind me to kill her when I get back to China."

"You should thank her. The fact that we found your mother before the Emperor or the British government, probably saved her from the gallows." Shirley held up the fan. "So, with this memento, do you trust me?"

Min grabbed the fan back. "I trust her, not you! Never you!"

"Well, however, there is no drama."

"But, I'm getting sick of sitting in this room. When can I see her? Or Mary!"

"I'm afraid neither of those is possible right now. Mary is in quite a bit of trouble with the law, and as for your mother, as soon as Mary makes a deal with me, we can reunite you two. But not until Mary hands over that book."

"She's not going to do that."

"If she doesn't, then you are free to go..." Min sat up in the bed. "...without ever knowing where your mother is...forever." Min sat back in the bed. "Yes, that's right. You have a stake in this as well. Perhaps you can convince Mary to change her mind."

"She won't listen to me!"

"It's in her best interest. Don't you think she wants to have a peaceful life without people trying to attack her?"

"Danger doesn't scare her."

"What kind of heartless person would keep a mother and child separated for her selfish reasons...over a magic book? Why is that more important than you? If I were you, I would give my life to see my mother again. My parents disappeared when they were looking for me years ago. If I had a chance, I would trade anything to see them again, even handing over a simple—little—book." Min looked disheartened. Shirley walked over and put her hand on Min's shoulder. "Don't worry. I'll do everything I can to reunite you and your mother." Min shook Shirley's hand off. Shirley started to leave the room. On a serving cart next to the door was an empty bowl. "Did you like the special Chinese food we prepared for you?"

"It was fine," Min said, unimpressed.

"I'm glad to hear." Shirley exited the room.

Min got out of bed, walked to the cart, and ate the last piece of stir-fried rice in the bowl. "This was good...It tastes like my mom's."

Mary rolled her chair from one side of the room to the other. 'I have to get out of here! Nothing will be solved by me sitting in this room!' She remembered sprouting wings when she had saved Thomas' life. 'At first, I was flying, and then I had wings—most likely connected. But how? How did that happen? Is it my Unus? If I could fly out of here, I wouldn't have to use my legs. At least until I landed.' She leaned forwards and concentrated as hard as she could. She expected the metallic wings to shoot out of her back. After a lot of grimacing and flexing, she gave up. 'I don't understand it. I can shoot fire out of my hands and turn swords into rope. But I can't control the metals in my own back! What am I going to do? I need a miracle to get out of here...' She sighed, rolled to her door, and turned the handle. The door was unlocked; 'Do they think I won't escape?' She traveled down the hallway, flanked by six-foot-tall paintings of angels. Their eyes seemed to follow her progress to the top of the stairwell. She looked down the stairs and then her chair. 'My old chair could navigate stairs all by itself...No matter, I can do anything I put my mind to.'

Mary moved forward, being as careful as she could, and inched the wheels of her chair carefully over the edge, hoping she could do a series of controlled drops onto each step. She thumped onto each step with ungraceful yet controlled drops. On the sixth drop, she lost control of the chair. It thumped down half the stairwell and turned sideways. She tumbled out of the chair, rolled down the rest of the way, knocked over a side table, and landed hard on her back. The chair rolled over her and jabbed her in the ribs. She lay on the ground surveying her bodily damage and contemplated what to do next. Her side and arm hurt, but nothing appeared broken. The chair wheels were bent out of shape and would now be useless as a transport device. She imagined herself crawling to her escape, but the absurdity of this plan wasn't debated for long when a pair of hands reached under her armpits and hoisted her upwards. Two butlers lifted her and began to carry her back upstairs while a third took her damaged chair away for disposal.

"I wish to leave!" She yelled.

"Sorry, Miss," said one of the butlers. "We received strict orders to keep you in your room so you can rest."

"I don't want to rest, I want out!"

"Sorry Miss, The President himself gave us these orders."

They opened her room, and sat her on her bed. "Now, if you need anything, Miss, let us know with this...." He rang a little bell on the side table. "Please rest and don't strain yourself anymore."

Mary was touched and infuriated by their helpfulness. But more angry at the failure of her plan. For a while, she lay on the bed. She mustered enough courage to try to leave again. Using only her arms to get herself off the bed, thumping onto the floor, and dragging herself across was exasperating. Without help, she wouldn't be able to lift herself high enough to turn the ribbed glass door knob. She pulled herself over to a side table and used one hand to hold onto it and the other to slide herself along the ground. She moved the furniture closer and closer over to the door. She had forgotten about the small vase on top of the table, and after too much wiggling, the vase tumbled off and smashed onto the floor near her.

One of the butlers opened the door. "Everything alright in here Ma—oh my! Miss!" The man lifted her off the ground. Another butler cleaned up the porcelain mess. She was carried back and placed gently on her bed. "I've told you, Miss. If there's anything you want, let us know. Don't strain yourself."

"I told you I want to leave! That's what I want!"

"You are to remain in your room until the President returns in the morning." The butlers left the room. It wasn't long before Mary had liberated herself from the bed again and traveled across the floor. Without worrying about the vase on its top, she pulled herself up on the table leg and reached the doorknob. 'I don't understand why It's so difficult! When my buttons are tight I'm as strong as an ox!' Shaking with instability, she reached out, turned the doorknob, and twisted before flopping onto the ground with a huge thump. In very little time, the butlers returned to the room. "What are you doing, guarding my bloody door?" Mary yelled.

Instead of being gentle as they had been before, the man hoisted her up and unceremoniously threw her onto the bed. "Get some rope, Henry," the butler commanded. While Henry retrieved a golden rope used for the window drapes, the other man held Mary onto the bed as she wiggled around. Her arms and legs were tied to the bed frame, rendering her even more incapacitated than she was before. One butler put the handbell in her mouth as a final act of provocation. "There, if you need anything, just let me know."

While the two men were leaving, one mumbled: "Next time I'm gonna thump her on her head, that'll keep her in!" Mary spit out the bell and wiggled around as much as she could. Her strength was less than average. She stared at the ceiling, feeling defeated, something she had never experienced since she first became Mary White.

She looked at the rope on her left wrist. 'Maybe I will just burn them off. A small fire, at the least, or I'll set the entire bed ablaze.'

The forge for lighting small fires like candles came instantly to her mind. 'Even before I was out of a chair, I could do small forges.' "Ganwull!" Nothing happened. She repeated and waited. Again and again, she repeated, wondering if she was saying them correctly. A part of her knew she was. It was not related to ego, but deep down, like the part that tells you your name is correct. After the tenth time, saying it through tears, the idea of being unable to forge took hold. "It won't work, I can't even forge! I'm powerless; I'm useless!"

A guard walked by Thomas' and Leo's cell and haphazardly tossed in two metal trays with moldy bread and suet, an imitation beef made from kidneys, and a serving of gruel, a mixture of: oats, boiled water, and hard cheese. Thomas picked up his spoon and consumed it the best he could; everything tasted terrible and matched its texture. He didn't know what to expect from prison food, but the vileness exceeded his expectations.

"You eating that slop?" Leo asked.

"Of course, one has to keep their strength up."

"Oh yeah, that's right, you're still expecting to get out of here alive."

I expect nothing, but I prepare for everything."

"Part of that police thing?"

"Actually, from the Army."

"Oh, an Army boy, eh? Where'd you serve?"

"Do you mind? The sound of your voice irritates me."

"Sorry, Chief, got nobody else to talk to,"

"Talk to yourself. You two seem to have a lot in common."

Leo chuckled. "Is that where you learned to fight? In the army?"

"Partly."

"And the other part?"

Thomas sighed. "If I tell you, will you give me 10 minutes of silence?"

"Make it good, and I'll give you 30."

Thomas sighed again. "When I was 16, I ran away and joined the army. They sent me to China at the tail end of the Boxer Rebellion. While there, I befriended a kindly old Chinese translator. He not only taught me Mandarin but also a bit of Wushu."

"Oh, so you're like Chinese kid?"

"If you mean Min, no, she's on a much higher level than any of us will ever be…except for that thing."

"What thing?"

"It killed my teacher in an attack…"

"Attack? I thought that thing was over in 1901?"

"It was, technically. It didn't mean we weren't vulnerable to insurgency. On one particular scrimmage, my teacher fought hand to hand with someone—something, dressed all in blue—he was considered a master, but that thing was—for lack of a better word —a demon—it brushed aside bullets as if they were flies, and before it could lay a fatal blow on me—anyway, that's enough."

"Ahh, you were just getting to the good part."

"30 minutes of peace, please."

"15, tops."

"We should be quiet. I'm still not convinced we aren't being observed."

Leo stood up. "Well, I think you had the right idea…" He took off his shirt. "It's possible. There could be someone in this block, listening for secrets…" He walked over to a sink and soaked his shirt under running water. "…But, they're not going to put them in a cell with us. There's too big of a chance of them running into us…" He walked over to his cell door while twisting and tightening his wet shirt

"What in the world are you doing?"

"The best place to watch us isn't in here…" Using his shirt as a whip, Leo snapped it outside the door into the hallway, and it came

162

into contact with something that morphed. A top-hatted guard dressed all in black appeared before their eyes, staggered for a bit, and acted unsure of which direction he wanted to escape in.

Leo used the delay to do another snap with the shirt. It wrapped around the man's leg, and with a quick yank, the man fell onto his back and took a silver knife out of his pocket. Leo flicked it out of his hand and down the hall. The man tried to stand up to retrieve it, but Leo wrapped the shirt around his ankle and brought the man onto the floor onto his hands and knees. He grabbed the man's pants leg and dragged him to the cell door.

"Leo, stop!" Thomas yelled.

Leo got the man's leg into the cell. Two other guards dressed in green hurried into the room. One focused on pulling the top-hatted guard away from the cage while the other kicked at Leo's head. After a third kick, Leo got knocked backward. The others dragged the man into the middle of the corridor. While laughing, Leo moved away from the cell door before a baton could crack his skull open.

"Think this is funny, eh?" The man in black said. He retrieved his knife, pointed it at Leo, and said: *"trydan!"* A small lightning bolt shot out and electrocuted Leo, and he convulsed for a moment and then lay limp. A whiff of smoke emulated from his tank top shirt. "Let that be a lesson to you!" The men left the block and slammed an iron door separating the wards.

"That didn't work out too well," Thomas said.

Leo chuckled. "Are you kidding? That worked out perfectly! "It confirmed my suspicions."

"And? What would those be?"

"All the guards are Dayfides, except for a select really low-level Forgers."

"That low level just electrified you."

"Are you kidding? That attack was weak! I faked injury—didn't even singe my shirt." Leo jumped up off the ground. "He was a level three at best. Even you can beat 'em."

Thomas sneered at the insult. "And the next confirmation?"

"We're not getting out of here alive."

"Poppycock, the judicial process calls for—"

"Malarkey! Forget about all that fair trial jazz! This isn't a normal situation, remember? Think about it! If this was just a cell block for Forgers, why haven't you seen anybody else in here but us two?"

"Perhaps it's a slow month?"

"Sure, because people with supernatural abilities never break the law in summer!"

"Maybe they're hard to catch with all of the powers."

"You saw how easily they rounded us up, I'm sure when you and the gang were hoisted into the paddy wagon, I bet there were some pretty powerful Forgers tossing you in there."

Thomas thought about Tibuta, Miss Moffitt, and the army of men with swords. "Perhaps...but that doesn't mean we won't get a fair trial."

"From who? They can't drag us into a Dayfide court and charge us with using magic to throw fireballs at people; the press would go nuts! They have to bury the front page story any way they can, to keep this stuff a secret as they've done for 1000 years! Gotta keep the Dayfides docile; easier to control!"

"This isn't the Middle Ages."

"Don't know how or when they'll do it, but if I were you, I'd start planning my last meal."

Thomas tried to dispute all of his facts, but it was strange that a jail for Forgers would have such weak security. 'If it were a prison for holding Forgers for long periods, they would require stronger guards to keep them in line. If Leo is right, this is a holding cell'. Thomas hated that he agreed with Leo.

He walked over to his sink, examined his toothbrush and safety razor, then sat on his cot and considered his options.

At 7:06 PM, Helga felt the same emotions as Mary when the guards came to get her out of her cell. She was escorted by a normal one and two of the top-hatted men. Her hands were encased in metal mittens, chained together like handcuffs, preventing her from even wiggling her fingers. The men escourted her to a metal gated elevator.

'This would be the perfect time to hit one of them in the face and the other in his neither-regions!' she thought. The regular guard seemed uneasy around the top-hatted men. 'I can feel no power emanating from him.'

The elevator door opened. Helga was pushed inside and readied her arms to lash out—there was a knife under her chin.

"Don't try anything, Helga of Pendle," one of the top-hatted men said. "You wouldn't be the first to try to escape in here!"

Helga halted her attack and tried to think of something else to do. Perhaps a better opportunity would come up later. She needed to get a better sense of her bearings. 'I need roomier fighting space!'

The elevator door opened. The guard shoved Helga into a long hallway. "Others have attempted escape in this area too!" one of the top-hatted warned.

At the end of the hall was a vault door resembling the one in White Manor, but instead of a silver elephant engraving on its door, it was three spirals converging into one point. One of the top-hatted guards reversed his key and inserted it into the door. It swung open with a heavy whine. Ignoring Helga's gender and age, the men shoved her into the room. Helga took note of this and promised an equal retort once she was free. Thinking about revenge only distracted her for a second. Her mouth opened aghast at the contents of the chamber. On multiple levels, rising at least 20 stories, hundreds of women and men were all chained to the walls of a cylindrical-shaped dungeon. Attached to the wrist of each prisoner were metallic tubes, each twisting and snaking, like vines, and converging to the lower level into a silver dome at the center of the room.

Some let out moans when Helga and the rest entered.

"Shut your yaps!" one of the top hat guards yelled. This only caused more of them to complain. Helga got shoved into a human-shaped indent on the bottom level occupied by a decaying corpse in a dress between two other women. The guard unchained the body, dragged it across the floor to the corner, lifted a metal grate, and tossed the corpse down a hole. "Looks like we're running low," one of the top hat guards said.

"Not to worry, we got a couple of spares upstairs," the other said. They pushed Helga against the wall into the space and started attaching her metal cast with silver chains. Helga made her move, but it was short-lived when one of the men said: *"trydan!"*, sending two bolts of electricity into her. She was only incapacitated for a moment and started struggling again. One of the men attached one of her arm chains to the wall, and the other one with a lot of group effort.

"She's strong!" the guard said.

"That's why she's down here," said a top hat guard.

"They'll get at least 50 years out of her."

"Pretty spunky." The man lightly slapped her face. "...I don't see why they just don't smelt her—" The top hat guard's words were interrupted when Helga lifted her legs, placed her feet on the side of his head, and with a quick twist, accompanied by a cracking sound, broke his neck. The man collapsed onto the ground, dead.

"You witch!" yelled the other top-hat man. He punched Helga over and over until the guard interrupted.

"H-Hey, can't you people use a special silver potion to heal him?" the guard asked.

"Doesn't work on us!"

Helga slumped down, battered and bruised, suspended by her upwards arms, a slight smile on her face. The man walked over to a spigot knob attached to the wall next to her with two tubes connected to it. One ran from it to the dome in the middle of the room, the other connected to a large metal hypodermic needle. The man roughly jabbed it into Helga's left forearm. Helga grimaced. He wrapped gauze around the device to keep it in place. He was satisfied it wouldn't slip out and turned his attention to the spigot. He slowly rotated it and then paused.

"If I had my way I'd turn this all the way up!" He and the guard dragged their dead comrade out and shut the large door.

Helga heard someone quietly laughing on her right. She turned her aching head and saw the person was Elzbieta, not looking in much better condition than she. "What's so funny?" Helga asked.

"I killed two of them...I finally beat you."

Helga laughed as best she could.

"Victoria!" The voice yelled. She groggily sat upright in bed, expecting her mother to be by her bedside. Instead, she found her room crowded with spirits, each of a different era and physical makeup. The one that first drew her attention was the little girl whose dress seemed to have been singed by a fire. Victoria was starting to get accustomed to the visitors. She felt unease, but her fear settled a little. Her concern was more with why they were here so early in the morning and such a large number. "What do you want?" Victoria asked, a bit crossed.

As always, no one answered. The figures all pointed to the direction of the prison, like last time. 'You want me to go back there, now?" Continued pointing was their answer. "It's so early!" She knew arguing was going to be useless. She tried to lay back down and close her eyes. They yelled her name again. She sat up, and to no surprise, they were all still in her sleeping area, pointing. She was unsure of the time; there were no clocks in the room, and it felt like 12 AM. If she got up, hurried down to the prison, and returned, she could make it back before the rest of the house woke up, but only if the trains were running. "There are no trolleys, I can't go down there right now." The little girl left the crowd and approached her. This action scared Victoria because they had never come closer or done anything outside of pointing.

"Go, now!" The girl said with a raspy voice before disintegrating into dust.

Things had changed more than she thought, for the spirits to be this aggressive. She feared what they would do if she tried to return to bed and ignore them. If they can now speak, what else could they do? With trepidation, she arose, lit a lantern, and got dressed.

When she passed her mother's bedroom on the way out, she paused and peered through the door crack. Her mother was still asleep. 'Only I can hear the voices...only I can see them.' Victoria continued through a pointing crowd of the unliving to the front door. She paused again and looked back: 'Why do I feel like I'm never going to see my family again?' One of the dead opened the door for her. 'Some of them can touch things!' She stepped backward in fear, took a breath, and then continued, letting them close the door for her.

Outside in the empty streets, she looked around, she knew there would be no trolleys, but she wished there was at least one car on the road. Perhaps a friendly driver could give her a lift downtown. Then again, she had heard stories of young girls getting rides from strangers and never being heard from again. Walking was the only option. By the time she would get to the prison, deal with whatever the spirits wanted, and return, her mother would be awake and in a panic. Victoria was about to start jogging to cut down on the travel time. She took a few steps but stopped when she heard some clopping sounds on the concrete street. The rhythmic echoes got closer and closer. She turned to find its origin. A horse approached her. 'Why is there a horse all alone on the streets at this time?' The animal got closer. It was in the same state as the others, still pointing towards the prison. She recognized it. Earlier in the week, the horse had a broken leg, and she'd heard the sound of its owner shooting it. The ashen, dirt-covered horse walked up to her and paused. "What? What do you want?" The animal gestured backward. She walked up to it and timidly reached out her hand. "Can I even touch you?" Her hand slid across the ice-cold skin of the horse's neck. She continued to run her hand along his back. "Am I supposed to ride you? I don't know how to ride a horse. How do I even get on? When I saw The Battle of Elderbush Gulch picture show, all of the cowboys had saddles. How can I ride you if I can't even get on you?" A pair of hands under her armpits lifted her onto the horse's back. She struggled a little out of surprise, but this did nothing to deter the large grey-skinned man dressed in a policeman's uniform. The man walked away from her, around a corner, and out of sight. When she had settled onto the horse's bony back, Victoria shook off the feeling of the dead man's touch. "He could touch me too!" Sitting on the dead horse didn't bother her as much. She was unsure why. Perhaps it is because she was more acquainted with the animal. She was there when he died.

The horse immediately started trotting down the street. Victoria tightened her thighs and grabbed onto his stringy mane for support. The animal took her on the same route as the trolly car. The sounds of its hoofs reverberated off the surrounding walls and empty streets. It wasn't long before she realized if anyone saw her, it would cause quite a shock. She would appear to be on the back of a dead animal, or silently floating down the street on an invisible one. This realization was proven on the face of a shivering dog when it watched her and the horse pass by without barking. 'Is he scared of us...' Victoria wondered. '...Is he just scared of me?'

Victoria Alexandria Vanderbilt. Age 13

Min got out of bed and pushed the button to cut on the light. She had fallen asleep while waiting for Shirley to return with news about her mother. "I'm hungry," she said. There was no chance of obtaining food at 12:01 AM in the hotel room. She was going to have to venture out. 'Can I leave?' She tried the door handle. Min had expected this, but when it failed to turn, a part of her was a little disappointed that Shirley had not told her the truth. 'I can leave anytime I want, eh?" The Waldorf's doorknobs were fancy but not made to resist an assault from a Wushu expert. It was a simple act for her to knock the knob off. She opened the door and stepped into the hallway, prepared to encounter a type of guard; there was none. 'I wonder if I was wrong. Not having an armed guard could be a sign of trust, and Shirley wasn't expecting me to leave. Min hesitated. 'Should I stay? Could Shirley really be in contact with my mother? If I left this room, I would mess up any agreements they have.' "What should I do? Shirley is a snake, but she did have that fan; she could have just stolen it—Mother would be dead before that happened—is she already dead? Maybe I should just kill Shirley when she comes back. Then I'll find Mary." Min groaned in frustration. She noticed a dining cart in the hallway from an earlier room service. She grabbed a half-eaten loaf of bread, bit into it, turned, and considered returning to the room to finish eating it. She paused because of the gasping sounds of two hotel patrons. A well-dressed man and a woman gawked at her from down the hallway. Neither one appeared suited for security.

"What is that?" the woman asked.

Min looked behind and realized they were referring to her: not her cheeks full of food, nor the cart. 'I've never before been referred to as 'that' before.'

'I think it's an Oriental girl!" the man answered.

"What is she doing in here? Is she stealing food?"

"I don't know! Maybe she's part of a circus or something!" Hanging around Mary and her friends had spoiled her. Min had forgotten only Asian men were allowed into the country. When she ventured alone, dressed as a male, she would usually be mistaken for a young Asian boy, but in the frilly white dress, she was an exotic doll. She quickly went back into her room. There was a conversation outside. Min was scared. 'I messed everything up!' She waited to see if anything would happen. There were footsteps outside; she knew what it was. The couple had contacted the hotel staff, and they were coming to investigate the strange sight of the Asian girl.

"This door handle is damaged!" someone outside yelled.

"She probably burgled in! Get the concierge!"

Min backed away from the door as though it had become a menace. She knew if anyone entered the room on their feet, they would leave on their backs, but this would not help. This situation may forfeit her contract with Shirley. She needed to protect it. She grabbed her mother's fan, tucked it in her dress belt, opened the window, and stepped out onto the sill. It was a long drop, ten stories down, but she was okay risking a fall over being caught by the police and sent back to China. She jumped, grabbed the floor ledge, and pulled herself up. After another leap, she reached a roof structure crowned with what looked like a separate building made of red brick and terra-cotta. A window on the top floor opened, and Shirley peered outside. Min ducked down behind a rooftop gargoyle. Shirley looked around and then returned inside. Min waited until she was certain Shirley wouldn't spot her, then jumped to the balcony of the open window.

Inside the hotel room, Min could see Shirley was having a conversation with two bellhops.

"I assure you she is not Chinese! She is White!" Shirley explained. "She's from Russia. Like myself, she is escaping the war. Now tell lady Faversham I'm sorry my guest frightened her. Good night to you." Shirley closed the door. "Damn that child!" She knocked a small vase off the table, it fell and smashed onto the floor. Shirley ground the heel of her shoe into the porcelain shards. After a long sigh, she left the main room and entered the bathroom. Min slipped into the window and hid behind the drapes. After a toilet flush, Shirley returned to the room and picked up the mouthpiece on the phone. "Yes, get me Park Row 6-4-9." There was a long pause until the call was placed and answered. "Yes, it's me. The girl has escaped…I don't know why…I made it quite clear that we have her mother. Perhaps I should have provided further proof; whatever the case may be, she's gone…I don't think she knows where Mary is…. Maybe she's heading to Tombs prison. If she does, it's going to complicate things, especially if she sees Azure Cloud there, n'est pas?"

Without any concern for Shirley seeing her slip away, Min jumped from the room to the stone balcony below. She looked around. 'Mother! Mother is locked up in Tombs prison!' "Which way is the prison!" She jumped downwards from ledge to ledge until she landed in the back of a truck bed. The truck traveled away from the hotel to an unknown destination. Up above, still talking on the phone, Shirley watched Min disappear down the street and smiled. A voice on the phone said: "Excuse me, Miss, would you like to make a call?"

"No, sorry." Shirley hung up the phone and watched the truck traveling away. "You're in for a big surprise when you get to the prison."

Thomas awoke when he heard the door to Leo's cell close. 'This is a rather late time for the guards to be visiting.' He thought. He saw Leo on the other side of the bars. He checked Leo's cell to make sure he wasn't imagining things. In the bed was a human figure made out of a pillow and some blankets."...How the hell did you..." Leo shushed him and held up a pair of keys. "...How did you..." Thomas whispered.

"I told you no jail can hold me." Leo whispered back.

"But...how?"

"My Unus."

"Your what?"

All Forgers have one natural ability we can do without forging; mine is pickpocketing."

"You took that guard's keys?"

"And a coin." Leo held up one of the coins Forgers used. "Not enough blessed metals to bust out of here, but enough to fight." Leo started to leave.

"Stop!" Thomas said.

"Shhh! What? You want me to bust you out, too?" Leo scoffed.

"No. I can't let you escape!"

"Here we go...How are you gonna stop me? From where I'm standing. You're still just a grouper in a cage."

"I could yell for the guards."

"Like a little kid? Is this the best you can do? I thought you were supposed to be Mary's knight in shining armor. And you're threatening to call for your mommy? Pathetic!"

"I won't let you escape!"

"Why?"

"You're a dangerous scoundrel!"

"Yeah, and so what? I'm also gonna free Mary from this whole mess! What are you gonna do to help her? Sit in this cell, waiting to die—for justice? Well, justice isn't a gift, it's a goal!"

"I can't have you on the outside with Mary!"

"You and I both know I would never harm her."

"That's why you made her float onto subway tracks?"

"I was only trying to make her go straight up. I don't know why she drifted to the subway tracks—maybe she knows how to fly. Or something; either way, her freedom and safety are my goals and always have been. You! You don't even know what you want! What's your role in her new life? Are you a savior or servant? I gotta go! You can go ahead and call for your mommy, it'll just slow me down a little, but no matter what, I will save her, with or without you!" Leo turned and hurried down the dark hall. Thomas watched him leave without saying another word.

At the end of the hall, Leo used the key he had stolen and inserted it into the lock of a metal door. It opened with ease. One of the top-hatted men was standing next to the elevator cage. The man lifted his billy club.

"Eh-ha- gu avuh!", Leo yelled. The coin he had stolen turned into a knife with a three-inch blade. He slid the knife right next to the

man's throat. "Make any moves, and I'll slit your throat!" The man froze. "Now, tell me, where is Mary White!"

The man was silent until Leo brought the knife closer to his jugular. "I don't know! They took her away this morning!"

"To where?"

"—I don't know!"

"To kill her?" Leo pushed his weight into the man's chest.

"No! I don't think so! She didn't go downstairs!"

"Downstairs? What's downstairs? WHAT IS DOWN STAIRS?"

"That's…"

"That's what?"

"I can't say…they…they'll kill me!"

"You sap! I'll kill you right now!"

The man was silent despite Leo sliding the blade close to his ear and shoving him. Leo put his hand on the man's head. *"Oo-aid vell ur wove ur aid dwaid!"* Nothing happened. "Looks like that won't work. The Ironsmith, is she down there?" The man gave Leo a strange look. He recognized it as when he played poker and had cornered his opponent. "Looks like she is. Is her giant sword somewhere in this building?" Leo peered into the man's eyes "… Great, looks like it is." Leo looked at the elevator. "One more question; guess that'll take me to both, right?" The man turned his head away. "You know, your non-answers give me more info than your regular ones. I think whoever they are, they're going to kill you anyway for squawking. If I were in your position, I'd go ahead and help me out. At least then, you stand a chance of getting out of here. Alive." The man seemed to be considering his options. He pushed hard into Leo and attempted to take the knife away from him. It was a feeble effort. Leo plunged it into the sides of the man's neck. After lots of thrashing around, countered by Leo pinning the man against the wall, he finally slumped and sat on the ground. "Don't say I didn't give you a choice."

Leo rummaged through the man's pockets. After confiscating all the money from his wallet, he found a handkerchief and wiped a large amount of blood off of his hands. He grabbed the billy club teclyn, waved it around, and then smelled it. "Your teclyns aren't pure—nonferrous. Is this deave and tun? Are you people even Forgers?"

Tombs Prison in 1915

Mary assessed her situation. The ropes were tight around her torso, and her legs remained useless. "Okay…I need to think. I need to get out of here! And somehow rescue Thomas, Min, and

Helga. First things first, get out of this room." She wiggled around in the bed. "These ropes are tight, but they've obviously never tied anyone up before—That's a good thing on many levels. If they had separated my arms using the posts, it would be impossible to escape. But, if I..." Mary began to inhale and wiggle, rest, then inhale and wiggle, over and over. It was a slow and arduous process as the ropes rubbed against her skin. The friction and movement caused her wrist to sweat, chafe, and bleed. She soldiered through the burning pain and eventually was able to loosen her restraints. With more movement and contorting her arms almost to dislocation, she freed one and then the other. She slipped off the ropes and shimmied until she was completely free.

She tended to her raw rope-burned wrist, tearing the bedsheet and making a makeshift bandage. 'Sorry for destroying your sheets, Alva. I'll reimburse you later.' She tore more of the bedsheet into pieces, attached them to the ropes, and bundled it all together. She cautiously tried to lower herself over the side of the bed, but she and the bedclothes slipped off and caused her to fall with a loud thump. She paused, waiting for the guards to come in and return her to the bed, rendering her efforts useless. All was quiet. She used her arms to pull herself and the bundle over to the window sill with great effort. The trip required a quick rest in the middle. 'Why is this so hard? Do I weigh more than I think? I guess having a spine made out of metal would contribute to that!' She glared at her wrists; they were still bloodied and stung. 'I'm not healing—all of my powers went away. Once I make it over there, then what? Am I strong enough to pull myself up? When this happened last time, I couldn't get off the floor! What chance do I have this time?' With a lot of stretching and grunting, she did a pushup, reached up, and grabbed the knobs of the balcony doors. It took every bit of energy she'd ever had to open one of the double doors. She lay on the floor for a while to catch her breath. Sweat beaded on her forehead and seeped into her eyes like vinegar, temporarily blinding her. She rubbed them off, opened her eyes, and peered outside.

Security was very light inside the grounds. There were no more than two police officers near the gate. Beyond that, she counted at least three armored automobiles and four top-hatted men with swords and rifles.

'Curious. They look like they're more concerned with keeping someone from getting in than out.'

She tied climbing knots into the ropes and sheets and fastened it to the decorative ornamental balcony. She cautiously pulled herself over the concrete railing, her arms shaking with stress until she was hanging by the rope. "I am so glad I was doing all of that upper body exercise in our gymnasium." Ignoring the massive weight her arms were supporting, she lowered herself three stories until she landed ungracefully on the ground behind some bushes. She rested, breathing as hard and silent as she could. 'Okay, Mary. Now what? I hope no one saw me. I have to get by those policemen and what I assume are Forgers and get to the prison and —what was I thinking? I can't even walk! How am I going to get all the way to the prison—and then what?' Mary looked around for any vehicles. There was a laundry truck about to leave. 'If I can make it to that truck, then I could hide in it and—" A pair of legs came into her view. She held still on the chance they hadn't seen her yet.

"Miss White, how did you get out of your room?" asked a male voice.

Elzbieta's tired and weak physical appearance made Helga feel nervous. The entire time she has known this person, she has always emanated an intense ember of Smithing power, and here she was, attached to a wall—a wild animal constrained. "Have ye been down here the entire time?" Helga asked.

Elzbieta pondered this question. It was like she had forgotten where she was. "Noo…first they put me in cell, but I find way to kill the weaklings.

"The ones with the top hats?"

"Yes! They fun to kill! Scream easily!"

"What are these things attached to our arms?" Helga looked at the tube and needle. "Must be made of ahrion because it punctured our skin."

"It make you weak every day. One day, die."

Helga turned her attention to the dome. "It all seems to be concentrating in the center over there. And…"

"You feel?"

"I do, under us, something is down there."

"Something down there. Something strong. Sometimes I feel weak, like thing in middle is taking more, and sometimes not at all."

Helga looked up to the upper levels at all of the other prisoners. Most were women; their ages ranged from teenagers to one she guessed was at least 100—all were in the same predicament. "Have you tried to escape?"

"Many times. But I grow weak."

"What about your teclyn? Have ye tried summoning?"

"I ask you. Same question."

Without their teclyns or access to pure metals, Helga wondered if anyone in this place has ever escaped.

"I tried to summon me teclyn since I was upstairs…" said a voice from the upper level. "…I know it's somewhere in this building, probably in something it can't break out of."

Helga recognized their voice. "Mausi!"

Mary was more sure than ever the man tying her to the bed again was not an employee of Alva's. She was also sure he was not a type of policeman—the word 'goon' came to mind. Instead of tying the rope around her chest as he had done earlier, now each of her limbs was tied to a different bedpost in an X shape. When he pulled and tightened the restraints until they hurt, any hope she could wiggle out of these harnesses was dashed. The man looked quite pleased with his accomplishment, as though making Mary miserable was his life's goal. He wiped his brow like he was working hard and sighed. "There. That outta do it," he said. "Now, to make sure you don't escape from this…" the man took a cloth and bottle out of his pockets.

"Wait, what's that?"

"Chloroform."

"What's that for?"

"To knock you out, of course. The President insists that you remain here until he returns. This will make sure you don't go on any more excursions!"

The man soaked the cloth with the liquid in the bottle and pressed it against Mary's nose and mouth. This brutish act caught Mary off guard. She wiggled her head around, but the rag remained on her face. After a minute, she closed her eyes and slumped down.

"This'll keep you out until noon." The man removed the cloth and left the room.

Leo descended inside the elevator to the next level. A top-hatted man was standing before him when the door opened. The expression on the man's face made him seem surprised anyone had ever appeared on this floor. Leo took advantage of the man's confusion and instantly rushed him before he could even touch his teclyn. The man was a lot stronger than the others on the upper floors. He pushed him against the wall and then tried to dig his fingers into Leo's eyes. The man stopped after realizing Leo had already used a knife to impale his heart from the side of his ribs. He wearily released Leo and came down on his knees. Leo looked down on him. "Do you want me to save you? Do you have any liquid ahrion? If you give me some information, I will heal you."

"...That won't...work..." the man struggled to say. He flopped down prone and died.

"Of course, it works...for Forgers..." Leo searched through the corpse's pockets and found a pair of keys. "I knew if I killed enough of you, I'd find some keys to get out of here."

He walked down the long hallway to a vault, its doors engraved with two gold snakes. 'This looks important.' Upon closer examination, he discovered it was a clo kefin—a reverse lock. "... Really important." He took each of the keys, and one by one, turned them around so they were handles first, and inserted them into a tiny slot where a keyhole would be. On the fourth one, the lock whirled, clicked, and clacked. The black metal door whined open. Leo wasn't sure what he expected to see, but another door with another clo kefin lock was not one of his predictions. He closed the outer door to prevent anyone in the hall from knowing he was in the vault and walked closer and closer to the inner door while listening to a rhythmic thumping. He placed his hands on the door. "What's in there?" As he had done before, he turned all the keys backward until he found one that fit. He was extra cautious when opening this one, afraid of what creature or man would come rushing out. The thumping sound stopped the second the door opened. A black void greeted his eyes. Leo took a defensive stance and cautiously shuffled his feet further inside the vault, hoping to get just far enough where his eyes would adjust so he could see what was inside. Darkness was the only reward for his prudence. Something touched his head. He reached up to feel a pull chain for a light. Without a second thought, he jerked it down, hoping it wasn't a trap. The light came on. The room displayed many objects: teclyns in their various resting states: scissors, canes, fans, knives, and jewelry. He rummaged through a silver chest full of jewelry and found his broken crucifix necklace. He said: *"Droo-so!"*, and it mended back together. He kissed it before putting it around his neck. A wave of energy and centeredness came over him, like a battery in a flashlight. He examined the objects attached to the wall by a one-inch thick silver chain. One was Helga's copper cane, and another was Elzbieta's sword in its parasol form. The copper cane and parasol started moving, undulating against the wall like wild animals trying to escape, creating the thumping sound he had heard from the outside. He unwrapped the parasol from its chain. His secondary nervous system made him duck down far ahead of his eyes. The parasol spun over his head, flew out of the vault, and slammed its metallic self against the outer door. The object shook and rotated as if being sucked against the exit in a vehement attempt to leave the room. He unhitched Helga's teclyn, and like Elzbieta's parasol, it flattened itself against the exit door. "I guess you two want to skidoo?" He walked over to the door and grabbed the parasol. Purple smoke emitted from the handle. An instant feeling of nausea enswathed his stomach, and he ran to the corner of the room and threw up. As quickly as it had started, the illness went away.

"Cursed!"

He went back into the vault and focused on any teclyn that didn't contain curses or tried to leave on their own. He pilfered multiple necklaces and rings, putting them in his pockets, and on his fingers. He admired all of the rings. "No wonder Professor White wore so many, I feel strong!" He removed one of the thick silver chains from the wall constraining Elzbieta's teclyn and wrapped it around his neck. "May need this to tie up a Forger later."

The second he opened the outer vault door to leave, the parasol and cane rushed out of the room, flew down the hallway, and slammed against the elevator door. "Looks like you two know where you're going." Leo summoned the elevator, and when its door opened, the animated teclyns entered the car and attached themselves to the ground. Leo now knew which direction he needed to go. "Like two hunting dogs. Is Mary down there, too?" He acquiesced, turned the elevator crank control to -13, and let it take them down.

A block away from the prison, Victoria's horse stopped and lowered itself to the ground. She hopped off before her legs got trapped under the animal. The horse didn't disappear like the other aspirations, it lay in the street and returned to a state of death. "Is this not a spirit? Was the man that helped me not one also?" Victoria asked. She touched the animal to see if that would make him crumble and petted his leathery skin. "Thank you." She stood in the middle of the street to center herself and tried her best, to surmise her experience. After looking back at the dead horse, she heavily exhaled her unsettling emotions. She walked the rest of the way to the prison, cautiously looking around for any witness to her earlier macabre event. The streets around Tombs prison were quite empty. Occasionally, a police wagon would show up and unload a bunch of drunken men, most likely the participants of a late-night brawl. Victoria knew she was not here to help them—there were no pointing spirits to guide her this time. Fritz was not in his usual spot. 'Did he finally go home?' She considered walking up to the prison door but had no idea what she would do once she got there. So, she waited. 'They have a reason to wake me up and bring me all the way down here. I'll wait for an hour and then try to get back home before everyone wakes up.'

Near her, something small hit the concrete with a meaty slapping sound. She moved closer to get a better look at the object. It seemed to be a sausage. She picked it up and confirmed it was organic. Upon further inspection, she saw something that looked like a fingernail on it. 'Is this a pig's foot? She rotated it to get a better look—it was a human finger. She threw it down and wiped her hand on her dress. 'Why did a finger fall from the sky?' She looked up to the top of the Criminal Courts building. Something sprinkled on her face like raindrops. She wiped her brow and looked at the blood smeared on her hand. "What's going on up there?" She started to back away from the building, fearing what else would fall on her.

Before she back any further, an EMF Model 30 automobile blocked her path. Four top-hatted men got out and rushed around her. 'Move! Girl!' one of them yelled. He shoved her out of his way. She almost fell but caught herself at the last moment. She felt both anger and curiosity. The men went to a locked side door. One of them said: *"Datglowee"*, it opened, and they rushed into the building. 'Whatever activity is going on the roof needs the attention of the mysterious men. Is it possible I'm here to investigate this?' Without any counterargument or spirits pointing her in another direction, she timidly fast walked to the side door, put her fingers in her ears and listened to the echos of steps and conversations in the stairwell of the men running up a flight of steps.

"Are you sure he's up here, 104?" Victoria heard one if them ask.

"Yes, I told 185 to report back if he didn't see anything! That was an hour ago! I sent 161, and he hasn't come back either!" answered another.

Victoria took a deep breath and waited until they were further away. With a lot of reluctance, she opened the door and followed the men up the stairs.

Moments later, a luxury model motor car with two passengers drove around the dead horse and pulled up to the prison entrance. The chauffeur walked to the back of the car and opened the door for Boss Murphy. He got out and looked across the street at the dead horse, the automobile, and then up at the Criminal Courts building. "Hmmm, Looks like the government may get to him first," he said.

"Shall I offer assistance?" the driver asked.

"No. That's Miss Wayward's problem ...I have my own." He put a cigar into his mouth, and they proceeded into the prison.

In addition to new forging powers, Mary also attained new physical enhancements. After drowning when she, Thomas, and Min fought the anghenfēls on the beach, she made a special effort to become better at holding her breath.

She exhaled a large reserve of stale air, and after a succession of rapid pants, her breathing returned to normal. There was not enough time to feel relaxed or clever for outwitting her captors, as they might have heard her loud exhales and realized the chloroform did not affect her.

Even before she set her eyes on them, she could feel someone's presence in the room watching her. A woman dressed in black materialized by the open window.

"Who are you?" Mary asked in a loud whisper.

"It's almost like yeh could see me while I was invisible." She took a drag on a cigarette attached to a long silver holder. "My name is Inga, of the House of Carrier." She walked towards Mary. "I was in the same coven as Helga. Yeh could almost say we were schoolmates."

"You're a friend of Helga's? Then, does that mean you're here to rescue me?"

"No..." She lingered over Mary and looked down at her. "I'm here to make sure yeh don't escape again. I've been keeping me eye on yeh and yuh little escape attempts. If yeh ever made it past the walls, I would have flown yeh back."

"I'm not simply trying to escape! I'm going to liberate Helga from prison before the President executes her!"

"The President. is not going to execute her if yeh hand over that God-cursed book."

"You know of the book?"

"Of course. We wuz going to come fetch it at yuh house before we wuz attacked by the Followers."

"Was one of them a woman fond of balloons and bombs?"

"That would be Mausi..." Inga took a drag on the cigarette holder and exhaled some smoke. "...She wuz also our mate. But she betrayed us and killed..." Inga turned her gaze towards the door. "She killed me friends, and me sister..."

"I'm so sorry."

"Thank you. Yuh jeopardizing the life of one of me last remaining friends. I won't let that happen."

"Even without me sneaking out of here, Helga's life is still in danger! The President has no interest in keeping her alive even when he gets the book."

"And how would yeh know that?"

"Because he's a disreputable man with a slanted agenda!"

"That he is, but I have far more faith in him freeing Helga than a Dayfide, stuck in here after being tied up. What are yeh gonna do? Once yeh escape out of here? You have no power, no legs—nothing! And yuh going to execute a prison break? Don't bloody make me laugh."

"I'm not powerless! I have..." Mary was about to expose her abilities to Inga but didn't know if she could fully trust her. "...I have many resources at my disposal. I just need to get out of this room, then I'll have a fighting chance to rescue Helga, as well as my other friends."

Inga scoffed. "The best thing yeh can do is sit tight and tell the President where the book is. Then, this will all be over."

"It will never be over! Please, release me! You don't have to help me beyond that—let me rescue our friend!"

"Yeh got stones, I'd give yeh that. Maybe that's why Helga defended you so much. Then again, I guess it was part of the job. She formed a contract with yuh family, right?"

"Helga is no longer an employee of the White household."

"Wot? Come again?"

"I released Helga from her contract of defending the book. She was working on her own accord."

Inga looked shocked. "Yeh mean without a bond? She was doing all this...because she wanted to?"

"Yes, is that uncommon?"

"It's certainly rare." Inga walked back and forth between the bed and the window. "I'm sorry, but I still can't help yeh. If I release yeh, and they find out, with one phone call, they'll kill Helga! And I can't allow that!"

"Please, I beg of you, help me...for Helga's sake!"

Inga opened the window and said: *"Headfan guyida!"* Her cigarette holder formed into a large kite and flew out the window, still attached by a silver string to her wrist. "I'm sorry... I don't know why Helga trusts you so much, but I can't gamble on her life with someone in your current state." Inga walked back over to the bed. "Apologies, but I need you to be asleep so you don't escape anymore. *Curse-kur!*"

"I told you! I'm not power..." Before Mary finished speaking, she felt herself passing out. Through her fading vision, she saw the kite pull Inga out of the window and into the sky.

Helga observed the inside of the chamber.

" 'ow many of us are there?"

Elzbieta looked up. "Five floors up, 13 per floor—65."

"Fast at maths, are we?"

"Always know who and how many are near me. So I can prepare for battle!"

"And yet, yeh keep dying! Why is that?"

"Each new life, Professor White always targeted me—always prepared, sometimes he hunt me down. Last time, I only made it to a little girl. This time, I come back strong, get trained by coven since birth—"

"Wait…he killed yeh as a little girl? I can't imagine 'ow he could do such a thing."

"It was after I get other kids to drown little Black Blood Mary. He show up in big iron fish in the middle of a pond. I walk away, but something struck me from behind, and I die again."

"A sneak attack? On a little girl? You are sadly mistaken! Even if yeh did try to kill young Mary White—which is appalling, by the way—Professor White would never do such a thing to a child. He was an 'honorable man!" Elzbieta laughed. "Wut?"

"You all think White family and Black Bloods are honorable! I be alive for 300 years, I've seen things."

"A Reincarnate?" Mausi asked.

"I'm almost 100," Helga said. "I've seen things too!"

"I gather none of yeh have seen anything like that?" Mausi asked. She gestured with her head to the dome in the middle of the chamber.

The three women turned their attention to it.

"Did yeh feel that?" Mausi asked Helga. Helga ignored the question. "Did yeh feel it?" Mausi repeated.

Helga sighed. "Don't talk to me, Mausi! It just ads more time to 'ow long I want to draw out yuh painful death!"

"Yeh felt it, though!"

Helga sighed again. "For the love of the Queen…felt wot?"

"That smelting on yeh coal…you felt it, right?"

Helga did feel something a moment ago, but she refused to answer.

"I feel it more than once since I've been down here," Elzbieta said.

"At least three times," Mausi said.

"What is it?" asked Elzbieta.

"I don't know, but I'm sure these pipes running from our arms into that thing in the middle has something to do with it," Helga answered.

"They're smelting us down," Mausi said.

"To wot end?" Helga asked.

"Does it matter? The end result is going to be the same!"

They all glanced at a mummified corpse hanging on the wall.

The Pendle Coven in 1860. In front: Mausi, Inga, and Helga

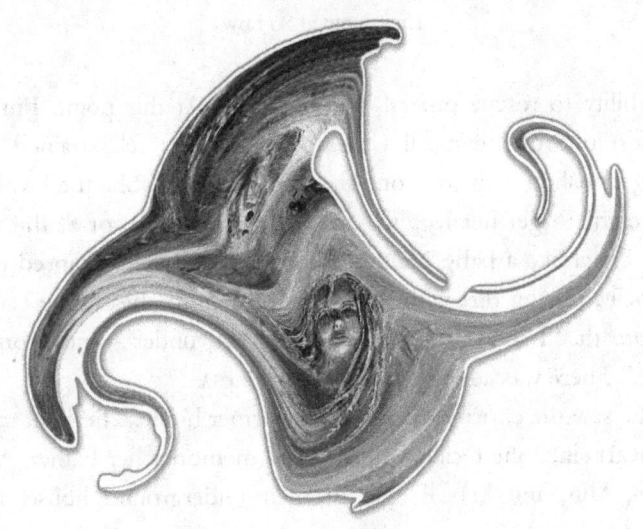

PART FIVE
THEY JUMPED SO LOW

Mary felt grass on her face. She rubbed her hands on it, took away a few blades, and smelled them. Even though it was hard to see details in the dim light, it was unquestionably grass. There was a slight breeze on her neck, warm and subtle. Where was she? Outside, somewhere. How had she got there? Unknown or why. She focused her attention on light sources, allowing her to see more and more details as her eyes adjusted. One detail was the moon, shrouded in blue and grey clouds. The other object was illumination, caused by multiple windows from a large manor not too far away. She recognized the mansion as the home of the Astors, her next-door neighbor. 'I'm at my home.' She looked behind and saw the wall of cars still there, blocking any view of Central Park, bathed in pale blue illumination. 'Why am I back home? Did Helga's friend change her mind? Is this a trick to get me to find the book for them? Are they hiding somewhere in the bushes, waiting for me to reveal my secret hiding place? 'It would be hard to search around without the use of one's legs.' She pushed up as high as she could. 'What am I supposed to do? If someone can rescue me from the Vanderbilt manor, they should also have the ability to rescue others! Why just me? At this point, I'm the weakest one of them all! Unless…' Her arms felt strained, like doing a pushup with someone sitting on her back. She tried with all her might to get her legs to move—to sit upright, or at the very least, crawl like a baby. Neither happened, and she collapsed onto her belly, mixing dirt with the sweat on her forehead. She caught her breath. "I didn't walk out on my own under some hypnotic forge." There was a long moment of stillness.

She saw the enormous crater, her former home. The sight made her heart sink. She recalled all the fond memories her Father, Abel, Helga, Min, and herself had in their underground house, now reduced to distant memories and rubbish. 'We won. But at what price? I guess living in an underground house didn't keep villains from coming after the Siv Myrddin after all.' She sighed

A feeling of unease engulfed her senses; she was not alone. It was the same feeling she got when someone was invisible around her, like being in a pool and someone else trying to slip into it without you noticing. This time, it felt different, like the person was not invisible, yet at the same time, not present. She gazed around to pinpoint the source of her unease. She had no idea how she had failed to notice the body not far from her. A large man lay on his back in a contorted prone position, suggesting a collapse instead of lying down. Mary crawled over to investigate the body, ignoring the possibility this could also be some sort of trap. The man remained still even when she asked: "Sir? Are you alright?" while shaking his cold body. She raised as high as she could to see his face. He was ashen but not yet decomposing, a sign he hadn't been dead for a long while. Mary furrowed her brow. "Why are you here? Is this all some kind of symbolic dream? To what end, though?" She pinched her arm. "No, not a dream—a fold? Gwenhwyvar said during dreams and hallucinations, you lose the ability for logic and to do proper maths: Five minus four equals one—No, not an illusion; therefore, somehow I've been rescued and taken back to my home —or what's left of it, with a dead man next to me.' She examined the body a tad more and found something metallic in his coat pocket. With some fiddling, a cap opened on the object. A lighter. She ignited the flame, bringing more details of her associate into view. His face was gaunt. His sunken eyes had a few insects crawling around them. She was taken aback but remained calm. 'I'm sure, before seeing horrific anghenfêls and so much death, this would have disturbed me even more!' She moved the light around over his clothing. "I thought he was wearing a tan suit, but it's actually white, just dirty. Was he buried and dug up?" The man had a silver arm. "Ahrion? He was a wealthy Forger…or one replaced his arm." Returning to the contents of his pockets, she found forging coins confirming his profession, an expensive pocket watch showing the time to be 4:09 AM, a French postcard with a woman in revealing undergarments, and some paperwork. 'Minus the naughty souvenirs, these are immigration papers. I recognize these from when we first came to the Americas.' "Maximilian Blanc…" The name on the papers was more shocking than the man's decomposing face. "That's…Leo made a paper doll of him with facial hair, but without a doubt, this is the Belgian!'

She crawled away from the body as fast as she could. Several feet away, she looked back to see if it was coming after her. The body remained still. "Perhaps he really is dead, but how? I don't remember seeing him fight in the confrontation with the anghenfêls and the elephants. But his demise could explain his absence. She slowly crawled back. She poked him twice. She noticed the large brown stains on his underside. "Is that dried blood? He was stabbed to death—more than once, but by who, or even whom? Notwithstanding, that's one villain I can worry less about.

"Hello?" she yelled. "Anyone out there? Anyone who can help? Help! A lone, disabled woman?" 'Did I do it myself? Another new skill? Unless the dead Belgian did it. A transference forge? I can't do forging very well, I don't know anyone powerful enough to do a transference, not even Gwenhwyvar. But if it's not 100% and not 0%, there's always a chance!'

'What can I do? What would I do before I had the emotions of doubt and fear? My mind has been such a jumble of emotions lately. I never realized how easy I had it between personalities. I've always had people rescue me. Both of my fathers from the elephant attack, Aunt Gwenhwyvar and her predictions—and Thomas at the party—No wonder Leo sees it as some kind of duty to save me! Like I'm some sort of weak damsel in distress! I might as well be that little girl again, still in her...wait..." Mary franticly whipped her head around, searching. She crawled as quickly as she could to the crater. Something told her where to go and where to start digging. "You should have come to me when I first lost the use of my legs!" Dirt and rocks wedged under her nails as she rummaged through the debris. "...but you were probably trapped underneath all this rubble..." She removed pieces of plates and cloth electrical wires "...But I bet you tried to reach me and did your best to get to the surface..." She removed pieces of furniture and an old doll. "...never giving up until..." a large handrail from what must have been part of the underground walkway " ...you made it to the surface!"

Mary gazed at the object she had uncovered. Even in the darkness, all available light reflected off the shining wheel as if it were made of pure silver.

When she entered the doorway of the Criminal Courts Building, Victoria heard what sounded like a wooden bat hitting a slab of meat. There was another, followed by some grunting and a quick 'Oof!' She followed the sounds 12 floors up, cautiously opened the door to the rooftop and came face to face with a brawl. Several men in top hats with lightning bolt knives were pummeling what appeared to be an enormous ferocious dog. They did their best to punch it, stab it and electrocute it. The beast shook off the volleys and countered with bites to their appendages, followed by a violent shake. The dog tossed one of the men through the air, and he landed, bleeding and moaning, not far from Victoria. she leaned down to see if she could help him, but the man slapped her hand away.

"Who the hell are you? How did you get up here?" he yelled. She didn't have much time to answer. There was a scream from another body flying against the door, forcing it closed, clipping the back of Victoria's heel. She looked down at the body blocking the exit, sealing her fate on the roof; trapping her. The trickle of blood coming from his mouth and his unnatural posture told of his passing. She felt like screaming. She backed away from the two men to find a less active location. From a spot near a brick chimney, she watched the dog shake off whatever damage the remaining men could do with their weapons. It returned their attacks tenfold. The last two men appeared to have been the strongest. Their knives shot out flames, and what she could best tell, was a magnetic force, throwing anything they guided at the dog. Victoria was hopeful their efforts would pay off. She feared how she could deal with the beast otherwise.

The fire bellowed out and forced the dog to the edge of the building. Victoria held her breath, anticipating their final victory when they would drive him over the edge and plummet to his death. At the last moment, the dog let out a huge bark. The volume and bass of the sound pushed shockwaves through the area, and Victoria felt it in her chest like being hit with a large rubber mallet. She fell back upon her rear, suffering less damage than the men. One was flung 20 feet away from the dog, landing on the roof, the other went over the side and fell to his death. The animal jumped on the man on the roof before he could get back on his feet.

Victoria shut her eyes. When she heard the sounds of breaking bones and the growls of the monster, it ended any hope she had of salvation.

The silence was the scariest part of the ordeal for her. She was aware as one of the only survivors, the beast would soon become aware of her and the injured man. She crouched down in hopes of remaining undetected. The dog stalked over to the bleeding man near the exit. His last word was 'No!' before a crunching sound and then silence. Victoria was shaking. She regretted so many things that had led her to this moment. If only she had ignored the spirits, if only she had stayed home, if only she had talked to the doctor as her mom suggested, If only—if only!

There was a stillness. 'Should I move?' She wondered. 'And where would I go?' The door or over the edge were her only options. Which was the worst fate? Having sharp teeth rip into her neck, cutting off her air? Or a 10-second fall? She considered the latter. She had to be sure of her upcoming decision. If she were going to die, she would examine all other options. A body was blocking the door, but she could push the corpse aside with enough power. If she was fast enough, perhaps she could do it just in time to get through the door before he could pounce on her. It was worth a try. If he came within a foot of her, that would be her clue to leap to the left and jump over the edge. The plan was set; perhaps the last plan of her life.

Peering around the chimney, she couldn't see or hear anything. Steadily, she tiptoed towards the door. The two bodies were still in the way; a part of her hoped the dog might have dragged them off to eat them. She put this morbid thought out of her head and focused on her plan. She was moving, but her legs were not. She wondered how this was possible. She looked down at her still legs —it was fear; the fear was paralyzing her bottom half. She took a breath, concentrated, and moved forward, trying her best to look in every direction. The dog was gone. It would be impossible to hide something that big. She considered the dog had done his business and jumped off the roof; this would be the best outcome. She hastened her pace to the door—no signs of a pursuit. With caution and dread, she reached down and grabbed the arm of the dead man blocking the door. Touching an inanimate body was a different level of discomfort than dealing with ghosts and spirits. She mentally held her breath, grabbed his arm, and pulled him sideways enough so that when the door opened, its weight would push him out of the way. She yanked the door open, and with each pull, the man's body inched more, opening a path to freedom. One more tug would create enough space to squeeze her between the door and the frame.

"What are you doing here?" Someone asked.

Her neck hurt from turning fast to see a new danger—it was Fritz. She put her hand to her chest to stop the rapid beating.

"You!" She said. "What are you doing up here?"

"What are you doing up here?"

"I came to investigate a bunch of men running—we have to get out of here! There's a giant killer dog on the roof!" Victoria resumed pulling the door open. "Quick, help me!" Fritz finished buttoning his shirt and tightening his suspenders.

"Are you getting dressed?"

"Yes…we'll I have to—"

"Pull him up, quickly!"

"What?"

"The body!"

He reached down, grabbed the corpse under the armpits, and slid him to the side.

With a great sigh of relief that stopped her hand from shaking, Victoria opened the door to liberate herself from the prior events. The door shut so fast its wind forced her backward. She looked at Fritz as though he had gone insane. "What in the world are you doing? We have to get out of here, now!"

"I didn't do that!"

"Then who…"

In the middle of the door was a very long red stick. They followed the end of the rod to its origin, originating in the hand of Miss Wayward, floating 30 feet away.

Victoria pointed. "Y-y-you're flying!" She looked at Fritz, who was unfazed. "She's flying! Who—who are you?" Victoria yelled.

Wayward flicked her arm. The red stick softened and took on the appearance of the red scarf. The scarf retracted and encircled in the air behind Wayward's head, and swayed around as if underwater.

Fritz placed himself in front of Victoria. "She smells powerful…and yet…familiar," he said.

Wayward came down to the rooftop and pointed at Fritz. "You…Cŵn Annwn! Come with me!"

"I can smell the blonde Black blood on you! You're working with her!" Fritz protested.

"And if I am?"

"I won't be going anywhere with you!"

"You seem to think you have options."

Fritz started to take his shirt off.

"What in the world are you doing?" Victoria asked. When Fritz removed his shirt, she covered her eyes.

"Do me a favor and gather my clothes!" he said.

Wayward looked at Victoria. "I don't remember them mentioning two of you."

"I have no idea what's going on! What are you, people?" Victoria said.

"You should have never come back here! Now your life is in danger!" Fritz said.

"My life was in danger the minute I started seeing gho—" There was a growling sound. She opened her eyes to investigate and witnessed Fritz transforming into a horse-sized dog. The rapid speed of his body's expansion almost threw her back. Once his frame enlarged and all his features morphed into canine appearance, he shook as though ridding himself of all traces of his humanity. He looked at Victoria. She pushed her back against the door. "H-help!" she yelled.

"Not to worry child," Wayward assured. "He won't be harming either of us!"

Fritz turned quickly at Wayward, growled, slowly circled, and assessed her. Wayward stood still as her floating scarf encircled her. Victoria never saw the dog move. Its attack was fast and forceful, like a wolf pouncing on nimble prey. After a slapping sound, he bounced back. The end of the scarf had moved even faster and launched him across the roof. He rolled along and quickly jumped up. After a long growl, he tried again. There were two whipping sounds. After the first one, he lifted briefly into the air, and after the other, he slammed hard on the ground and flattened out. Fritz tried a low attack. Another whipping came down upon his head. His chin bounced off the roof. His body was tossed backward by the other end of the scarf when it slipped underneath him. He flipped himself over and landed on his feet.

"I should get out of here!" Victoria said. She turned around and began to descend the stairs. She thought about the boy who knew a lot about what she was and the woman who might know even more. She returned and watched the dog try to attack, over and over, and get physically refuted.

Fritz backed away and hunched down.

Victoria had seen this earlier before he let out his huge bark. She was about to cover her ears and warn the strange floating woman, but there was no need. Before the dog could unleash a thunderous sound, one end of the scarf wrapped itself around his snout and closed it shut while the other end lifted him in the air and cocooned his body in red silk.

The woman smashed the red bundle onto the roof over and over. Victoria couldn't imagine a regular creature surviving such an onslaught. She was amazed when the scarf unraveled, and Fritz shakily lumbered away to regain his composure. Victoria felt glad he was alive, a strange reaction to a murderous monster.

"How are you able to do this? Is this magic?" Victoria yelled.

"This does not concern you, child! Run along, return to your Dayfide world!" The woman said.

"I would greatly appreciate an answer!"

The red scarf twisted around Fritz and restrained his paws and legs. His struggles were ineffective. The cloth lifted him into the air. Instead of slamming him to the ground again, the woman turned her back to Victoria and began to walk away with Fritz in tow.

Victoria knew this was the last time she would see them. Once the woman made it over the ledge, this would end her chance to know what she is. "Stop!"

"What is it?"

"I need answers! Who are you? Who is he? What am I?"

"You? You're a person having a dream. Now go back home and sleep!" Wayward took a position to launch herself off the roof. A strange feeling came over Victoria. It was like her body had suddenly expanded, and she could feel all the air, even as far as the woman. In the air, there was substance, like solid areas in the nothingness. These forms connected to her like strings from a puppet. Victoria sent her current thoughts through the strings and into the forms. They materialized 14 of the ashen ghosts. They grabbed Wayward around her waist and legs and anchored her to the roof. Wayward was confused as she moved around, trying to free herself from the many grasp of ghostly hands.

"What? What is this?" Wayward yelled. She looked back at Victoria "Are you doing this?"

"I'm sorry, I don't know why they are doing this! I urge you not to leave until you can answer my questions!"

By her clumsy movements to release herself, Victoria could tell the woman could not see the ghost as she did. They brought her body flat onto the ground. Victoria walked closer to her. "Now, please, can I have some answers?"

"I have more questions for you, child!" Wayward held her scarf. "Eh-ha- gu avuh!" It turned into her Chinese war hammer, releasing the unconscious Fritz from its grasp and depositing him onto the roof. She lifted her weapon. With one swing, she dissipated the ghostly bodies into a gray mist. She stomped over to where Victoria stood. "You're a Forger?"

"That's what the boy told me."

"But, you didn't use words…And you're not at a high enough level to do that…" Wayward seemed to realize something and then stepped back in fear.

"What? What is it?"

"When I was bound, did you see anything?"

"I could see the ghost holding onto—"

"Ghost?"

"Yes. I can see ghosts, and spirits, and ghouls. They're helping m—"

"Blacksmith!"

"What?"

"The cursed ones!"

"Huh?"

"Eh-ha- gu avuh" Wayward's war hammer transformed into a Chinese qiang spear. She bought it backward, preparing to strike."

"No! Wait? What did I do?"

"Better to put you out of your misery now before you come into your powers!" Wayland brought the spear down to sever Victoria's head. Victoria closed her eyes and prepared for the hereafter.

In the basement of the building next door, Boss Murphy, escorted by two top-hatted men, arrived on subfloor 13. The elevator door opened. The man standing next to him was suddenly pushed against the wall by a large gust of wind. Before the other man could act, he had a dagger in his head. The first man's body was slammed against the ceiling and the floor numerous times until the wind released his lifeless body onto the elevator floor. Boss

Murphy knew he was going to be next. He closed his eyes and prepared for an end that didn't come. After cautiously opening his eyelids, he saw Leo wiping blood off of the knife onto one of the dead bodies.

"Don't worry..." Leo said. "I'm not going to kill you...yet!"

"Who, who are you?" Boss Murphy said, more nervous than he wanted to appear.

"No matter who I am. I know who you are. You're Charles Murphy, right?"

"How do you know..."

"Oh come on! Do I look like a goof? Can't live in New York without knowing who the big eggs are. You're more powerful than the mayor."

"What do you want, money?"

Leo scoffed. "Figures, that'll be the first thing you think of. Money would be nice. But, for now, since the keys I have didn't work on this one, I'm guessing the fact that you and those milquetoast Forgers are down here means you have a key to this Clo Keffin. Leo walked closer to Murphy. "I'll take the key, please."

"How do you know I'm not a Forger?"

"Because I know who you are. Someone told me Forgers want all the gold but none of the attention. Kinda explains why we ain't mentioned in the history books. Dayfides do all the work, and Forgers collect all the rewards, 'cept now and then they reward one of you with the illusion of leadership." Leo patted Murphy twice on the chest, turned around, and walked towards the large vault door engraved with three spirals. Boss Murphy put his hand into his suit pocket and looked confused.

Leo lifted the key in one hand. "Are you looking for this?" He held a small derringer in the other. "...or are you looking for this?" Boss Murphy looked embarrassed. Leo continued walking to the door of the Clo Keffin. "Don't try anything, you've already served your purpose!"

Leo inserted the key into the Clo Keffin. Helga and Elzbieta's Cane, and parasol began to rattle against the door like anxious dogs yearning to go outside. "Guess the owners are behind this door, am I right?" Murphy didn't answer. "If that's true, and they get these teclyns, they'll probably use them to murder me, right?" Leo removed the silver chain from his neck. "This was keeping them from flying around." He carefully wrapped the chain around the cane and the parasol's handles without touching them. The objects stopped moving and became docile. "Hmm, that's better."

The door opened. Leo gestured to Boss Murphy. "After you, Boss." Murphy entered first to the sound of jeers all around the chamber. Whistles and catcalls joined the jeers as Leo trailed closely behind. "Who's that', and 'Let us free!' were among the words. As he took in the sight of all of the Forgers bound to the walls by tubes, converging to the dome in the center, Leo's mind swirled with thoughts

"Wha-what is this place?" he asked. Boss Murphy didn't answer. Leo turned to him. "What are these people doing down here!?" Again, no answer. Leo walked over to Murphy, grabbed him by the collar, and glared at him. "What are you damned Dayfides doing to them?" After a brief silence, Leo lifted the dagger to Murphy's eye. "Tell me! Or I'll use a forge that'll make this feel like a red-hot poker!" Murphy's continued silence infuriated Leo. He yelled: "*Roy are don!*" The dagger glowed red. He brought it closer to Murphy's face. Before it made contact with the skin, someone said: "Leo?" distracting him from continuing. Off to the side, he saw a couple of familiar faces. He released Murphy and walked over to confirm his summation. He smiled when he saw Mausi, Elzbieta, and Helga bound to the wall.

Victoria wondered if a ghost had stopped the spear from impaling her head. When she opened her eyes she saw a short Chinese girl in a frilly white dress, using her clapped hands around

the blade to stop the spear mid-strike. Even with the gauze covering her eyes, Wayward's expression seemed as surprised as Victoria's. The girl tried to kick Wayward with her right foot, but Wayward flew backward into the air and landed several feet away. Fritz awoke, transformed into a boy, and lumbered over to Victoria.

The Asian girl crouched, and took a stance like an archer pulling back a bow.

Fritz shook off as much of his beating as he could. "Q-Qing Min?" he weakly said.

"Are you alright?" Min asked.

"What are you doing here?" he asked.

"I heard my mother was around here. What are you doing up here?" she asked back.

Fritz gestured across the street. "Elzbieta is in there."

He pointed to Wayward: "...And she attacked us. Wayward's spear came downwards, ready to cut through Victoria's head. Min blocked it again with a palm hit to the side of the blade. Wayward's curled fist struck Min in the chest with such force she pushed into Victoria. They both slid a few feet and landed on their backs. Wayward spun the spear and then tried to impale Victoria. Min used her feet to kick the shaft upwards, then backflipped and used her arms to stop a barrage of spear attacks on Victoria. No matter how frequently Min swiped the spear to the side or deflected low blows using her feet, Wayward continued her attack and increased her ferocity and speed. Min countered using clawed-hand tiger fist so she could grab the spear and disarm Wayward. There were numerous opportunities to do this, but Wayward twisted the spear away or used a feint until Min released her weapon. Min aimed for Wayward's bandaged face, assuming it was an injury. Wayward moved her head and attacked with a foot strike, forcing Min to jump into the air. Wayward did a two-fingered hit on Min's chest, sending her reeling backward into a chimney pipe, bending it. Min fell onto the ground in pain.

"What? What's wrong? Victoria asked, picking her up.

"She's…Really strong!…and knows Wushu!"

"Then we'll fight her together," Fritz said.

"Are you ready for this?" Min asked.

"More than ready, I'm angry!" He transformed back into a large dog. They each picked a different side of Wayward and circled her.

"Watch out for her scarf!" Victoria said. She never saw Wayward throw the spear. It came within one foot of her neck before Min deflected it, and it embedded in some pipes, an inch from Victoria's head.

Min freed the spear and pointed it at Wayward. Victoria fell onto her bottom, onto Fritz's pile of clothes in shock.

Wayward pointed her hands at the spear. It yanked out of Min's hands back into Wayward's. Min appeared unfazed and got into a combat position.

"Ouch!" Victoria said.

"What is it?" Min asked.

"I sat on something sharp." Victoria took Min's hairpin out of Fritz's pants pocket and held it up. Min saw it with her peripheral vision, it beckoned her, and she sensed it.

Min reached out her hand. "Give it to me!" Victoria handed it to her. She smiled when it touched her fingers. "Fritz! Why didn't you tell me you had this?"

Wayward's spear flew towards Victoria's heart.

Min yelled: *"Eh-ha- gu avuh"* Just as she finished the last syllable, the hairpin transformed into her qiang spear. The blade extended, deflecting Wayward's spearhead towards the sky, barely missing Victoria's face. Min spun her spear and stood in front of Victoria. Fritz had jumped at Wayward and latched his teeth onto her arm. She swung him back and forth, but he held on and chomped down harder. After a strike with her other fist to his head, he let go and rolled to the roof's edge.

"Fritz!" Min yelled.

Dizzy and confused, he tried to shake off the punch, but it was evident to all that it had almost rendered him unconscious again.

"Why does she want you dead so much?" Min asked Victoria.

"I don't know. She called me a Blacksmith."

"I don't understand what that is, but if she wants you dead, you must be one of the good ones."

"I'd like to think so."

Wayward's spear spun from the sky back into her hand. Before she could attack, Min struck first at the heart, head, legs, and arm. Wayward blocked all, and she countered with equal force on Min. The clashing weapons caused sparks and metallic resonances in the air. Wayward jabbed at Victoria. Min used her spear to come underneath and deflected Wayward's spear upwards. Wayward continued the rotation and used the butt of the staff to hit Min in the chin. Min flipped backward and landed on her back. She rolled sideways, avoiding a blunt end downstroke from Wayward, so powerful it cracked the concrete roof. Min swung her qiang sideways to cut off Wayward's legs. Wayward jumped upwards and the qiang swept under her feet. Min sprung forwards but was stopped by a foot to the chest, forcing her into the metal door of the exit.

Wayward brought her spear shaft down to incapacitate Min. Two inches away from Min's leg, the stick stopped midair as though it had struck something solid.

Wayward was confused at first, then looked over at Victoria with scorn. Unlike the others, Victoria knew what had happened. Standing between Min and Wayward was one of the gray ghosts, taking the full force of the staff. Wayward waved the spear around, and the ghost dissipated into dust. She stepped back and pointed at Victoria.

"I...They did it, I didn't do anything." Victoria responded.

As Fritz leaped into the air in a surprise attack to land on Wayward's back, he was unfortunately heard. Using her spear's blunt end, she stopped him with a blow to the chest. He yelped and fell. Min jabbed at Wayward's lower half. Wayward lifted her leg and planted her foot on the spearhead, preventing Min from moving it further. Wayward reeled her spear back like a batter preparing to hit a home run on Min's head. Min steadied herself for the attack, knowing even if she blocked it, the blow was going to hurt.

"157?" yelled the top-hatted guard entering Thomas' cell block. "Are you in here? The man walked down the hall and discovered the corpse Leo had left in front of the elevator. "157!" The man bent down and checked for vitals that weren't there. "157! What happened?" In a state of panic and anger, the man looked around and landed his gaze on Thomas, sitting on his bed. "You! What did you do? Did you kill him?"

"Me?" Thomas said. "I'm afraid you have me confused with my neighbor."

The guard unlocked Leos cell, entered and bought his baton down on the pillow doll. He ripped the doll apart in frustration and walked back into the hall. "Where's the other prisoner?" He yelled.

"I have no idea. Maybe he actually managed to escape?"

The top-hatted man quickly unlocked Thomas' cell and entered.

"What are you doing? Shouldn't you sound an alarm or something?" Thomas asked.

The man pointed a knife at Thomas, yelled: *"Mellt!"* and fired a lightning bolt at him, throwing Thomas off his bed, and onto the floor.

"Where's the other prisoner?" The man yelled.

"I...told you...he escaped..." Thomas struggled to say.

The man fired another bolt into Thomas, causing him to convulse.

"Tell me!" He placed the knife against Thomas' head.

Thomas knew if he fired, it would lobotomize him, and it would be over. 'I'm going to die in this cell, never being able to help Mary!'

206

The man was about Forge 500 volts of electricity into Thomas, but yelled in agony. He looked down and saw a trickle of blood running from his ankle. "What..." Thomas swiped something sharp against the man's other Achilles tendon. The man screamed, his legs buckled, and his face contorted in pain and confusion. He brought the knife down to stab Thomas in the head, but Thomas blocked it with his arm, rotated the man's hand and bent their thumb backward in a joint lock. The guard dropped his knife. Thomas picked it up, and struck the handle to the side of the man's head, rendering him unconscious. Ensuring the man was immobilized, Thomas stood and examined the makeshift weapon he had used to slash at the guard—a toothbrush with a razor affixed to it. He tossed it aside as he stepped over the man's body. 'What am I doing? My police career is most definitely over.' In the hallway, he wondered where to go. 'I can't let Leo near her.'

There was a silver blur in front of Min's face. Something had grabbed Wayward's spear and held it steady—the end of a large metallic crab claw. The claw grabbed Wayward's spear, and with a quick yank sent it, and Wayward backward. Wayward did a backflip and landed on her feet and then one knee. Everyone forgot about their fight and focused on the strange form. The metallic crab claw retracted and joined legs underneath the velvet cushioned seat of a wheelchair. Mary sat in the chair, beaten, soiled and exhausted. "Mary!" Min yelled.

"Hello, Butterfly!" Overwhelmed by seeing Min alive, Mary's face lost its composure. Min showed more happiness than Mary had ever seen in her. They remembered the attacker and steadied themselves. "...Min, when this is over, I'm going to hug and kiss you until you pop, understand?"

"Yes," Min said. Min picking up her qiang.

The crab chair walked sideways to get in between Wayward and the children.

"Didn't expect to see you here," Min said

"Quite honestly, I didn't expect to find myself here either. But alas." Mary addressed Wayward: "Now, if you would please refrain from trying to murder these children, I'm sure all of our lives would be much better."

"She's not trying to kill them, just me," Victoria said. Mary looked back at her. "Oh, Hello Victoria? Does she really want you dead? Did you do something to her? Steal apples from her orchard?"

"No Ma'am, I don't know her! I was brought here...I think to help the dog boy!"

Fritz stood next to Mary; she reached over and petted his head, "Hello Fritz, good boy."

The group began to circle around Wayward.

"That woman is tough," Min said.

"Good to know," Mary said. "Doesn't matter. The strong will always beat the tough."

"Are you an optimist or crazy?" Victoria asked.

"I like to call it willful ignorance." Mary accessed the unwavering, silent Wayward, staring at them behind her gauze. 'She can fight without sight? How powerful is she?'

Victoria moved closer to the back of Mary's chair, briefly studying the turning gears of the legs underneath. "Are you really a witch?"

"I'm not sure what I am, dear. Do try to stay behind us."

"Don't worry about her, Min said. "She can make something invisible that stops attacks. That woman called her a Blacksmith."

Mary had a slight expression of fear. She looked over at Victoria. "Ex...extraordinary—"

Wayward took advantage of the distraction and jabbed straight at Mary's neck. One of the crab claws rose fast enough to block the assault.

Five more jabs flew at different areas of Mary's body and the chair. Its claws and many legs blocked each attack. Mary realized Min had paused and was focused on the volley of jabs.

Fritz used Wayward's attack to his advantage and lunged onto her back. Wayward reached backward and threw him over the side of the building.

"Fritz!" Mary yelled. "Chair! Save him!" The chair made a bell sound, and with a prodigious leap, it jumped to the edge of the building and held on with one of its claws. The other claw stretched with an accordion extension and grabbed the falling Fritz by his neck. He yelped in pain; Mary grimaced. "Sorry!" The crab arm lifted him, threw him backward into the air, and he landed back on the roof. "I'm sorry, Fritz," Mary said again. "Better than falling to your death, right?" Fritz growled at her.

Min had re-engaged Wayward, protecting Victoria from her new attacks. Wayward groaned in frustration from not advancing her mission. Her red scarf stretched down and pushed her into the air. It continued to expand until it reached the group, like two scarlet tentacles. The scarf flexed and grabbed at them while Wayward assaulted with her spear, creating a three-pronged attack. Min took on defending against the spear as Mary and Fritz fought off the scarf. The fierceness of Wayward's attack increased. Even though the chair and the other two were able to match the onslaught blow by blow.

'We can't fight her all day!' Mary thought. 'She's so strong—it's like she's holding back! I'll never have enough time and strength to defeat her and rescue the others! She said she was only after Victoria...' "Victoria!" Mary yelled.

"Yes?"

"Do you think you can do anything with your ability?"

"I still don't know what's going on," Victoria answered.

"Something is protecting you, right?"Min yelled.

The red scarf came dangerously close to hitting Mary in the head. "We don't have much time! Do you think you can attack her? Or at least delay her?"

"I don't know!"

"Just try! It's important!"

"I'll do what I can!"

"Fritz! Is it okay for Victoria to be on your back?" Mary asked.

Fritz growled in disapproval and snapped at the red scarf.

"Please! If you do, I promise you, I'll rescue Elzbieta when I rescue the others! You have my word!"

The scarf slapped his side, and he skidded sideways for a second. He looked at Mary, nodded, and barked with an expression of pain.

"Min! I'm going to need you to work on my buttons!"

"Can't do...that...and fight her...at the same...time!" Min yelled between blows.

"Not to worry, I'm going to create some time! Okay, Victoria, whenever you're ready! Do whatever you can to stop her from attacking us!"

Wayward briefly withdrew the scarf; it reformed itself with sharp ends. "Prepare yourselves!" she yelled.

"Wait—" Min said as if Wayward had said something familiar.

"Victoria, now!" Mary yelled.

Victoria closed her eyes and tried to recreate how she felt each time the ghost intervened.

A scarf spear stabbed into Mary's wheelchair seat, an inch from her shoulder. The other end scraped Fritz's rib. Min, displaying a look of distress, was pushed backward by Wayward's spinning spear.

"Victoria?" Mary asked.

The scarf attacks started turning into a red blur of death. Mary could almost count down the number of seconds they had before Wayward found an opening. If one of them faltered, it would be enough to distract the other two, leading to other exploited openings. "Victoria?"

Victoria still had her eyes closed and seemed to be talking to whoever had been helping her all this time. "Please...please..." she said.

"Victoria?"

"I'm trying!" she yelled back. "I can't do anything! Someone else is doing it..."

On sub-level floor 13, all of the Forgers restrained to the wall slump down and weakened in unison.

"What's going on?" Leo asked. He looked at Murphy. "What is happening to them?"

The tubes leading to the dome in the middle of the chamber moved and constricted. Leo walked over to it, laid his hand on the surface, and felt a part of himself being ripped away.

Victoria opened her eyes in time to see the pointed end of the scarf heading towards her face. Something stopped it. The scarf had dealt a fatal blow and impaled them through the heart. In shock, Victoria surveyed who had sacrificed their life for hers. All members of their party were still alive. The scarf withdrew, and the living corpse of one of the top-hatted men immediately slumped to the ground, dead again.

"My word!" Mary exclaimed.

"I—I didn't do it!" Victoria said with fear and remorse.

Wayward was about to attack again, but five more reanimated corpses jumped at her. She withdrew her scarf and spear to protect herself from these new foes. She beheaded one of them, but the other four grabbed onto her legs and waist and tried to pull her down.

As fascinating as it was watching this scene unfold, Mary knew there would only be a brief window of opportunity to take action. "Min, step on the back rail and grab onto the back of my chair! Victoria, get on the dog!"

Everyone did as asked: Victoria wrapped Fritz's clothes around his neck to use as a reign, and Min collapsed her Qiang spear back into a pin and placed it in her hair.

"Chair! Escape her!" Mary yelled. "Everyone, follow me!" Her legged chair rang a bell and leaped over the side of the building. It bounded down onto different ledges before landing on top of a top-hatted men's vehicle, collapsing its roof. With Victoria holding on to Fritz for dear life, he followed the same path.

Mary and Min raced down the street, the metallic legs of the wheelchair rapidly tapping away. Fritz and Victoria galloped close behind. Mary looked back and saw Wayward peering over the roof ledge. She had dispatched her adversaries faster than Mary expected. The scarf formed itself into two red bat wings. With a few flaps, Wayward lifted off the roof and pursued after them.

"Where are we going?" Victoria yelled.

"Away from her!" Mary yelled. "By the way, Min, dear, you wouldn't happen to have your key on you, would you?"

Min pulled out the key on a chain from her blouse and showed it to her. "That's the bee's knees! I'm going to need you to do me up." Mary leaned forwards a little. Min opened the back of Mary's blouse, inserted the key into one of the rivets, and turned it. There was a ping sound. Min almost turned the next one but had to be sure Wayward wasn't a threat. She saw the woman forming the scarf into the shape of a giant blade, two yards long, and swinging it downwards to cut Victoria and Fritz in half. Min jumped into the air and landed behind Victoria on Fritz's back. The dog buckled a little from the downward force. While balancing on the galloping dog, Min reactivated her spear and deflected the giant knife off to the side, where it cut a telephone pole in half. She parried two more slashes. "She really wants you dead!" Min said to Victoria.

"I don't know why! It's not my fault I'm like this!"

Min fended off another blow to the side. "Can you do the thing that made her stop? Again?"

"I told you, I'm not the one doing it!"

The legged wheelchair jumped backward over the others and landed behind them, facing Wayward. It continued to run in reverse just as fast.

"Min, my buttons!" Mary yelled.

"What about us?" Victoria said.

"What about them?" Min asked.

"I'll try to fend her off. If my buttons get tightened, I can do forging!" Min jumped off the dog onto the back of the wheelchair. Fritz turned the corner, and Mary's chair automatically followed. Min turned another button and barely had enough time to block the downward slash of the large blade.

"Four more!" Mary yelled. She felt her full strength returning already, like her body was remembering itself.

Wayward was doing a double-prong attack, making the ends of the scarf jab downwards. Mary's chair stretched its two crab claws, using scissors extension arms, and they grabbed onto Wayward's shoulders. With a whip to the left, they sent her crashing through the window of a nearby office building. "Good job, chair," Mary said. The chair jumped and turned forwards again. Min resumed turning rivets.

Mary sighed. "Two more!"

Some people were starting to appear in the early morning hours on the side streets. They looked in shock and awe at the crab-legged vehicle and a child riding on the back of a giant dog down the street.

"I can't make the same mistake," Mary said. "We need to take this fight elsewhere, before someone gets hurt and we destroy New York!"

"Where?" Min yelled.

"To the docks! If I can forge again, I can do a Vorago on the river and send us all to England!"

"England? What are you talking about?" Victoria asked.

"Don't think too much about it!" Min answered. She was about to insert the key into the last two rivets but was interrupted.

"LOOK OUT!" Victoria screamed.

A Model T car fell towards them, crashed, and flipped forwards a little, coming within a foot of hitting Fritz's tail. Up in the sky, Wayward was floating in the air. The gust from her scarf wings lifted vehicles into the air and rained them downwards on the group. One after another, the cars smashed onto the pavement with a booming impact and flipped towards them.

They ran in a zigzag to avoid being hit, getting sprayed by metallic debris, glass, and pieces of the street.

Min tightened another rivet.

"One more..." Mary said. "...then I'll throw fireballs at her!" A car came dangerously close to squashing them. The crab chair jumped to the left as Fritz jumped to the right. The car flipped between them. "Any time, Min!" Mary yelled.

Min tightened the final rivet, and replaced the key around her neck. "That's all of them!" She yelled.

Mary put herself in deep concentration. She took a deep breath, lifted her hand, pointed it at Wayward, and yelled: "Roy are don!" There was a long pause. Wayward temporarily halted throwing automobiles at them; nothing happened. There was no fire or even a change in air pressure. Mary yelled the words to the fireball forge again. Wayward flinched, but it was unnecessary.

"What's wrong?" Min asked.

"I...I don't know. Maybe it's the wrong words!" Mary tried once more, leading to another failure. "No! It's not working! Unless..." Mary scooted upwards in her seat and then plopped back down. "It didn't work!"

"What didn't?"

"I should be able to walk again, but I can't! It didn't do anything! I'm still helpless!"

"Should we try again?"

"No! It's not the key, it's me! I feel like it worked…It may take some time because it's been a week!"

"What do we do now?"

"Try not to die!"

The chair jumped back and forth to avoid another rain of cars.

The feeling of being drained stopped.

"What's down there?" Leo yelled.

He held a knife to Murphy's neck. Murphy's continued silence let him know that no matter what Leo did to threaten him, there was no chance he would explain anything about floor -13.

Leo walked over to Helga. She lifted her head and barely acknowledged him. "Helga. Where's Mary?"

"She's not down here. Yeh backstabbing nutter!"

"Hmm, that guard was telling the truth." He looked up at the rows and rows of prisoners. "What is this place? What is that thing in the middle of the room?"

"Even if I knew, do yeh think I'd tell yeh?" Helga answered.

"I guess not." He started walking and examining the faces of those constrained to the wall. He stopped at a mummified corpse of a woman. "Some of you have been here longer than others—I was right…this room…this prison… this isn't a prison for Forgers, this is a death penalty." He pointed his knife at Murphy. "What do you think, witches? Should I just burn him where he stands?"

There were multiple rumblings of support in the chamber.

"Don't call us witches!" Helga said.

"Do you think I'm responsible for all this?" Murphy asked. "I didn't build this—do you know how old this part of the prison is?

"If not you, then who?"

"You don't know anything about your history, boy!"

Leo placed the knife to Murphy's throat again. "Educate me! What is all this? Why are you people doing this?"

"My people?...Your people...OUR people!"

"My people...I doubt Forgers would put their own people in here. An army with magic convicts is still a magic army. Being in here is a waste of talent."

"It's not all going to waste," Mausi said.

"Shut yuh yap, Mausi," Helga yelled.

Leo walked over to the women. "What do you mean?"

"When yeh touched that thing in the middle. Yeh felt it, right?" Mausi asked.

"I did...I felt something."

"Like the life being sucked right out of yeh?"

"Yes."

"That's what they're doing, mate, sucking the life out of us!"

"And doing what with it?"

"Don't know. But it's all going down there!"

"Down where? Inside the dome?"

"No luv, it's not the dome that's doing it. It's what's under the dome!"

"Under the dome? There's another level?"

"Under the floor. There's something under this chamber. I've seen 'em going down a stairwell off to the side."

"And what's down there?"

"Mausi! Shut up!" Helga yelled.

"So you do know something, Helga. Tell me!" Leo yelled.

"Sure Leo, just bring your ear close enough for me to whisper it to yeh."

"No thanks, and have you bite it off or something?"

"I can tell yuh," Mausi said, "But wot's in it for me?"

"I won't kill you?"

She chuckled. "Are yeh having a laugh? Do yeh think I'm afraid of death? The only thing the Followers of Myrddin are afraid of is the Dayfides ruling the world for another thousand years."

"I suppose you're right. What do you want?"

"Chained to a wall, being smelted? Missing me 'and? Are yeh so clueless as to what I'd want?"

"I don't have a key."

"It's the same one yeh used to open the door to 'ere, ye wanker. Assuming they made these locks as well. A key for a Clo Keffin will open any lock created by that particular Forger."

Leo pulled out the key he had taken from Boss Murphy. "That means someone else made the Clo Keffin on the Virginia... probably Gwenhwyvar—how do I know You won't just kill me once I let you loose?"

"Forgers honor."

"Leo was taken aback. He considered something.

"What?" Mausi asked.

"Forgers' honor? You won't try to kill me?"

"Yuh not me enemy... 'e is." Mausi looked at Murphy.

"We can work together."

"Pardon?"

"If I free you, you'll work for me?"

"What? No! I pledge the Followers of Myrddin!"

"Temporarily then? Until we get out of here, you will follow my orders."

Mausi thought for a moment. "Temporarily?"

"Yes."

" 'ight, Forgers honor, I'll follow ye until I escape from here."

"And you won't kill me once we're outside?"

"Fine—why are you so paranoid, luv? Ok. I won't kill you once we're outside."

Forger's honor?"

"For the love of the queen—Forger's honor!"

Leo used the key and unlocked Mausi. Once freed, she placed one of the top-hatted men's dagger on her stump. *"Cumeskey kuday kudalid"* The knife fused, grafted onto her bone, and became a sharp hook. She stepped over to Helga grabbed her by the cheeks with her remaining hand, squeezed, and laughed" 'ello 'elga, o'right? Should I slit yeh throat right now? To put yeh out of yuh misery?"

"Mausi…yeh slag!" Helga struggled to say.

"Leave her for now," Leo said. She's not going anywhere… unless you want to pledge loyalty; what do you say, Helga? Mary got you thrown in here, can't do worse by me?"

"I'd assume pledge loyalty to the Devil's bollacks!"

"I figured you'd say something like that. "What about you, Ironsmith?" You want to get out of here?"

Elzbieta looked up. "Will get out of here Apple Man, and when I do, I peel your skin off," she quietly said.

"That sounds like a no. No matter, I just need to know where your sword is. I didn't see it in the vault, where is it?"

"Go ahead, take it; big surprise for you." Elzbieta laughed.

"What does that mean?" Elzbieta ignored his question. Leo paused in thought, rolled his eyes, and then plunged his dagger into her side. She grimaced.

"Elzbieta!" Helga yelled.

Leo poked the knife handle. "I'll just leave that in your gut. Give you some time to think about what you want to do. Don't take too long. Anyone else want to die in here?" he yelled. "If you follow me, you can all be free!" He yelled, his voice echoing throughout the chambers."

"You fool!" Murphy yelled. "Some people in here are insane— mass murders!"

A metal gag prevented a pink-haired woman on the higher levels from speaking. She did her best to raise her chained hand.

Leo spotted her and climbed up a rusty metal ladder off to the side and then another until he reached her.

"That's Carmun, she terrorized all of Ireland with her banshee voice—leave her!" Murphy yelled.

"You willing to pledge loyalty to me?" Leo asked her.

She nodded yes. He used the key to release her gag.

"Aye," she said with an Irish accent. "I'll follow you to hell n' back, just as long as I can kill as many Dayfides as I can! Forger's honor!"

Leo unlocked her other restraints and gave her some ahrion. She quickly sucked it down. He touched her chest and said the words to the healing forge: *'Gwessla orga-na.'* Seconds later, she looked healthier and younger. Her hair turned from pink to blood red.

"Anyone else?" Leo yelled.

"Me!" A grey-haired woman on a higher floor yelled, with an Italian accent.

"Chi sei (who are you)?"

"Canidia."

"Don't free her, Leo!" Helga yelled.

"Why not?" he asked.

"More than most, she deserves to be in here. That Bronzesmith is quite infamous in the history books for kidnapping, murder, magical torture, and poisoning—bad as they come!"

"And what of us? What did we do to get in here?" Leo yelled.

"Yeh 'onestly don't remember all the 'orrible things yeh did?"

"Even so, how many of them are in here because the Dayfides just wanted to get rid of people like us? As long as she pledges loyalty, it doesn't matter who she is! Everyone deserves a second chance. Will you pledge?"

"Yes! Forger's honor!" the woman answered.

Leo climbed the ladder, freed her, gave her ahrion, and said the healing forge. Her hair turned black as ink.

"Me too!" A woman with greenish skin yelled.

Leo had heard stories of her. "Jenny Greenteeth, you loved drowning people for fun," Leo asked her to pledge loyalty, and she agreed to follow him. This scenario went on over and over: thieves and mass murderers all pledging their loyalty.

"Yuh releasing evil back into the world, Leo!" Helga yelled. "That one there is Rosina of Leckermaul! Yeh ever hear of Hansel and Gretel?!"

"Sometimes, in order to fight a man with a knife, you need a bigger, rustier knife," Leo said. He started handing out some of his rings to the higher leveled Forgers and felt even more empowered. He thought of what Maximilian had told him:

'What would happen if we could free the most dangerous Forgers in the world? Getting them to swear on their honor to follow me? Now that would be an army!'

Leo couldn't help but grin.

Mary could feel her powers returning, but it was too slow. At the level she was at now, she could probably light a candle or levitate a coin, things they tried to teach her when she first learned forging. But those abilities didn't have a chance of stopping a flying woman with a living scarf from throwing a horse and cart at her. The hay cart crashed to the ground, followed by the neighing horse. The animal landed on the cart contents and rolled to the ground. "That poor horse!" Mary said.

They were heading towards the Hudson River docks area. Mary knew at this time, there would be fewer civilians in this area than in the inner city. She also knew without being able to do a Vorago, escape was limited. Wayward's scarf made a swipe at Victoria and Fritz. He jumped into the air, and the scarf smashed a used clothing store window. He ducked and dodged another swipe, causing the scarf to break the window of a meat shop on the other side of the street, whose logo was a dog eating a sausage. This scenario gave Mary an idea. "Min, Fritz!" She yelled.

"What?" Min answered.

"She's definitely targeting Victoria and Fritz! I need you to hop onto Fritz, and when we reach the end of this block, I want you all to make a left! When you do, she'll follow you, and I'll be able to get behind her and attack her from the rear—maybe we can get her in a pincer attack!"

"Okay," Min said.

"Now then, hop on to Fritz!"

Min was about to jump but stopped and moved to Mary's seat back and did the best she could to give Mary a rear hug.

Mary reached her hand back. "I love you too! Go on then!" There was an air-piercing scream from behind them. Mary looked back and witnessed Wayward increase her attack in throwing things at them: Postal boxes, man-hole covers—anything not tied down was thrown and dodged by them. "She seems crossed at hugs!"

Min jumped backward onto Fritz, and they all galloped to the end of the block. When Mary arrived at the intersection, she looked back and yelled: "Now!"

Fritz, Min, and Victoria took a sharp left turn, and Mary went to the right. Unexpectedly, Wayward did not follow Min and the others.. It took Mary a second to realize what had happened. "She's targeting me, now?" Fritz came to a sliding halt, and he and the girls witnessed Mary and her crab chair running down the street, being chased by Wayward. They started to follow. "Maybe we can do the rear attack!" Min yelled.

"No!" Mary yelled. "Fritz! Go in the opposite direction! She's after me!"

"What about you?" Min yelled.

"Don't worry about me—vamoose! Find someplace to hide!"

"But—"

"Go! I'll catch up to you later!"

. They watched Mary and Wayward go out of sight.

"Let's get out of here before she comes back!" Victoria yelled.

"Where?"Min asked.

"I know a place! Just go!"

Fritz started running again. Min looked back. A feeling of deja vu and despair churned in her chest.

Thomas watched the elevator rise with the two dead, top-hatted men in it. 'This came from down below. That's where he's heading.' He dragged the bodies out and checked the men's identification. "A special Forger division of the government law enforcement. How long have they been in operation? As if I don't have enough to contend with in a world of smithing and beast-men, now I have my own government running some kind of shadow police force!"

Thomas got inside the car, and pulled the lever to take him down. On the next floor, he came across the open Clo Keffin vault with all of the Forger's teclyns, and in one of the drawers, he found a handful of forging coins. He took some and placed them in his pocket. There was a rattling sound coming from one of the other drawers. Thomas opened this one, and his ink pen immediately flew out of it into his hand. "Oh, that was unexpected!" He returned to the elevator and pressed the button to take him to floor -13.

On arrival, Thomas crept down the hallway, sticking close to the wall. He noticed Helga's and Elzbieta's teclyns bound to the side of the door by chains. 'Is this a bad thing or a good thing?' He let them be for now and carefully peered inside the vaulted prison. He could see Boss Murphy get pushed by Mausi into the middle of the room. Although Helga and Elzbieta were chained to the wall, dozens of other Forgers were roaming free. 'I don't see Mary. Where's Leo? This looks like a jailbreak—whatever it is, I shouldn't rush in. I don't want to endanger Helga, and I'm vastly outnumbered by what I assume are Forgers.'

Leo unlocked the last of those willing to pledge loyalty to him in exchange for freedom. He descended a ladder, stood on the dome in the middle of the chamber, and started counting his recruits. There were 39, varying in strength, from level four up to a couple at level nine, happily relishing in their liberation and the return of their powers. Leo lowered their chatter with a raise of his hand. Like newly trained wild dogs, they reluctantly complied and quieted down.

"Ladies, gentlemen...and others. I am your new chief, Leopold Bianca." Some in the crowd cheered. "Now, the first order of business: how do we get out of here?"

"Elevator!" Mausi said, pointing towards the hallway.

Thomas panicked, flattened himself against the wall, and hid further from the vault door entrance. He looked at the elevator and wondered if he could get inside it and escape before they could catch up to him; the thought of leaving Helga kept him stationary. "The elevator only holds five people—tops," Leo answered. "So we all can't escape all at once. Besides. The bodies I left in those have probably got the guards attention. The first group up is gonna get ambushed. If that happens, the elevator will be shut down and the rest will be stuck down here!"

"Then we destroy it! And we all fly up through the shaft!" Canidia countered.

"I'm sure it's been forged, like the bars and everything else in this place."

"If we can find some water, we can just use a Vorago, right?" asked a guy in the back.

"Do you see any water down here?" Leo answered.

"Then there's no other way out of here!" A woman yelled."

"I disagree...right? Boss Murphy?"

Boss Murphy crossed his arms.

Leo gestured at him. "I'm sure most of you are familiar with someone who actually runs New York. The head of Tammany Hall, I present to you: Charles Francis Murphy."

Everyone looked at Murphy.

"What is he going to do?" Cayman asked.

Leo stomped onto the dome. "He! Is going to tell us about the big bad under this prison and how to get to it!"

"Never." He mumbled.

"I'm sure you won't tell me now, but I bet any one of these Smiths knows a whole assortment of creative torture techniques to get it out of you."

"Why do we need that...thing under the floor?" Rosina asked.

Leo Jumped off the dome and walked up to Murphy. "What is it?" Murphy ignored him.

"11...12...13? Ah, your nose flared! That means I hit the nail on the head! That thing under us is a level 13!"

There were uproarious comments among the group. Some expressed disbelief.

"Yes, a level 13! How do we know this? Because only a level 13 could cast a forge on this entire building, strong enough to prevent us from leaving, and the fact that its forge is still going on for however many years this place has existed means they're still alive and on the premises.

"So, what do we do, kill it?" Mausi asked. "Are you daft? A level 13 will clean our clocks!."

"True...although we might stand a chance if we all attack at once or if I can get ahold of her sword!" Leo gestured to Elzbieta. "...How are you feeling, Iron Smith? Still alive?"

"O' right?" Helga asked Elzbieta. She didn't respond. "Chin up deary! Yeh can't let him beat yuh just yet. I know yeh can feel yuh teclyn like I do. It's close by, right?"

"If she dies, she'll just come back to life," Mausi said.

"What are you talking about?" Leo asked.

"She's a reincarnate."

There was gasping and murmuring in the crowd.

"Really? I thought those were religious myths!" Leo asked.

"Yeah, she claimed last time Professor White snuck up behind her and killed her when she was just a little girl." Mausi laughed.

"Can yeh imagine? Everyone talked about 'ow honorable he was." She laughed some more.

Leo looked stressed. "I...I can understand how he'd do anything to protect Mary's life....anyway, my plan—my dream is: if we don't have to fight that thing below and it's a prisoner like us, we free it like I did with you and get it to join us," Everyone mumbled in agreement. "Talk about bringing a bigger knife to a fight! We'll have one of the biggest in history! Am I right?" There was cheering from most.

Mary was one block away from the pier. Without being able to forge, she was going to be boxing herself in. The flying woman bore no evidence of tiring from throwing large objects at her or trying to slash her with the long red scarf. As the chair was the thing that was avoiding the onslaught, Mary had no other way to protect herself. 'What can I do?' I can only run away for so long. If she manages to damage this chair in any way, my options will be nonexistent. I hope the children are safe. No matter what I do, I can't let her get back to harming them.' She realized she was back in the area with the Olympic. 'Oh no, this is not where I wanted to end up! If I get near that ship again, I'm sure there are many armed men—then again..." At the end of the block, the chair made a right and ran along South Street, heading towards the Olympic. This area only gave Wayward different objects to throw at her; smashing large wooden crates, small boats, and barrels.

'I need to get close enough to the Olympic so they'll notice me!'

A crewman on the Olympic noticed the traveling racket approaching them. Kapitän! Mehr Hexen nähern sich! (Captain! More witches are approaching!) he yelled.

"Ich wusste, dass sie zurückkommen würden! (I knew they would come back!) Captain Schwieger yelled. "Laden Sie die Kanone, bereiten wir den Hexen ein echtes Willkommen! (Load the cannon, let's give the witches a true welcome!)" While others ran towards the railing with rifles, a couple of men uncovered the newly installed cannon and began loading it with a silver mortar.

Mary's chair jumped over a stack of barrels, which were immediately smashed by a downward slash from the scarf.

'She doesn't give up, does she?' Mary glanced back. 'She hasn't done any attacks except physical ones. Is she an Iron Smith? It would be a lot easier to hit me with a lightning bolt.' Her chair jumped in the air before Wayward's scarf grabbed two automobiles on either side of her and sandwiched them together. "Definitely into physical attacks!" Mary got closer to the Olympic. Dockworkers scrambled out of the way of her chair. It maneuvered around the vehicles and crates. Mary glanced again at the cannon on the deck, tracking their movements. 'If they don't fire and kill their own men, I assume they are waiting until we hit that open dock area up ahead.' Before Mary could arrive there, Wayward's scarf clipped two of her chair's crab legs. The wheelchair tumbled forwards and crashed into a dry-docked sailboat, knocking its stern off. Her chair's metallic claw blocked a downward slash. Mary knew significant damage had been done to the internal machine works by the sound of contact. 'This is it!' She panicked. Wayward landed on the ground and slowly walked towards her. Mary became assured this was a victory walk, like a predator playing with their fresh, terrified catch. Her chair picked up the boat parts and tossed them at Wayward. Mary didn't see what she used to block them because it moved so fast. This happened over and over as Wayward got closer, Mary throwing objects, only to be slashed away. Mary glanced at the men on the ship with the cannon. She didn't know much about cannons, but when the men hurriedly moved away from it, she knew it was ready. "Chair! We have to get out of here!" she said. There was no bell sound as an acknowledgment. The chair did its best to circle until Mary's back faced the sea. Mary was confused as they had moved away from a possible escape route to where the sea was their only option. As she had never used her chair in water, she was doubtful it even floated. "Chair! Wrong way! We have to go the other way!" The chair ignored her and continued to block Wayward's fast attacks, causing dents and dislodging pieces of itself to fly away. Mary heard someone on the ship yell something that sounded like the German word for 'fire'. "Chair! We have to go!" She turned her attention back to Wayward. She had converted her scarf into a red sword to destroy parts of her chair. The blade extended with every slash. "Chair! We need to go! Now!" There was no bell sound; the chair hunched down like it was giving up. Wayward raised her red sword in the air. Mary saw a cannon flash from the boat. "Chair!" Her chair leaped forwards at Wayward with what seemed like using all of its reserved energy, wrapped every appendage around Wayward, and restrained her arms and legs. "No!" Mary yelled.

She was flying backward through the air after an enormous flash, followed by the boom of the cannon. She was still seated in her chair, but only in the red velvet cushions, carrying her backward through the air towards the Hudson River. She felt the sensation of heat and debris from the dock, just before the back of the cushions hit the water. She prepared herself for the worst. She knew in her weakened state, she couldn't tread water very long and especially not swim to shore; she was going to drown. Water sloshed briefly on her back, but her front remained dry. With understandable confusion, she grasped her inflated seat cushion. Flaming pieces of the dock and what she assumed were chair parts fell all around. Flakes of burning ash snowed down on her, stinging her face. Wooden objects were the last to hit the water. All became quiet.

She looked up at the smoldering dock and sparkles of floating embers. Sounds of cheering came from the boat; the Germans were happy with their success. She was alive, but what about Wayward? She waited for signs of movement from the dock. There was no follow-up shelling from the Germans. She assumed nothing had survived their first attack. Moving her arms like oars, sheЯed LevelЯed Levelbackpedaled towards a ladder on an undamaged part of the dock. It took a lot of effort, but rung after rung, she pulled herself up the ladder until she returned to the street level. She lay prone on the dock, breathed, and suppressed her exhaustion. 'I still have a lot of work! What am I gonna do now, without my chair? I can't fight anyone; I'm sorry, Thomas and Helga, but there won't be any Germans to trick into destroying the entrance to a prison.' She felt along her lower back. 'Why didn't Min's key work? Is my apparatus broken? Whenever something goes right, something immediately goes wrong—is this what it's like to be normal? It's like I'm fighting myself! And I'm my worst enemy! So, what can I do? Lay here and wait for the Germans to come over here? To make sure I'm dead? Crawl to the prison and accomplish absolutely nothing—throw myself into the water? Death? Wouldn't that be easier? Why does this feeling of despair keep happening?' She buried her face in her hands and felt like crying. Amongst the sounds of a blowing breeze and a small crackling fire, she heard a quiet metallic whirl and an occasional clicking. The noise got closer and closer to her. Something nudged her on the elbow. She raised her head from her hands. Next to her was a golden metal box with spinning sprockets and gears. She deduced it was the last remaining part of her chair. She grabbed it to get a closer look. It continued to work, producing the whirling and clicking sounds. She rotated it and discovered the key she had inserted many years ago to bring the chair to life.

She rubbed her fingers over the box, then delicately pulled the key out. It was the same type used to tighten her buttons and open the Clo Keffin vault at the old manor. The motor gradually came to a halt. The heart of her machine stopped working. Mary felt she had lost one of her friends. "Thank you. Thank you for taking care of me all these years. I hope by your actions, you are allowed to obtain a soul." Mary put the key in her dress pocket. "So many with so little have given so much. I can't stop…I won't stop! As Min's mother said, they can bring me death, but I can bring them death and hell!" There was a loud pinging sound from her back,

"Oh!" Mary sighed heavily. Her feet, calves, thighs, and pelvis tingled as blood flooded into these areas. She wiggled her toes. "This ..." she got onto her hands and knees and pushed herself up until she stood. She inhaled a long breath of stale, smoky air and coughed it out. "Oh my, not the freshest of air." She glimpsed at the crew on the Olympic and hoped no one noticed her. Splashing sounds were coming from the river. "Now, what?"

With labored movements, she limped over to the edge of the dock to investigate, "It has been a long time since I've walked."

In the water, Miss Wayward struggled to stay afloat. Her arms were flailing about, and her head kept going under.

"Is she...drowning?" Mary continued to watch the struggling woman. " I guess Min was right. Why bother learning to swim if you can run on water? This will at least take care of one problem..." Wayward went under, came up a few moments later, and went down even longer.

Mary sighed. "I am quite daft, aren't I?" She rolled her eyes and then dived off the pier into the water.

"So, how do we get to that level 13?" Leo asked Boss Murphy.

"The entrance is over there." He gestured to a floor grate on the opposite side of the room.

"He's fibbing!" Carmun said. " I've seen them throw dead bodies down there!"

"Oh yeah?" Leo walked over to the grate and examined it. "Hmm. There do seem to be some steps leading down. He lifted the grate. "Shall we all go down here? He looked at Murphy. "Or... you really are bad at poker, and the speed you squealed was a little too fast—forget it!" Leo placed his hand on Murphy's head. *'Oo-aid vell ur woove...!'* Leo stopped midway through the Mind-bending forge and laughed. "Just as I thought, that nervous look on your face means your mind isn't protected! Don't worry, I don't need to bend your mind to tell what you're thinking, I know this is probably a trap."

"It could also be an exit out of here," Murphy said.

"How so?"

"Bodies are taken down there to dispose of them. It also connects to a mile-long tunnel that leads all the way to the Brooklyn Bridge.

"Why would that be there?"

"It was built back in the 1870s by Anthony Oechs, to be used as wine cellars. Now they just use it to dump bodies."

Leo got close to Murphy's face. "Hmm, that time you were telling the truth. But that doesn't tell me where that Level 13 is."

"That's because he doesn't want you to release it, you wanker!" Helga said.

"He'll tell me, or he'll die," Leo answered.

"If you're so good at reading people—and yuh not, yeh'd know 'ed rather die or let you lot go free than tell you how to get to that Level 13. Torturing 'im won't make "im spill the beans. Yeh should just take the exit and bugger off!"

Leo thought about it. "Okay, it's true. It could be a way out of here, or it could be a trap. Tell you what, anyone wants to volunteer checking it out?" No one said anything.

"Ha! Such loyalty!" Helga said, laughingly.

"Shut up!" Leo looked at all of his Forgers. "Nobody? I thought you were the toughest of the worst down here. Are you all afraid?"

"I'll go," Mausi said.

"What?"

"Yeah. I'll give it a go. If it turns out to be the exit, then as soon as I leave this place, I won't be under contract whiff you, and I'll be free, I will!"

"I'll go too!" A woman said.

"Me too," another said.

"And me!" A man chimed in"

"You're not afraid?" Leo asked him.

"It's like she said, if we make it out of here, and you get captured or killed, we won't be under contract with you anymore! We'll be free!"

There was some rumbling from the crowd. More and more people volunteered to leave.

Leo raised his hands to quiet them down. "I'm so touched. You're all so willing to serve me." He heard Helga chuckle. "But we can't have everyone leaving! Tell you what, anyone else below a level five can go! You're all useless anyway!"

13 Forgers volunteered, walked down the steps, and headed into the unknown.

Watching from the hallway, Thomas did a headcount of the remaining adversaries. 'Still around 25 or 26 people who would kill me in an instance if I make myself known.' He studied the teclyns on the wall. 'That's Elzbieta's sword in disguise, I remember that from the dock fight she lost, and I'm pretty sure that's Helgas teclyn. Did they subdue them and take away their weapons?' I saw what happens when that sword is touched, but I wonder if I could somehow use Helga's teclyn.'

Leo returned to Elzbieta's side. "You're still alive? Jeepers! You are one tough dame. Last chance to pledge loyalty." He grabbed the handle of the knife and pushed it in. Elzbieta groaned and breathed hard.

"Leo, stop!" Helga yelled.

"Why don't you just kill her?" Someone said

"I think the chances of her pledging to me are not zero. If she's a reincarnate, she knows if she doesn't complete whatever keeps bringing her back, she'll have to do it all over again. This may be her last chance to break the curse! Right? Ironsmith?"

Elzbieta ignored him.

Leo looked towards the escape route. "I guess if they come back, and it really is an exit, we won't need to fight the big bad under the dome. That will make you and your sword useless.

Except…She was probably lying. How would a sword make someone fall in love with you?" Leo turned his attention to the dome. He felt around it and tapped it.

"What are you doing?" Murphy asked.

"Seeing if this is a secret entrance to Level 13. Maybe it's hollow inside."

"I could tell," Carmun said.

"What?"

"I can use sound to see what's behind walls, like how bats see where they're going in the dark."

Can you do that for this entire room?"

"Aye, lad, but I warn yuh, it might hurt yuh ears.

"It's okay."

Carmun took a deep breath and then sang a high E6 music note. The sound filled the entire chamber.

At first, the sound was annoying. The vibrations continued to flutter in everyone's eardrums and became irritating and a little painful. The unchained ones covered their ears, and Helga and Elzbieta winced.

When Carmun had finished, she studied the mummified body on the opposite side of the room Leo had seen earlier.

"No wonder you were gagged," Leo said.

Carmun pointed to the body.

What? Leo asked

"This floor is all solid. Not even sound can penetrate it. But that area over there; there's a hollow space behind that body."

Leo walked over to examine it. On its bottom left was a doorknob shaped like a small skull. He glanced back at Murphy, whose face had a slight look of panic. "I see, it's a door. How do we get in there?"

"Just open it!" said the guy with an eye patch. He walked over and grabbed the knob.

"Wait, no!" Leo yelled.

Within a second, the man froze and fell onto the ground. Leo looked down at him. "Are you okay?" There was no answer. Leo bent down on his haunches and checked the man's pulse. "He's… he's dead!" A collective gasp filled the room.

"Cursed!" Someone said.

"Level 13 or not, what kind of forge can instantly kill you?"

"That's why 'e doesn't want you to release that thing," Helga said. "Only one kind of Forger can cast a curse like that!"

"A Blacksmith," Leo said.

With the gauze only covering her eyes, Miss Wayward's mouth was free to cough up water.

Mary was about to pat her on the back but stopped. "You know," she said, "I've always wondered why you would hit someone on the back when they are choking. It's obvious they are still breathing, am I right?"

Wayward was too weak to sit upright. She looked to her side and saw her scarf had been blown to pieces, rendering it useless. Even with her eyes covered, she still conveyed a look of scorn. "You…you saved me," she said with a raspy voice.

"Yes, I suppose I did."

"Why?"

"Because you were drowning."

"But…I wouldn't have saved you."

"Well. It's a good thing our situations weren't reversed."

"Why would you save an enemy?"

Mary thought for a moment. "I like to believe everyone is your friend until you know otherwise. Although you are quite formidable, I don't consider you an enemy…You're more of an… obstacle."

"You think I owe you my life now? Don't you?"

"Not necessarily. If you give someone a gift, it's their choice if they want to accept it." Miss Wayward turned her head away. "But, if you want to do me a favor, you could explain who you're working for." There was no response. "Alright then, how about your name?"

"I'm Miss Wayward."

"Wayward? Hold on, of the Wayward sisters?"

Miss Wayward nodded yes.

"Extraordinary! Are you sure?"

"Pardon?"

"Oh! I'm just surprised by your accent and your lovely skin...I thought the Wayward sisters would be more... Scottish. Rather, that's how Shakespeare portrayed you...that and haggard—sorry. Alright, then." Mary stood up and walked to the ladder that led down to the water.

"Wait! I still don't understand. Why would you rescue someone trying to kill you?"

Mary took a breath. "Hmm. I'm not sure. It was a spur-of-the-moment thing—I've been very impulsive lately, mostly towards the negative. It felt good to go in the other direction. I guess you could say it has to do with seeing that adorable little Asian girl again, the one you were trying to kill."

"I wasn't trying to kill her!"

"Really? Be that as it may. Her upbringing was entirely based on the premise of killing people who look like me. Lo and behold. There she was, risking everything to protect me and the others; I love my little Butterfly."

"Do you think you're her mother?"

"Oh, heavens no! She has a mother. Until we find out if she's alive...or not, I would never stand in the way of that relationship. For now, I'm happy to be the eccentric aunt..." Mary pulled her hair back, bent down, picked up a piece of Miss Wayward's old scarf, and used it to tie her hair into a bun. "...But remember, if you ever come after her again...without hesitation...I will kill and die for her. Now, if you'd excuse me, pip-pip, cheerio." Mary started to climb down the ladder. She stopped when she heard celebratory noises coming from the Olympic. "If you do feel compelled to pay me back, you can always do something about those vexing Germans over there that blew us up! Just a suggestion.

Mary climbed downwards to the water, put her hand into it, and started swirling it clockwise. *"Cray giât deem kurk fan!"* The area around her fingertips glowed. She took her hand out of the water, and it spiraled into a whirlpool. The surface of the spiral got wider until it was shoulder-width. Mary took a couple of deep breaths and jumped from the ladder into the center. The Vorago rapidly sucked her down, and within seconds she had disappeared.

Mausi and the other 12 Forgers treaded through a dark, echoing tunnel that led to the wine caves and the Brooklyn Bridge. Thanks to the Headvan Tân forge, small firefly lights circled and illuminated their path.

"Do you think it's a trap?" a woman asked.

"Sure is dark." another stated.

"Shut it!" Mausi said. If it's sound-activated, you lot would have killed us all!"

They continued, serenaded by the sound of dripping water in front of them. Mausi stopped and looked around. She looked puzzled"

"What are you looking for?" a man asked.

"They said this tunnel was used for dumping bodies, right?"

"Yes."

"Then, where are the bodies?"

Everyone looked around.

"No bodies, no skeletons? Shouldn't there be evidence of some kind?" As they continued, no matter how hard they searched, there were no signs of corpses.

With caution, they advanced further down the tunnel. Mausi stopped when she stepped on something crunchy. She bent down and examined the object.

"What is that?" Someone asked.

"Studying it closer, it was completely void of its flesh. "It's a skeleton," Mausi answered.

"What type?"

"Rat."

Everyone continued down the hall but Mausi studied the rat skeleton more.

"Come on, let's go! Never seen a rat before?" Someone yelled.

Mausi felt there was something off about the skeleton, something emanating from it. Afraid of being left behind, she got up and hurried after the others. The rat skeleton twitched.

They entered a newer, more developed part of the tunnel.

"This must be the wine cellars they were talking about," someone said.

"Hey look!" an old Forger yelled, pointing down the tunnel.

About 50 yards away, they could see blue light slipping in at the end of the tunnel.

"It's the exit!" someone yelled. Everyone started to jog and run towards the light. Mausi, not being as fast of a runner, lagged behind and tried to keep up.

Even though they were getting closer to the exit, the blue light seemed to get smaller and smaller, like an aperture closing. Eventually, they got within a few inches of the exit and realized something was covering it; something huge preventing them from advancing any further.

"What's that blocking the end of the tunnel?" Someone asked.

"What is that?" One of the men said. He took the lead. One of the floating firefly lights flew over to assist. It was not a solid white object but made up of multiples. He put his face even closer to it to focus his vision.

"Well! What is it?" Mausi asked.

"It looks like..." He put his face within a few inches of the white wall. "...More rat skeletons."

"Do what?"

The spot the man was looking at showed two tiny blue lights. They multiplied and spread outwards, eventually covering the wall.

"What is that?" a woman yelled.

"Eyes! Millions of them!"

The glowing blue eyes spread out from the barrier and covered the walls all around them."

"They're everywhere!"

Mausi was the first to back away. The rest of the group followed suit and immediately began to reverse course.

"Ow!" Someone yelled.

"What?"

"One of them bit me!"

"Let's get—"

Like a wave of annihilation, thousands of rat skeletons with glowing blue eyes crashed onto the man's body. Within an instant, they bit, chewed, and ripped at his flesh. His screams became a horrible battle cry for the other rats in the chamber to take action as well. They flowed into the small space like macabre water, squeezing out of any crack or crevice.

Another man got consumed before he could even scream. A woman pointed her ringed finger at the horde and yelled: *"Roy are don!"* Flames emitted from her hand and covered the approaching mischief.. The skeletons ignited, giving the woman a moment of hope. She realized even on fire, they didn't stop advancing. Tiny flaming rat skeletons swarmed around her, their charred bones crackling as they lunged with jagged teeth and sharp claws. She was ensnared in a nightmarish frenzy, a victim not only of their relentless assault but also of the searing flames that flickered around them, turning the air into a hellish inferno.

The number of rats dropping from the ceiling and exploding out a side wall increased. The Forgers cast fire, wind, and lightning. Some forges exploded a large portion of the horde. One of the Smiths discovered a wind forge was useless, as it only delayed the rats for a moment before they dragged him to the ground screaming. Lightning was far more effective, blasting hundreds of the creatures into bits, but there were always a thousand replacements from all directions. Surrendering eventually to inevitable defeat, The Forgers died, shooting multiple bolts in a random pattern of chaos.

Mausi was far ahead of the others. Two were running close behind her, but it was only a matter of time before they fell to the ground. That will signal the last five seconds of Mausi's life. She only had one weapon that she could use, it didn't matter if it would doom the others to a horrible fate—she was going to survive. She took one of the foraging coins Leo had given her and said: *"Gwen fwadenlarge!"* The coin enlarged and formed into one of her small, round bombs. Its fuse lit instantly, and she tossed it behind her. It exploded, killing one of the Forgers before the rats would have killed them. The explosion shockwave collapsed the ceiling. Bricks and beams fell and sealed off the tunnel behind Mausi. She continued running, even though nothing was chasing her. She was concerned only with getting away from the sounds of screaming behind the wall she had created.

Abel was already on edge. After everything he had to deal with, a bunch of mud-covered ghosts was the last thing he thought would manifest in their world. He moved an old globe to the corner of the room, nested the crystal ball on its stand, and set it on the mapping table. he spent a fair amount of time rubbing, thumping, and flicking his fingers at it, but it remained in its decorative state. 'Why did they give this to me? Is it going to do anything?' He paced back and forth. 'It needs something to activate it, I assume, or someone. Forgers could probably do it. In which case, they gave it to the wrong person.'

The sound of bubbling water was coming from downstairs. Abel grabbed his spyglass teclyn and tiptoed down to the hull level. The bubbling got louder. 'Is there a leak in the bathroom?' The noise stopped by the time Abel reached the white-tiled room. He had forgotten Helga had him fill up the tub so they could return. "Finally!" He stood next to the tub and watched the water spiral. eager to ask why it took them so long. A hand reached out of the water. He waited to grab it and pull it out: 'This might not be a friend!' The hand grasped the side of the tub. Mary pulled her top half out of the water.

"Mary?" Abel reached inside and helped her lift the rest of her body out of the tub. As soon as she was out of the water, it settled, and the tub returned to normal.

Mary plopped onto the floor and caught her breath.

"Are you alright?" he asked.

"Oh, Abel?" What are you doing in London?

"This isn't London, it's the Virginia."

"The Virginia? Why did I end up here? I was aiming for the manor in London."

"Well, at least you made it halfway across the Atlantic."

Abel helped her stand. They embraced, and she she kissed his cheek.

"What took you so long?" He asked.

"Sorry. So much—too much has happened!" She took the ends of her dress and wrung some water into the tub. "Oh, Nuts!"

"What?"

"River water!"

"Pardon?"

"I jumped in the Hudson River."

"Ah, I see. Helga mentioned something about that."

"Oh well, still glad to see you." When she once again wrung out her dress, she found the key in her pocket. "Oh, right…" She fast-walked to the bridge.

"Where is everyone else?" Abel asked as he hurried behind her. "Did you rescue Min?"

"Yes and no. She's free. The rest are in Tombs prison."

"Prison?!"

"Yes, unfortunately. The Americans want me to hand the book over to them as a trade, which we can't do even if we wanted to. I was actually on my way to London. In the hope of getting aid from Aunt Gwenhwyvar—could use her muscle to break them out, or at least give me the key to this safe, unless…" Mary moved the painting that covered the clo keffin and inserted the key into the hole; nothing happened. "Curses! This key doesn't work either!"

"Is that from Aunt Gwenhwyvar?"

"No, it was for my old wheelchair."

"Well, of course, it's not going to work. He didn't make that safe."

"I know. It was still worth a go. I guess it's back to plan A."

"You're going to do a prison break? Is that wise? We'll all be hunted fugitives!"

"Far too late for that—let me change out of these wet things, and I'll regale you with all the particulars."

"Hurry back, I have something to show you."

Mary entered the ship's salon wearing a black swimming suit resembling a medium-length sailor dress with a wide collar embroidered with an anchor. She sat on a stool, dried her hair with a towel, and occupied her time, trying to attach the key to a necklace she had found in her berth.

Abel bought out a tray of tea and some molasses cookies. "Why are you wearing your old bathing suit?"

"Well, I figure I'm going to go back in the Vorago again and again, so I might as well wear something that can get wet."

"Good point."

"Anyway, as I was saying, everyone's in prison, I'm going to break them out—hopefully with your help, or else they will all be executed at noon."

"Of course, I'll help. What about Min? Can she help?"

"Yes, she was quite helpful when Fritz and Victoria—oh! Thomas' niece Victoria is a Blacksmith! The kids are together and hopefully hiding from one of the Wayward sisters—"

"Wait! Stop! A Blacksmith?!"

"Yes, I know! They're like a handful of those in the world, correct?"

"Four usually. And the Wayward sisters? From the Shakespeare story?!"

"Yes, Just one, not as old as you would think…nor Scottish, but she was blind…I think."

Abel stood up and walked over to the crystal ball. "Perhaps she's looking for this…A group of mud monsters delivered this to me recently."

Mary stood up to get a better look at it. "Is that, is that a real crystal ball?" She rubbed her hands over it. "Fascinating! Where did this come from?"

"I told you, mud creatures crawled out of the ocean and placed it on the deck.

"I thought mud creatures was a weird metaphor?"

"No. I think I have now officially seen everything. Helga said our adversaries had this, and that's how they've been spying on us."

"Were the mud creatures anghenfels with sharp teeth and the sort?"

"Not really, more like forms covered in sea mud."

"Invisible?"

"Perhaps."

"Could they touch you?"

"Yes…probably."

"Those were ghosts. And they gave you one of the Eyes for some reason."

"A good reason…no one can spy on us anymore."

Mary started pacing.

"Mary?"

"Miss Wayward was trying to kill Victoria because she's a Blacksmith."

"Understandable, they're not very popular. Father used them as a bogeyman to get us to behave."

"They deal with the dead, right?"

"Manipulation of ghosts, spirits, corpses, illusions, dreams, and —"

"Dreams!" Mary looked scared.

"Pardon?"

"My dreams—all of those visions I had inside the Vorago—a manipulation! Victoria said someone else was using ghost manipulation instead of her. Assuming she's not that strong, only one other person can do that, a higher-level Blacksmith!"

"So…they're helping us?"

"Of course! Those mud monsters were probably covered ghosts doing their bidding!"

"But why would a Blacksmith help us? I've never heard of the Grim Reaper helping anyone."

"Unsure, but they're definitely on our side. They helped me and the kids escape, gave you that eye to keep it out of the hands of our adversaries, withheld my status as a Forger from everyone, and gave me visions of Elzbieta's history with my father before she even attacked us!"

"A warning?"

"Exactly! And…"

"And?"

"I was freed from captivity and wound up next to the body of the dead Belgian,"

"The Belgian?! The Belgian is dead?"

"Yes, apparently stabbed to death.

"My, how much did you go through?"

"Quite a lot. But it makes me wonder if the Blacksmith can use corpses…" Mary shivered. "Never mind that. But the Blacksmith does seem to be helping us."

"It's a little unsettling having death on our side."

"I'll take all the help I can get."

"How are you getting in and out of the prison?"

"Getting in will be easy. Vorago."

"How so? Will that work?"

"When I left the prison, I asked the Warden if I was invited back inside, and he said yes."

"So."

"The Warden sometimes stays at the prison; he had a bed."

"Pardon?" Abel raised an eyebrow.

"I saw it on the way out, you goof! Do you understand? An invite into his residence? A Vorago only works if you are…"

"Invited into a residence; cunning!"

"Thank you. Getting out, on the other hand…"

Leo could order the others to use the master key to open the cursed door. Commanders in wartime; often used their loyal soldiers to further the mission. But, getting one of them to sacrifice their life would look like cowardice. They would all lose faith in his leadership abilities. "I sent those others on a suicide mission," he said quietly, thinking about Mausi and the group. Perhaps this would be his punishment. If he is to be their leader, he will live. If not, instant death. Without procrastinating, he jammed the key into a hole under the skull-shaped door knob and turned it. He exhaled and took a breath, and then another and another. Fate had chosen him to be their leader.

The door creakily opened by itself. Another set of steps came into view, curving downwards. Leo cautiously poked his head in the doorway. No traps were activated.

"Ok. it's clear," he said. A mumbling of agreement emanated from his crew. "How come none of you noticed Murphy and others going in and out of this door?"

"Quarda qua! (look, here)", Canidia answered," drawing Leo's attention to the side of the door where a person chained to the wall would have observed the entrance. "Un illusione!(an illusion!)"

Leo walked over to the spot. The door still looked closed. Only by looking at it head-on could he see it opened. "Level 13s are a real corker! Okay crew, let us head out!" Everyone started to follow Leo down the steps. He stopped. "Wait a minute, I think I'll leave a couple of you back here to prevent someone from attacking us from the rear. Leo pointed to two remaining lowest-level Forgers, "You two. We'll come back for you if that level 13 is copasetic. Kill anyone that gets off that elevator." Leo realized Boss Murphy was holding back. "What do you think you're doing? Grab him and put him in front." Murphy struggled a little as they moved him forward. He stood agitated in front of Leo. "Don't want you to miss the party, right Boss?" Leo pushed him forward. He stumbled a little and started walking down a long flight of steps. Everyone else filed in behind them and headed down the stairway.

'This is an improvement,' Thomas thought, watching the scene. 'I stand a much better chance against two than 24.'

One of the remaining Forgers looked at the other. "You know," She said. "That elevator can hold us. We could easily take it and be out of here?"

"That's true…I'm sure they'd never see us coming. Soon as we kill anyone coming down, our order will be complete and we could escape!"

Thomas panicked at the thought of them coming into the hallway.

"I'm sure it's not a normal jail cell for Forgers and Strykers," Abel said. "Helga can easily bend bars with her bare hands when she's cross."

"On my way out, I saw a special wing of the prison, with bars made of hi-yaguh and an elevator that went 13 floors underground."

Abel sighed. "13 floors? That's a lot of potential unknowns to contend with."

"I know." Mary put her hand on his. "But I have faith in us."

"Your faith in me may be misguided. I'm not so sure how much help I'll be. Elzbieta said if I fight any powerful Forgers, they'll mop the floor with me."

"I wouldn't listen to that ruffian, I saw another Forger mop the floor with her! I'm sure she's in that prison as well."

"That's even worse! When someone who can beat you gets beaten by someone else! I have no chance of defeating that!"

Mary sighed. "Abel, my dear brother. You shouldn't listen to the wrong people, they're not on your side!"

"She had a point: the Belgian grabbed me and bent my mind, Leo and Shirley took advantage of my naiveté, that anghenfël who threw a ship's anchor at me and broke my ribs—if it wasn't for Helga, it would have killed me—Even Africa, I wasn't able to save myself from being abducted or my father from being killed, or the men in the cage at the circus..." He felt like crying. He tightly closed his eyes, took a deep breath, and stopped the tears.

Mary pulled him to her chest and held him tight. "There, there. It is a lot to endure."

"You seem to be handling it, though."

Mary snorted a laugh. "I'm really am good at putting on appearances, aren't I?" She held the key on the chain up. "I think the reason why—Do you remember eight years ago when I played Olga in Tchaikovsky's Eugene Onegin at Carnegie Hall?"

"Yes, you were brilliant."

"Thank you. But, what you did not see, was me being a nervous Nelly at home."

"You?"

"Yes, and this was when I was still the super optimistic, confident version of myself. I felt like I was going to pass out! I've never performed in front of so many people before, and this was that opera's American debut!"

"But you still performed well."

Mary put the necklace around her neck. "Yes, thanks to something Father said to me. On the carriage ride over, he said: 'I know you're nervous, but remember, no one goes to a show to see performers fail. We all want to see the best show ever and are rooting for everyone on stage; we're on their side, and that's why, at the end of their performance, as a sign of gratitude they accept their support by taking a bow.'"

"I'm not sure I understand."

Mary poked his chest with her key. "Everyone is rooting for us, and I think it would be disrespectful not to do the absolute best we can. If we fail, we fail. But if this works, we will take a well-deserved bow. So, do the best you can, Abel, for them. For me. And yourself! And stop acting like you're not a skilled performer! Remember, If you don't have faith in yourself, you can borrow my faith in you! I have plenty to spare!"

Abel smiled and nodded.

"And besides…" Mary started to rub the crystal ball. "We also have the help of a high-level Blacksmith! Double, double toil and trouble; fire burn and cauldron bubble…." The crystal ball started to glow. "Oh! Oh my!"

"What did you do?"

"I was just mucking about! I had no idea that was a real thing!"

The sphere glowed and then was filled with gray swirling smoke, settling into a blueish-gray color.

"What should I do?"

"You're asking me?" Abel said

"Aunt Gwenhwyvar told me crystal balls use a type of extrusion forging, meaning it's a Goldsmith technique. But I'm not a Goldsmith!"

"I beg to differ."

"Pardon?"

"Your back contains ahrion, cop, and eyve. You should be able to master all."

"I'm afraid so far, all my skills are being force-fed to me, probably from our Blacksmith friend. I'm drawing a blank on how to utilize ancient artifacts."

"I've seen illustrations where soothsayers rub their hands over it while issuing commands. Should you try that?"

"Worth a go." Mary began to rub her hands around the crystal. The smoke inside moved around and glowed intermittently. "It's reacting! Now what?"

"Well, they used it to spy on us. Let's try that!"

"Okay, show me...show me...President Wilson!" A blurry image hazily came into focus inside the ball. It eventually showed President Wilson sitting on a toilet. "Good heavens! Show me something else!" The image went back to grey smoke. "Let us never do that again!"

"Agreed. Let's focus more on our friends."

"Show me, Thomas." Nothing changed inside the sphere. "It didn't work."

"Full name? Perhaps? There must be a million people named Thomas."

"Show Me Detective Thomas Alexander Vanderbilt." The image of Thomas faded in. He was in the hallway of the -13th floor, spying on the activities inside the vault.

"He's free! But...Where is he, and what is he looking at?"

Abel looked closer at the sphere. "I think he's trying to listen in on something. Does this thing have sound as well?"

"It appears not—look! In the other room, is that a type of dungeon? Is that Helga chained to the wall?" Mary rubbed the sphere. "Show Helga of the House of Pendle." Helga dissolved into view. "It's Helga and Elzbieta! That must be a special wing of the prison!"

"It looks like the two women in front of them are some kind of guards."

"Is Thomas outside trying to free Helga?"

"It appears that way. We should find a way to get to him as soon as possible, I'm sure he would appreciate the help."

Mary thought for a moment. "Not yet. I don't think he's foolish enough to barge in there without a plan. I trust in his abilities as I do in yours. Before we execute our plan, I want to be as fortified as possible. Perhaps getting help from Gwenhwyvar and Min. "Show Me Gwenhwyvar of the house of White." Aunt Gwenhwyvar's image was projected inside the sphere, seated at a table, and appeared to be writing a note. "Look! There she is! But where is she?"

"I recognize that painting behind her! She's in the kitchen of the London house!"

"Thank goodness! She's safe!"

"You should Vorago there, right now!"

"In a moment. Show me Quing Min, daughter of Azure Cloud..."

Min watched Fritz exit the alleyway, buttoning his shirt.

"It must be annoying taking off your clothes every time you want to turn into a dog," she said. Fritz ignored her comment. "You should get someone to make you magical clothes that don't rip," she added.

"Where are we?" He asked Victoria, as she lead their group down the street.

"My neighborhood," she answered.

"Why?"

"I'm going home!" Victoria said curtly.

Min stopped walking. "Wait, you can't go home!"

"Why not?"

"If that woman comes after you, she'll kill your family!"

"She won't!"

"Why wouldn't she?"

"Because my mom won't let her!" Victoria walked faster.

Min grabbed Fritz's arm and stopped him. "Tā fēngle! (She's crazy!) We can't let her lead that woman to her home!"

"Who cares, it's not my family." He shook off Min's arm.

"What's wrong with you? She helped us! Don't you want to pay her back?"

"I don't need her help!"

"That's not true! That woman was going to clobber you if we hadn't helped!"

"I don't need anyone's help! I can rescue Elzbieta, on my own!"

"You're a fool! The only way we'll rescue anybody is by working together!"

"Where you there to save Elzbieta?"

"What?"

"Did you come to the prison to help me save Elzbieta?"

"No, I heard Shirley talking about how my mom is in there."

"You came to save her?"

"Yes."

"And I came to save Elzbieta; not your mom, not that girl, not the Black Blood or anyone else in your household—Elzbieta only!"

"Still, we can't let that woman kill innocent people!"

"My original reason for coming to this city was to kill Mary White so Elzbieta would stop dying, over and over again, and we could live a normal life! Anyone standing in my way is a stepping stone! That includes you and that girl's family!"

The speed at which Min punched him surprised even herself. He flew into metal garbage cans and lay on his back in a pile of rubbish.

"You are without honor!" Min started to walk away but stopped. "I should have let that woman kill you!" She stomped away to catch up to Victoria.

"Why do you think Min hit him?" Mary asked.

"Puzzling. Obviously something she's passionate about."

"Quite."

"Where are they?"

"I recognize that neighborhood! That's where Thomas' sister Thelma lives. I've been there for dinner a couple of times."

"That accounts for everyone."

"Yes, this is good! With the exception of Helga, who I hope gets aid from Thomas, it will be harder for the government to execute them if I don't meet their noon deadline."

"I don't think you should use this as an excuse to be complacent."

"Of course not, but it does give me enough of a window to visit Gwenhwyvar and bring her back."

"Well then, shall we get started?"

Shirley's luxury auto parked under the Bridge of Sighs, between Tombs prison and the Criminal Courts Building. A chauffeur opened the door for her. She noticed a bit of activity across the street, now accentuated by police automobiles: a sheet covered body being carried from the side entrance, and what appeared to be a horse carcass on a flatbed truck.

Shirley walked closer and tried to do a quick examination of the scene. A policeman blocked her.

"Excuse me?" she asked him. "What happened?"

"There was some kind of a brouhaha on the roof, bodies everywhere."

"Were there any women or children injured?"

"No ma'am, just men."

"Thank goodness for that." Shirley turned around and walked back to the prison. "Where did they all go?" she mumbled.

She approached the receptionist desk and asked for the associate warden. He was retrieved from an office off to the side. "Miss Blanche, you're back again…and at this early hour," he quipped.

"Oui, I was wondering if you had seen Boss Murphy come in here for a visit?"

Yes, ma'am. Came in about an hour ago," he answered.

"Hmm. Do you mind having someone escort me to him?"

"Sorry, but you're not allowed in the area he went to. Besides, prisons aren't a place for a lady."

Shirley took her spiral necklace from around her neck. She began playing with it, reflecting the light into the eyes of the associate warden. He became interested in the jewelry and then fascinated by it. "Are you sure? I think you may want to make an exception for me.

"Sure…sure thing, ma'am. I'll see if one of the G men is available."

Shirley put her necklace away and patted it.

The man made a phone call to the operator. After a long wait to be connected, he gave up and hung up. "That's queer?"

"Is there a problem?" Shirley asked.

"None of the guys answered; maybe they're busy."

"Could something have happened?"

"Naw," he laughed. "Nothing ever happens down there. Tell ya what. I'll take you down."

He guided Shirley inside the prison and towards the elevator. She felt nervous and unassured.

Inside the caged elevator, they watched red-painted numbers on the doors show which levels they were passing.

Shirley watched the number for sub-level five rise up and away "I don't think I've ever been down this far. Is this where they keep the Forgers?"

"Yes, madam. In the old days, every floor underground had cages full of them, but one by one, they all disappeared. Now there's only the ones on negative floor 13."

"Is that why security is so light on the upper floors."

"Yes ma'am, no one left to guard, and on the bottom floor, there's no escape."

The elevator landed on the -13th floor. A shocked Thomas turned around to see who had arrived. Inside the vault, the two Forgers Leo had left in charge were also alerted to Shirley's arrival.

"Hey!" yelled the guard. What are you doing down here?" He fiddled around, trying to find his pistol as though it was the first time he'd ever had to use it. One of the Forgers yelled: *"Pigan larul!"* On the floor, upward concrete spikes spread forwards in a wave, getting bigger and bigger until they reached the same height as the guard. He took out his gun but it was thrown into the hallway by an upward spike. His punctured vocal cords prevented him from screaming as he was impaled in place. Thomas looked back at Shirley. He didn't understand why he was concerned for her well-being. After all of the things she had done. It would be perfect to let her be the next target of the wave of spikes. His legs had already taken action, forcing the rest of his body to follow. He grabbed the chains on both sides of the door, restraining Helga and Elzbieta's teclyns, and yanked them away. The teclyns rattled for a moment, dislodged themselves from the side of the door, and flew into the vault. Elzbieta and Helga took notice that their teclyns had appeared. One of the guarding Forgers was in the middle of launching another attack, but the spikes never got further than a few meters. With just a look, Elzbieta transformed her teclyn into a large sword. It smashed through the tops of all of the concrete spikes, flew between the Forger's head and her body, and curved to the side until its hilt attached itself to the metal-covered restrained hand of Elzbieta. The Forger's body fell onto the floor, followed by her head. The other Forger was at a loss for words. Helga took advantage of the hesitation and guided her teclyn over her head. When she yelled: *"Mellt!"* The cane transformed into a copper staff. Lightning bolts sizzled down on the woman and fried her. into a smoking heap. Like Elzbieta's sword, Helga's teclyn flew across the room and attached itself to her covered hands.

Thomas picked up the gun and looked back at Shirley. She had already taken the elevator back to the top floor. "Damn it! I was too late!"

"Language, Detective," Helga said.

"Oh, sorry." He ran to give her some aid. "Helga!?"

"Detective Vanderbilt. My dependence on you is starting to get a bit needy."

"I can live with that. Are you alright?"

"I've been worst for the wear."

Thomas looked at the chains holding her to the wall and the vine puncturing her wrist. "Let's see, I don't have a key for your chains. Maybe I can break them off of you. He pointed the gun at the chains.

"That'll just bounce off and 'it me in the face! Her sword could probably do it, but if you grab the handle—"

"I saw that. Maybe I can use your staff to break you free."

"Don't think that'll work. Her sword is a Chamfer."

"A what?"

"A Spell Breaker."

"As in—"

253

"Exactly what it sounds like. You saw how it slashed through those webs of Little Miss Moffitt."

"Maybe I can get the key from Leo."

"Are ye going to brawl with 27 Forgers? Yeh got some stones on yeh, Stryker!"

"You're right. But I have to do something." He reached over and tried to pull Helga's teclyn away; it didn't move. "Can I borrow this?"

"Oh, sorry. It's okay, teclyn. I trust him."

Thomas pulled the copper staff away from the wall with ease. Holding it like a sword, he lifted the rod and brought it down on the solid metal cast covering Helga's left hand.

"I'm telling yeh, Detective, you're wasting your t—" Helga looked down at the restraint, broken in two. She lifted her arm, and the chains fell onto the ground, broken. "Bloody...How...how?"

"Guess the chains are weaker than you thought."

"No, no! Those were forged, Those should be unbreakable by regular weapons!" Thomas broke the other chains. Helga shook her hands to get blood circulating in them again. She pulled the vine out of her arm. "All these years, I had no idea I had a Chamfer!"

"Where did you get it?"

"Professor White gave us all of our teclyns."

Thomas took out his pen. "What about this pen? Is it one, too?"

"Maybe. That explains 'ow Abel and I wuz able to block 'er sword's attacks. Helga gestured to Elzbieta.

"Here, do you need this?" Thomas handed Helga a vial of ahrion."

She drank half of it. Thomas touched her wrist and said: *"Gwessla orga-na!"* Her tube-punctured wrist healed over in an instant. She was about to give the other half of the liquid to Elzbieta.

"Stop! What are you doing?" Thomas yelled.

"I was going to heal her. She has a bloom'n knife in her side."

"Are you mad? Have you forgotten that she's the enemy?"

"Yes, well…she's 'urt."

"So what? Isn't she trying to kill us?"

"She is, but—"

"Leave her! Leo probably did us a favor!"

"De-tec-tive Vanderbilt!"

"What?"

"Where's yuh sympathy?"

"Thomas got close to Elzbieta. "Tell me, if we let you go, are you going to stop trying to kill all of us?"

"No." Elzbieta answered.

"You see?" Thomas gestured at her. "The minute we set her free, she'll run us through with her giant sword!"

"Not her, you!" Elzbieta said. "I no attack Helga until I kill Apple man, Boom Boom Lady, Dee-tec-tive, Blonde, and then Redhead Black Blood."

Helga sighed. "Elzbieta? Do yeh think yeh can 'old off on attacking Detective Vanderbilt? Like yeh been doing with me? So that we can perhaps work together to get out of this cursed place?" Elzbieta was silent. "If yeh don't, you're going to bleed to death, and if you die without killing Mary, we all know what happens then.

"Even if she does," Thomas said. "The minute this is over, we'll have to fight her, and I'm not okay with someone trying to kill Mary the first chance they get."

Shirley exited the elevator at ground level, and pulled a lever, cutting the elevator operation off. She hurried down the hallway and entered the lobby.

"Ah, Miss Blanche, you're back." The receptionist said.

"May I borrow your phone, please?" The receptionist set it on the counter. Shirley called the operator. "Yes, I'd like to call

Mulberry Street, 122, please." The operator made the connection, and Benjamin Strong, governor of the Federal Reserve, picked up the phone. "Yes, Mr. Strong, this is Shirley Blanche. Sorry to call you so early in the morning."

"No worries," He said. "After all the catastrophes, I haven't slept a wink."

"Of course. Mr. Strong, I was wondering if I may borrow some of your strongest Forgers?"

"Borrow? What for?"

"I have a little project which may require a bit of force."

"You need goons, in other words."

"Not so roughshod, but yes. A little bit of coercion may be necessary."

"Why don't you use your own men? Aren't you the head of the European Gold Foundation? You have Miss Wayward to start."

"Miss Wayward is already on…another mission. All of my other helpers are in Europe right now on much more important missions.

"I see. Is this related to getting the book? Or the Eye back?"

"Of course, always."

Strong thought for a moment. "Okay, I'll lend you two. But no more. We still need some to guard the transition of gold to the new location."

"Of course. Have them meet me in front of Tombs prison. And thank you."

After The call ended, Shirley went outside to wait for the Forgers.

Min cooled herself with her mother's fan "You didn't have to come with us!" she told Fritz. "You're free to go wherever you want!"

"I smelled food, and I'm hungry," he responded.

Victoria opened the door to her apartment.

Otto walked past the entrance. He had a toothbrush in his mouth. He looked at Victoria with an expression of indifference. When he saw Min and Fritz standing behind her, he seemed more interested. "Mom!' he yelled. "Here she is!"

"Okay," Thelma said from the kitchen. "Victoria? Where were you? Come sit down for breakfast."

"Mom!" Otto said. "She's not alone."

"For the love of—What are you talking about?" Thelma walked out of the kitchen, wiping her hands on her apron. When she saw Min and Fritz, her face had the same expression as Otto's. "Victoria? Who are they? Are they friends of yours?"

Stress and emotional nausea rose in Victoria's stomach, filled her chest, and came out as tears. She ran to her mother and embraced her. Thelma was caught off guard but eventually caressed her daughter and comforted her trembling body. "Victoria? What happened? You're a mess." Victoria's voice was too shaky to explain anything coherently. "You two!" Thelma looked at Min and Fritz "...What happened?"

Min started to speak but hesitated. She looked at Fritz for support, but he was content with being silent. "Uh-mm..."

"I was attacked!" Victoria said.

"Attacked?" Otto asked."

"Otto! Get ready for work!" Thelma said.

"But Ma..."

"Git!"

The boy went into his room.

Thelma looked intently into Victoria's eyes. "Who attacked you? Did they do anything to you?"

"It was a woman."

Thelma seemed puzzled at the answer. "A woman? A woman attacked you? Does she live in this building?"

"No, she was a witch."

"I bet! What kind of person would lay a hand on you? Is the boy and—is she a Chinese girl? Are they involved in this?"

"They…they saved me."

"Where is this woman? Is it someone in their building? We should call the police!"

"The police won't help! She's too powerful!"

"I don't care how wealthy she is! No one touches my daughter and gets away with it! Is she still outside? Where did this happen?"

"Mom, please—"

"Victoria! We can't have someone going around abusing children—"

Victoria tightly hugged her mother and started crying again, "Mother! Please! I just want to forget all about it!"

"Victo—"

"PLEASE! For now! I want to pretend that everything is normal…for now…please. Just for this moment…please."

They embraced again. Thelma pulled away first. "Are you hungry?"

Victoria nodded. "You two, are you hungry? Min and Fritz looked at each other and then nodded. "Come along, plenty for all. Thelma guided them all towards the kitchen.

Mary swam downwards towards the exit of the Vorago, illuminated by the upside-down sun rippling on the water. This part of leaving the Vorago was always unsettling. Swimming downwards while wearing the bathing suit was a good idea, as doing this in a dress took longer. As she had discovered, the first thing to do when coming out of a Vorago is to reach around for a ledge. If you are exiting a swimming pool or bathtub, this makes climbing out a lot faster. She grabbed down and outwards and touched a stone surface. The minute she put her hand through the wall of water, her orientation transitioned from the light being on the bottom to the top. The blood flowing to her head now rushed to her feet. She lifted herself upwards into the sunlight onto a fountain ledge in front of White Manor's courtyard, flopped onto the ground and took in a breath of oxygen. By her guess, it was almost 11 a.m., London time. She wasn't sure if she was in the right place. Lots of cobblestones leading to the main gate were disheveled. Old vines punctured through in random places. She looked back at the front unlatched gate. 'Someone has been here...someone uninvited.' She rushed to the front door. It was opened with little effort. She stopped in the doorway, listened, poked her head in, and looked around. There was broken glass on the ground. The door appeared to have been forced open. She looked down at her bare feet. "I should have worn shoes." Next to the entrance was the mud room, used to store shoes too soiled to enter the rest of the house. On the shelf was a pair of green gardening boots. Mary slipped them on. They were a little big, but she knew she didn't have the luxury to be picky. She cautiously crept through the main hall, her fist ready to strike anything that was not friend or family. As she had expected, the great hall was in disarray. If were possible for objects to be turned over or thrown on the ground, they were. Someone had pulled down some paintings by artist Elizabeth Nourse and leaned them against the wall in a neat stack. "Not a robbery... someone that respects fine art; someone educated trying to gain access to a hidden wall safe—Hello?" she yelled. "Hello ?" Mary checked the drawing room and sighed at the overturned Rococo furniture. In the unruly library, every book was scattered and splayed. Mary tried to remember where she had seen Gwenhwyvar in the projection. "The kitchen!" Before she entered the room, the smell of rotting food and stagnant spices reached her nostrils. Like the other areas, everything was scattered all along the floor, peppered with broken ceramic dishes. She felt a breeze and shivered briefly. "Why is it so cold in here?" she asked. She picked up the broken half of a cup she remembered as one of her favorites. The kitchen drawers and cabinets were all opened. The pantry was also not spared, with the addition of the opened jars of spices, pickled vegetables, and dried fruit thrown around the little room.

"Aunt Gwenhwyvar?" Mary yelled. 'Did she leave? Did we not see her in here less than an hour ago?' "When did this all happen? It wasn't recent. Some liquid items look like they had dried out and grown mushrooms.' Among the mess, a white note on the table stood out. Mary picked it up. "Is this what she was working on?" She unfolded the paper and read it:

Hello Dear:

I hope this letter finds you well.
As you can see, it appears we had visitors at one point. By my estimation, this appears to have happened back in Spring. If you search the rest of the house, you will see all the other rooms have been marred in the same manner.

They really did gain full access to our facilities. I'm sure at one point, they realized the Sir Myrddin was not here and moved to our other abodes. As to who did this? I can only ascertain it was someone armed with a Chamfer or a Spell Breaker if you will...

As I'm sure, you wished to sit down for tea with me as we did last time, I'm afraid I can't stick around for that right now and will be unable to facilitate. As grandiose as it may sound, I am currently working to ensure the survival of the entire world.

If you are visiting to procure advice, rest assured I have the ultimate faith in your abilities as a Forger, a champion of good, and as my loving niece to be triumphant. Just remember. Even though I can't see you like we did last time at the table, you're the apple of my eye.

And most importantly, don't despair, even the abyss has a light.

I will try to rendezvous with you at a later date when you need me the most. In the meantime, have a cup of your favorite sage tea, and I will see you next time.

Love always, Gwenhwyvar

'When I need you the most? I need you right now! For someone who can see the future, she left no advice on the best course of action!' "And what did she mean, my favorite tea is sage? It's…"

Mary entered the pantry; it was completely disheveled. Even though she wore boots, she subconsciously tip-toed around the broken glass and dried beans, crunching underfoot. She walked over to the shelf used to house the large tea jars. Next to a box of matches, the bottom half of one of the containers remained. Inside were some tea leaves; it was no surprise they were sage. "It looks like she picked this off the ground and put it back on the shelf."

'I'm sorry Aunt Gwenhwyvar. I prefer my tea not to have so much broken glass in it.' She noticed the matches. "Why did she put that there?" She picked up a pinch of the sage leaves and smelled them. 'When I was talking to Shirley, she lit this on fire…." Mary returned the leaves to the shelf and walked out of the pantry. She looked around, turned, and walked back in. 'It's only cold in here.' She lit the match and set the pile of tea leaves on fire. It burned briefly, then smoldered. The temperature in the room went from cold to warm in a second, as a warm breeze had just blown into the little room.

'So. That's what this is about!' Mary looked at the labels on the shelves. The broken jar of sage was in its proper place. 'My favorite tea is Lapsang Souchong...' She ran her hands along the shelves and read the alphabetized tags. "Everyone in the house hated it, but I liked its campfire taste—reminds me of the time I was in the American West..." The shelf that would have housed Lapsang Souchong was as bare as the rest. "Did she redirect me just to get me to light the sage on fire?" Mary rubbed her hands along the Lapsang Souchong shelf and the wall behind it; there was a bump in the wallpaper. She rubbed her finger over it and then used her fingernail to peel away a bit of the paper. She removed enough of it to tell what had been causing the bump. "Is that a keyhole?" She grabbed a large piece of the paper and tore it, revealing a little door in the wall. "And there you are!" She ran her finger over the metal keyhole. "Clo Keffin ?"

She removed the key from her neck and looked at it. "This key won't work if Aunt Gwenhwyvar made this safe." She sighed. "Father, is this your doing?" She inserted the handle into the hole and turned. The lock whirled and clicked. A little door popped open and expelled dust into the air. "Oh my!" She peered inside the little safe and then reached in and felt something. "What is..." she removed the item. It was another large tea jar. She rotated it and read its label: "Lapsang Souchong...but it's empty." She squinted and looked closer at it. "What is this supposed to be? All of that security for an empty tea jar?" She lifted the jar up and down. "Hold on...it feels weighted." She took the lid off and put her hand inside. It touched something. The object inside faded into view. It was a book with a silver elephant head on it. "Whoever did this went through a huge effort so that this does not fall into nefarious hands. She flipped through the pages. "Is this a journal?"

Mary uprighted a chair, placed it at the kitchen table, sat down, opened the book, and read some of its hand-written pages:

> March 31, 1880
>
> My love has died. Although I have so many endowments, neither I nor my sister-in-law, Gwenhwyvar can save her. What use is it to be given gifts by Nephilim, if we can't heal our most important organ?

'This was written by Father! He's talking about my English mother. They tried to have a child together but it never made it. She died eight years before I was even born. Mary flipped to the middle of the journal:

> February 5th, 1898
>
> I have almost gathered enough ahrion for Mary's operation. I hope it is not too late. Getting the second half of the book costs more than just lives. I will have to use forged silver rivets as reinforcements all down her back. With proper training, perhaps these can be turned into an enhancement one day.

'Enhancement? The angel wings? A clue on how to activate them would have been greatly appreciated! This was a few days before my operation. He changed my memories so that she died... when my actual mother died. Let me see what else he says about welding my mind...' Mary flipped between pages 8 and 12.

> February 11th, 1898
>
> I know it is wrong, and I will take full responsibility for it, but my daughter's happiness is the only non-materialistic thing I can provide her. After I nearly got her killed in the train attack before she was even born. Or unable to prevent her mother and uncle's death at the circus, what else could I do?
>
> Calculus Remotio extracts a high price. After experimenting with her cousin, spirits proved the best option...

Mary sighed. "I see. He really did do the same deplorable thing to Shirley. But what did he use for her false memories?" Mary flipped months past her transformation from Mary Black into Mary White.

The Green Dragon Crescent Blade
Ruyi Jingu Bang
Durendal
Thuận Thiên (Heaven's Will)

Each has proven ineffective.

'Durendal was a legendary sword. Ineffective for what? Is he looking for something to destroy the Siv Myrddin? Is Shirley right?'

When Mary exhaled, she could see her breath. "What's going on? She looked around the room. The tea leaves she had set on fire were still smoldering. There was a slight frosted coating on some items. She ran her finger over the surface and picked up small shards of ice crystals. "Why did it suddenly get so cold in here?" She stood up and walked into the kitchen; it was even colder. As she kept walking, the temperature got colder and colder the closer she got to the front door. Larger ice crystals formed towards the entryway. A blanket of ice completely covered the front door. She reached for the doorknob; it was so cold it numbed her fingertips. She yanked the door open, shards of ice splintered away from the frame, and tiny snowflakes blew over her face. "Is it not summer?"

The courtyard was a contained winter event. The structures: fountains, statues, cobblestones, and gates were white and sprouted ice stalagmites. The gate was open, and an ice arch framed a figure holding a cane.

"Miss Wayward? You recovered fast." Mary looked down and realized her feet were becoming frozen to the ground. She pulled her boot up and severed the icy seal. "So much for honor. I would think saving your life would have gained a bit of a respite from you —at least for an hour." Wayward remained silent. Mary squinted her eyes to get a better look at Wayward's face, to gauge her reaction the best she could through the bandaged eyes. "Why did you follow me here? I thought your mission was to kill those children?" Wayward remained silent and concentrated on sending waves of frozen energy down her cane towards the house. Mary took notice of Wayward's cane: 'She didn't have that teclyn before…then…' Mary hurried back inside the manor, slamming the door shut. A thick coating of ice and stalagmites was forming from the entryway and flowing towards her as fast as she walked away from them. The freezing speed increased and started covering every still object: Walls, furniture, and ceiling developed a thick coating of ice. "She's going to freeze the whole house!" Across the room, a grandfather clock had its hands frozen at 1:12 p.m. 'It's already past 8 in New York! I don't have time to muck about with Miss Wayward and then free the others!'

She started running but slipped and fell onto her hip. She soldiered through the pain and ran into the kitchen. 'I have to hurry!' She grabbed her father's journal and started to leave but stopped herself. "Vorago will destroy it…" She hurried back to the kitchen, and put the book inside the empty tea jar. The encroaching ice had turned everything in sight into a wintery morgue. She noticed the ice had not reached the stairwell. Walking was difficult, and running was not possible. She settled for sliding towards the stairs, sloppily ice skating in the main hall while being chased by winter. So much ice was building up behind her that it weighed down a chandelier and sent it smashing to the ground behind her. She looked up to the top of the stairs. As she hoped, it had not yet succumbed to the frozen terror.

She started to go up the stairs but slipped down. She flopped onto her knees and belly. She quickly got up and tried again with the same result. 'It's far too slippery!' She looked up the stairs. 'I wish my wings would come out when I need them!' She concentrated momentarily, causing her boots to freeze to the ground again. She tried to pull them up, but the seal was too strong this time to break. Ice rose above her ankles and was about to flow inside her boots to touch her bare skin. 'I can't fly…" Mary crouched down. "...But I'm still a good jumper!" She leaped out of her boots, flew over the flight of stairs, and landed on the upper floor, collapsing onto her elbows and knees, doing her best not to smash the tea jar into the ground. She got up as quickly as she could and ran to the nearest bathroom. She grabbed one of the knobs of the claw-footed tub and turned it on, and the faucet made a strange noise; nothing came out of the spout. "What's going on?" Mary turned the knobs harder and then hit them with her fist. A drop of water trickled out. "Why isn't this working!" There was a cracking glass sound coming from outside the room. The ice attack had reached the upstairs. 'The pipes, the pipes are frozen!" She stood up and tried the sink. Nothing came out of its faucet, as well. The toilet was her last resort, but the water inside it was already a block of ice. "Oh no!" She went back to the bathtub. "Should I just fight her? I could use fire—I should have used that on my boots—wait, fire—heat!" Mary put her left hand on the faucet. "*Roy are don!*"

Her hand glowed red. Steam began to come out of the faucet. After a sputtering sound, water trickled out. When the water touched the tub, it started to freeze again. Mary put the tea jar on her lap and put her right hand in the tub. "*Roy are don!*" Her right hand also glowed red. The water thawed and slowly expanded to fill the tub. 'There can't be more than 10 millimeters in this tub! I need at least 20 for a Vorago to work!' Mary continued heating the pipes and thawing the water as more and more noises came from the outside hall. She took a peek and saw a large section of the ceiling give way. Wood beams and icicles bigger than her all came crashing down. A gust of cold air gave her a warning; she was next. She watched helplessly; the sink, the mirror, and the toilet all ceded to the spreading freeze. She stopped her fire forge and put her hand in the water. 'This looks like at least 30 millimeters; "*Cray giât deem kurk fan!*" The water bubbled and glowed for a second. But it stopped when ice crystals formed around the edge and moved towards the center. Mary returned her hands to the faucet and said:

"Roy are don!" Again, the water began to flow, and the ice in the tub thawed. The ice forming in the room began to envelop her tiny space. Larger ice shards began to fall on her; one scraped her cheek, producing blood. Mary held her position and ignored the stinging pain. Her feet were starting to get numb from the cold; she knew with the speed of the drop in temperature, she would yield to frostbite at any moment. "Come on, stop freezing!" She yelled at the water in the tub. She concentrated on the heat and exerted as much melting power as she could. The water expanded to an area she believed would be large enough to dive into. She yelled as quickly as she could: *"Cray giât deem kurk fan!"* The water in the tub bubbled and glowed around her right hand, and a whirlpool formed in the center. She knew she only had seconds before it froze over. She removed her left hand from the faucet. The pipes immediately froze over, and the water stopped flowing. She grabbed her jar, stood up, and set her numb feet into the tub. At the same time, the water's edges were solidifying and rapidly closing off her escape route. Her feet were pulled into the whirlpool, drawing the rest of her body downwards. When her face entered the water, she could see the ice surface, inches away from her eyes. She dunked in and started to spin but stopped moving downwards. 'Something's wrong!' She looked down and saw the whirlpool tugging at her spinning yet stationary body. She looked up and realized the ends of her hair were still in the manor, held captive by the frozen sheet inside the tub. She reached up and pulled with her free hand; it did no good. She yanked harder and harder, but she just stood still, spinning. She tried to tear her hair, but it had twisted into a reinforced rope; the more she struggled, the more oxygen she exerted. By her estimation, if she did not free herself in the next 10 seconds, she wouldn't have enough air to escape from the Vorago. Trying to separate the hairs was futile; she panicked. She felt something come out of her back; an object reached up and severed her long hair in half, freeing her from the ceiling of ice. Mary spun downwards into the darkness of the Vorago. As best

she could, she looked behind her and saw what looked like a skinny metallic crab leg, with a sharp pointy end, shrink and withdraw into her back.

"What kind of monster am I?' She wondered.

In London, an unexplained localized ice storm was seen in the summer of 1915 in Westminster.

PART SIX
THEY STUBBED THEIR TOE

Leo and his companions entered a spacious hall with a high stone ceiling arched like a cathedral. Their footsteps echoed throughout the chamber as they moved steadily towards a large, black metal door. Two enormous winged, metal elephant head statues adorned both sides of the frame.

"Did the Silversmiths build all this?" Leo asked.

"Silversmith architecture but Goldsmith money. Rosina of Leckermau said.

"And how would you know that?" Leo asked.

"One thing I know is architecture."

"Oh, right. You made a house out of sweets. To kidnap and eat kids."

"That's all just a rumor! It was just made to look like it was made out of sweets."

Leo was about to touch the surface of the large door but stopped. He looked back at his Foundry members and picked what he thought might be the weakest one. "You," he said, pointing at a skinny teenage boy. Leo walked over and handed him his key. "Open this door."

The boy looked at the key and then Leo. "No, thank you."

"What!"

"No thanks, this might be a trap."

"So, what if it is? You have to follow my orders!"

"No, I don't, not if it's stupid!"

"Looks like you have a bit of a leadership problem," Boss Murphy said.

"I'm not—do you understand what'll happen If you don't follow my orders?" Leo yelled at the young man.

"No. But I know what'll happen if that door is a trap."

Murphy chuckled, as did a few of the Forgers.

'This isn't good,' Leo thought. 'They don't have faith in me!'

"You have to be willing to sacrifice yourself for your Foundry! Didn't you see me open the last door!"

"So, that was all for show?" Murphy asked.

"What?"

"You did that to show how tough you are?"

"Listen! You little bas—" Leo noticed that the teenager had a pale complexion and a look of shock on his face. "What? What's wrong with you?"

"Stop! go away!" the boy yelled.

"What is he going on about?" Rosina said.

The boy writhed around as though trying to remove something sticking to his skin. His movements became erratic, and he ended up on the ground as something ripped at his soul and pulled it out, causing him to endure a pain worse than having his flesh ripped off. The boy screamed and shook. He slumped down, breathless and still, with an expression of surprise.

"Cosa gli è successo? (What happened to him?)" Canidia asked.

"It's Forger's honor," Leo answered. "Maybe this is what happens when you go against your vow. You get dragged to hell! Anyone else want to challenge my authority?" Everyone looked surprised and in shock. The entire scene unnerved Leo. One hundred-year-old Forgers were seeing something new that scared them.

Fritz gobbled down his fifth bowl of porridge.

Thelma seemed reluctant to give him a sixth. It wasn't that she was against being charitable, and this poor boy seemed to be starving, but it was getting close to 9 a.m., and she would be late for work. She obliged anyway, gave him another bowl, and sighed. Her son Otto announced his impatience of waiting around for them to finish eating. Thelma sent him on ahead. When Miss Flo arrived to care for the younger siblings, this was an obvious prediction for tardiness.

Thelma collected empty bowls from Min and Victoria. "Okay, I need to get ready for one of my jobs, and you kids need to run along. Right? Do you two work at the mill?"

Fritz and Min didn't answer; neither understood the question. Victoria looked down solemnly. "Victoria, darling, are you sick?" Victoria nodded her head. "Oh, poor thing. You can rest up in my bed." Thelma guided Victoria into the master bedroom. "You two can go on ahead," she said to Min and Fritz, "Victoria is going to rest up."

As Fritz and Min were leaving, Fritz looked at Miss Flo. She was in the kids' room, changing one of the twins' shirts, lifting it over their heads while holding the baby in her other arm.

"Do you want anything to take with you? "Thelma asked them. I can give you some bread and cheese if you want." Fritz nodded. Thelma returned to the kitchen to prepare the food, leaving The kids alone.

"You were a little late today, Flo. Is everything alright at home?" Thelma yelled from the kitchen.

"Home is fine," Flo answered. "It's the streets that are all messed up. There must'a been another gas explosion or something. 'Cause there were cars and garbage turned over all over the streets. A taxi driver got himself killed when another car landed on his!"

"Oh! My!"

Fritz Pointed to Miss Flo.. "She looks different than them. Is she part of their family?" he asked Min.

"Her? No, she's a bǎomǔ."

"A what?"

"Nanny? A babysitter?"

"What are those?"

"Haven't you ever had a babysitter?" Fritz looked confused. "Someone that watches you when your parents aren't there?"

"Elzbieta has been taking care of me most of my life."

"What were you doing before then? What happened to your parents?"

"My parents were…"

"Were what?"

Thelma came from the kitchen and handed them a napkin with food inside. "This should hold you, at least through lunch. If you get hungry, drop by later. Least I can do for you helping Victoria."

"Can I have a word with her before we go?" Min asked.

"I suppose. But don't stir her around too much! She's not feeling well."

"I know, we won't."

"We?" Fritz asked.

"Yes, you're coming with me."

"Why? I might be late for the mill."

"Wŏmen zŏu ba (come on, let's go)!" Min grabbed Fritz's arm and dragged him into the master bedroom.

Victoria lay in the bed and stared off into the distance.

Min looked back and noticed Thelma had followed them into the room. "Can I talk to her…by ourselves?"

"Anything you can say to her, you can say it to me!" Thelma said.

"It's okay, Mother," Victoria said.

"Thelma ploddingly left with obvious reservations

Min waited before speaking. "You can't stay here!"

"What are you talking about?"

"That blind woman! She's going to find you and hurt your family!"

"Where else can I go? The police?"

"No, like you said, she's too powerful. She'll destroy the police station; we have to find Mary."

"Why did this have to happen to me?"

"I don't know. But now we have to do something about it!"

"No, we don't! Maybe Mary White took care of her!"

"We don't know that! If we don't leave, your family could be next!"

"And you don't know that!"

"These people are monsters—actual monsters!

"And what are you? What is he?" Victoria pointed at Fritz.

"We're not monsters. We're the ones that fight the monsters! There's also Helga, Abel, and Thomas. They're all very strong! They can—"

"I never wanted any of this! I just want things to go back to the way they were! No ghosts, no crazy witch ladies—no—those men —those men—were killed—he killed them!" She pointed at Fritz. He looked down. She started to cry.

Thelma entered the room. "Okay! That's enough! I think you kids should leave!"

"But..." Min said.

"Go on, leave her to rest!" She nudged the kids out of the room and towards the front door. "Once again, thanks for your help. Now, run along!"

When the front door was open, a figure was standing in front of it, preparing to knock; it was Mary, dressed in her black bathing suit and a pair of red lace-up boots, dripping water onto the hallway floor.

"Oh, hello, Thelma," Mary said.

Thomas descended the rusty metal ladder and returned to the ground floor of the chamber where Helga and Leo's gang had been captive. Everywhere he went, the remaining Forgers chained to the walls pleaded with him to let them free, some even haft heartedly pledging loyalty without saying: 'Forger's honor'. Thomas ignored them all, knowing most would kill him if given a chance. Helga came from the side where she had been feeling along the walls and ignoring her solicitations.

"Anything?" Thomas asked her.

"'Fraid not, Detective. Looks like Leo and Mausi's gang took the only exits out of 'ere."

"Unfortunate. It would be a lot easier not having to fight our way out."

"Nev'r do mind, Detective, I can 'andle at least two of them."

"Don't be so sure, Helga. I have faith in your abilities, but when I hear words like: 'Infamous in the history books' when describing our opponents, it does give me pause."

Helga sighed in agreement. "It would be a lot easier if it were three of us…" She looked over at Elzbieta. "Don't suppose you'd reconsider?" Elzbieta didn't respond. Helga walked over to her. "Elzbieta, are yeh still whiff us?" Helga examined her further and was about to pull the knife out."

"Stop!" Thomas yelled.

"I was just going to pull out the knife."

"If you do that, she'll just bleed out faster!…learned that the hard way."

Helga went back to examining Elzbieta's pale skin. "Elzbieta! Yeh don't have much time left. Let us save yuh!" Elzbieta lifted her head and groggily shook it no. "Stubborn as a mule, Yeh is! Do Yeh want to die down here, never finishing yuh job? All we're asking for is to put aside yeh little vendetta until we get out of 'ere!"

"I'd refer her to forget about it altogether," Thomas said.

"We can renegotiate later. Right now, we need 'er manpower. If we go down in them tunnels, or an army comes down that elevator, things are going to go all to pot!"

Thomas looked at the elevator. "They haven't come down yet. I wonder why?"

A taxi arrived at the front of Tombs prison where Shirley was waiting patiently. Inga exited the vehicle. Not that far away, Tibuta walked from a trolly and joined them.

"I thought you'd both fly here," Shirley said.

"There's already been enough commotion with Forgers," Inga said.

"You wouldn't know what happened across the street, would you?" Shirley asked.

"Across the street? I was talking about the car wreckage down the way."

"Shirley furrowed her brow. "Hmm. Anyway, you're probably wondering why I bought you two here."

"Yes. Is this related to Mary White?"

"Bien sûr. As you may or may not know, she has until noon to tell the President where the...thing is."

"Yes, go on."

"And you may or may not know her friends are locked up here."

"That we are."

"There seems to be a problem. When I went to check in on Boss Murphy, after he failed to return from a visit to the -13th floor, not only did I not see him, but Mary's friends had broken out! They were running around freely, along with other Forgers."

"What?! Then there should be all kinds of alarms going on right now!" Inga gestured to the prison. "Have you told the guards?"

"No."

"Are you daft? This is an emergency! Have you heard the rumors about who they got locked up UNDER the prison?"

"Yes, the one they've been using to spy on everyone."

"Spying is the least of our problems! If they manage to set her free...God help us all—last time was millions! How many deaths will it be this time? And what will happen if she teams up with the other three? Cor blimey! Why haven't you told anyone? We should get every Forger over here and lock this place down before it's too late!"

"I can see you're concerned. But she's not our priority."

"Are you having a laugh?"

"No. Our main priority isn't her, it's retrieving the sword of the Iron Smith.

"How would that be more important than letting a Blacksmith run free in the world?"

"There are already three of them running around in the world. But if she does cause trouble, that sword is also Caliburn."

Tibuta gasped.

Inga looked at Tibuta and then Shirley. "As in?"

"Yes. So if that Blacksmith escapes, if we don't secure that Chamfer, we won't stand a chance against her."

"But I heard people that touched that Ironsmith's sword down by the docks, got the lurgy and such!"

"Yes, it's probably cursed. But we all know how to remove curses, right?"

"Okay, but why do this alone?"

"Because a contained fire does what you want it to. Unless you want whatever chaos happened down the street to happen to the rest of the city, we will contain this without getting the Blacksmith's attention."

Inga looked at Tibuta. "You agree with all this?" Tibuta shrugged her shoulders.

"I'll take that as a yes," Shirley said.

"Ladies, if you will." She led them inside the building.

" 'old on, yeh going too?"

"Of course. I'm going to supervise. I've already sent two people to do simple tasks, and they've never returned!"

Before Mary could speak another word, Min had already jumped into her arms and hugged her so tight it hurt a little. She bore the pain, hugged her back, and gave several kisses on the forehead.

"Hello, my little Butterfly, " Mary said, pulling away.

"H-how did you find us?" Min asked.

Mary hugged her again. "I'll explain later. Are you two alright? Is Victoria alright?"

"Mary White, are you acquainted with these children?" Thelma asked.

"Oh! Hello, Thelma, nice to see you again."

"Charmed, I'm sure. What are you doing here…Dressed like that?"

Mary looked down at her swim-dress and her lace-up red boots. "Oh…oh this? I…I was swimming earlier."

"Hmm, I've heard rumors you swim to the Statue of Liberty; is that true?

"Today I've come from much further. May I please speak to Victoria?"

"How do you know she's here? Were you involved with her attack?"

Mary looked at Min for information.

"We told her she got attacked by a crazy lady, and we saved her."

"That is the truth," Mary said. "Although after confronting her attacker again, I have to say there's far more to the story."

"And would you be willing to share some of that with me?" Thelma asked. "Or perhaps the police? Victoria was terrified! Who was this woman? Is she one of your acquaintances? She said it was someone powerful!"

Mary noticed Fritz was walking away towards the stairs. "Fritz! Where are you going?"

"This has nothing to do with me."

Mary hurried to him and grabbed his arm. "Please, don't go! I need your help as well."

"For what?"

"I think. If we work together, we stand a far better chance of accomplishing our mutual goals."

"I don't need your help."

"From what I've...seen recently, I can tell that Elzbieta is in no position to..." Mary looked back at Thelma. "...to leave her current facilities...where she is...now, you stand a far better chance of helping her with my assistance."

"Are you saying his mother is in the hoosegow?" Thelma asked."

Mary rolled her eyes. "I see the Vanderbilts all have the detective trait inheritance." She put her hand on Fritz's shoulder. "Yes. I promise. I can help get her out of jail, but only if we all work together."

"Why would you do that?" Fritz asked. "She wants to kill you? I want to kill you!"

"Whoa-whoa,-whoa!" Thelma yelled. "The mouth on that rag-a-muffin!" Thelma walked up to Fritz. "I don't know what your mother did or why she hates Mary White...or even why Miss White came straight here dripping wet from swimming, wearing red boots—but if she has the resources to help bail your mom out of the pokey, show a little gratitude, young man! It's not every day that someone you hate can ignore all that and still be charitable!"

"Thank you, Thelma," Mary said. "What do you say, Fritz? Should we call a truce? After all, we were a great team when we fought the...Crazy Lady."

"So, you are involved in that!" Thelma said. "Perhaps you can give me more information about what in God's name is going on?"

Mary paused in thought. "I...the—how can I explain this?"

"Aren't you late for work?" Min asked Thelma.

"Trying to change the subject I see," Thelma said.

"It's not that Thelma," Mary said, "it's just the truth is far more complicated than you could ever believe."

"I'm sure no matter what you tell me, it can't be anything I haven't heard before."

"...But." Mary looked at the clock on the wall, her hand, and then Thelma's head. 'It's 9:31. If I do a mind bend on her, it will save me so much time!' She started to reach for Thelma's head. "Hold on, Thelma. You have a string in your hair…"

"What? Where?"

She almost touched Thelma's head but was interrupted by the sight of Victoria.

"Victoria? What are you doing out of bed?" Thelma asked.

"Can I speak to her?" Victoria asked.

"Sweetie, you need to rest."

"Please, Mother."

Thelma groaned. "I swear, we're getting all kinds of visitors today! Is my brother outside as well?"

"No. He's in p—he's busy downtown." Mary answered."

Thelma looked back at Victoria, Mary, and then back to Victoria. "Okay. You can talk to her while I get ready for work. But when I leave, I want them all out of here! All! AND I expect a full explanation when I come back, understand?" Victoria nodded. Thelma got close to Mary's ear and whispered. "I know my brother thinks you're the bee's knees, but if one of your socialite friends hurt her and you're protecting them, I don't care how much money or power you have, I'll make sure all of you end up sharing the same cell with that boy's mom!"

Mary got a chill from the threat. "Of…of course."

Victoria returned to the bedroom and lay on the bed.

Mary entered the room, shut the door, and sat on a nearby chair. "So, I'm sure you have a slew of questions, as do I. It's interesting, in just one family, you have a Forger and a Stryker! The odds of that happening ar—"

"What's a Blacksmith?" Victoria interrupted.

"Well—"

"That's what she called me, and when you heard that, the look on your face was fear. Like how it is now."

"I apologize. I didn't mean to put you at unease. It's just a Blacksmith is a very rare Forger and—"

"What's a Forger?"

"Let me ask you, first. When did you first come across your abilities?"

"The ghostly stuff is recent, but everything else started...when I turned 13 and...and, you know….."

"When you first started having your courses?"

"Yes, that's it."

"That's usually when it starts, unless you have an early exposure to ahrion as I did."

"What's ahrion?"

"It's—I wish I could go into a full explanation of everything, but I fear our time is limited by how long it takes for your mother to get ready for work."

"Then give me the basics! What am I?"

"Alright. The way it was explained to me: Just as smithies forge metal, we forge everything. In your case, that includes ghosts, spirits, the re-alived, dreams, and fear."

"Magic?"

"No. Magic is 10% illusion and 90% delusion. Forging is real."

"But, I thought only God or the Devil could do that?"

"If Jesus was good at chess and you're good at chess, does that make you a demigod, or does it make him a human? Labels like gods, miracles, and even monsters are something the Normalu–normal people use to explain things they don't understand from our world."

"But, there's no mention of Forgers in the Bible!"

"I beg to differ." Mary saw a Bible on the nightstand, under another book. She picked up the top book and read the title: "Dreams by Sigmund Freud? I know him! He has peculiar issues with women." She tossed the book onto the floor, picked up the Bible, flipped its pages towards the end, and read:

"Acts 8: 9-13: Simon Magus. A certain man named Simon had been holding practicing magic in the town and holding the Samaritans spellbound. He passed himself off as someone of great importance. People from every rank

of society were paying attention to him. 'He is the power of the great 'God,' they said. Those who followed him had been under the spell of his magic over a long period."

She handed the book to Victoria. "Typical Goldsmith behavior."

Victoria sat with a concerned look in silence for a while "Are you a witch?"

"I'm not really sure. I have the elemental powers of a Coppersmith—that's the more proper word for witch, by the way, I also have the manipulations of a Silversmith and the proprioceptions of a Goldsmith. None of my current skills existed until I had contact with a high-level Forger, I suspect a powerful Blacksmith."

"The one under the prison?"

"It's at the prison? Have you also had contact with it?"

"She kept sending spirits to me, saying my name and pointing at the prison; a dead horse carried me to the prison to save the dog boy—he could smell her, even though he said she lacked a smell. It's almost like she used me to fight that bandaged woman and the men in top hats—like a puppet!"

"Hmmm."

"What is it?"

"Nothing, you said: it's a she, but carry on. Do you think you can do some of the things you did earlier? Without her help?"

"I don't know, this is all going too fast for me."

"I understand. This is much too fast for anyone. But if you are able to do even a minuscule amount of what a full Blacksmith can do, we will have a much easier time getting into that prison."

"Is that why she keeps dragging me back there? Why would I want to do that? She scares me! I just want her to leave me alone!"

"She's not going to do that. She needs you...she needs us."

"For what?"

282

"I'm not sure. However, if she continues summoning you, she's not going to stop until you meet her face-to-face."

"What if I just ignore it all? Isn't there a way I can go back to being normal?"

"I did that for 17 years, but eventually, the person you are catches up to you."

"How about a way to get rid of these powers?"

"Death?"

"WHAT?"

"Sorry. I didn't mean to sound morbid, but this is who you are from now on.

"BUT, WHY ME?"

"Victoria, why not you? There can only be a few Blacksmiths at a time. You came across your abilities when one of four of them died. Other Forgers, although not as rare, are still only as common as mechanical ice boxes in houses. Why me, as well? Perhaps God is manipulating our lives to fit a particular narrative. In any case, we can't help the way we are born. All we can do is: make the best of it, do things we don't like doing for the things we want, and keep failing our way to the top."

Victoria sat on the bed in silence for a long moment. Mary reached over and tried to grab her hand, but she pulled it away. "I know how you must feel. When my father told me I had the potential to be a Forger, the only thing I could think about was this was not supposed to be me. I'm not special. At the time, I was very frail and emotionally broken, so much so that to better train me, he forged my mind and took away all of my bad memories."

"Pardon? He did that? Just to train you?"

"At first. But instead, he decided to raise me as a normal girl for the next 17 years. No one would ever guess that I was a Forger— oh!"

"What is it?"

"He was hiding me...in plain sight."

"What?"

"Nothing...I just realized something; anyway, here I am, and here you are."

"Your father sounds like a horrible person!"

"Pardon?"

"For him to erase the memory of his own daughter? For training! He sounds terrible!"

"Well, he did what he thought was right. He still provided for me, and was always there....that's more than I can say for some parents."

"What do you mean? My mother is wonderful!"

"She is, and she's not the one I was referring to. Your father has been missing for quite some time right?" Victoria didn't answer. "When was the last time you saw him? Thomas said he last saw him in a pool hall in Flatbush—"

"Get out!"

"Excuse me?"

"I've had enough of you people!"

"Victoria, you are one of you people."

"No, I'm not! I'm not dealing with any more ghost goblins or whatever else is trying to kill me!"

"I'm sorry I insulted your father; it's my vanity, I'm not used to dealing with negative emo—"

"Leave! Now!"

Mary stood up and walked to the door, and stopped. "I know I can't force you to come with us. Actually, that's not true. I could quite easily force you to come with us, but I'm not going to. Please, think about it. You know where to find us. Mary left the room.

A moment later, Thelma entered. "Are you alright?" She asked Victoria. Victoria nodded. "I swear, these aristocrats. Okay, I'm heading off. I'll try to be back before 10. Unless they let us out early." She kissed Victoria on the head. "Get some rest. You're home now, and nobody can harm you." Thelma patted Victoria's hand and then left the room.

Thelma ushered Mary, Min, and Fritz out of the house in the most passive-aggressive manner she could portray. Mary didn't protest. She knew Thelma had the right to be protective of her daughter. Once outside, Min inquired about their missing party member.

"She's not coming," Mary answered.

"Why not?"

"She wants to be a normal girl."

"So, what do we do now?"

"Now? We find the nearest fountain, rain barrel—or whatever we can all fit into, and make our way to the prison…" It started to rain. "…Or, the closest puddle."

Leo was about to pick someone else to open the door but remembered they had a hostage. "You!" he pointed at Boss Murphy. "You've probably been down here before—open this door!"

Boss Murphy took a moment to decide his next move. He took the key from Leo and inserted the handle into the mouth of the right side Elephant medallion. The door opened with the same rusty whine as the others. Everyone was wary and backed away, expecting something horrible to appear. The inside of the large chamber was oval-shaped and dimly lit, 112 yards wide by 157 yards long, with a curved ceiling reaching 148 yards high. 1 inch of rippling water covered the ground, distorting the only light source projecting from above. They walked towards a lit object at the far end, illuminated in an almost angelic fashion. Leo stepped on something bumpy. He looked down, tapped a vine with his boot, and followed it to its origin. Hundreds of twisting vines reached the far ends of the chamber in a spiral and converged at the glowing center. As they walked past some of the vines, white bulbs on them opened into flowers.

When they got within 100 feet of the main object, they had stopped walking on water and were only stepping on vines covering the ground.

"What is all this?" Leo asked Boss Murphy. He didn't answer.

Leo went ahead of the group to see what the light source was shining on; twisting vines and sprouting flowers converged to form a glowing oval nest. In the center, a very elderly sleeping woman lay inside, clad in a long white gown. Her white hair reached beyond the bottom of her feet, the ends turning into twisting dread locks that continued out of the nest to connect to vines on the ground.

Her limbs were free, but her torso was wrapped and restrained in a silver chain, shiner than any other ahrion metals Leo had ever seen. 'A strong Brightsmith created those chains,' he surmised.

"Who is this?" Leo asked Murphy. Murphy gave Leo a look of disapproval. His continued lack of answers infuriated Leo. He grabbed Murphy by his collar. "Is this the Blacksmith? This old crone? She looks weak and dead! I thought she'd be locked away, like a wild beast! Instead, this looks more like a corpse!

Victoria finished the latest entry into the Mysterious Book of Mysteries. The recent events had given her pages of information. All the puzzle pieces of the unexplained events suddenly made sense; Be it the sight of a weird creature or death by odd circumstances, now it was all connected to the existence of Forgers. One contradiction she was having trouble with was how her Christian faith fit into this new world. 'Were all religious figures Forgers? Is God just a powerful one? Is it possible for a Forger to be so powerful that they could cause the death of everyone's firstborn child? or cause a worldwide flood?' She wondered about the powerful Blacksmith under the prison. 'Why would someone so strong need my help? What would they need help against?' Victoria felt guilty for not going with Mary and the others. 'No! I've had enough! I want all of this to just go away!'

She lay back on her pillow, closed her eyes, and tried to rest. She could hear her siblings and Miss Flo playing in the other room. 'I wonder if any of them have strange abilities as well? Miss White said there are two in our family. Who was she talking about, is it Mother?' The Blacksmith should ask for their help instead. I don't think I can take much more of this.' She set down the Mysterious Book of Mysteries, picked up her mother's Bible, and continued to read where she had left off.

Then Saul said to his servants, "Seek out for me a woman who is a Medium…"

"There is one in Endor," they said.

So Saul disguised himself, putting on other clothes, and at night he and two men went to the woman. "Consult a spirit for me," he said, "and bring up for me the one I name."

But the woman said to him, "Surely you know what Saul has done. He has cut off the mediums and spiritist from the land. Why have you set a trap for my life to bring about my death?"

Saul swore to her by the Lord, "As surely as the Lord lives, you will not be punished for this."

Then the woman asked, "Whom shall I bring up for you?"

"Bring up Samuel," he said.

When the woman saw Samuel, she cried out at the top of her voice and said to Saul, "Why have you deceived me? You are Saul!"

The king said to her, "Don't be afraid. What do you see?"

The woman said, "I see a ghostly figure[a] coming up out of the earth."

"What does he look like?" he asked.

"An old man wearing a robe is coming up," she said.

Then Saul knew it was Samuel, and he bowed down and prostrated himself with his face to the ground.

Victoria closed the book. "They truly are in the Bible."

She noticed it had started to rain. Snaking trickles of droplets against the window slithered down to the wooden sill, adding more moisture and mold to the wood.

She got out of the bed and walked over to the window. As the rain showered and bathed the soot-covered buildings and streets, she felt she was also being cleansed from the earlier events. "Was it all real?" She considered the possibility of hallucinations; perhaps her brain was broken. She needed the help of the famous German doctor. Seeing witches and flying cars would indicate insanity. "Is any of this real?" She touched the window; it felt cold. She put her mouth close to the glass and breathed out. She could see her breath fogging up the glass. She wiped the condensation off. Another hand slapped against the window on the other side. Victoria screamed and jumped back. Before she shrieked again or ran out of the room in a panic, she recognized the person on the outside. "Gertrude?" Victoria asked.

Her friend stood, unresponsive, outside on the wooden fire escape.

Victoria opened the window as fast as she could. "What are you doing outside in the rain? At my mother's window?" She grabbed Gertrude, and pulled her inside.

Gertrude started walking around the room, occasionally picking up random objects and setting them down. "Gertrude?" There was still no response. She picked up the Bible and seemed to study what Victoria had just read. "Gertrude! You won't believe what I've been through! It's true! It's all true! Witches, goblins, ghosts! It's all true! A witch tried to kill us—Mary White is a witch—I think! I'm a witch too!" Gertrude leisurely turned the pages. "Gertrude, are you even listening? I'm telling you it's all true! The stories are all true! Even the giant monster dog—It's the boy! That boy can turn into a dog! And there was a Chinese girl! Swinging a spear around—like whoosh! I'm not sure what she was, but she wasn't normal either!" Victoria walked over and shook Gertrude's shoulders. "What's wrong with you? I'm telling the truth! It's all—"

"I'm not Gertrude, child," she said. Her voice sounded different, very mature and controlled.

Victoria released her shoulders and stepped back. "Gertrude, this is not funny! If you knew what I've been through, you wouldn't joke around like this."

"Not a joke, child. I've known everything you've gone through since you were 13."

"This isn't funny! Why are you doing this?"

"After all you've seen, you doubt I can't take control of your little friend?"

"Are you…Are you the one? What did you do to her?"

"We are both aware of who I am. Do you know who you are?"

"I…I'm like you."

"Nothing like me. No one is like me." Gertrude walked over and stood a few inches from Victoria. "Why are you still here, child?"

"Here? In the apartment, or here, alive?"

Gertrude smiled. "The Black Blood and the children are coming to me. Yet, you remain here."

"Black Blood? Is that Mary White? I'm not going with them. It's suicide. I'm lucky to have survived that scarf woman!"

"You saw so, yourself. With my help, you can defeat all enemies that stand in your way."

"No! You have Miss White and the others! You don't need my help! Now, release my friend!"

"I need her…I need you. If you do not help me, I will use her to help me in your stead."

"What do you mean?"

Gertrude went to the window, opened it, and stepped out onto The fire escape.

"What are you doing? Where are you going with her?"

"I'm going to use this girl to free me."

"You're taking her to the prison? Gertrude has no powers! She's clumsy! You'll kill her!"

If you care for your friend, I suggest you accompany her."

I—this isn't fair! Why are you doing this to us!" Gertrude began to descend the fire escape. "Stop!" Victoria heard one of her siblings let out a cry.

"Everything in there all right, Victoria?" Miss Flo asked.

"It's fine, Miss Flo!" Victoria gazed out the open window as the rain poured down and pattered on any metal parts, like the sound of many ticking clocks. She stood up and walked over to the window. 'I wonder what would happen if I just closed it and went to bed? This will all be over.'

With an expression of extreme curiosity, Gertrude stood on the sidewalk and looked up at the pouring rain. she held out her hands and felt the drops pool in her palms. A few passersby glared at her, and some even commented, telling her she should go inside or get an umbrella. None stopped to help. Footsteps ran towards her.

"If we were to walk in this rain, we'd catch a death of cold!" Victoria yelled, coming from behind her.

"No need to worry. A ride has already been procured."

"Another dead horse? We can't do that! There are too many people walking about—someone will see—"

A black taxi cab pulled next to the curb. Gertrude let herself in. Victoria hesitated. She noticed the collapsed part of the roof over the driver's side. She took her seat in the back next to Gertrude. The driver sat in a slightly contorted position under the imploded ceiling. Victoria looked at Gertrude, gazing out of a broken window. "I don't have any money."

"You don't need anything. You have me," Gertrude said.

The driver put the car in gear, and they plodded away.

The second the elevator started producing operational noises, No matter what was making its way down to the -13th level, Thomas knew it wasn't good. He rushed over to Helga, still trying her best to convince Elzbieta to call a truce. "Helga! We have to go!"

"I know, Detective! I'm waiting on an answer from 'er to see if we have a deal!"

"You're not going to get any agreement out of her! All she can think about is murder—let's go! We have to decide on a direction!"

"O'right. Elzbieta? Is it a yes or no?"

"Why…would…she……agree t-to that?" Elzbieta struggled to say.

"It's irrelevant! If she doesn't, you get released from Forger's honor, and you can chop us all to bits!" The elevator got louder as the car came down further.

"We're running out of time, luv! Yes or no?"

Thomas ran to the hatch Mausi and her companions had gone through, then over to the secret door Leo had taken. He knew one probably led to instant death while the other may have slightly better odds.

"Elzbieta!" Helga yelled.

"T-thinking…" Elzbieta struggled to say.

The bottom of the elevator slowly descended into the site. "Helga! We have to go!" Thomas yelled.

Helga quickly walked over to him. "Which door are we going through?"

"Either one is bad. You choose."

"I say pick the one Leo went through. No matter what happens, at least I'll get to kill him before we die!"

"That works." She and Thomas trotted over to the secret door. Thomas looked to the elevator to see what trouble was coming down; the car was empty. "Hold on!" They stopped running. The gate door opened by itself. "What's going on?" He cautiously stepped closer into the hallway.

"Detective! We need to leg it!"

"Wait! Why is it empty?"

"Who cares! It just bought us some time!"

"But if we can take this, we might stand a better chance."

"Unless they sent it down here, like a stupid worm to catch stupid fish!"

Thomas got closer to the car. He stopped one foot away. "You're probably right, it's a tra—"

"Detective?"

Thomas was slammed against the wall. He held his hands up as though he seemed to be choking and grabbing onto something under his neck. He took one of his hands and struck low. It came into contact with something. Inga faded into view. She held a staff under Thomas' neck. His hand had struck her in the neither-region.

"I'm not a bloke, but that still 'urt!" Inga complained.

"Inga! Let him go!" Helga yelled. She pointed her techlyn at Inga. "I said! Let—him—go!"

"I heard you, Helga. But I can't do that. He's an escaped prisoner."

"So am I!"

"Don't worry, I'll deal with you later."

"You'll deal with me now! *Mellt!*" A lightning bolt shot out of her teclyn. Before it could strike, Inga jumped back. The bolt went between her and Thomas and hit the wall. Thomas yelled: *"Eh-ha-gu avuh"* and his pen turned into a bayoneted rifle. When it expanded, the blade almost cut Inga's cheek. She jumped back and deflected the blade with her staff. Thomas circled away from her. She pulled her staff apart into two smaller ones joined by a chain.

Helga aimed her weapon at Inga's head and wondered if she had it in her to hurt or even kill her long-time friend. "First, they use yeh as a security guard, and now yeh some kind of bloodhound! What happened to yeh, Inga? I used to look up to yuh."

"Sorry to disappoint," Inga said. "I guess me job's not as glamorous as a maid."

"There is a lot of faffing around, but at least my boss isn't a twit!"

"Your boss is willing to let you die! Just so she can protect that bloody book!"

"Understandably. We're not 'olding on to a recipe for Shepherd's Pie! It's the fate of the world! Did they tell you why they need the book?" Inga remained silent. "I thought so! Not going to share what's actually going on with the worker bees!"

"If she'd just turned it over, none of us would be here...and my sister would still be alive!"

"That's not fair! Mausi is responsible for your sister! Your sister died for the same reason you're down here—risking your life for people who consider you pawns!"

"We're officials on the side of the law! We're not expendable!"

"Not yet!"

"What?" Inga asked.

"Have you not taken a gander since you came in here?"

"Inga did a quick gaze at the ceiling. "So—it's a prison!" She said nervously."

"A prison? A prison with tubes running into the arms of the prisoners and going into the ground? Just yuh ordinary prison! I beg to differ!"

"What...what is all this?"

"This is what yuh government does to us when they want to get rid of us!" When Inga got closer to the half dome in the middle of the room, she tapped it with the side of her boot. "We think there's a Level 13 down there, sucking all our powers out and using it to keep this prison going, probably ever since it was built! That's how much the Dayfides respect us, Inga! Stay in line, or they'll send you down here to be smelted, and used as coal!

"St-still. If you break the law, there has to be some kind of punishment."

"It's inhumane!" Thomas said. "No matter who you are or what you did, you at least deserve a fair trial. And if you're found guilty, even execution is more humane than what they're doing down here —this is torture!"

"That includes leaving a knife in someone?" Helga asked Thomas. He looked away in embarrassment.

"No…this…" Inga noticed the Forgers still chained to the wall. "They—they must have done something really terrible!"

"What about me?" Helga asked. "Do Yeh think I'd ever kill someone for fun? Do I deserve to automatically be tossed down here and be smelted for 50 years? Until I look like that!?" Helga gestured to the mummified body. Mausi killed your sister, Inga! And they put her down here right next to me! Legends, bread stealers—even youngsters; all down here! Equally! We're all the same to them!"

"Not all the same." Shirley's voice suddenly said. Thomas and Helga looked all around. Shirley materialized from the hallway and walked into the room.

"You!" Thomas yelled.

"The Snake!" Helga yelled. She pointed her teclyn at Shirley and said: *"Bêl tân!"* A fireball shot out of her staff towards Shirley. It deflected when it got within 2 feet of hitting her. Tibuta materialized into view, standing in front of Shirley, spinning one of her spiked balls on a chain. Some residue flames dissipated off the weapon, and she stopped spinning it.

Thomas walked backward until he and Helga were next to each other. "Helga?" He said.

"I know, Detective. Just remember, I said, I don't care if I die! I'm up for it, as long as the blonde cow dies first!

Shirley held up her hands and walked around Tibuta until she was between the two groups. "Now, now, mes amis. (my friends), we don't have to start fighting immediately." She looked at the dead bodies on the ground and the hallway. "Ooh, la la! Why do Forgers always want to solve all their problems with combat?"

"You're one to talk, slag!" Helga yelled. "You blew up White Manor and tried to kill everyone!"

"That had nothing to do with me. I just took advantage of the situation."

"Is that what you call it?" Thomas asked. "Why are you down here?" "Coming to take advantage of the current situation? The book is not here, and neither is Mary!"

"I know. She is safe and comfortable outside."

Thomas and Helga looked at each other. "Yeh think she's telling the truth?" Helga asked.

"Probably not."

"Whether you believe me or not is not relevant. Right now, I'm here to fix a more important problem."

"What the devil are you talking about?" Helga asked.

"This prison break of yours has the potential to release a Level 13 Blacksmith back into the world."

"We know that!" Thomas said. "Leo is already on his way to do just that! Right now, he and a bunch of Forgers are heading towards it to get it to join his gang; I doubt they'll be successful."

"Good heavens!" Inga said. "We can't waste time any more with these two! We have to hurry up and stop him!"

"Go ahead, be our guest," Helga said. "He went in that secret door near that mummy!" She pointed at the place against the wall.

"We can't just yet," Shirley said. "To confront a Forger on that level requires the assistance of a weapon of equal power."

"Well, you won't find many weapons like that in a prison," Helga said.

"Oh? Au contraire (On the contrary)." Shirley said. "Remember how that Ironsmith was able to cut through forged metal? Only a Chamfer could've done that." Helga and Thomas tightened their grips on their teclyns.

"So, yeh come here to kill Elżbieta?" Helga said. "That's the only way you can get a hold of that weapon."

"Bien sûr. (of course). Now, please, we have wasted enough time talking. We need to catch up to Leo. Can you tell us where Elzbieta is?"

Thomas looked over at the spot where Elzbieta was. Now, just broken chains. "Helga?"

"She's not here," Helga announced. "I guess she accepted the deal."

"What deal?" Thomas asked. "Helga? What are you talking about? Did you free her? That's—"

"Keep yuh hair on, Detective! Bottom line: Mary and us are now safe from 'er attacks…for now."

Shirley looked frustrated. Allons-y! (Let's go!) She rushed to the location of the secret entrance and moved around until she could see it."

"What about these two?" Inga asked Shirley.

"Forget about them! We have to catch up to Elzbieta before she escapes! Otherwise, we'll never get that sword!" Shirley disappeared into the doorway.

As they left, Inga sadly looked back at Helga. Tibuta paused and did the same, but her expression informed them how lucky they were, not having to fight her.

Thomas turned to Helga. "Where is she? Where did she go?"

"I said, don't worry 'bout 'er, Detective. She won't be coming after us or Mary, for now."

"What did you say to her?"

"It's between her and Mary now."

Thomas looked angry. "I wish you would have included me in that conversation!"

"Right. Let's leave it out for now and focus on getting out of 'ere."

"Mausi didn't come back. So there's the possibility her group found the exit and escaped."

"That or they all perished."

"Let's take the easy way out, then." They walked around all the bodies and the spiked floor in the hallway to get to the elevator. They both stepped inside. Helga was about to lift the lever to take the car up. She paused for an unexpected amount of time. "Ah, bugger!"

"Helga? Is something wrong?"

Helga took a deep breath and stepped out of the elevator.

"Helga?"

"Shirley is right."

"What! Right about what?"

"A Blacksmith convict would be dangerous out and about."

"Why? What can happen?"

"The last time a Blacksmith acted up was in the 1300s. Almost 200 million people died back then."

"200 million! Good lord!"

"Yeah. So yuh see, I can't risk one getting out of here. Especially beholden to Leo! My conscience won't allow it."

"But what can you do?"

"Whatever I can. We have Chamfers as well. Even without Elzbieta, I should at least be able to slow it down. Besides, they imprisoned it down here somehow." Helga started walking backward. "You go find Mary, I'll 'andle this."

"Don't be ridiculous!" Thomas left the elevator.

"What are you doing? You don't have to come! Take the elevator upstairs. You can probably 'andle the guards—but I don't think you can 'andle this thing."

"And neither can you, alone!"

"Detective...Thomas. This thing may kill you with the wave of their finger!"

"After all we've been through, you think I'll abandon one of my mates?

"Mates?"

"Yes, that's what you British call good friends, right?"

"Yes...Mates." Helga smiled and then walked off in a huff. "Fine then, crack on! Try to keep up, and don't blame me if you get killed!"

"Of course."

Helga and Thomas entered the secret passage.

Mausi materialized in the hallway. She was out of breath and sweaty. "Coor! Holding a forge that long really takes a lot out of yuh." She entered the elevator. "Don't mind if I do." She lifted the lever and started her ascent.

"153?" The man in the top hat called out. "153?" He unlocked the metal door leading to the special wing for Forgers. "153? Where are you? Your shift is up!" He yelled. He carefully looked around. "Are you invisible? Where are you?" He arrived at the cells where Thomas and Leo had been. Inside one of them, a groggy man winced in pain and held his ankle. "153?" The top-hatted man unlocked the cell and entered. "What happened? He glanced around the room. "Where are the prisoners?'"

"…Escaped…" the injured 153 struggled to say.

"Escaped!? Both of them!?"

153 nodded.

"A prison break! We gotta sound the alarm!"

In the shower room of the regular part of Tombs prison, a group of convicts cleaned themselves with lye soap. The acidic cleaning material and the cold water were unpleasant, but the prisoners still seemed to take pleasure in washing away all the sins they had committed inside and outside the prison walls. On the floor, the overworked drains clogged into a pool of stagnant water. Standing in it was annoying, but the prisoners tolerated it, well aware that any complaints resulted in mocking indifference.

Everyone stopped. The sound of a hand crank siren alarm blared through the complex. The alarms were used seldomly, except during riots or escapes. Everyone here knew this hadn't happened since the 1800s.

"Lockdown! Lockdown!"a guard yelled, rushing into the shower area. "Back to your cells! Back to your cells!" He waved a baton in the air. More guards entered the room. The slow speed of the prisoners grabbing towels and drying themselves infuriated them.

The guards hit them on the back with their batons. "Move it! Move it!" They yelled. The prisoners scrambled to leave. The guards struck any man not moving fast enough.

The sound of slamming cage doors and yelling from the guards echoed through the halls as they forced prisoners back into their cells.

A slow drip from the inferior shower heads trickled down to an inch-deep pool of water in the empty shower room. The surface stirred and swirl into a whirlpool. Mary, Min, and Fritz pulled themselves up out of the Vorago, and stood.

Mary regarded the alarm. "Sounds like they're aware of our presence.

"Eww! Min complained. "This water is worse than that mud puddle we came out of!"

"Mary wrinkled her nose. "Still better than a toilet…a tad.

"Where are we?" Fritz asked.

Mary noticed the dripping shower heads. "The men's facilities." "Looks like we just missed bath time. Thank heavens for that, not in the mood to witness men's credentials. Come along then, we have to figure out how to get to the underground area." She lead the way to the hallway. Three guards in the hall finished locking cell doors. Their facial expressions were just as shocked as Mary's group, when they spotted a woman in a bathing suit, a boy and a Chinese girl in a white frilly dress inside a prison

"What in Saint Peter's name?" One of the guards yelled.

"Oh, hello," Mary said. "We seem to be lost. Can you please show us the way to the elevator?"

The guards looked at each other. One gestured to Mary with his baton. "Nab 'em!" They rushed to attack with their batons in the air. Before Mary could speak another word, Min had ignited into action and stopped the lead attacker. Using only one arm, she turned the man's weapon behind his back and then used her foot to kick him into one of the cell doors, knocking him unconscious. The prisoners burst into cheers and jeers.

"Min! Don't kill them!" Mary yelled.

Min rolled her eyes and continued with restrained strikes.

The other guards focused on attacking her. She flipped one onto the ground and did an axe kick to his head. She halted the other's baton and followed up with a fist strike to his chest, incapacitating him. With each hit, the prisoners roared in approval.

"Alright then, we need to get to the lift," Mary said. "Take your bow, and let's go." Min bowed a little to the applauding prisoners, then followed Mary and Fritz..

As the alarm bells rang, more guards tried to apprehend the strange group that had suddenly appeared in the middle of the prison. Mary said: *"Qwithie gwint!"* A large gust of wind came from her hand and pushed the men against the wall, knocking most unconscious. The others were too disoriented to stand and pursue.

They made it to the end of the hall. Mary pressed the button to call the elevator. The gears and levers clicked and clanked, signaling its approach.

"Hmm," she said.

"What is it?" Min asked.

"This is relatively easy. I expected at least one Forger."

They got inside the elevator car. Mary was about to pull the lever but paused.

Fritz exited. Mary followed, pulling Min out by the hand.

"What is wrong with you two? Min asked.

A figure appeared inside the elevator.

"Mausi!" Mary yelled.

"Fiddle Sticks! I wuz hope'n to slit yer throats before yuh noticed me." Mausi stepped out. She held up her hook hand. Min pointed her quiang at her. "'Old on, no need for all that." She held up one of her small bombs.

"If you do that, you'll probably collapse the floor in here," Mary said.

"Most likely. I don't want any trouble. I just want to slip past you."

"And escape?" Mary asked. "Never! You deserve to be in here for all of your crimes!"

"Believe me, dearie, there are far worse people on the -13th floor. But as much as I'd like to discuss justice and morality...why don't yeh three get in the lift, go do whatever daft thing you're here for, and I'll be on me way. Otherwise, I'm gonna bury us all under tons of rubble!"

They cautiously re-entered the elevator as Mausi backed away into the hallway. After Mausi was far away, her bomb thumped onto the floor, and rolled towards them.

"I knew it!" Min yelled.

"*Crafanyo dül lo!*" Mary yelled. "In an instant, hundreds of concrete hands morphed out of the floor and surrounded the bomb in a dome. A second later, a contained explosion cracked the dome and expelled smoke like a cherry bomb. They fanned the smoke away and closed the gate of the elevator. Mary pulled the lever and they descended.

"Why did you let her go?" Fritz asked.

"Sometimes you have to sacrifice a chess piece; she's the perfect distraction. While everyone is busy with her, they'll ignore us."

When the taxi made a left and steered towards the docks, Victoria almost told the driver he was heading in the wrong direction. She realized it meant they were not going to the prison, and why would she protest that? The taxi left the road and bumped over a rocky beach. When it arrived underneath the supports of the Brooklyn Bridge, she could not contain her growing curiosity. "Where are we?"

Gertrude exited the taxi. It started rolling forward, towards the East River. Victoria leaped out when the water flooded inside, and reached her ankles. "What are you doing?" She yelled at the driver. The automobile continued into the water and disappeared underneath the surface. "Was he trying to kill me?" Victoria yelled at Gertrude.

"For now, there is no advantage to you being dead," Gertrude answered. She walked around discarded wine barrels, and broken bottles towards a cave entrance obstructed by tall grass and rusty iron bars.

"What is this place?"

"The prison."

"This isn't the prison entrance."

"This is <u>our</u> prison's entrance."

The battle-scarred floor and the impaled and decapitated bodies left Mary, Min, and Fritz aghast when the elevator door opened.

Mary tried not to waste too much time standing around in awe at the inside structure. "Thomas? Helga?" she yelled.

"They're not here," Fritz said.

"You said they were down here. Where are they?"

Fritz sniffed the area as Mary and Min searched for clues to their friends' whereabouts."

"I know where they went…" Said a voice from up high.

Mary found a bent ladder off to the side in good enough condition to climb up to the sound's source. At the top, Mary found a 100-year-old man chained to the wall.

"Where did they go?" She asked. "What happened here?"

"You think I'll give you information for free?" He scoffed.

What do you wish?"

"What do you think? You stupid girl! Release me!"

"I have neither a weapon nor a key that will work on these chains."

"What about the one around your neck? Idiot!"

"I'm fairly certain my father didn't build this prison!" Mary cast a glance at her key. She removed it, inserted it into the lock on his chain, and twisted it. "Observe! It doesn't — His arm chain came loose and hit the floor with a thump as the lock opened. "Hold on... That isn't feasible! Did my father craft these chains?"

"I don't care who made what, you ridiculous girl! Loosen my other arm and free me! Before she finds out! Fool!"

"Yes, of course. But could you please refrain from your insults? It gives some justification for why you're down here in the first place!"

Mary put her key in the lock to free the man. His eyes widened in terror.

She felt dread mixed with a chill between her shoulder blades. "What is this?" she asked.

The man gasped for air. His skin became more and more wrinkled. Mary noticed the wiggling silver cord connected to his arm. "Is this hurting you?" She pulled it out, and he stopped moving and slumped down.

"What? What just happened?"

"Is he dead?" Min asked

Mary checked his pulse. "Quite." She noticed an aged woman chained nearby and approached her to get answers. Before she could come within a foot of the woman, all life was physically sucked out of her body "Oh my!" Mary yelled. "That time I didn't even touch them!" She glanced at the others, chained to the wall. "These poor souls! It's like they are being sucked dry of all their life energy."

"Stay away!" A prisoner yelled from another level. A few others yelled similar commands. They didn't need to warn her away; she had already chosen not to attempt any more rescues. She touched the hand of the recently deceased.

"Through here!" Fritz yelled.

"What?" Mary asked.

"They went this way!"

Mary climbed down to meet him and Min at the mummified body. She watched as Fritz went beyond the illusion and entered the secret entrance.

"Fritz?"

Mary and Min followed.

Every remaining prisoner convulsed and screamed in agony as the silver tubes connected to their arms constricted. Their bodies shriveled, and they all expired in a wave of mass executions.

The further they walked, the darker the lighting in the stone tunnel became. Victoria tripped and stumbled on a rock but kept herself from falling. "Where are we going?" She asked Gertrude.

"Just a bit further. Patience, child."

"I can't see anything!"

Gertrude sighed, then stopped walking. Victoria wasn't sure if she was upset.

"Wh—"

Gertrude held her hand up to quiet Victoria. After a long moment passed, Victoria was about to speak, but a sound caught her attention; skittering and pattering echoed all around the tunnel. "What is that?"

"They're here."

Hundreds—thousands of tiny blue lights swarmed towards them. Victoria took her place behind Gertrude even though Gertrude was shorter than she. The little lights surrounded them and illuminated the inside of the cave. When she had got a better look at the light source of animated rat skeletons, Victoria felt her fear vindicated. She clutched Gertrude's shoulder and looked around for a means of escape.

'Do not worry, child, they're merely more vessels you can choose to do your bidding."

"Why would I ever choose such horrid creatures?"

"It's normal for the living to fear the dead. Yet, have you noticed? The way they light our way to our destination. Is it not beautiful?"

Assured they were not in danger, Victoria released Gertrude. They walked through the glowing blue tunnel. Gertrude was right. If she ignored the source, the path created by the dead was almost relaxing. Victoria moved closer to the wall to get a better look at one of the creatures. It hissed at her.

Leo and his foundry felt along the walls of the chamber. "Anything?" Leo yelled.

"No way out except that door!" said Rosina.

"How do you know?"

"I told you. I know architecture. Don't question my skills again."

Leo returned to the woman in the nest of vines.

"If you've seen what you came to see, then you can leave," Murphy said. "Use the water and Vorago out of here."

"No, not yet. Not until you tell me who the woman in the nest is." He waved his arms around."...and this."

"All you need to know is there's no way you'll ever be able to break those chains. And even if you could, someone like her would never join forces with someone like YOU."

"Someone like me? Someone like me? Leo angrily said. "And what is someone like me? Someone like me now has one of the most powerful foundries in the city—maybe the world! Someone like me is about to bust out of a place I'm sure no one ever escapes from! And someone like me can easily bend your smug, stupid Dayfide brain, get all the info I want, and then send you off to go walk in front of a trolly!"

"That would be much more desirable than watching some sidekick goop acting like he's a leader."

"I am a leader!"

Murphy scoffed. "Admit it, boy! You're just a plug-ugly simp! Out for himself! Now stop all this nonsense and leave this place before you get the other half of your men killed!"

Leo held a knife to Murphy's neck. "You really want me to kill you, don't you?"

"Then do it!"

Leo paused for a long moment. His heart was racing.

"What are you waiting for?" One of the women said.

Leo looked nervous. He looked back at the others. Something was different. He did a quick count. "Wait...What? Where did..."

"Something wrong?" Murphy asked.

Leo put the blade to Murphy's eye. "What happens to the other half of my men!?" Leo's hand was shaking as he waited for an answer. He looked back. Even more of his gang were gone. The rest began to look around and steadied themselves for battle.

"Okay, have it your way. Leo said. He put his hand on Murphy's head. *"Oo-aid vell ur woove ur aid dwaid!"*

Murphy's eyes turned red.

"How do I get out of the prison?" Leo asked him.

"No one comes in or out of here without her permission."

"Then get her permission!"

"I can't control her and neither will you."

"What happened to my men?"

"They are probably dead. I don't know what she does with them."

Leo panicked. There were now only three others left

"Who is she?"

"Death."

"Enough with the bunk! Who is she really?"

"Pestilence."

"No more flip answers! What's her real name!"

"En—" A vine wrapped around Murphy's mouth.

Only Leo and Murphy remained. Vines grabbed onto Leo's legs.

He remembered being in a situation like this, back at White Manor in London, restrained by vines, then ice from Miss Wayward. He struggled to free himself. *"Roy are don!"* A small fire flared up on one of the vines. The vine retracted into the water, put itself out, and snaked around his leg. *"Roy are don! Roy are don! Roy are don!"* Leo yelled. Multiple flare-ups attacked whichever vines were slithering up to his neck. They retracted and tried again at unprotected areas. He remembered; in London, it wasn't the vines or the ice that did him in, it was Max's betrayal. He felt something he had tried hard to oppress: great sadness. An image of Shirley Blanche's face came into his mind. He was being dragged down, like the boy outside. 'Am I going to hell?' he thought. He looked up at Murphy.

A last-minute feeling of anger came over Leo. "Shirley was there with Max! Since the beginning—they all betrayed me! Everyone betrays me! I've been a fool to believe in any of them! To believe that Mary could love me! I'm here because of her!" Leo sunk further and was losing his battle against the vines and himself. Murphy stood emotionless, his red eyes still looking down judgmentally at him. With the last bit of his fortitude, Before his throat was tightened too much by vines to speak, Leo yelled as loud as he could with a raspy voice: "Kill…yourself…"

His world went dark.

The President's motorcade filed in line in front of Vanderbilt Manor. After one of the top-hatted men opened the door of the luxury auto, Wilson stepped out. He took a cleansing breath, checked his watch, and smiled: "Beautiful day, isn't it?" he said. To the top-hatted man. The top-hatted man looked taken aback by the comment. He reluctantly agreed. The President checked his watch again. "In…about 30 minutes, I'll be able to accomplish what no President has done."

"And what's that, Mr. President?"

Realizing he was talking out loud, the President cleared his throat. "Don't worry about it. As long as she agrees. But at noon, everything will go as planned."

"Yes sir."

They walked into the manor, were led into the parlor room, and served tea and biscuits. "Where is Miss White?" he asked one of the maids.

"I think she's still in bed."

"In bed? At noon? It's a rather important day to be sleeping in. Make sure she's up! I don't want to be kept waiting!"

"Yes, sir." the maid went off to relay the message.

Alva came in, greeted Wilson, and was about to sit across from him.

"Mrs Belmont, I'd prefer you not be here," the President said.

"Pardon?"

"I have a sensitive matter to discuss with Miss Mary White."

"Oh? But I'm sure whatever it is, I can offer her support. And..." Alva noticed his face had become stiff and unwelcoming. The two top-hatted men looked rather stern and intimidating. "Oh...I see. Well then, I shall take my leave. I'll see you later in the day."

When Alva stepped outside the room, the maid who had gone to check on Mary returned. "M-Miss Belmont," she said nervously.

"Yes, what is it? Is something wrong?"

Alva followed the maid upstairs to Mary's room. The door was open.

"What's going on?" Alva said with frustration and a little bit of fear in her voice.

"I was going to go in and give her some lunch. She didn't answer the door when I tried to give her breakfast! I figure she was trying to sleep!"

She pushed past the maid, entered the room, and saw the bed, all disheveled with ropes attached to its headboard. A pair of muddy footprints lead from the bed to a bloodied bed sheet rope hanging out the open window. "Dear heavens! Call the police!"

The President stood when Alva returned to the parlor. He was about to restate his desire for her not to be there, but Alva cut him off.

"She's gone! I'm afraid something nefarious has happened to her!"

Without regarding Alva, the President and his men rushed upstairs. They then hurried outside to see the bed rope reaching to the ground. On the bottom lay the bodies of the men in charge of guarding Mary, their heads facing backward.

"You think she escaped?" the assistant asked.

"No you idiot, she couldn't even walk! Think she could break out of those ropes, crawl all the way down here, and then kill both of these fellas? She's not even a Forger! She was either taken or rescued!"

"By who?"

"I don't care! Call the prison and execute her people!"

"Mr. President?"

"It's been 24 hours! She didn't hand over the book. I'm a man of my word! Get me the prison, we're going to teach her a lesson about sneaking off!"

They returned to the parlor room. The secretary retrieved a long corded phone and stretched it to the President. The operator connected him to the Warden's phone. The President could hear an alarm blaring from the earpiece. "What's going on over there?" he asked, snatching the phone from the assistant. "Hello? Hello? What in the hell is going on over there?"

"I'm not sure sir it—well, the—" the Warden said. "I can't talk right now! We're having an emergency!"

"I don't care if your own mother is dying! This is the President speaking!"

"I know, Mr. President. But somebody got inside of the prison!"

"Why would anyone want...if they broke into the prison, it should be easier to catch them! And lock them up!"

"Yes, sir, of course."

"Listen, I don't want to keep you, I just have one simple order: Execute Helga of 'Pendel' on negative floor 13!"

"The British lady?"

"Yes. Is there a problem with that?"

"Well...Yes. We think the break-ins headed down there."

"To negative 13?"

"Yes sir."

"That sneaky..."

"Sir?"

She's sending her henchmen to try to take away our bargaining chip! Listen, I'm sending the toughest Forgers I can find to come down there and quench your break-in."

"Thank you, Mr. President."

Just hold tight! The Calvary is on the way!" He hung up the phone and turned his attention back to the secretary. "Get me every powerful forger in New York we have!"

"Unfortunately, sir. Most of the ones that work for us are still guarding the transfer of the treasury. The others are looking for Gwenhwyvar."

"Then talk to Shirley Blanche, I'm sure she can spare some of her Forgers!"

"Maximilian. Was the only one we could confirm that was working for her. She claims the rest are in Europe fighting against the Germans."

"That's a lie! What about Miss Wayward..."

Three lifeboats full of German survivors rowed away from the smoldering dock which used to be their base. Captain Shwieiger surveyed the destroyed dock, with his spyglass.

War es wieder der mit dem großen schwert? (Was it the one with the big sword, again?)" he asked his first mate.

"Nein, diesmal nicht (No, not this time.)" the First mate answered.

Captain Shwieiger sighed. "All that work…I hate this country so much."

On the aft deck of the RMS Olympic, Miss Wayward stepped over the body of a German. She spotted Shwieiger and his crew off in the distance. She considered pursuing them for a moment but restrained herself. In the empty bridge, an unanswered phone rang constantly.

Mary, Min, and Fritz arrived at a tall door. The last thing they expected to see was someone searching the body of a young man.

"Who is that? Is he helping that injured lad?" Mary asked. "I think I know that man."

The man took a knife out of the boy's pocket and pointed it at his own throat.

"Hey!" Min yelled

Like an autonomic response, Mary slipped into her fast state. By the time Murphy was halfway to stabbing himself in the throat, Mary was already upon him. She grabbed the knife, preventing it from going any further. The two began a suicide tug-of-war; Mary held the wiggling knife back, and Murphy tried with all his might to end his life.

Mary noticed his red eyes. "Mr. Murphy! Please stop!" She yelled." Her words were just air to him, and he continued to struggle with her.

Annoyed with the scene, Min walked over, and with one smack to the side of the head, Murphy fell sideways and released control of the knife.

"Thanks, Min...I think," Mary said. "You didn't kill him, did you? That would be counterproductive."

"He's fine. See."

Murphy shook his head and groggily sat upright. "Wh-What... Where?"

"Mr. Murphy? It's Mary White. We met when my father worked with you to improve working conditions in factories."

"Oh...yes...How did I get out here?"

"Not sure. Your eyes were quite red, and you were trying to stab yourself."

"Red eyes? Stab myself...Oh, right..."

Mary examined the dead boy next to Murphy, she frowned after finding no pulse."Poor lad. Who was he?"

"One of Leo's subordinates.

"Did you say, Leo? Is Leopold Bianca somewhere down here."

"Murphy pointed towards the chamber. "In...in there."

"All right, let's go, everyone." Mary stood and started to leave. Murphy grabbed her arm.

"Are you insane? I have no idea how you got down here, but don't go in there! Something very dangerous is in there!"

"I know. It's been a part of my life for the last 17 years. I think it's high time I met her face to face."

Murphy sighed and let go of her. "You're just like your father.""

"Thank you."

"Listen. I'm sorry that everyone is trying to get that book out of you—I regret ever helping Wilson get elected. But I owe you for saving my life. If you ever need anything, you can come to me, and no matter what the President says, I'll make sure you always have a safe harbor in New York."

"Thank you, Mr. Murphy. Take care of yourself.

"You too!"

She scanned the entryway. "Safe to assume we're not going to be run through by a spiked booby trap."

"Booby what?" Min asked.

"It's a type of bird…" Mary noticed Fritz had stopped at the entrance and stared intensely at the darkness. "Fritz? Are they in there? And alive?"

"They are."

"What ever-so is the matter, child? You look like you've seen a ghost."

"Worst than ghost"

"Pardon?"

"I can smell everyone in there. Floating inside an empty ocean."

Mary looked down at Fritz's fearful and ashen face. "It's the abyss. Shall we go?"

"You're still going in there?" Min asked.

"Yes. It can't be avoided. She's in there."

"What if it's a booby thing?"

"Hmm, true. Tell you what. You stay out here and slowly count to 900. After that, call out to see if we're okay."

"900?"

"15 minutes."

Mary turned to leave, but Min grabbed her arm. Mary patted Min's hand away and continued into the darkness.

Mary and Fritz treaded carefully into the dark chamber. They stopped when they noticed the spot-lit woman off in the distance. "That must be her," Mary said.

They walked towards the light on the layer of water covering the floor.

Mary looked up. "I don't think that light is from the outside or electric. My aunt said: 'If you look towards the light, darkness will always be behind you.' Even in the abyss, there is light.

She looked at her reflection in the water. "Is this an underground well or something? We're nowhere near the rivers or a lake."

"That's not just water," Fritz said.

"Not water?"

"It smells like people...lots of people.

"What are you going on about?"

He bent down onto his haunches, dipped his fingers into the water, and smelled it."

"Is it like old bath water?"

"No...it's...it's not just people; bugs, rats, plants—living things all...all in here."

"A soup?"

"Everything soup."

He started to walk again, and Mary nervously grabbed his arm.

"Wait! Let's not rush into this. Can you still smell Elzbieta?"

"Yes."

Mary looked around. "Let's put some light on the stage and see what we're dealing with. *Headvan Tân!*" A dozen little firefly lights came out of Mary's hand and flew away to opposite sides of the chamber. The lights spot-lit the ancient concrete walls covered in white vines, stretching up to the ceiling light source at the top of the dome "Those vines, I've seen them before. They look similar to the ones that protected our houses in the UK. I don't see anyone. Where did our friends go?"

Fritz was traipsing on the water and looking down. He stopped at a certain area. "Here."

"Pardon?"

"Man that smells like peppermint is here."

"What? Who?"

"Thomas."

"Thomas? Thomas is where?"

"Here."

"Where?"

"Down there."

"In the water?"

"I don't know, but his scent is strongest. Right here."

Mary joined Fritz and then got down on her hands and knees. She rubbed her hands over the ground under the water. "I don't feel any irregularities. If he's down there, we can't get to him. But, maybe she can…" Mary looked at the vine nest and then at Fritz, who was now gone. "Fritz?" She stood fast. "She waved her hand around. The firefly lights traveled to wherever she pointed. "Fritz?" She yelled. Without further instructions, the fireflies returned to Mary's side and circled her. "Drat!" She took one last gander around and then at the entrance. "Min! Don't come in here! It's a trap!" There was no response. She hoped she had reached her before she had finished her counting. 'Why didn't she answer?' Mary waited. 'Whatever had snatched up my friends is going to come for me next!' Nothing happened. The object in the spotlight was not that far off. If she walked towards it, would it activate the trap? Could she even reach it? She took a chance. With steady, calculated strides, she traveled to the person in the nest of vines, waiting for something to happen. At the end of her journey, she paused and looked back again. The ripples from her footsteps traveled across the reflective pool, from her to the far ends of the room, like sound waves. She looked down at all of the twisting white vines and followed them to their destination. Unlike Leo, Mary was not surprised to see the mummified woman in the center of the light. 'Of course, someone so powerful they could enter dreams and manipulate the dead would be old, and the chains wrapped around her explained the only reason they wouldn't be out in the world!'

"Hello?" Mary said. "I assume the fact that I am standing here means you meant for it to happen." She moved in close to get a better look at the figure's skin, coated in a white crust, like an ancient statue left unattended for hundreds of years. "I'm not sure if introductions are in order, but my name is—"

"Mary White?" yelled a voice from behind her. Mary turned around.

Victoria and Gertrude were walking towards her from the entrance.

"Victoria? You came!...and?"

Gertrude walked past Victoria and Mary and examined the body. "It's a strange thing. To see oneself from this angle," Gertrude said.

"Oneself?" Mary asked.

"She's using the body of my friend Gertrude," Victoria answered.

"So this is..."

Gertrude turned her attention to Mary. "Pythonissa."

"Pythonissa?" Mary asked.

"Like a giant snake?" Victoria asked.

"No," Mary said. "Pythia is an ancient word for the first soothsayers. Pythonissa was the first...the first witch, also called... Endor...You're the Witch of Endor."

Victoria took a step back. "From the Bible?"

Gertrude went back to looking at the body. "Yes. Among many names, I am what you call in your book of tales: 'The Witch of Endor.'" She turned to Mary. "You don't seem surprised."

"For someone to accomplish the things you've done, I surmised you must be someone of great power. My only query is, why would someone in your position need my help? Or even the help of two young girls?"

Gertrude gestured to the body. "Do you not see for yourself?"

"Your freedom? Is that what this was all about? The visions? Hiding my forging from the authorities? Even going so far as to give us the Eye of Graeae? Impeding on Victoria's life and using her to fight? All so we could make it down here and free you?" You do realize there are only two kinds of people in prison? Those wrongly convicted and those who are guilty. Which are you? Why would an innocent person be chained up in the sub-basement of a prison, inside a clo keffin? Blacksmiths aren't exactly known for spreading world peace!"

"You are correct in saying I deserve to be here. Your father saw to that."

"My father?"

"Yes. He built this place to hold me after I was captured, in 1666. They later built the prison on top of it."

"That's over 200 years ago! Just how old was my father?"

"Older than you think. Only those that belonged to the Round Table were powerful enough to capture me."

"A knight? So he put you in here? All the more reason not to let you go!"

"Oh, you misunderstand my reasoning. I didn't bring you down here to free me...I bought you down here to kill me."

It took Mary a moment to comprehend what Gertrude had said. "Kill you? All of this was to get someone to kill you? I'm sure many visitors in the 200 or so years you've been down here could have easily been tasked with that! Why me? Why them!" Mary gestured to Victoria. "And what did you do to my friends? And Leo, and all those Forgers I saw in the Eye? I'm sure any one of them would be quite willing to grant your wish!"

"Only a Blacksmith can kill another Blacksmith."

Mary looked at Victoria. "There are at least two others in this world besides her!"

"They refused."

"Why?"

"They would rather see me out in the world, causing chaos again. If one Blacksmith dies, another takes their place. That new one may not be prone to destruction or population control and may even work against them."

"Population control? Is that your metonymy for it? Did my father put you in here for your practice of population control?"

"It was my greatest count of creating the balance. Back then, I was known by another name: Pestilence,"

"1666...the end of the Great Plague...that was you!"

Gertrude didn't answer.

Mary's heart raced. "Not many can say they've looked death in the eyes! Victoria? What do you think? Are you willing to end her life?"

Victoria looked disgusted. "No, of course not!"

"I didn't think so. It seems your plan is awash in failure, Pestilence. I'm sure you'll get another chance in 200 years with someone else. Now, please! Release my friends, and let us be on our way."

"When you kill me, I will release all of your friends."

"Ah, a hostage negotiation. I wish I was the one tasked because I would literally kill for my friends. But as I'm not a Blacksmith and Victoria is too innocent to dispatch anyone, I doubt we can be of help."

"Please, help me."

"Why are you in such a rush to die? You're over 1000 years old! A couple of hundred years down here couldn't have soured your taste for reaping so much, your guilty conscience would rather die than cause any more harm?"

"Love."

"Love? You fell in love? With who, or whom?" Gertrude looked Mary in the eyes. "With...Me?...With my father?"

"I'm sure you're well aware of the deal he made with me to change you from Mary Black into Mary White?"

"Yes. He allowed a woman he once loved to...Oh.......Oh God, no!".

"Miss White?" Victoria asked. "What are you two talking about?"

Mary walked unsteadily over to the nest and examined Pythonissa's face. She then woefully came down onto her knees. "No…"

Gertrude walked over and put her hand on Mary's head. "It's okay, child. Until I died, I enjoyed every moment of our time together."

"No …it wasn't real…" Mary muttered, tears welled in her eyes.

"Of course it was real. What is reality but the story your mind tells you?"

"Why didn't Gwenhwyvar tell me…"

"To keep you away from your mother."

"It wasn't real!"

Gertrude got down on her haunches. "Remember in Wales when we would sit in the garden among the African daisies, the warm sun on our faces? You would lay on my lap, and I would put a daisy behind your ear and read The Brothers Grimm, or The Adventures of Tom Sawyer. Oh! How you loved hearing about life in the colonies—"

"Stop!" Mary yelled.

Gertrude stood. "It was real. As real as you want it to be."

"I don't understand what's going on," Victoria said. "What are you two talking about?"

"It's nothing, child." Just a mother-daughter spat." Gertrude said.

"What?"

"Back to the matter at hand." Gertrude got down on her knees and held Victoria's hands. "Please, release me from this eternal prison. I beg of you."

"I…even if I wanted, there's no way I can! Murder is a sin!"

"Is it really murder if I'm asking you to do it? Or is it a charitable act? When they shot that horse, would it have been better for him to keep pulling a cart with a broken leg…in constant pain? Do I not deserve as much mercy as a horse?"

"Still…I won't do it!"

"You've heard her," Mary said. "Now, release everyone!"

Gertrude stood up and walked over to the body. "When I die, everyone will instantly be released. You may go if you want, but your friends will remain down here, slowly being smelted for the next 50 years."

"Fifty years?" Mary yelled. "What did you do to them?"

The sound of breaking branches emanated from the nest outwards towards the walls. Victoria ran to Mary. Mary put her arm around her and spread out her firefly lights to get a better view of the entire chamber. Around the room, roots under the floor rose from the water in arches. The end of each arch pulled something up and out of the ground; large dripping shapes rose and became giant white and green lilies with milky-white, translucent elongated beans hanging from their centers. Mary counted at least 23 of them. When the Lillies finished rising, the vines rested around them, like sleeping snakes.

"What in God's name?" Mary asked.

"An anghenfêl plant." Gertrude answered. "200 years ago, this was just a fungus. But when it reached my body and fed on my coal, it transformed over time to what you see here."

"I knew these roots looked familiar." Your vines protected our houses."

"Yes. So you see, I've always been on your side, protecting your family...my family from the outside world."

Mary walked to one of the lilies while looking down at the roots. "If these stretch all the way to Britain...these aren't roots... rhizomes?"

"Is there something inside that one?" Victoria pointed to one of the lilies.

Mary joined her. Victoria was right. There was a figure inside the translucent bean-shaped objects. Mary put her face to its side, as close as she could, without feeling too uncomfortable. The face of the figure came into blurry focus. "Leo!"

"Uncle Thomas!" Victoria yelled from another plant. Mary ran over to her and put her hands on the bean's surface. "Thomas! Can you hear me? Although stressed, Thomas seemed to be sleeping. "What did you do to them!" Mary yelled at Gertrude.

"They're sleeping, as they will do until their slow demise."

"Not if I have my say in the matter! Mary pulled her fist back

"I wouldn't do that!" Gertrude yelled. Mary stopped and looked back at her. "...Even if you had the power to punch your way inside the pods, the minute you do, the other pods will smelt the life force of the others, instantly killing them, including Min, and Helga."

"Min? You claim to be on my side, yet you would kill some of the same ones you protected!"

"I simply want to show you how committed I am. I don't want to hurt anyone; if I did, they would already be dead. But I will do everything I can unless you prevent me from doing it! Victoria, is the life of your uncle and the others worth saving mine?"

"I..." Victoria rubbed her hand over Thomas' prison. "It's ..."

"Is it the act? The method? Here!" One of the lilies leaned downwards. The elongated egg opened like a burst balloon, and liquid gushed out, followed by the metallic thud of something falling out of it. Mary and Victoria walked over to examine the object. "Is that a parasol?" Victoria asked.

"It's a special weapon in disguise," Mary answered. "Caliburn, King Pendragon's sword, to be precise. Victoria reached down to pick it up. "Don't do that! It has a curse on it!"

"She will have no problem touching it," Gertrude said. "Curses don't work on Blacksmiths. Go ahead."

Victoria hesitated, looked at Mary, and then reached down and grabbed the handle. The second she touched it, the parasol transformed into an English longsword. Victoria held it aloft and had a look of wonderment.

"It didn't turn into a gigantic sword," Mary said.

"This is its original form. Elzbieta preferred the berserker style.

"Why do you need that particular sword?" Mary asked."

"It has to be a Campher."

"But, there are others in the world. Why Caliburn?"

Your father searched far and wide for just the right one. Each failed. He finally narrowed it down to the sword of Pendragon."

"He was collecting Chamfers…"

"As part of our arrangement, to free me from this long torment."

"So, all of this was to get that sword and this girl here?" Mary pointed to Victoria. Gertrude didn't answer. "And what's my part in all this?" Gertrude remained silent. "Oh, I see. Everything you've done: processing my mind, warning me about Elzbieta—what else did you do? Did you kill my parents at the circus? My father on the Lusitania? Was that part of your plan?"

"Your father was on his way to England because he heard a reincarnate Ironsmith was there wielding Caliburn. He knew she would try to hunt him down as she had done in the past, but unfortunately, the Germans ruined his plan."

"So he really was looking for a weapon."

"For me…he did all of this for me."

Victoria was still looking at the sword. "Miss White…what should I do?"

Mary put her hand on Victoria's shoulder. "I don't know, Victoria. We can't let the others die, and I know my father was probably trying to help her, but there's still something off about this whole thing. I'm sure this is all quite overwhelming for you. It's not an easy decision to take a life, even if they ask you to. Recently I had to take the life of a literal monster, and I still think about it. I believe you must act in the best interests of yourself and the others. If you truly can't do it, we'll find another way to rescue everyone. I'm sure we can come up with something in 50 years—"

"And what about your friend Gertrude?" Gertrude interrupted. Mary and Victoria looked at her. "Shall I walk her outside into the river? Jump from the nearest building?"

"No!" Victoria cried.

"Don't let her manipulate you Victoria," Mary said.

"She's going to kill her!"

"Oh, not just her…" Gertrude walked closer to Victoria. "I can influence those on the outside as well…your father for example."

"My father? What about him?"

"Right now, imagine him in a poker hall, desperately gambling away the last of his earnings. If he loses, he will fall into despair, and it will be quite easy to push him into desperation and even violence…"

"Victoria! Don't listen to her!" Mary yelled.

"How easy…" Gertrude continued, "…it would be to send him to your house…"

"Stop!" Victoria said.

"He asks your mother for more money, she says no, and he strikes her…"

"Stop!"

Gertrude began to circle Victoria. "He gets desperate—searches the house—finds nothing—she tries to stop him and in his rage —"

"NO!" Victoria stomped over to the body of Pythonissa.

"Victoria!" Mary yelled, "She's using the power of desp—" A vine-covered her mouth. She tried to remove it, but other vines restrained her arms.

Victoria stood by the body and paused.

"Your mother's last word will be to call your name…Vic-tor-i —"

With her heart overflowing with fear and rage, Victoria brought the sword down. It easily cut through the chains and buried itself in the center of the corpse's chest, causing it to flinch. A silvery dust emanated from the gash.

"Thank you," Gertrude said. She closed her eyes and collapsed onto the ground.

All became quiet.

"Gertrude!" Victoria released the hilt and ran over to her friend. "Gertrude!" She shook her to awaken her. "Gertrude, wake up!"

All around the room, the pods opened up and released their victims. Body after body fell onto the ground, coughing and wheezing. The pods withered away into the water. When Mary was released, she hurried over to Victoria, who was shaking Gertrude.

Victoria looked at Mary. "She's not waking up! What's wrong with her?"

Mary looked sorrowful. "I was afraid of this."

The different groups stretched, shook off the affects of their paralysis, and began to congregate with their kind: Leo and 14 of his Forgers; Thomas, Helga, Min; Elzbieta, and Fritz; Shirley, Inga, and Tibuta.

They searched the ground for their weapons, released from their pods. Thomas, Min, and Helga found their teclyns, but Elzbieta searched desperately around. "Where's Cali?" She yelled. "Where my Cali?"

"Can't you feel it?" Helga asked.

"No!"

Thomas ran to Mary. "Mary! Thank God! You're all right!"

They briefly hugged before she pulled away, Mary whispered: "Thomas, we've got to get out of here!"

"I know, we're surrounded by evil miscreants!"

"No, not them, her!" Mary pointed to the corpse.

Helga joined them. "Let's leg it fo' they get organized!"

Min tightly grabbed Helga around her waist. "I've missed you!"

"Yes Everyone, Mary said. "There'll be plenty of time for hugs, kisses, and cake later! For now, we need to skidoo!" Mary hurried over and grabbed Victoria's arm. "Come along, dear!"

"Why won't she wake up?" Victoria said with tears rolling down her cheeks."

"She's not going to wake up."

"How? I saved her! She said she'd release her?"

"She did, I'll explain later. We need to leave!" Mary tried to pull her up but failed when Victoria resisted.

"No! Not until she wakes up!"

"Victoria…"

Helga walked over and yanked Victoria upwards. "Sorry dear, too dangerous in here!"

Off to the side of the room, Tibuta started spinning a spiked ball on a chain, preventing part of Leo's group from approaching Shirley and Inga. Another group started circling Mary and the others. "Too late!" Thomas said.

Mary's group covertly moved over until they joined with Shirley's.

"So nice of you to join us," Shirley said.

"The enemy of my enemy and all that," Mary said.

Leo's foundry encircled them, brandishing their techlyns.

Ignoring everything, Elzbieta continued searching for Caliburn. She stopped when she realized Fritz was near her, also searching. She gave him a shoulder hug and rubbed his head before continuing.

Helga stood next to Inga. "Watch yuh self! Some of these Forgers are legendary!" she said.

"If we beat them, then we'll be legendary as well," Inga responded.

The circle of convicts became smaller.

"Those children look tasty," Rosina said.

"Was that the Witch of Endor?" Shirley said, pointing at the stabbed corpse.

"It was," Mary answered.

"You killed her?"

"Someone else did."

"With Caliburn?"

"Yes."

"At least that's one less worry."

"Unless I'm right."

325

"We'll!... Well...WELL!" Leo yelled. He stood in front of the nest. All eyes turned to him. "What do we have here? It's so nice for everyone to come together to celebrate me becoming the biggest egg of the most powerful foundry in the world. Also, the soon-to-be deaths of my most hated enemies!"

"Leo! Let us go!" Mary yelled. "The longer we stay here and fight, the less chance we'll be able to leave here when it's too late!"

"Too late? Too late for what? That thing that captured us is dead! Thank God for that. She didn't seem like the type to follow orders."

"Is that my Cali?" Elzbieta pointed at the long sword.

"How are you still alive?" Leo asked her. "You are one tough dame! May have to get two of my gang on you."

Elzbieta fast walked to the nest and the long sword sticking out of it.

"Someone?" Leo asked.

Carmun flew up and landed between Elzbieta and Pythonissa. Fritz transformed into a dog, haunched down, and sprang at Carmun. She shrieked, and a gelled wave of air came out of her mouth, sounding like a hundred nails on a chalkboard. Fritz collapsed and writhed in pain. Elzbieta put her hands over his ears. Her face looked stressed, and a trickle of blood came from one of her ears.

Carmun stopped screaming.

"Good job," Leo said. "Anyone else wanna try challenging my men? Not so tough without that sword, are you Ironsmith? Carmun, why don't you do the honors and finish them off."

Carmun walked over to Elzbieta and Fritz, smiled, and then inhaled deeply to release a scream powerful enough to kill them. Her exhale abruptly stopped when Elzbieta punched her so hard in the diaphragm that there was a cracking sound, similar to a thick tree branch snapping. A lump from her lumbar poked out of her back. A spritz of blood sprayed Elzbieta's forehead. She wiped it off with her hand, creating red stripes on her face. Carmun's shocked face looked down at Elzbieta. who stood up, grabbed Carmun's shoulder, and pushed her onto the ground.

A laugh echoed throughout the stone chamber. Everyone looked around to see where it was coming from. Much to Thomas and Helga's surprise, the source was Tibuta, showing the first true sign of emotion they had seen from her.

Elzbieta stepped on Carmun's back and continued towards Leo.

"Now, hold on, Ironsmith," Leo said. "I got more where that came from." He started to back up and grabbed his crucifix. "Someone stop her!" He looked over at his foundry. No one moved. "Hey! Stop her! I command you! You have to do as I say!"

His words inspired no actions on their part. Elzbieta got closer to him. Leo was about to launch into a wind forge but stopped when she started to back away.

"Oh," Leo said. "You come to your senses?"

Everyone was looking behind him. cracking and breaking sounds echoed throughout the hall. The corpse gradually raised its hand and pulled out the sword. It grabbed the side of the nest, lifted itself into a sitting position, moved forwards until it was on its hands and knees, and began crawling. Strands of its dreadlocks attached to the vines snapped like thick cables. Leo looked unsurely down on the form as it struggled to move towards the reflective pool of water.

Mary tapped Thomas on the arm. When he looked at her, she gestured to the exit. He understood and motioned to the others. As they backed away towards the exit the body lowered its face into the pool of water, like a wild animal come to a watering hole. It started washing its face, hair, and arms. Years of dust clouded the reflective pool. Pythonissa crawled over to Leo and grasped his leg. He stood petrified with fear, her presence exuding an unsettling power. She pulled herself up his leg, hip, chest, and shoulders until she was upright. She patted Leo on the shoulder and then gently yet firmly pushed him aside, like the gradual, relentless pressure of a freight train, moving steadily and inexorably forward.

She stopped, put her feet together, bent down, and touched her toes. She stood upright, spread out her arms, and began a series of stretches. Everyone stared in confusion. Mary and her group couldn't resist watching and wondering what Pythonissa was doing.

Leo ran out of patience when her stretching produced a loud unsettling bone cracking sound. "Hey you!" he yelled. She ignored him and bent down. "Hey!— I'm talking to you!—Hello?" Can you hear me? Are you—"

Pythonissa stood upright, moved her hair away from her face, put a finger to his lips, and said: "Shhhhhhhhhhh." She bent back down and continued stretching.

Mary had paused when Pythonissa revealed her face. It was indeed her deceased British mother, doing yoga stretches in front of the most dangerous Forgers on earth. Thomas whispered "Mary!" and grabbed her arm. Within a few more feet they will reach the exit.

"Hey! Don't shush me!" Leo yelled. "Do you know who I am? I'm the Chief! I came here to ask you to join us, but after your little stunt with the plants, I can tell we may have to show you what happens when you mess with us!"

Pythonissa seemed annoyed as she stood up, glared at him, and then gave him a dismissive look. She turned away and surveyed the others.

"Don't you dare turn your back on me!" Leo yelled.

Pythonissa poked Leo in the face with her Thumb, index, and middle finger at incredible speed. He staggered briefly and then put his hand up to his right eye. Pythonissa held up his eye so that his remaining eye could see it. Leo screamed.

"LEO!" Mary yelled. She ran over to him.

"Mary! No!" Thomas chased after her.

Leo reached out his shaking hand to get his eye back. Pythonissa dropped it into the pool, and as he reached down to get it, she squished it with her bare foot.

Helga pointed to the exit. "Min, you take Victoria and head out that exit!" Helga ran after Thomas.

"You heard her, scram!" Min said to Victoria before she followed Helga.

"Leo!" Mary bent down to comfort him. "Oh no! Do you have any ahrion?"

He held his bleeding socket and glared at her. "Get the hell away from me!" He swatted her off of his back.

"Leo, I'm sorry—" Mary looked at Pythonissa. "Why did you do that?"

"Mary...Berry?" Pythonissa softly said, a wistful smile gracing her lips.

Mary remembered her mother calling her that. For a moment, she had forgotten why she had run over there. "Why?"

"He...was being......rude."

"That's not a reason to do that!" Mary gestured to Leo, moaning in agony.

"After all...the trouble he has...caused you?"

"Him? What about you?"

"Mary!" Thomas warned.

Pythonissa walked over and put her hand on Leo's head. Leo winced and shook. He took his hand away from his socket. It had fused shut."

"She did that without ahrion," Helga said.

"Or speaking. She's casting." Inga said."

Pythonissa stood up "See...all better."

"All better? He's still missing an eye!" Mary yelled.

"A lesson for the future..." Pythonissa turned her attention to the crowd. "...a lesson for all." She raised her hand and gestured for everyone to come closer. They all complied.

"WHY AREN'T YOU ATTACKING HER!" Leo yelled. I gave you an order! You have to follow my orders! Or you'll die! Why aren't you dying? You should all be dead! Why aren't you dead!?

"Forger's honor…is a curse put on Forgers by Myrddin Wyllt…"Pythonissa said. She turned to Leo." Blacksmiths have the ability to break curses…Right now, I am holding back the curse…" She studied the faces of the Forgers. "I am Pythonissa, known to Dayfides as…Pestilence, or the Witch of Endor." There was a gasp among the crowd, "If you wish to continue to follow Leopold Bianca, I will reinstate the curse…and you can continue to follow him, living as common criminals until your inevitable demise…or you can follow me without a death curse looming over your heads, doing it for glory…for honor…for freedom, a better world…and a better life yet to come."

The freed Forgers looked around at each other in agreement.

"What are you planning?" Mary said.

"Eventually, as for all things, it will become apparent…Have patience, Mary Berry."

"Stop calling me that!"

"Oh darling…so much anger."

"I have my doubts any of this is a good thing."

Pythonissa spread out her arms to Mary.

"What?"

"Come…give Mother a hug." She gestured with her hands.

"Pardon?"

"A hug. It's been years."

Mary stood in silence.

"Not even a hug to welcome me back? Please?"

Mary felt like running, but at the moment, the sight of Pythonissa holding out her arms was inviting, like looking at a missing part she needed. She walked forward.

"Mary! Don't" Helga said.

Mary paused but continued until she tentatively embraced her mother with the delicacy of hugging something that might break. She expected a rigid texture or foul odor from someone who had been asleep for 200 years. Instead, Pythonissa was soft, warm, and smelled fresh and floral, like laying in a field of African daisies. A wave of sadness and joy entered Mary's heart.

There was a scream off to the side.

Mary pulled away.

Elzbieta rubbed her smoking hands. The long sword lay on the ground before her.

"It burns!" she yelled.

"Of course, it burns. It has a curse on it." Pythonissa said.

"What did you do to my Cali!" Elzbieta yelled.

"Caliburn now belongs to me."

"Cali! Mine!"

"Do you believe I'll allow you to continue to chase my daughter around with that thing? I think not."

"Give me back my Cali!!" Elzbieta stomped towards Pythonissa."

"Elzbieta, hold on!" Helga yelled.

Two of the giant lilies rose out of the water behind Elzbieta, and in less than a second, they swallowed her and Fritz inside its petals.

"Don't hurt her! We made a deal!" Helga yelled.

'I know." Pythonissa said. And I don't like the conditions of that deal! Don't worry, I won't kill her. If I do, she'll just be back in a couple of years to cause more trouble." She looked at Leo, still hunched over on the ground. "Isn't that right, Leo?" He balled his fist and scowled up at her.

"What do you mean?" Thomas asked.

"Oh, right he never told any of you."

Mary shook her head.

"When your father and Leo rescued you from the ice, Leo took it upon himself to follow the little girl who instigated the event; that was actually Elzbieta in her previous life, by the way…" Mary looked at the petal. "While Elyan took you inside to revitalize you, Leo, without his permission, followed her and Fritz. He snuck up behind her, took a large rock, and—'

"Ok, that's enough!" Mary said, looking emotionally drained. "Leo and Elzbieta both deserve punishment."

"Excuse me…" Shirley said. She stepped forwards through the crowd. Tibuta and Inga followed. Pythonissa looked a little annoyed. "Excuse me…" Shirley curtsied. "…Your Highness. I'm sure you know who I am… who everyone is—"

"Yes, Shirley, what is it?"

"I was wondering, are you planning to get revenge on the world or just all who imprisoned you down here?"

Pythonissa stepped forwards and got a closer look at her. "Savez-vous quelles sont les deux choses les plus importantes de l'univers (Do you know what the two most important things in the universe are?)" Shirley shook her head. "Temps et informations (Time and information). You'll get neither. Now, get back in line. You've also caused my daughter a fair amount of trouble."

Shirley withdrew into the crowd.

"What did you do to Gertrude?" Victoria was kneeling by her Friend's body..

"Victoria!" Thomas yelled. He ran over to her.

"I told you to leave!" Min said.

"I told you both to leave!" Helga said to Min.

Pythonissa walked over to Victoria. "Of course, you couldn't leave. Your curiosity is far more powerful than your fear. I understand. Your family has always been like that. Such a thirst for knowledge! Maybe that is the attribution that creates so many Forgers and Strykers in your family." She touched Gertrude's head. "One day you'll be able to talk to your friend, whenever you wish. I can teach you how if you want?"

"What do you mean?"

"You thought I had hypnotized Gertrude to do all of those things. When I threatened you with your father losing his money in a pool hall and coming home and harming your family, truth be known, an hour before you met up with her, that was what happened to Gertrude..." Victoria looked afraid. "...I'm sorry, Blacksmiths can only control the dead.

Victoria started bawling.

Thomas pulled Victoria up and away. "Stay away from her!" He yelled.

"Sorry For your loss, Victoria. You'll get used to it." Pythonissa walked over to Mary. "So, are you ready to leave?"

Mary wiped away a tear. "Excuse me?"

"You seemed like you wanted to leave. Earlier? I saw you and your companions sneaking off. Do you not want to leave?"

"I do..."

"Having second thoughts?"

"No, but..."

"All right then, let me help you all along." She bent down and put her hands in the water.

The water around her fingertips glowed. When she took her hand out, the water spiraled into a whirlpool. The surface of the spiral got wider until it was ten feet wide. "This should take you far from here. Just think about where you want to go." Mary was in deep thought. "Dear? Was this not your goal, to rescue your friends and escape?"

"Y...yes."

"You can take Shirley with you."

"Me? Shirley asked, confused.

"Yes. The last thing I need is you mucking about. Go with them. I'll deal with you later."

Shirley joined Mary's side and looked into the Vorago. "I have to say, she's nothing like what I expected."

"No...she's not." Mary watched Pythonissa talking to Canidia. Mary turned to Thomas and Helga. "Thomas, take Victoria and go! Helga, you and Min as well."

"And leave you behind?" Thomas asked. "I think not!"

"Not to worry, I'll be fine. She's going to need me."

"For what?"

"I have a few speculations—but she's right; my number one priority is to get you and Helga out of here."

"Appreciate it Miss…" Helga said. "But I want to make sure the Blacksmith that caused the Great Plague isn't all sixes and sevens." She looked over at Pythonissa, who smiled at her.

"You need me," Min said to Mary. "You're terrible at fighting,"

"If any of you fight, you will all die," Shirley said. "I'll take my chances with the Vorago. I wonder if Japan is far enough from here?"

"Hey!" Min said. "You lied! You said my mother was at the prison!"

"Oh? Did I? À plus tard (see you later)." Shirley jumped into the Vorago.

"How does she know that's not a booby?" Min asked.

"Pythonissa doesn't need to kill us, we're not a threat," Mary answered.

"That's rather insulting," Thomas said.

"And true—Thomas, go! Right now! Victoria is the most vulnerable and valuable! Take her, and go far away from here!"

"We go together, or we don't go at all! We nearly had a moment together! I'm never going to leave your side again!"

"Oh, Thomas." Mary sadly said. "Thank you for everything." She walked up to him and kissed him on the lips. The whole room became silent, with only the sound of the whirlpool.

When Thomas pulled away, his lips tingled. "I L—" Before he could finish what he was going to say, Mary pushed Victoria into the whirlpool. "Mary!" he yelled.

"Go! Protect her!" Mary yelled.

He jumped in after a screaming Victoria and spun down into the water.

"Yeh Sure you don't need them?" Helga asked."

"For now, I need them both alive," Mary answered.

Inga and Tibuta approached Helga. "You're not going in?" Inga asked.

"Neither are you and Big Girl."

"We have to monitor whatever unfolds here."

"Why don't yeh just arrest 'er and put 'er back in chains?

"We both know that's never going to happen again.

Pythonissa walked to the side of the whirlpool, bent down, and touched the edge of the current.

"What are you doing?" Mary asked.

"Please don't get in my way, or you'll be punished," Pythonissa warned.

The diameter of the whirlpool started to enlarge. Anyone close to the edge moved away from it. The surface became even more turbulent, and water sprayed out, followed by small, white sparks of electricity."

"Should we stop her?" Min asked." No one responded. They all watched the water and light show; a spinning upside-down tornado. There was a metallic moan from below. Something large and black began to surface out of the maelstrom. Everyone stepped backward further except Mary, Helga, and Min. They recognized it. The Virginia ascended like a black whale and settled. The water became calm and returned to its smooth, flat, reflective plane, interrupted by multiple ripples from the dripping ironclad ship.

"I can't believe it," Inga said. "Such power."

"How did she find it?"Helga said. "Vorago needs a personal object to lock on, to bring something to you!"

"The Eye of Graeae," Mary answered. "It's been hers all this time. That's why she gave it to us."

"Like a fishing lure. Stupid bait."Helga said.

Pythonissa staggered a little. Some vines came out of the water and wrapped around her wrist. She gestured to the Virginia. "Canidia, Rosina, go to the bridge! "

"What about the crew?" Rosina asked."

"There should only be one man on board. He won't offer much resistance."

The Forgers jumped onto the deck."

"Now, should we do something?" Min asked.

"Steady," Mary answered.

Everyone waited until Canidia reappeared. "There's no one on board," she said.

"Hmm," Pythonissa said. "Where did you go, Abel? It's fine, just bring me the crystal ball next to the safe." she glanced at Mary. "You're being rather complacent, dear. I expected you to at least say something like 'I knew this whole thing was about getting the Siv Myrddin', or 'How did you Vorago it? It can't be transported!'"

"Did you ever do anything for me that wasn't related to; escaping from here or getting that book?" Mary asked.

"Don't think I'm doing all this just for some nefarious purpose."

Rosina came from below deck holding the Eye of Graeae. She jumped off the deck to Pythonissa and handed her the sphere. "There was no safe."

"WHAT?" Pythonissa yelled. She dropped the sphere. It briefly flashed when it hit the ground.

"There was no safe. Just a big hole."

The vines released Pythonissa's arm, and she jumped onto the deck. She slumped down briefly, got up, and fast-walked to the bridge.

When she arrived, instead of seeing a safe in the back wall, there was a large, crudely cut hole. She stomped back to the deck, jumped off, and landed in front of Mary. "What did you do with the clo keffin!" She yelled.

Four Hours Earlier...

Abel was loading ahrion bullets into his cannon gun. He heard the familiar splashing in the bathroom tub down the hallway. he ran back to help Mary, if necessary. Mary was already out and gasping for breath. She haphazardly set the tea jar on the floor.

"What's that?" Abel asked.

Mary saw a little water had seeped into the jar. "Oh No!" She yelled. She reached in and took the book out. It felt damp. "Good heavens! no!"

"Mary?"

Mary held up her hand as a gesture for Abel to stop speaking. "Can I have some sage tea and more of those scrumptious cookies you made, please?"

"Now?"

"Yes, please. Oh! And some footwear." She wiggled her toes.

"Oh...alright." Abel left the room.

Mary opened the book. 'Some of the pages got smeared!' She sighed. 'It's fine. From what I saw, I think I got enough information to understand what's going on.'

Abel brought her a pair of red, lace-up boots.

"Where did you find those?"

"Your costume collection." He left again, retrieved the tea from the kitchen, and was about to put the leaves in a teapot but Mary grabbed them from him and set them on a plate. *'Roy are don!'* She put her hand over the leaves and ignited them. They burned briefly and smoldered. The room became a little warmer. "Just as I thought."

"What? What's going on?"

"We were being spied upon. Apparently, spirits hate the smell of sage."

"There were spirits in here?"

"There are spirits everywhere. These particular ones were working for our so-called Blacksmith friend."

"Why?"

"As soon as I found fathers journal in the London house, I was attacked by someone I think was the real Miss Wayward.—"

"The real one, then who attacked you earlier?"

"No idea, but their skills were different. Maybe the Blacksmith has the sisters working for her in exchange for the Eye of Graeae

—anyway, the Blacksmith has been using us all this time. It's like she's moving checker pieces around like chess pieces!"

I'm unsure if she's after the Siv Myrddin or this journal. "I hazard a guess that ghosts aren't strong enough to rip a safe out of the wall."

"How so?"

"Remember how Elzbieta got through the manor's door without a key? Not by chopping through it, but by chopping around its supports? The safe can't be opened. But the wall around it is weaker. When her ghost came on board, they could have…"

Mary went into deep thought.

"Mary?"

"That's it!"

Pythonissa looked angry and then smiled. "You couldn't have done anything with the clo keffin without me seeing it."

"We have a lot of sage tea on board—fathers doing, no doubt."

Pythonissa sighed. "Good try, dear. Unfortunately for you, Blacksmith can not only control deceased humans, but we also can control dead animals, including sea life. It will only take but a moment to find the safe, by searching the sea floor with ocean spirits."

Out in the middle of the Atlantic, the ghosts of dead whales and dolphins emerged from decayed bones on the sea floor and entered the world of the living, joined by millions of ghostly fish. They swam along the waters, looking for anything that resembled a safe.

Pythonissa closed her eyes. Her face became angry again. She opened her eyes, smiled, and strolled towards Mary. "What did you do with the clo keffin?"

"I'm sorry. Are the dead fish not performing as you had wished ?"

"Mary? Dear? What did you do with the clo keffin?"

"It's gone! And you'll never find—"

Mary was in the air. When she hit the ground and rolled to a stop, that was when she realized Pythonissa had struck her. 'This is pain.' entered her mind. 'Fighting the anghenfēls was sparring.' Her face hurt, her neck hurt, and she tasted blood. She spat, and a tooth came out into her hand. She spat again.

Helga and Min activated their weapons and were about to attack "Helga! Min! Stop!" Mary yelled. They halted.

"I'm so sorry! I'm so sorry! I'm so sorry!" Pythonissa cooed as she ran over and comforted Mary. She put her hands on Mary's face. "I'm so sorry darling. Do you want me to heal you!"

Mary pushed Pythonissa's hand away. "I got it." Mary picked up her tooth and placed it back in its socket. "Gwessla orga-na." She could feel the roots reconnect; it still hurt.

"So sorry, dear." I lost my temper. It's because I've waited so long for this moment, and now…"

"What are you going to do with it?" Mary felt her stinging, swelling cheek.

"I can't tell you, Dear." She stood up. "Why would I do that? If I tell you anything, you'll just get my way. I want you far away from all of this, married, growing old, and living happily with my grandchildren. Not battling Forgers that you have absolutely no chance of defeating; kind of what Leo has always wanted for you…" She looked over at him. He narrowed his eyes at her. "…

So, just tell me what you did with the safe. I promise you, no harm will come to you and your friends."

"And the rest of the world?" Mary asked. Pythonissa tightened her lips. "I thought as well."

"It won't be as bad as you think." She put her foot on top of the Eye of Graeae and rolled it back and forth.

"I don't know about that, I can think of some pretty horrid things."

"Mary dear, please. You have no chance of fighting against me. I know more about you than even you realize. Even with my forging knowledge inside your head, you're still a level five."

"It doesn't matter..." Mary slowly stood up. "...I'm not going to let you cause another plague! I don't care how weak I am, or how strong you are. I'm never going to give up! Part of your powers are despair, you were depending on that to manipulate me! But Father saw through that—made me hopeful—to hide me from you and your influence! In his journal, he wrote you had died because he couldn't heal your most important organ. I'm sure he was speaking metaphorically. He meant your heart! Your love! He wasn't trying to kill you because he loved you! He was trying to stop you from destroying the world, and I'm going to continue his goal, even if I have to fight every last one of you!"

Pythonissa sighed. "As you wish. I didn't want to hurt you or your friends, but some things are even more important than a mother's love for her child."

"Only the bad mothers."

Pythonissa pointed towards her. Mary felt a presence behind her moving in the blink of an eye. She jumped to the side. One of the giant lilies crashed down behind her, its petals open for capture. Min cut the top off the one that tried to grab her, and Helga vaulted backward over hers before setting it on fire with a lightning bolt. Tibuta smashed the one trying to swallow her with one iron ball while using the other to destroy the one attacking Inga.

"You're all prepared this time," Pythonissa said.

Leo charged at her with his knife. She quickly pivoted, allowing his momentum to carry him past her. As he moved to her side, she struck him on the back, sending him sprawling. He fell flat on his face, landing in the water across the chamber, right next to Mary and the others.

Mary rolled him over to prevent drowning. "Abel! Now!" she yelled. A flash came from the ship's bow, then the sound of cannon fire. A projectile traveled to the Eye of Graeae, hitting it. There was a blinding explosion, followed by a multicolored shockwave that threw everyone off their feet. Shimmering pieces of Eye of Graeae dispersed into the air.

After the ringing in her ears had stopped, Mary got up as quickly as she could. Pythonissa still lay on the ground, surrounded by unconscious Forger convicts. On the deck of the ship, Abel materialized.

"Abel?" Min yelled.

" 'ow long as he been 'ere?" Helga asked.

"He was on board the whole time, invisible thanks to a coin," Mary said. "Back to plan A. We need to get the Virginia out of here!"

"What about 'er?" Helga pointed to Pythonissa."

"Attacking her will be pointless., only a particular Campher can kill her!"

"Looks like Leo didn't get the message."

Leo had gotten up and was heading towards Pythonissa, his knife ready.

Inga rushed over to Mary. "What did you do?"

"I bought us some time! We need to Vorago this ship out of here before she wakes up!"

"Why didn't you just leave? Through that door?" Inga gestured to the exit.

"Because if she gets her hands on this ship, she'll be able to find the Siv Myrddin!"

"It's on this ship, isn't it?"

"Of course not! It can't be Voragoed, right?"

"I guess...Why didn't you tell me you knew so much? Or even could walk? I just might have let you loose!"

"Because no matter what happens, I'm still not going to give that book to any of you! But if you help me, I'll make sure at least she doesn't get it and start another plague!"

"How are we gonna get that out of 'ere?" Helga asked. None of us has the power to make a Vorago that big!"

"What if we work together? A level five plus a level seven equals a level 12!" Mary said.

"That's not 'ow's that works!" Helga said."

"But she's right," Inga said. "If we work in a congregation, we may be able to do it! There needs to be at least three of us. So we can surround the ship in a triangle. If we each forge a Vorago and get them to touch each other, it should form a giant one."

"Sounds like a plan," Mary said. "Min, you protect Helga! Tibuta protects Inga, and..." Mary looked up at the ship's deck. "Abel, protect me!" Abel waved to her.

"Shouldn't Tibuta protect you?" Helga asked. "Strongest protect the weakest and all that!"

"It's never about strength, it's about bonds! Min and Abel would die to protect us!"

"She's right!" Min said.

Helga put her hand on Min's head. "Pray it doesn't come to that, Luv."

While he made his way towards Pythonissa, Leo transformed his teclyn into a lancer spear and randomly stabbed anyone on the ground. "This! Is what happens! When you betray me..." he stabbed a low-level Forger. "...Remember this lesson in your next life!" He stabbed another. After the third one, he made it to the high-level ones. He raised the spear and brought it down to kill Jenny Greenteeth, but her body quickly sank into the water as though it were many feet deeper than the one inch it was. He saw her swimming around like a fish under a thick sheet of green ice. He tried to jab her, but his spear only hit the concrete floor.

Off to the side, Elzbieta and Fritz were released once again from their flower prison. "I want my Cali!" Elzbieta yelled, stomping over to the unconscious body of Pythonissa. A mid-level male Forger tried to stop her by throwing a fireball at her. She brushed it off like a burn from a candle and punched him in the jaw. He flew 20 feet away into the darkness. A low-level woman tried electricity. The conductivity of the water under both of them caused her to harm herself, and she collapsed. Elzbieta was almost in punching distance of Pythonissa's body. A spiked-covered concrete wall formed between them and rose 60 feet into the air. Rosina stood on top, forging the structure.

"You in my way!" Elzbieta yelled. She was about to jump at Rosina, but a painful feeling in her right leg stopped her. When Elzbieta looked down, silver snakes were biting her on the leg. She collapsed and felt dizzy. She grabbed each one and threw them far away. Fritz grasped some with his jaws, snapping them in half. When destroyed, the silver pieces liquified, and returned to Canidia, who recreated hundreds more by saying: *"Na-droid!"* They continued to slither towards Elzbieta with their mouths open for biting.

Mary, Helga, and Inga surrounded the Virginia in a triangle. Mary stood in front of the stern. Each said: *"Cray giât deem kurk fan!"* and put their hands in the water. Whirlpools formed around their hands and expanded. Helga's and Inga's were twice the size of the one Mary had formed.

"You have to do better than that," Inga complained.

"I'm trying," Mary said. "I've never had to transport anything larger than three people."

Helga's and Inga's whirlpool grew large enough to merge, forming one large one, covering ⅔ the area under the Virginia. The ship buckled and dipped a little.

"Up to you now! Miss!" Helga said.

"I'm trying!" Mary concentrated.

Elzbieta became frustrated with the constant onslaught of snakes slithering towards her. The poison from the bites was starting to make her dizzy. With what felt like using all her reserves, she slapped the water surface as hard as she could with her fingers pointed upwards towards Canidia. A powerful spray of water hit Canidia in the face, and she relinquished the snake forge. She staggered back. Without wasting the opportunity, Elzbieta launched forwards and hit Canidia in the face. She fell onto her back. Elzbieta was about to deliver a finishing blow, but her fist was hurting. There was a burning green liquid on it. Canidia sat up, green acid drooled from her smiling mouth. Fritz latched onto her neck to crush her windpipe. He jerked back, yelped, and fell to the side, writhing in agony.

"Fritzy!?" Elzbieta yelled.

There was a claw mark on his belly. Canidia held up her hand, displaying her sharp, green fingernails.

"You! Nothing but poison!" Elzbieta yelled.

Canidia smiled and said: "*Moog Gwen-noting!*" Her green eyes flashed. She exhaled, and a cloud of green smoke bellowed out of her mouth towards Fritz.

"No! Elzbieta started running towards her. The venom in her blood caused her to collapse. "No! I kill you! You hurt Fritz!"

A cannonball hit Canidia. She flew sideways into the wall that Rosina had created. Elzbieta looked towards the ship. Abel cocked his cannon gun. He nodded at her. She returned the gesture. Shaking and dizzily, she crawled over to Fritz and dragged him away towards the Virginia.

Like a fisherman waiting for his game to appear, Leo held his spear and searched around the ground. Many feet underground, he saw Jenny's swimming, light green form, easily slipping through the rippling stone when she came close enough to the surface. When he lost track of her, he knew what would come next. The splashing sound behind him confirmed this. As fast as he could, he turned around and stabbed. He was sure he would get her in the belly. There was nothing there but splashing water. Two slimy hands wrapped themselves around his throat and torso and dragged him down until his nose was beneath an inch of water. A mixture of shock and disbelief filled his thoughts. It felt impossible to be drowning in such shallow water, but her hands pulled him down beneath the liquified floor just enough to cut off his air supply, just enough to cause him fear, and just enough to entertain the laughing Jenny Greenteeth.

"Abel! Save him!" Mary yelled after witnessing the entire scene.

"No!" he yelled back.

"Abel!"

He ignored her.

"Abel! You're not him!"

Abel rolled his eyes, transformed his cannon gun into a rifle, and aimed at Jenny Greenteeth with a regular bullet.

Abel's shot was perfect. Despite how tightly Jenny's hands wrapped around Leo, the bullet only hit her and not him. She relinquished her stranglehold on him and retreated down into the water.

Leo coughed and got up as quickly as he could. With his remaining eye, he looked at Abel onboard the ship with such disdain and hatred that Abel felt like he wanted to take another shot directly at him with an ahrion bullet.

Jenny popped her head out of the ground, looked back at Mary, sneered, ducked under the floor, and started swimming towards her.

Leo watched the figure. Mary looked over at him, and they made eye contact. The image of her kissing Thomas flashed through Leo's mind. He turned his gaze away and continued towards the wall around Pythonissa.

Abel took shots at Jenny, but they ricocheted off the ground above her as she swam closer.

"Mary! Concentrate!" Inga yelled. "Your part is shrinking!"

345

"I'm trying! Rather large amounts of distractions in here!"

Behind Mary, Jenny burst out of the water and was about to grab onto her neck to pull her down. Abel jumped from the ship's deck and slammed his rifle butt onto Jenny's head, sending her slumped body floating down into the green.

"Thanks, Abel," Mary said.

"No problem." He watched Elzbieta laboriously dragging Fritz towards them.

When Leo was getting close to the wall, Canidia began to release green smoke into the air again. Leo choked, fell to his knees, and then created a wind forge to blow it away from himself while he recovered.

"Ok, now there's a problem," Abel said.

"What is it."

"Poisonous gas headed our way!" Abel aimed at Canidia. Rosina forged A small stone wall, blocking his shot of her. "Damn!"

The green cloud wafted over the little wall and drifted towards Elzbieta and Fritz.

"Looks like they're done for."

"I made a promise I would help him!" Mary yelled.

"I'll get them."

"Are you sure?"

"Concentrate!" Inga yelled.

"I'll be fine! Abel jogged out to meet Elzbieta and Fritz. He reached down and helped her up. "No! Get Fritz first!" she yelled.

He laid her down, grasped Fritz by the scruff of his neck, and dragged him over to the edge of the Vorago. Elzbieta struggled to stand but collapsed into a crawl. Abel ran back for her. The green cloud was only a few feet behind her. He grabbed her by the wrists and started heaving her across the floor. A pair of green hands reached up and fastened around her hips. He could see Jenny Greenteeth's sinister grin under the floor. He said: *"Eh-ha- gu avuh cledeath"* and his gun transformed into a bayonet. He swiped down to cut off Jenny's hands. She ducked into the water and switched to a different part of Elzbieta's body. Whenever he tried to hit her, she moved again, at least three more tries, as the poison cloud inched closer to them.

Mary's whirlpool was finally large enough to merge with the other two. When they intermingled, a single oval-shaped whirlpool formed, and the ship gradually sank into it.

Inga stopped forging and pointed her hands at the ship. "Quick! Levitate it before it leaves!" They all said: *"Urf ur caa fael"* and pointed their hands at the vessel. It rose a little and then hovered one foot over the water.

Mary looked over to Abel, struggling to be let loose. "Abel? Time to leave! Abel?"

"Working on it!" He yelled. Jenny's grabbing and letting go of Elzbieta kept his advancement at a snail's pace. He looked back at the approaching cloud of poison. 'She's delaying me, trying to set me up!' He raised his sword over his head. *"Qwee-tha!"* the blade rapidly inflated and grew.

"Min! Help Abel! Mary yelled."

"Looks like he's got it!" Min said.

Abel was floating rapidly towards them, holding on to the rope of a giant silver balloon with one hand and his other arm wrapped around a dazed Elzbieta. Under the floor, Jenny followed, looking up at them in anger and frustration.

Leo made it to the wall Rosina had created around Pythonissa and began to climb it. Rosina looked down at him from the edge of the wall. With the wave of her hand, she fabricated multiple spikes along the wall's surface. One of the spikes struck his leg, causing immense pain. He took a coin out of his pocket. *"Gwinade freedro!"* The coin transformed into a silver apple. Leo threw it at Rosina, and it exploded with a blinding flash, sending her reeling away from the wall's edge.

The sound of pitter-pattering splashing began to fill the chamber. "What's that?" Mary yelled.

Through the doorway, they saw hundreds and thousands of tiny blue lights coming towards them. More came into view, and the form of the rat skeletons became clear.

"Are those...rats?" Helga asked.

"She's waking up!" Mary yelled.

"Bloody Hell!" Helga yelled. "Can yeh do double forges?"

"This one is already draining me!" Mary yelled.

"Me too!" Helga yelled.

Min placed herself in front of Mary, facing the rat skeletons.

Inga stopped forging. Her part of the ship slowly sunk into the whirlpool. Mary and Helga felt as if they were lifting a hundred extra pounds.

"What in the world are yeh doing?" Helga asked.

Inga jumped on board the ship. "If this ship is so important, we need to leave! If you want to get out of here alive! I suggest you come on board! Now!"

"Inga! Yuh slag!" Helga yelled. "We're not leaving without Abel!"

Abel was about to land on the ship's deck and drop Elzbieta off. A red fire swarmed around him and baked his skin with powerful heat. He could feel burning in his lungs when he breathed. He ungracefully dropped Elzbieta onto the deck, and he thumped down afterward. When he looked towards the wall Rosina had created, there was no sign that Pythonissa had caused the attack. In front of him, Inga pointed her cigarette holder techlyn at him. "What are..." he asked.

"I won't allow her on this ship!" Inga, gesturing at Elzbieta.

"She's no danger! She has a truce with Helga!" Abel rubbed the pain from the burns off his shoulder.

"She has no truce with me! So either she goes, or you all go!"

"There's a wall of poisonous gas headed our way, a creature swimming through the ground, as well as god-knows-what, coming from the other direction! We don't have time for this!"

"Tibuta, come!" Inga yelled.

Tibuta looked at Inga. And then Mary and Helga, struggling to keep the ship in the air. She started fast walking towards the approaching wave of rats.

"What are you doing? You stupid brazier! I told you we need to go!"

Tibuta ignored Inga and continued.

A wave of tiny clattering bones skittered closer to them. Tibuta activated the two spiked balls on chains out of her sleeves and then began to spin them away from each other like two propellers. Soon, they were spinning so fast, that they turned into blurred disks. Blue sparks flew from the disk off to the sides and grew until a long wall of electricity formed and separated them from the rats. Whenever the skeletons got within two feet of the wall, their bones disintegrated

"Mary!" Helga yelled. "I don't know 'ow much longer I can keep at it. Feeling a bit shagged, and me coals feels like it's burn'n low!"

"I know! If we stop now, the ship will drop and instantly go away! As soon as Fritz and Tibuta are on board!" Mary answered.

Min looked down and saw Jenny swimming under Mary like a shark, surveying her, trying to find the best angle for attack.

Leo scaled the top of the wall and looked down at the unconscious body of Pythonissa. On the other side, he could see Rosina hiding and Canidia exhaling poisonous smoke towards Mary and the rest. All were an easy target with one knife throw to the head. He raised his arm and threw. It was a perfect throw aimed right between Pythonissa's eyes. A grey shape rose between her and Leo. Rosina had once again created a little wall to thwart him. Spikes jutted out of the wall. They gouged his legs, and he jumped off to the side. More spikes sprouted under him. Leo yelled: *'Urf ur caa fael!'*, and floated towards the ground.

Longer, sharper spikes extended to him, close enough to puncture his shoulder. His arm felt numb from the injury. Blood trickled down his leg. He grabbed all of the leftover coins and rings he had and tossed them at Rosina's enclosed area. *"Gwinade freedro!"* The ahrion objects turned into silver apples and exploded in a barrage, sending pieces of stone everywhere. When the smoke cleared, he saw Rosina's arm slumped over a pile of rubble. Leo had a burning sensation in his lower back. He put his hand on the area and realized it was a stab wound. One of the low-level Forgers he remembered specifically killing had snuck up behind him. "What in the world?" He was so focused on the Forger that he failed to notice someone else grabbed him around the neck, and tried to squeeze the life out of him. Leo remembered killing him when he first saw Boss Murphy. "Re-alived..." He put his hands on their ice-cold heads. *"Roy are don!!"* Heat, smoke, and then fire emanated from their heads. The rest of their bodies combusted faster than the time he had set Il Capo on fire. Like burning kindling, the bodies slid down and disintegrated into gray ash on the spiky ground. "Need to...hurry...before she brings Carman... back!" Leo struggled to say. He painfully limped over to Pythonissa.

"Get that beast off of the ship!" Inga ordered. She gestured at Elzbieta.

"That cloud is almost here!" Abel yelled.

"Then I suggest you move!" Inga yelled, "Or be burned to death! *Flama-cohl"* Red flames snaked from her hands all around him and Elzbieta.

Abel tried to pick up Elzbieta and move her to the inside of the ship. The heat was intense. If he stayed by her side, he felt he would join her in death. The need to abandon her grew stronger and stronger. He remembered the fire at the circus. The Nigerian men in the cage, the consuming flames, his helplessness. "N-no!" He pointed his techlyn at Inga. She heated his techlyn so much his fingers began to smoke. He dropped his weapon and focused all his energy on picking Elzbieta up and moving her to the inside of the ship. Inga increased the intensity of her attack. He felt his skin simmering. 'Is this what those men felt before they died?' he thought.

The heat subsided faster than it had begun. Abel glanced back to see why Inga had stopped. She was clutching her chest and coughing; the poisonous cloud had traveled far enough to affect her. He carried Elzbieta to the bridge and closed the airtight door. Through the window, he could see Inga turn her techlyn into a gas mask. It was far too late. She dropped her mask and went down on her knees, violently coughing and wheezing.

Abel transformed his techlyn into a mask, put it on, and ran outside. He put Inga's mask back on her face, carried her inside the ship, and sat her on the other side of the room from Elzbieta. He got some tubes of liquid ahrion out of a first aid box, gave it to them, said: *"Gwessla orga-na."*, and returned outside to get Fritz.

With an expression of bewilderment on her face, Inga watched him leave.

The cloud enveloped Mary, Helga, and Min. All three held their breaths, knowing they each had less than a minute before they would have to breathe. The air around Mary suddenly became clear. She examined her surroundings before she took a breath. Min was waving her mother's red fan and gracefully doing a tai chi dance. The strong wind from the fan collected the dark cloud and accumulated above her head. Jenny Greenteeth breeched to latch on to Min's leg, and drag her down to the concrete waters. A sharp object impaled Jenny's shoulder. She shrieked and writhed around, trying her best to release herself from the small harpoon. On the deck of the ship, Abel held a rope attached to it. Jenny sporadically swam along the ground, pulling Abel's arm around like he had hooked a giant fish. No matter how much she struggled, Abel held on and managed to lift her out of her watery base. Jenny screamed, grabbed the rope, and began to climb up. Abel didn't know what to do. The frenzied speed she was climbing to reach him was motivated by a murderous desire. She got closer. 'If she gets onto the deck she could dive inside the ship, and will hinder our escape!'

Abel thought. *"Dückweh luhg!"* His harpoon and rope turned back into its default magnifying glass. Jenny and the techlyn fell close to the edge of the ship. She writhed around, trying her best to grab onto the side. She missed, fell into the Vorago, and spun out of sight, followed by Abel's techlyn. He sadly watched his weapon disappear, hoping it was the right decision

After more graceful turning and twisting moves, Min swirled the cloud into a small whirlwind above her head. With a quick fan flip, she sent all the gas funneling downward into the Vorago.

Leo finally reached Pythonissa. He transformed his techlyn into a long sword and raised it. "Let's see if you can come back without a head!" He brought the sword down. It hit something hard and stopped. Leo's eye scanned from the blade to Pythonessia's index and forefinger, pinching the edge of the blade and preventing it from moving. Pythonissa glared at him. She regarded the blade and grabbed onto it, producing no blood from the contact. The blade deformed into a long staff. Leo let go when the hilt elongated into a long curved blade. His weapon had become a scythe. He stepped back and stumbled on some rocks.

"You always were a hindrance," Pythonissa said. "I Never understood why Gwenhwyvar tolerated you." She raised the scythe.

On the ground, Canidia forged hundreds of silver snakes and sent them slithering through the water. Min skimmed the surface with her spear and cut them into pieces before they could reach Mary, and Abel as he hoisted Fritz onto the ship's deck. As before, once destroyed, the silver pieces returned to Canidia, and reformed into snakes.

"This is endless!" Mary yelled. We'll never be able to board with this constant onslaught!"

"And I'm almost empty!" Helga yelled."

There was a scream from Canidia behind her protective wall. Over her head, a circle of flames was menacingly lowering towards her. The heat was so intense the water surrounding her was steaming, and the snakes she had forged ceased and disappeared.

On the deck of the Virginia, Inga stood next to Abel with her arms spread.

"You…" Abel said. "You should be resting."

"I don't like…owing people…favors." Inga struggled to say. She concentrated more. The ring of fire lowered towards Canidia, causing their clothes to burst into flames. Canidia screamed and rushed from their enclosure, blanketed with fire. She dove onto the ground and rolled around in the water to extinguish herself. Inga moved the ring over Canidia and continued the attack. Canidia fought against the heat from above and the boiling water below.

Inga's fire ring ended suddenly.

Abel looked over at her, wondering if she had fainted from exhaustion. She stood still for a moment, her eyes wide with surprise. Behind her, something was hovering and spinning. From what Abel could tell, it was a large blade of some sort, a spinning scythe. Inga's body fell forward. Abel was about to grab her until he realized her head and body were separated. In shock, he hesitated and watched the parts fall off the deck and spiral in a red swirl into the Vorago.

The spinning scythe flew away from the ship, over the battlefield, and was caught by Pythonissa, standing on the wall, surveying everything like a Queen over her kingdom.

"What was that?" Mary yelled.

"Inga…Inga's dead." Helga said, closing her eyes and looking away. Her end of the ship started to lower and skimmed the surface of the Vorago.

Pythonissa reached down, picked something up, and threw it towards them. It flew in the air and landed between Min and Mary with an organic thud. Mary wondered what new horror was being unleashed upon them. It was a figure missing an arm. "Who is…?" The person slowly raised their head, and she now saw his bleeding disfigured form. "Leo!" Mary started to reach down to him.

"Mary!" Helga yelled when the ship started to lower into the water and rotate. "I'm already carrying two weights as is!"

Mary regained control as best she could. Leo's leg appeared broken. He tried to crawl, leaving a cloudy trail of red in the water. He raised his remaining hand towards her.

The whirling sound produced by Tibuta spinning her iron maces halted. She had stopped and seemed to be struggling, but there was no sign of any foe. "Tibuta?" Mary asked. Pythonissa had her scythe raised and was pointing it at Tibuta. 'What is she doing to her?'

Tibuta acted as though something was restraining her arms and legs. Mary felt a chill and remembered what she had seen when Victoria had stopped Wayward. "Ghost!"

Unseen to all except Pythonissa, hundreds of ghosts from the convicts who had died inside the prison swarmed on top of Tibuta, weighing her down and restraining her limbs. The rat skeletons crossed the barrier Tibuta had created and started jumping onto her, nibbling and scratching. She thrashed around, sending ghosts and rats flying away, only to be replaced by double the number.

Mary looked at Tibuta, writhing around in agony, Helga at her weakest and down at Leo. Her heart felt trifurcated. 'He ended up this way because he wanted to save me from this life. I've killed him!' She looked back at Tibuta, struggling with ghost and rat skeletons. 'What was I thinking? It was a stupid plan! She's going to kill us all, get the book, and then millions of deaths will follow, and it will all be my fault!'

Min got closer to Mary, her spear at the ready. 'What do we do?" She asked.

A feeling of dread filled Mary's stomach in a nervous mass. Every negative emotion seeped into her mind like black tentacles wrapping around her heart. "It's hopeless." On the wall, Pythonissa looked down at her. "This is...this is what death does...fear... disparity..." she looked at Min. Her face wasn't one of bravery, but she had a steadiness—prepared for whatever came in their direction. "Min..."

"Yes?"

Mary stared at Leo. His eyes conveyed something she'd never seen in him before: fear. "…Min…"

"Yes?"

"…Save Tibuta."

Leo's expression turned to shock. Mary looked away from him.

Min leaped over to Tibuta and brought the fan down, billowing Tibuta in a powerful gust. The rat skeletons flew off Tibuta's body, and the ghost dissipated.

Min constantly slashed away with her spear at the rats she could see and the fan for what she could not. Tibuta gritted her teeth. Blue sparks flew down her arms, into the chains coming out her sleeves, and into the giant spiked balls at the ends. She brought her wrists together, forcing the spheres to collide and merge into one giant spiked mace sphere. She reached over and shoved Min away from her and onto the ground several feet away.

"Hey!" Min protested. "Don't you want my help?"

Tibuta ignored her, lifted the giant iron sphere, and spun her body around. The enormous sphere sparked and formed a powerful energy mass around her circumference.

With the rat skeletons not being able to get near them, it was obvious to Min that she was no longer needed. She rejoined Mary. "What is she doing?"

"I don't know," Mary answered. "But I think it's time to go!" She looked down to see if Leo was alive; he was gone. "Leo?" She turned her attention to the others. "Helga! Tibuta! Let's go!"

"Okay, on three!" Helga yelled.

Spiked vines emerged from the ground and tried to entangle themselves around their legs.

"Three!" Mary yelled.

Helga, Mary, and Min jumped into the air and landed on the deck of the Virginia. Vines wrapped around Mary's legs and began to drag her off of the ship. She yelled: *Bêl tân!* and burned them away.

"Why aren't we sinking?" Helga asked. She looked over the side at the vines, twisting and wrapping around the hull, raising the ship in the air just enough to prevent it from touching the Vorago. Off to the side, the vines trying to capture Tibuta couldn't get around her giant spinning spiked sphere.

Abel watched the vines snake their way over the deck. "What now?" he yelled, trying his best to remove them by hand, but he could only tear a few at a time.

Helga lay slumped on the bridge. "Sorry..." she said. "I'm knackered."

Pythonissa had her scythe raised and waved it around.

"She doesn't give up!" Min said.

"But, she's still not full strength!" Mary said

"Looks bloody full strength to me!" Helga said.

Mary noticed Tibuta, still spinning the giant Mace. "She's going to hit her with that..." Mary turned her attention to Min. "When I give the word, throw your spear directly at Pythonissa's heart!"

"Hǎo de (okay)!"

"Will that do anything?" Abel asked.

"More than Tibuta will."

Tibuta let go of her mace. The flaming ball emitted blue electric bolts and traveled across the chamber, raising the water in its wake. Pythonissa took notice of the object and put her scythe in front of her. The ball hit her with explosive force. Sparks flew from the impact and illuminated the room. Even across the chamber, Mary and the others felt a gust of hot air from it. Pythonissa was thrust backwards but unsteadily held her ground, deflecting the spinning massive sphere.

"Min! Ready!"

Min raised her spear.

Pythonissa continued to fight off the spinning sphere of energy. Mary knew it was only a matter of time before it would dissipate. She looked up to the chamber ceiling at the unknown light source. "Tibita! Send it up! Towards the light!

Tibuta raised her hand. The energy ball rose into the air. "Min, now!" Min threw her spear across the room. It landed directly in Pythonissa's chest. The ball continued to climb upwards and collided with the white light in the ceiling. Like an electrified spiderweb, the energy dispersed from the center to the far edges in a chain reaction and stopped. A deep rumbling echoed around the room.

Pythonissa was still standing but visibly shaken. She grabbed the spear shaft and struggled to pull it out.

"Did that do it?" Helga asked.

"No," Mary said.

"Then what was the purpose ..."

There was another rumbling echo. Tiny pieces of rubble started falling from the edge of the room, followed by a guttural cracking sound. The entire ceiling broke loose in a massive solid, falling bolder and descended to crush all under its force.

Every sub-level floor, from -1 to -12 started collapsing. Those on ground above experienced a level 5 earthquake, shaking guards, convicts, and all who were still dealing with Mausi's breakout.

"Inside! Now!" Elzbieta yelled, holding the door to the bridge open. Exhausted, Tibuta leaped and joined them on the deck, almost slipping off the side. Abel grabbed her arm and pulled her up. They all scrambled into the bridge.

Pythonissa looked up at the large boulder with surprise and pleasure. The second the top landed on her, all vines holding the Virginia in the air withered away. The ship made complete contact with the Vorago and started spinning downwards. Above, the collapsing ceiling came closer, threatening to turn everything around them into rubble under its massive weight.

In the bridge, Abel pushed the boat control lever forward. The Virginia spun and dived down faster, avoiding being landed on by the collapsing ceiling. As pieces of the rock touched the Vorago, they broke off and swirled towards the descending Virginia, putting the ship inside a whirlpool of giant boulders. Abel turned the wheel, sending everyone against the walls. Bricks and boulders pelted the hull. Some of the hits were severe enough to cause a breach. Water squirted inside. Elzbieta touched the walls and said: *"Sel-yo!"* The cracks repaired themselves, but more boulders slammed into the walls, creating new ones. The ship continued to spin around. They tumbled around like clothes in a washer. The lights gave way, engulfing them in darkness. The noise of the boulders hitting the side of the ship transitioned into rocks and then pebbles, and finally, just the sound of swirling water. The Virginia rose out of the water like a black whale, 30 feet into the air, and came down onto the surface with a massive splash.

With a gasp for air, Victoria emerged from underwater. She immediately knew where she was by the room's interior design: her home, inside a full bathtub.

The door swung open. Miss Flo held one of the twins, wrapped in a towel, ready for their bath. They both looked wide-eyed at Victoria. She looked at them and then at herself and realized she was interrupting bath time by being in the tub with all her clothes on. She quickly pulled herself out and walked past them, dripping water from her dress onto the wooden floor. Miss Flo and the child watched her without comment.

Water flowed from the bottom of the bridge door when Mary opened it. Despite the numerous dents and small rocks scattered along its deck, the ship was afloat and still intact.

The others followed behind her, looking around to see where they had ended up. For a destination, a Vorago used either the desire of the creator to bring someone to them or the will of the person who travels inside it. Seven people inside the Virginia, with seven potential individual destinations, had collectively agreed on the same place. Mary looked up at the enormous Statute of Liberty towering overhead, its copper coating shining bright in the late afternoon sunset of New York Harbor, raising her torch high in the air, welcoming them back.

The sight was too overwhelming for Mary. She got down on her knees and began crying. First Min, then Helga, and then Abel all bent down and caressed her in a group embrace.

6:07 PM

Mary knocked softly on Victoria's front door—she knew her appearance would anger Thelma, but she didn't care, it was more important to settle her peace of mind. As luck would have it, Victoria answered the door. She entered the hall and quietly shut the door.

"Oh! Thank god!" Mary embraced her as she hugged her back. "Are you alright, dear?" Victoria nodded. "Where's Thomas?

"I came out of the bathtub, but he wasn't with me."

What? That's impossible! I assumed he would be with you! I told him to protect you! Did you let go of his hand?"

"I never saw him in the thing. I just spun around and ended up here." Mary looked worried. "Is he alright?"

"I don't know…maybe If I use one of his personal items, I can do a tracking forge on him. I'll go to his apartment—assuming Elzbieta didn't destroy it.

"What?"

'It's nothing…He's probably fine—hopefully. As long as you're okay."

"What happened with Pythonissa?"

"She's gone, for now."

"For now?"

"We buried her, but I'm sure she will eventually dig herself out. Without a special weapon and a Blacksmith, we can't completely stop her,"

"But, I can't—"

"I know. I'm not saying you need to do anything. We have a little breathing room, even without your help. There are other Blacksmiths out there, remember?"

"And Gertrude?"

"Gertrude?"

"Is she really gone?"

Mary sighed. "I'm sorry, dear." She hugged Victoria.

Victoria began to break down. "Can I bring her back?"

"Not in the way you wish."

"Can I at least see her again?" Victoria said between sobs.

"Maybe…with training, I'm sure."

"Then, train me!"

"That's more of a Helga thing."

"Then she can train me!"

"I wish there was enough time. But we're leaving tomorrow."

"What? Where are you going?"

"We need to find the right Chamfer—the special weapon my father was looking for, the only one that can destroy Pythonissa."

"Take me with you!"

"Victoria, you just said—"

"I want to talk to Gertrude again! I want to say I'm sorry for ever involving her. I have to see her!"

"That's very honorable of you, dear. But we're going far away, to Europe. Knowing your mother's opinion of me, I highly doubt she'll allow us to pinch you off for the summer."

"But—"

"It's fine. You should stay here, mourn the loss of your friend, and live a normal…"

"What is it?"

"Nothing...I sound like Pythonissa—anyway, if we survive, when we come back, Helga can give you a proper training." Mary gave her one last hug. "Right! Off I go then, take care of yourself. If your uncle shows up, tell him we'll be repairing the ship off the shore of Battery Park until one o'clock." Mary walked away, waving her hand goodbye.

The blue sparks emitting from Elzbieta's hand smoothed the last piece of dented metal on the Virginia. She stepped back and admired her work.

"All done?" Abel asked as he approached the ship from shore, carrying a wooden crate full of supplies.

"Better than it was before. Poor ship."

"Your foundry definitely has an affinity for machines. Thank you for doing that."

"Now I pay you back. Owe you nothing."

"I never said you owe me anything. I'm glad to be of help. What are you going to do now? Are you still bent on killing Mary?"

"Depends on what she says about our deal."

"What deal?"

"Between us. Not you."

Mary and Helga came from the bridge onto the deck. Mary held a white straw boater hat.

"What say you, Black blood?" Elzbieta asked.

Mary stared into the distance, looked at the hat, and took a moment to think. She looked at Elzbieta and nodded her head.

"Forger's honor?"

"Forger's honor."

"Good. Now I only have to kill Blonde Black blood."

"Or you can make the same deal with her," Helga said.

"No, I want to see her dead!"

"It's good to have goals," Abel said. "I guess this is goodbye. Thanks again for repairing the ship." He began to leave, but she grabbed his arm.

"Stryker!"

"Yes?"

Elzbieta looked around embarrassed. "I...I...Sorry for calling you weak...You. You're strong...Strong like Forger.."

"Thank you." She punched him in the arm.

"Ow!"

"Don't get big head! I still beat you and Helga!"

"Wot's that about beating me?" Helga yelled from the deck.

"We fight when we meet again, Helga of Pendle! Find out who is strongest!" Elzbieta yelled.

"Anytime luv! Stay alive until then."

"We battle after I find my Cali."

"You're going back there? Are you off your trolly?"

"Snake lady is strong. But will be defeated. She doesn't have what we have."

"And wots that luv?"

"Przyjaciele (friends)"

"Come again? Wot does that mean?"

"Fritzy! Time to go!"

Fritz came from the bridge with Min.

"Any luck with Thomas' scent?" Mary asked him.

Fritz smelled the air. "He's too far away...but..."

"What?" Min asked.

"There is a familiar smell that comes and goes...I remember smelling it when you showed me your old clothes back at the underground house."

"MY MOM'S CLOTHES?"

"Yes, that's it. I kept smelling that when we fought that woman with the bandages."

Min was happy for a second and then realized something. She pulled out her mother's fan. "That woman was working with Shirley, and Shirley had this."

Fritz smelled it. "Oh...Yes. I guess that was it...Sorry."

"It's okay, I found out she was alive. That's good enough for now."

"Fritzy!" Elzbieta yelled"

"Gotta go. Goodbye, Quing."

"What? Don't call me by my first name, you're not family! And we're not married!"

"Really? What about when we kissed?" Fritz laughed.

Everyone heard something hit the water. With frustration, Elzbieta rolled her eyes and watched Fritz swim to and climb up onto the shore. "Stop playing around, Kochanie! We have to go!" He rung out his shirt and looked back at Min. She smiled and waved goodbye.

Mary and Helga watched Elzbieta and Fritz walk away.

"Are yeh sure you're okay with the deal you made with 'er?" Helga asked.

"Yes.

"What about Thomas."

"It's not his decision."

"He seems like a pretty traditional man."

"Guess we can have that discussion when we find him."

"Any luck?"

Mary lifted her hand with Thomas's hat. "Almost...I'm starting to get an image. Last time I did this for Leo, it didn't go so well..."

"O'right?"

"It's just...Leo." Mary closed her eyes and sighed.

Helga reached over and grabbed her hand. "Yeh never know. Yuh thought I was dead, remember?"

"A terrible part of me hopes Leo's not alive. So he won't remember how I betrayed him."

"Pythonissa knew yeh would try to save him. It was a trap; 'e was bait. For now, let's do what we can in the present. Focus on finding Thomas. Just keep concentrating. Think of yuh connection to him."

"Yes...you're right. Focus on—wait! I see him! I think."

"Yeh think?"

"He's in a very strange place..."

Thomas waded out of what he assumed was a swamp, full of tall grass growing out of the water in what seemed to be an intentional pattern. He arrived at an elevated path and stepped out of the water.. A group of Asian men wearing what appeared to be coats made of hay and conical hats on their heads stood over him. they held wooden weapons shaped like sledgehammers with long handles. Before he could completely crawl out of the swamp, one of the men pushed him back in with the sledgehammer. When he tried to leave again, they pointed the weapons at him and yelled in an unfamiliar language.

"Zhōngguó rén (Chinese)?" He asked. The men got angrier. Thomas asked again.

"No," said a female voice from the side.

Thomas watched as Shirley approached the group of men. Her muddy dress let him know she had arrived in this strange land the same way as he had.

"Don't worry, they're just rice farmers wearing raincoats."

"Shirley?" Where are we? Where's Victoria?"

"I'm more interested in the fact you followed me here. Do you love me that much?"

"No! Of course not! I probably had this place on my mind when you..."

"When I said I wanted to go far away." Shirley addressed the group of men: "Kare wa daijōbu, watashitoisshoni imasu (He's okay, he's with me.)"

The men lowered their sticks.

"Shirley? Where the Devil are we?"

Japanese rice farmers in the 1900s.

"Japan?" Mary asked.

"Sound's like it," Helga said. "Never been there. 'eard they're not too keen on foreigners, especially Russians, so 'e should be okay.... Less they think. 'e's Russian. Oh well. It's horses for courses, I suppose. Should we get 'em out?"

"Japan is a big country. In the time it takes to find him, Pythonissa may be able to dig herself out and be on the loose. As much as I love Thomas, I can't waste time on vague leads; we need to pinpoint his exact location."'

"May take a while. I can 'azard a guess that old hat 'as no real value to 'im."

Tibuta came from below deck.

"All better?" Mary asked.

Tibuta nodded her head.

"Good. Are you going to arrest us now for escaping from prison?"

Tibuta shook her head, reached into her dress pocket, pulled something out, and placed it in Mary's hand.

Mary looked down at a metal disk engraved with a winged elephant on one side and three spirals converging into one on the other. "A Forger's coin? You're giving me a coin?"

Tibuta nodded and held out her hand. Mary shook it. Tibuta looked annoyed.

"I'm sorry, what?" Mary asked.

"I think she wants to do Copper coding," Helga said. " 'ere, let me 'ave a go." Helga opened her hand, and Tibuta placed her hand in hers and began moving her fingers as if she were typing in Helga's palm. "She says…" Helga translated. "…*Thank you for saving my life and healing me. Use the coin if you ever need my help. It will find me, and I will find you.*"

"Oh! Thank you!" Mary said We can use all the help we can get! Do you want to come with us?"

Tibuta shook her head, and Helga continued to translate. "*No. My place is here. You need a friend on the inside.*"

"That's 'elpful," Helga said. "Our very own mole."

"*Before I go.*" Tibuta tapped, "*I have to ask, how did you know that glowing light would bring the ceiling down?*"

"I didn't," Mary answered.

"Do what?" Helga asked.

"To be quite honest, I knew something would happen. But nothing that dramatic." Tibuta looked confused at her. "When he built that prison, my father forged that light at least 200 years ago, and it was still burning bright. I remembered something my aunt told me: 'If you look towards the light, darkness will always be behind you.' It was a clue. I figured destroying it would create a nice distraction, and we would simply slip away in the chaos.

"*So, it was luck?*"Tibuta typed.

"Oh yes. Never discount the power of luck. It's one of the reasons any of us are here in the first place." Tibuta sighed. "Not to worry, Tibuta, next time we'll find a way to properly defeat her." Mary put her hand on top of Tibuta's and Helga's. "With you on our side, our luck has just increased, exponentially." Tibuta smiled, nodded to her and Helga, turned around, and departed towards the park.

Shall we go ahead and shove off then?" Helga asked.

"Yes...or...maybe not?"

"Come again?"

Mary pointed towards the shore. Two women were approaching them, one holding a suitcase. They asked Tibuta something, she pointed at the ship, and they continued towards it.

"Now wot?" Helga asked.

They came into focus. Mary rushed down to the shoreline. Thelma? Victoria? What are you doing here?"

"I'm coming with you!" Victoria said.

"What? No! How? Excuse me? Thelma? Are you okay with this?"

Thelma walked up to Mary, grabbed her arm, and pulled her aside. "Is it true?" she asked Mary.

"What is? Did she tell you about me?"

"Yes!"

"I know it must sound unbelievable, but it's all true—"

"So it's true! You know Doctor Freud?"

"Dr. Freud? Dr. Sigmund Freud?"

"Yes."

"Well, I once had a heated argument with him. About women."

"Can you get him to see her?"

"I'm sorry, see who?"

"Victoria said you're going to Europe. If you take her with you, can you take her to see Dr. Freud?"

"If we go to Vienna, I guess if it's not 100% and not 0%. There's always a chance. But, why would you want her to see him? and most importantly, trust her with me?"

"I'm at the end of my rope, Miss White! Victoria is seeing things! She got caught taking a bath with all of her clothes on! She's going through something! The last time this happened, they took away one of my family members! I'll be damned if I let that happen to my precious little girl! I will make a deal with the devil himself for her! Sending her to Europe with an eccentric aristocrat in that weird boat is a much easier choice!"

"Thank you? I think?"

"I admit I'm weak, Miss White! I'm not rich, I'm not smart like you people—there's nothing I can do to help her!" Thelma started to tear up but stopped herself.

Mary put her hands on Thelma's shoulder. "You're not weak, you're not poor, and you're certainly very smart, in the most important way! You're just exhausted. You're working long hours while raising five kids all by yourself and providing everything they need! That takes a tremendous amount of strength. In a house, rich with love, which is more valuable than all the silverware in the Vanderbilt mansion! And it's not a weakness to admit you need help. Only a brave person is willing to set their ego aside for the benefit of others, and only an intelligent person is smart enough to know their limits and to tap into the vast resources of human knowledge that others can provide. That's how the smart people I've met do things, especially the brave ones!"

Thelma wiped away a tear. "So, how about it? Can you take her to see Dr. Freud?"

Mary looked over at Victoria. She smiled at Mary, raised her eyebrows, and clasped her hands together to plead. Mary sighed. "Okay, I'll do my best."

"Thank you so much!" Thelma hugged Mary; she was caught off guard and then hugged her back. "Please take care of my girl. I trust you."

"I will."

Thelma went over to say goodbye to Victoria as Helga came over to confront Mary.

"Is she coming with?" Helga asked.

"Apparently."

"Are you sure?"

"She's a Blacksmith that can kill Pythonissa and see ghost spies."

" 's that right?"

"And she needs training; congratulations, Teacher Pendle, you now have your own apprentice."

"Bloody hell, the last thing I need is a Penny-Welding Swarf."

Thelma kissed Victoria's cheeks more than once. "Be good and listen to Miss White…"

"I will."

"…And Dr. Freud!"

"I will."

Thelma gave her a long hug. "Telegram me the second your foot touches the shore!"

"I will."

"And come back to me."

"I will."

"Come back to me, all better!"

"I'll come back better than ever."

They released each other, and Victoria walked to the ship, watched by her mother.

"Hello, Min," Victoria said. "Where's Dog Boy?"

"He rescued his Elzbieta. They just left," Min answered and looked at Victoria's suitcase. "You changed your mind. Are you okay with fighting?"

"No. But, sometimes you have to do things you don't want to do, to see your friends again."

"All to shore that's going to shore!" Mary yelled, leading everyone on board. "Welcome Victoria to the refurbished C.S.S. Virginia."

"What an interesting black ship," Victoria said, touching the iron wall. "Wait, the Virginia? I read about this in school! It was in the civil war! It battled the Monitor and used to be called the Merrimack!"

"Really?" Mary asked. "How delightful!" Mary led her onto the bridge. "We'll start our tour here: this room is the bridge."

Victoria marveled at all the cherry oak finish and red velvet interior; one area took her aback. "What happened over there? She pointed towards the giant hole where the safe used to be.

"Oh! I forgot about that." Mary pointed her hand at the hole. "Wait. First. Victoria, are there any ghosts or spirits in here?"

Victoria looked around. "No."

"Good. *Dat-galey!*" The wreckage began to shimmer and wave, and the missing wall safe reappeared, completely intact in the space.

"You cheeky devil!" Helga said. 'Ow did you do that? It can't be voragoed or turn't invisible!"

"It can't. The book had a curse on it to prevent Vorago. That is how Pythonissa could transport it, by removing it. But curses have nothing to do with preventing invisibility."

"I'm confused. Come again?"

"Aunt Gwenhwyvar gave me a clue! Quid Vis Videre! Or, what do you want to see? We don't have to make the book invisible. We only have to make it appear that way to everyone. Invisibility is a Gold forge, an illusion cast on the viewer, not the object. We can't create an illusion for the book, but what about its housing? A way to make us see <u>around</u> it to the other side. A curved mirror. The biggest mistake Pythonissa made was giving me her knowledge, including illusion Forges."

"Does that mean we can beat her?" Victoria asked.

"I don't know….. We didn't win this time—at all! We escaped! I'm sure the next time we meet, she's going to be: stronger, wiser, and angrier. But, the good news is, we will be stronger, wiser, and braver! We barely made it out of there alive…Some of us didn't…" Abel and Helga grabbed her hands. "…but I have the audacity to believe that we've already succeeded, we've already won, and the only thing we have to do now is remove all of the dust and dark clouds in the way until we can clearly see the blue sky." Everyone looked at each other in agreement.

"O'right," Helga said. "Enough of this treacle. Let's go save the bloody world."

In Battery Park, Thelma wasn't leaving until she was sure her daughter couldn't see her waving. She could still see Min and Victoria on the deck of the Virginia, waving back as they grew smaller and smaller, and cruised away from the New York shore towards the Atlantic.

A white-haired woman dressed in black approached and watched the boat disappear. Thelma noticed the bandages wrapped around their face and eyes.

"Are they gone?" Miss Wayward asked.

"Yes, they left a while ago. Do you know anyone on board?"

"Only a couple."

Thelma looked at the boat, now impossible to see without a spyglass, and then at Wayward. "May I ask…and excuse me if it's a sensitive question, what happened to your face?"

Wayward touched their face. "I've been wearing this for so long, I forgot I was still wearing it. Guess I don't need it anymore."

Wayward pulled her hair off, revealing a white wig over her black hair. She began to unravel the bandages. Thelma grimaced, imagining what type of disfigurement lay under the bandages. Wayward unraveled the final gauze and tossed it onto the ground.

Thelma was in shock, but not from disgust. The stranger was a beautiful Chinese woman.

"You...Do you know the little Chinese girl on that boat?" Thelma asked.

"Of course, ever since she was born." She put on a pair of dark spectacles and walked away.

Photo of Azure Cloud, leader of the Hongdeng Zhao (Red Lanterns Shining)

Don't Miss Book #4!

MARY & I
Spell Breaker

About the Author

Alexander G. J. grew up in Charlotte, North Carolina. He moved to Atlanta, Georgia to study commercial art, then to San Francisco, California, to bolster his writing and fine arts skills. He currently lives in Richmond, California.

Novels by Alexander G. J.

Mary & I: The Real Story of Miss Mary Mack
Mary & I: Black Blood
Mary & I: The First Witch
Mary & I: Spell Breaker (due by 2028)
Flaming Jackass: Sex, Drugs, and Pizza
Flaming Jackass: In Love
Flaming Jackass: Returns
Flaming Jackass: Detox
Why Did the Chicken Cross the Universe?
Xiene!
Life with Xiene (due by 2026)
Tina and the French Boar (due by 2027)
Flaming Jackass OMFG! (due by 2026)

Blog: marymackandi.blogspot.com
Facebook: facebook.com/rabbitstudiosbigpush
Author's page: amazon.com/author/alexanderg.j
Instagram @Alexscafe